Advance Praise for
The Girls from the Revolutionary Cantina

"Who needs sisters when you have friends like *The Girls from the Revolutionary Cantina*? Padilla's debut novel delivers plenty of laughter, a pinch of intrigue, and a whole lot of drama. Readers will be so eager to find out what happens next, they won't be able to put this down."

—Margo Candela, author of *More Than This*

Praise for
Hard Language: Stories

"Padilla's writing is intimate, evocative, and often heartbreaking and surprising."   —*Booklist*

"Fresh and free of cliché . . . shed[s] a warm light on Latino lives in the U.S."   —*Publishers Weekly*

"This collection, with . . . avowedly realistic stories about contemporary Mexican-Americans—both in California and Tijuana—[and] people struggling in love, work, and life, shows off the sharp talent of a fine new writer. . . . Padilla has a keen sense of what goes on between men and women on both sides of the border."

—Alan Cheuse, National Public Radio

The
Girls
~ from the ~
REVOLUTIONARY
CANTINA

ALSO BY THE AUTHOR

*

Hard Language

The Girls from the REVOLUTIONARY CANTINA

M. Padilla

THOMAS DUNNE BOOKS
St. Martin's Griffin
New York

This is a work of fiction. All of the characters, organizations, and events portrayed in this novel are either products of the author's imagination or are used fictitiously.

THOMAS DUNNE BOOKS.
An imprint of St. Martin's Press.

www.thomasdunnebooks.com
www.stmartins.com

Book design by Kathryn Parise

ISBN 978-0-312-59308-7

First Edition: July 2010

10 9 8 7 6 5 4 3 2 1

In memory of Richard V. Piper
and for
Alicia and Peter Padilla

⤛ Acknowledgments ⤜

Thanks go first and foremost to the supreme Tod Goldberg. I might still be toiling at the beginning were it not for his insight and encouragement. Everlasting appreciation also goes to my agent, Joy Azmitia, and my editor, Toni Plummer, for championing this story and for their thoughtful notes; to Mark Coggins, Tom Steele, Ronnie Vasquez, and Bob Nymoen for reading so many drafts and solving so many problems; to Elsa Francis, Sam Francis, Claudia Aguilar, Susan Johnson, and Paul Kraus for all they brought to this book; and to the California Arts Council for the generous grant that helped launch this project. Finally, very special thanks to Chris Erickson and Stephen Suess for seeing me over a couple of big humps, and to Dan Faltz for supporting me in more ways than I can count, and for the final push that got the manuscript out the door.

The
Girls
～ from the ～
REVOLUTIONARY
CANTINA

1

Risks and Opportunities

Even now Julia cringed to think about it: how she must have appeared to him, caught standing in the middle of his office, riffling through his things. Monica from his sales group had assured her he was gone for the day, so how could she resist peeking in to see what she could learn about him—this company hero with the stunning gray eyes, ese hot papi chulo, as her friend Concepción called him. She'd wanted a closer look at the photo on his desk, the one of the San Fernando Valley beauty queen rumored once to have been his fiancée. Satisfied that she was only marginally beautiful, Julia had lingered. She'd taken the jacket from the back of his chair and pressed it to her nose, enjoying the sweet scent of cologne. That was when he had appeared in the doorway with a look of shock, eliciting from her a sharp gasp. And the lie she had come up with: She was looking for a lighter. A lighter! She wasn't a smoker; he and everyone else she worked with knew it.

"Be thankful he's not in your sales group," Ime said when Julia called the next day to lament her blunder. "Imagine if you had to work with him every day."

"I don't think I could feel any more humiliated," Julia said.

"You need to talk to him. Make nice, but not so nice that he thinks you're stalking him."

"Maybe I should take up smoking," Julia said.

Ime laughed warmly. A knot of tension loosened in Julia's chest. She could always count on Ime to make her feel better. Her laugh alone was sometimes all it took. Friends since the age of seven, they had grown up together in the northeastern part of the San Fernando Valley, daughters of hardworking Mexican parents reaching for an American Dream that always seemed a little out of reach. Of all Julia's friends, only Ime, with her burgeoning real estate career and fearless financial risk-taking, had broken through to a life that resembled what their parents had dreamed of. Julia was not far behind, a fact she owed to Ime demanding her company on the way up the ladder of success. Julia was grateful for her encouragement. She owed Ime in more ways than she could count.

"I'm heading over to Marta's now," Ime said. "Why don't I swing by and get you?"

"I'm too far out of your way. I'll meet you there."

"It's no trouble. It'll give us a chance to talk without those chismosas knowing every bit of our business."

"Those chismosas are our friends," Julia said.

"You signed a lifetime agreement with them," Ime said. "I'm on month-to-month."

Julia told Ime she'd be waiting for her outside her apartment in ten minutes. At her bedroom mirror she ran a brush through her hair and applied a little blush. She examined her face from several angles—the tawny cheeks, the expensive new salon cut. She didn't think she looked like a pervert. She looked like someone who deserved success.

At her closet she slipped into the Marc Jacobs jacket Ime had given her for Christmas, then went to get her good Celine pumps from where she'd left them under the coffee table. She snapped one onto each foot, practiced a few of the salsa steps her friend Concepción had taught her, then tugged her belt to a fresh notch on the way out the door.

Outside, the day was cool and bright and dry. The San Gabriel Mountains stood clear and sharp in the distance from the winds that had blown through the San Fernando Valley the night before. On the sidewalk she dodged a couple of kids chasing another kid with fronds that had broken loose from the towering palms in front of her building.

When Ime pulled around the corner, Julia understood immediately why she'd been so eager to pick her up. She was behind the wheel of a new silver BMW 5 Series. She pulled up to the curb, rolled down her window, and propped her sunglasses on her head.

"Show-off!" Julia said, stepping up to the car. "¡Híjole! It's beautiful, Ime. You didn't tell me you were thinking of trading up."

Ime flashed a proud grin. "Not bad for a girl from Pacoima, eh? It's got ten-speaker audio and heated seats and a three-liter dual overhead cam—ha, whatever that is!"

Julia's gaze followed the car's contours as she circled to the passenger side and got in. She ran her hands over the buttery leather seats, breathed in the pungent mix of leather and plastic. "My God, Ime, are you sure you can afford this?"

Ime rolled her eyes. "I knew that's the first thing you'd ask. To make it in my business you have to look the part. I'd let you drive, but with your record . . ." With a mischievous smile, she put the car in gear and tore out with a squeal of rubber.

"Careful," Julia said, tensing. "Kids."

Ime took San Fernando Road through downtown San Fernando, then cut south on Van Nuys Boulevard past the commercial districts of Pacoima, Arleta, and Panorama City, where shop signs alternated between English and Spanish. The wide, flat boulevard had been their weekend cruising grounds as teenagers, before any notion of themselves as "career women" had begun to take hold.

A few minutes later, the abandoned GM plant appeared on their left. The sight of the old, fading buildings always made Julia feel heavy and knotted. Her and Ime's fathers had worked assembly there until '92, when the company sent its production jobs to Canada. Though the plant's closing hadn't been a surprise, it had marked the beginning of Julia's father's struggle to find permanent, stable work. She remembered the shame in his face after long days of searching but coming up empty-handed. She remembered her mother's anxiousness every time a bill came in the mail. Seeing her once bright, happy parents weighed down by worry had led Julia to promise herself this—that she would build enough security to never have to be in that position herself.

Ime was a part of that security, as were her other friends. Julia held Ime close because she knew she could be counted on, in spite of her flaws, in spite of her self-absorption. She was her safety net. When they were both in their early twenties, Julia's father had announced that he and her mother were going to have to sell the little two-bedroom house Julia had grown up in; they could no longer make the mortgage payments. Julia had just started taking business classes at Valley College, which she believed would put her on track for the kind of career and security she wanted. A sinking feeling had overcome her as she realized that the only way to help her parents save their house was to quit school to work full-time. Ime, already making great money in her second year selling houses, had stepped in—not only with the money to help them catch up on their mortgage payments but with enough cash to pay off the house. Knowing Julia's parents wouldn't have accepted the money directly from her, she'd funneled it through Julia, letting her be the hero. When Julia offered to sign something promising to pay her back, Ime had cut her off firmly. "The only thing I want in return," she'd said, taking Julia's hand and squeezing it hard, "is a promise to stick with me. Successful Latinas don't get support from anybody but each other."

A sudden tap on the brakes brought Julia back to the present. With a nod toward the plant, Ime said, "They're turning that into a mall."

"Really? A mall?" It was hard for Julia to picture the plant as anything other than what it had been.

"Everything in the Valley eventually gets turned into a mall." Ime said this optimistically, without sorrow or nostalgia. The past never blurred her view of the opportunities that came with change.

Approaching the Revolutionary Cantina, Ime started searching for a parking space out front. Failing to find one that would allow her to keep an eye on her car from the bar, she settled for a spot two blocks south. She and Julia got out and hugged, then started walking quickly side by side down the street. They talked over pedestrians and each other, breaking apart to pass people and coming together again still in conversation.

"There's something I wanted to ask you," Ime said as they came to a light. "A little favor that shouldn't put you out too much."

Julia slumped her shoulders in frustration. She knew what was coming—the same favor Ime brought up every few weeks.

"I want you to introduce me to some of your co-workers," Ime said. "You know, just to get my business card out, plant a few seeds."

"Ime, how many times do I have to tell you—"

"I know, I know. You think it puts your co-workers in an awkward position—"

"Exactly! There are millions of other prospects out there. Please stop bugging me."

"I didn't get to where I am today without bugging a few people," Ime said.

Julia said nothing. Silence was the only way to get Ime to change this subject.

"Fine," Ime said after a few seconds. The light turned and they stepped into the street. They were almost at the Cantina when Ime said, "By the way. How are your mom and dad doing? I happened to drive down their street the other day. The house sure is looking nice with all that new landscaping."

Julia wagged her head in disbelief. "You're unbelievable, Ime. Un. Be. *Liev*able."

At the Revolutionary Cantina, first Ime, then Julia pushed through the glass doors. As usual during the afternoons, the narrow little place, decorated with framed photos of determined-looking mustachioed Mexican revolutionaries like Emiliano Zapata and Rodolfo Fierro, was nearly empty. At nineteen, Julia and Ime had started hanging out here because it was the only bar that looked past their flimsy fake IDs. In the years since, they had become good friends with the bar's owner and several of the regulars. The Cantina was their default meeting spot for birthdays and canasta, and their first stop on the weekends before heading out for a night on the town.

Concepción, Julia's loudest and tallest friend, was hanging yellow streamers from the brass lamps above the bar. Julia had nearly forgotten that today's gathering had originally been planned in her honor, to celebrate her new job with Ostin Security Systems. She had already been working there for eight months as a sales rep when Concepción decided that it was a milestone that needed celebrating.

"Any excuse to have a few beers, eh?" Julia called to Concepción.

Concepción came down from her step stool and minced over in

heels and glitter stretch pants. She pinched Julia's cheeks. "Congratulations," she squealed. "You're really giving Ime a run for her money. I'm so happy for you!"

"I'm just glad to be working again," Julia said. She felt her face turn red. It still embarrassed her to recall the way her last job had ended.

Marta, the squat, older, frowning bar owner, slipped down to the end of the bar and turned the music up. An Obie Bermúdez remix that was popular in the clubs sent Concepción into a shimmy. She took Julia's hand and made her dance with her. Concepción taught Latin dance, mostly to Anglos trying to get in on the salsa craze. Over the years she had tried to teach Julia to ballroom dance, with limited success.

A few minutes later Marta swatted at the women with her bar towel, herding them to a table near the window where she had laid out a tray of beers from the tap. Settling into her chair with a cigarette, she took a double deck of cards from her apron and shuffled, then started firing cards around the table with her muscular hands.

Against Julia's protests, Ime related the story Julia had just told her about getting caught in her co-worker's office. Julia's cheeks burned.

"Well, I can't say I blame you," Concepción said, drawing up her cards. "That co-worker of yours is pure hotness." Concepción was the only one of Julia's friends to have met him. Dropping by Julia's office unannounced (a habit Julia had yet to break her of), she'd seen him coming out of the men's room and had begged Julia for an introduction.

"What you should do," Concepción continued, "is invite him to my Cinco de Mayo party."

"Why would she want to do that?" Ime said. "She wants to impress him, not humiliate herself even more."

"I'm not inviting him and I'm not trying to impress him," Julia said. "I just need to make sure he understands it's not going to happen again."

"You never want us to meet the people you work with," Concepción blurted.

"She's ashamed of being Mexican," Marta rasped. "You pochas are all like that."

"That just isn't true!" Julia said, and it wasn't. She'd always been proud of her heritage. Ime, on the other hand, often downplayed hers. She pronounced Benevides, her last name, with three syllables instead of four. She referred to her ethnicity as "a mix of Latin and some other things."

"It's why she doesn't like us coming by her office," Concepción said to Marta.

"I've told you before, I'm not comfortable mixing work with my personal life. I can't explain why exactly, but it just feels safer to me that way."

"I'll say it for her," Ime said. "You guys can be a little embarrassing at times." She drew a card and threw it down without much thought. She had little patience for card games, played recklessly, and often won.

"Your personal life and your work got pretty confused at your last job," Marta said to Julia with a smirk.

"If you want advice about what to do with your co-worker, you should think about going to see Pilar Chávez," Concepción said.

Marta frowned at her. "That vieja bruja you go to? Are you kidding?"

"Don't underestimate her," Concepción said. "Just last week she predicted that I was going to have a brush with celebrity. Sure enough, guess who I saw coming out of Bloomingdale's on Saturday?"

"Who?" Julia said. She drew up another card.

"Diego Ramirez."

"I've never heard of him."

"He's that Chicano that does the action movies," Marta said. "The one they're trying to sign as the first Latino James Bond."

"I think I know the one you're talking about," Ime said. "Didn't he marry that woman, la huera?"

"That's him," Concepción said.

"Don't tell me you tried to talk to him."

"Sure, why not? I had to tell him how much I love his movies."

"I'm sure it was the highlight of his day," Marta said. "I'm sure he doesn't have enough crazed Mexicans bothering him in shopping malls."

"Naturally, I invited him to my Cinco de Mayo party," Concepción said.

"Good God," Ime said. "You couldn't possibly think he'd want to come to your party."

"Why not?" Concepción said. "My parties are famous."

"Because there's always a fistfight," Ime said. "Someone usually ends up in the emergency room."

"Diego Ramirez is a womanizer and a drug user," Marta said.

"How would you know that?" Concepción said. "Oh, wait, I forgot what a magnet this place is for celebrities. Isn't that Meryl Streep over there?"

"I know more than you think," Marta said. She squinted and released a pencil-thin shaft of smoke over Ime's head. "His ex-wife disappeared two months ago and there's talk that Ramirez might have had something to do with it."

"He's a terrible actor," Ime said. "What was that movie he did with that woman?"

"*Midnight Blood,*" Concepción said.

"A Latino vampire movie. Ha!"

"At least they've started to make more movies with our people in them," Marta said. She drummed her stubby fingers on the table. "Who's holding up the game?"

"Just a minute," Concepción said, reordering her cards. "Don't hurry me, don't hurry me. OK, how's this?" She laid down the first canasta.

Marta slapped her cards down. "How do you always manage that?"

"You give me good cards," Concepción said. "There's nothing I can do about that."

The women played a couple of games of canasta and went through a couple more rounds of beer. Toward the middle of the afternoon, Concepción pushed back her chair and stretched her longs arms overhead, sending her plastic bracelets to clatter down around her elbows. "Well, that's it for me," she said.

"Already?" Marta said. "I'm only ten points behind. You should give me a chance to catch up."

"I've got a class to teach," Concepción said. She stood up and with a swirl of her hips said, "If I want to eat, I've got to teach the gringos the Latin beat."

"And I've got a house to show," Ime said. "It's for a couple that just found out they're pregnant with twins. I need to convince them they can still afford a three-bedroom in Chatsworth—or else give them a lift to the abortion clinic. I didn't say that. The devil made me say that."

"The devil makes you say a lot of things," Marta said.

"I know," Ime said, threading her arm into her jacket. "We're pretty good friends."

The women exchanged hugs and promises to call. Concepción left first, then Julia followed Ime out.

"I hope you're not mad I told them that story," Ime said as they walked back to her car.

"No," Julia said. "I just hate it when they accuse me of things."

"You mean about being embarrassed of where you come from?" Ime laughed. "It's just jealous talk. Don't let it bother you." She waved vaguely to indicate the neighborhood. "Are we really missing so much by leaving *this* behind?"

Ime hooked her arm through Julia's and pulled her close as they walked. "I worry about you," she said after a minute.

"Because of what I did at the office?"

"No, not that."

"What then?"

"Sometimes I think . . . you miss things."

"What kinds of things?"

"Opportunities."

"Opportunities?"

"When I see something right in front of me, I don't hesitate. I take it before somebody else does."

"I've done all right," Julia said.

"You could do better," Ime said.

"If I weren't so practical?"

"Something like that, yes."

Julia smiled. She appreciated Ime's concern. But Julia had never been a risk-taker. That was Ime's talent, not hers.

"Well, thank goodness I have you to point opportunities out to me so I don't miss them," Julia said.

They stopped at Ime's car. Ime handed Julia the key. "You drive."

"Are you sure?"

"I trust you. Take the 405. Let's see what she can really do."

⌒ 2 ⌒

Invitations

On Monday morning, Julia set off to work with two goals in mind—to formally apologize to her co-worker Ilario, and to convince him that there was no need to say anything to her boss or to file a complaint with Human Resources. Getting dressed, she chose a soft-shouldered chenille turquoise jacket and skirt to wear, because she had read in a women's business magazine that cool colors and soft fabrics elicited forgiveness more quickly from the opposite sex. A half hour after leaving her apartment, she pulled into the lot adjacent to her office, confident of the words she intended to use and the manner in which she would deliver them.

Ostin Security Systems occupied the first and second floors of a three-story building that reminded Julia of a Rubik's Cube with two of the top corners missing. The building was the cleanest, newest, and most spacious she had ever worked in. She loved the way the mirrored, rose-tinted exterior reflected the trajectories of planes taking off from the nearby Burbank airport without warping them. She loved the even spacing of the banana palms that lined the path leading up to the front entrance, and the fact that the glass doors were cleaned twice daily. Even after eight months, as she entered the building lobby each morning and took in the smell of fresh paint and new carpet, she still silently said a few words of thanks to Ime. It had been she who found the opening through one of her clients.

Julia loved her job, too. From the moment Ime'd read her the job description—selling security systems and service agreements to medium-size businesses—she'd felt that the job was right for her. Security was an idea she could get behind in any form, a product she could sell.

Stopping at Ilario's office, which was just down the hall from hers, she found his lights off and his door closed. On his door was a note explaining that he would be at a retreat for the day with the rest of his sales team. Julia was disappointed but also a little relieved. It was not just his silver eyes and good looks that intimidated her. It was also his reputation as a company star, consistently outperforming all the other sales associates and bringing Ostin Security some of its biggest clients. Though he had been with the company only a year longer than she had, his peers treated him with a deference usually reserved for management. The few brief conversations she'd had with him—and the dozen or so she'd overheard—convinced her that he was smart and personable, but not very humble. She supposed, however, that anyone as talented as he was was entitled to a bigger-than-average ego (Ime shared similar traits), and that a bigger-than-average ego was necessary to make the most of exceptional talent.

In her office (a sliver of space, but her own office nevertheless), she sat down to answer a couple of phone messages. She had been on a call for no more than five minutes when she heard the *ka-chink ka-chink* of plastic jewelry that so often announced Concepción's arrival. Wearing headphones, she half walked and half danced into Julia's office. She sported pumpkin-colored capris and a tight black sleeveless belly shirt that showed off her pierced navel, and she was munching from a Styrofoam plate of taquitos mercilessly gobbed with guacamole. Setting the plate down on Julia's desk, Concepción tossed a nylon dance bag into a nearby chair. Digging through it, she began piling things on the desk— knee wraps, tampons, a V-shaped hand strengthener, cotton balls, a copy of *American Rider*. A minute later Julia got off the phone and Concepción pulled off her headphones. "I need your approval," Concepción said.

"You have my approval about everything except those pants and the fact that you always show up here without calling."

"I'm talking about this, tonta." She handed Julia an invitation to her Cinco de Mayo party, then bit into a taquito while Julia perused the invitation, designed to look like an oversize U.S. green card. On the back was the image of a Mexican flag with a lopsided eagle perched on a cactus, a bottle of beer in its talons. Julia wasn't sure whether it was intended to look drunk or was just badly drawn.

"A green card?" Julia said. "Don't you think some people could be offended, C?" C was Concepción's nickname. Over the years it had shrunk from Concepción to Connie to just the letter "C".

"Only people with no sense of humor. Who wants them at my party anyway?"

"And why do you need me to OK this?" She noticed her name on the invitation. Concepción had listed her as a hostess. "Never mind. I get it." She reached for her checkbook. "How much do you want?"

"If you could see your way clear of covering the cost of the band . . ."

"A band? What kind of party are you throwing?"

"One that's going to teach that big puta Remedios once and for all that she can't throw a Cinco de Mayo party on the same day as me and expect anyone to show up."

What had started out as a small gathering of friends for drinks and chips had ballooned in recent years into hundreds of guests trafficking in and out of Concepción's one-bedroom Van Nuys apartment with its sparkly cottage-cheese ceilings and brightly painted furniture. Over the years Concepción had come to demand more and more of her friends' time and money in order to ensure that her party outdid the competing one thrown by her onetime friend and longtime rival, Remedios Salazar.

Julia tore off a check and handed it to her. "How's this?"

"Quite generous. Here's your stack of invitations to distribute. Please, this year, no senior citizens, no sober freaks, and no religious fanatics. No gringos who think they can dance, or gringos who know they can't but think it's cute when they try. This year I want Fun. I want Hotness. And I really, really want you to invite that co-worker of yours. What's his name again?"

"Ilario—but I told you, *no* co-workers."

"See? I was right. You're embarrassed of your friends." She looked around distastefully at the walls of Julia's office. "This environment is so stuffy. It's not good for you, it's making you too uptight. You've been working much too hard and we hardly get to see you anymore."

Julia *had* been working hard. She had learned long ago that her talent as a salesperson lay not in her ability to dazzle customers with flashes of personality but in being able to listen and empathize. Nurturing clients in this way worked well for her, but required greater patience and longer hours. She worked hard, too, out of concern that anyone might accuse her of benefiting from the company's diversity policy. It had happened before. In her first sales job out of college, selling "waste management solutions," she'd overheard two co-workers at the company picnic wondering out loud about how she had been hired over people they knew who had more experience. Never mind that her ability to speak Spanish gave her an advantage in dealing with many of the company's clients.

She realized then that no matter how friendly her co-workers treated her, she would have to prove herself in ways that the other sales reps didn't.

Julia's desk phone rang. She took the call. "Mr. Guzman, hello! What can I do for you?"

Mr. Guzman was the owner and founder of Guzman Industries, a firm in Oakland that made cooling systems for high-tech devices that had to be stored and used at precise temperatures. He had patented a new cooling invention that required less space and was more efficient than standard methods, and his business was exploding. Julia had been trying to get his agreement on a two-year contract since her first week at Ostin Security. High-strung and indecisive, Mr. Guzman had taken up hours of Julia's time yet still hadn't committed to an agreement. Landing the account would mean the largest commission Julia had ever received. More important, she believed it would secure her place with the company and restore the self-confidence that had been so badly shaken at her last job.

While Julia spoke to Mr. Guzman, Concepción took a pen and wrote something on one of the invitations. Then she slipped out of Julia's office. Julia craned her head out the door, stretching the phone cord, and looked down the hall to see where she was going. She caught Concepción pushing the invitation under Ilario's office door.

Julia put the receiver to her chest. "What are you doing?!" she hissed. "C, come back here! . . . I'm sorry, Mr. Guzman, what was that? I didn't catch that last thing you said. . . . OK, that will be fine, we can talk again in a few weeks. Muchísimas gracias, eh?"

When she finished her call, she said, "What did you write on that invitation?"

"What invitation?"

"I saw you push something under his door."

"I just left him a little note from you saying that you'd love to see him at the party, and also that you were too shy to invite him face to face because you're madly in love with him and you're looking forward to an opportunity to declare your feelings."

"You did not."

"No, but I should have. I wrote that you hope to see him there."

"Shit, that invitation could be taken the wrong way. Besides, I don't think your party is the kind of thing he'd be interested in."

"Try and get him to come anyway. What a great addition he'd be. Híjole, I don't know how you can concentrate with that kind of hotness right down the hall."

Julia grabbed a file folder from her desk drawer. "I have a meeting. Let me walk you out before you cause any more trouble."

"Fine," Concepción said. She refilled her bag with her things. She examined some company pens from Julia's desk and threw those in as well.

Once Julia had seen her out, she went back to retrieve the invitation from Ilario's office. He had locked his door. She stomped her foot. Now she was going to have to apologize *and* explain the invitation.

The next morning, Julia rose early in hopes of beating Ilario to the office. But as usual, he was there before her. She found him at his desk, paging through a spiral-bound report. Julia saw the invitation on the top of his in-box. She knocked on the doorjamb to get his attention.

"Hi, Ilario. Listen, I just wanted to say how sorry I am about Friday. It was really wrong of me to invade your private space, and I just want you to know it won't happen again."

He tilted his face up at her. "So I shouldn't send an e-mail to your boss?"

"I sure would appreciate it if you didn't."

He gave a thin smile. Julia wasn't sure how to read it. She cleared her throat. "And about that invitation. That was kind of a mistake. A friend of mine was here and she put it under your door by accident."

He stopped paging through the report. "So I'm not invited?"

"Oh, no, I didn't mean that. I just mean that I hadn't meant to invite you. . . . I mean, I hadn't *thought* about inviting you, but you're more than welcome to come if you want to. . . . I *would* have invited you, except I didn't really think it's the kind of thing you'd be interested in. . . ."

His handsome gray eyes gazing up at her didn't help untie her tongue.

Then, finally (her face flashing one last shade of red): "It's going to be a fun party. I hope to see you there."

She turned on her heel and left his office.

She was going to kill Concepción.

≈ 3 ≈

Hotness

The days leading up to Concepción's annual Cinco de Mayo party were always stressful for Concepción, and by extension, Julia. The primary source of Concepción's preparty anxiety stemmed from the rivalry she shared with Remedios Salazar. Nothing less than a complete triumph over her former friend would satisfy her, and she invariably drove Julia to distraction obsessing over plans and preparations.

This year, the timing of the party could not have been worse for Julia. In trying to keep her sales numbers up at work, she had been devoting weekends to researching new potential customers. But she knew from experience that she would suffer a lengthy tirade from Concepción if she failed to show up. So the morning of the party, Julia rose early and headed over to Concepción's Blythe Street apartment in Van Nuys to help her set up.

When she arrived, she found her friend in a state the likes of which she had never seen before. Concepción was pacing frantically in front of the small stage she had paid to have constructed under the sprawling jacaranda of her apartment building's courtyard. The band, which she'd hired based on Marta's recommendation, turned out not to be the Latin hip-hop band she'd expected, but rather a mariachi band consisting of five timid-looking teenagers in traditional traje who bore a remarkable resemblance to Marta. They stood in a lineup in front of the stage, looking at Concepción with wide eyes as she ranted and ran tense fingers through her hair.

"Look at them!" she said to Julia. "Marta sent a bunch of her nephews and nieces! A bunch of fucking mariachis! What was she thinking?"

The boy who appeared the oldest of the group took a courageous step forward. His Adam's apple rode up and down his long, pimply neck as he said, "Señora, if you'll let us play for you, I think you'll like what we do. We play Cinco de Mayo parties all the time, and quinceañeras and weddings, and last year we even won first place in the junior division of the Mid-State Mariachi Festival."

Being called "señora" did nothing to appease Concepción, who turned red and said, "Mariachi music is the most horrible, depressing music in the world! How could I have trusted Marta with something so important?"

Julia took Concepción by the elbow and, as though shutting off a spigot, forcefully turned her away from the musicians. "I want you to give them a chance," she said. "There's nothing we can do now, and anyway, there's nothing more appropriate for Cinco de Mayo than mariachis."

Julia turned back to the boy and asked him to play something from their repertoire. He cued the other teenagers, and on a four count they began a respectable rendition of "Cielito Lindo." Concepción covered her ears and screamed until they stopped.

Julia sent her inside to change. She crossed her palms over her chest apologetically. "Please ignore my friend," she said to the musicians. "She doesn't handle stress very well. You guys are going to be perfect. I'll do what I can to keep her out of your way."

The color flowed into their faces and they picked up "Cielito Lindo" again, enlivening the tempo as though in appreciation of Julia's intervention.

Julia found problems in the kitchen as well. In her fit over the mariachis, Concepción had left a tray of appetizers in the oven and they had begun to burn. Concepción was smacking at the smoke with a Minnie Mouse oven mitt while the smoke detector buzzed overhead. Julia marched Concepción to her bedroom and told her not to come out until she had changed. Then Julia opened a window, climbed onto a chair to remove the battery from the smoke detector, and threw the burned appetizers in the trash. She removed plastic tubs of marinating chicken skewers from the refrigerator and carried them out to the barbecue, then did a quick inventory of liquor and supplies at the makeshift bar Concepción had set up outside her first-floor apartment. Concepción came out a few minutes later in a lavender spring dress with a crimped hem.

"You look great," Julia told her, and it was true. The dress flowed nicely over her hips and brought out the deep color of her legs. "What about your neighbors? Did you get permission from everybody to use the courtyard?"

Concepción nodded.

"No problems with the Pentecostals?"

"I told them I'd babysit their kids for a month if they didn't complain about the noise."

Julia glanced at the Mexican flags Concepción had hung from her neighbors' balconies and the red and green streamers that flew out from the jacaranda tree in the center of the courtyard. She pulled a couple of beers from the ice chest next to the bar and handed one to Concepción. "Five dollars says Nina gets here before anyone else."

"Ten says she's still moping about her breakup with Roberto."

As predicted, Nina was the first to arrive. She came through the gate in her usual modest slacks and yellow, buttoned-up cardigan that bunched around the waist but was too tight in the arms and shoulders. It was the same outfit she'd been wearing when Julia, Concepción, and Marta had met her at Dodger Stadium a few years earlier. They'd noticed her sitting alone a few seats down, listlessly waving a pennant as the Mariners hammered the Dodgers with a 7–0 lead. Striking up a conversation with her, they'd learned that she'd had to come to the game alone because her boyfriend had just started working nights and slept during the day. They invited her to go drinking with them afterward, and she'd become a kind of ongoing renovation project for Ime and Julia. Trying to get her to spruce up her look, they'd bought her some new clothes and introduced her to the proper use of makeup. But since breaking up with her boyfriend two months earlier, she'd reverted to wearing the same lifeless slacks, the same weepy-yellow cardigan.

The emotional strain of the breakup still showed on her face. Julia took her hand and tried to get her to dance. Nina reluctantly stomped out a few steps, then retreated with a wave of her hands to a nearby folding chair. "Please," she said, "nobody wants to see me dance."

"What nobody wants is a sad face at a party," Concepción said. "Have a beer or something. I don't want you bringing my guests down."

"I'm sorry," Nina said. "I'll go if you want me to."

"Don't listen to her," Julia said, giving Nina a side hug. "You're staying. Maybe you'll even meet a nice guy to get your mind off Roberto."

Concepción gave Julia a look. Don't get her hopes up, it said. Be realistic.

"Here, Nina, drink this," Concepción said. She handed her a

beer from the ice chest. Nina took a couple of sips. Within seconds, this made her have to go to the bathroom.

With Nina out of earshot, Concepción said, "Please don't let her ruin my party."

"How's she going to do that?"

"By talking to people," Concepción said. "She's like a black hole sucking up everything around her."

"Give her a break," Julia said. "She'll get over Roberto soon enough."

"She wasn't that much fun before the breakup, either. Remind me why she broke up with him?"

"He cheated on her."

"And she won't take him back?"

"She won't even talk to him."

"Who would have guessed she'd hold out so long?"

No one would have. Roberto was a broad-faced, mustachioed man of thirty-five who boasted machismo with every step but whose affection for Nina bled through his macho front like water through tissue paper. After a night of drinking with friends, he had shown up at Nina's door with a terrible confession. Years earlier, during the first few weeks he and Nina had been dating, he had cheated on her with another woman while he was in Tijuana visiting his grandparents. The guilt, he said, was eating him alive even now. He wanted to marry her but knew that he had to come clean first. His remorse was so complete, and Nina's prospects for marriage so limited, that none of Julia's friends doubted that she would take him back. Julia had urged her most strongly of all to consider reconciling. But Nina was resolute, and ever since had been adrift on her own sea of sadness.

. . .

By two o'clock, with still no guests other than Nina, Concepción threw up her hands and said, "That's it. Remedios has won. She's probably been spreading terrible rumors about me. She's that sneaky."

But moments later, her fears were allayed as a large contingent of friends who frequented her favorite nightclubs came pouring through the gates, including Paz, the muscular bartender from the Mayan; Tumi, the cigarette and candy girl; and Coco, the deaf coat-check girl who always wore glitter in her makeup. Within the hour, with more and more guests arriving by the minute, Concepción was laughing, flirting, and dancing with anyone who would agree to be her partner. Even Nina had begun to smile a little and sway to the music.

A mild wind shook the top branches of the jacaranda, sending down a shower of purple blossoms over the crowd. Julia said a little prayer of thanks. She closed her eyes and imagined the party as a flower blossoming all around. She kept her eyes closed until she felt a presence, friendly but insistent, coming toward her.

Ime was threading her way through the crowd with a briefcase in one hand and a clear garment bag holding a suit slung over her shoulder. She wiggled her fingers at people she knew, then set her briefcase on the ground near Julia. Julia kissed her, then said, "What's with the suit?"

"I have to show a house in an hour."

"You're not staying? C is going to be furious."

"Not if you cover for me," she said. "I'm going to mingle and make sure she sees I'm here. Then I'm going to change and sneak out without her noticing. Tell her I went out to get ice if she asks where I am."

"We have plenty of ice."

"Make something up. I've got the perfect house for this nice Jewish couple in Valley Village. Let me go hide this. I'll be back."

She slipped out of sight through the crowd. A minute or two later Concepción sidled up to Julia and swung a long arm over her shoulder. Her face was glowing from dancing. She looked at Julia with affection that was no less sincere for having been brought on by drinking and said, "Isn't this wonderful? Everyone's here and I'm here and I'm happy."

"There's no way Remedios could outdo this," Julia said.

"I don't even care about that," Concepción said. "I'm just glad to have so many friends here. I wish Marta didn't have to work, but I forgive her. I forgive everyone for everything bad they might ever have done to me. And thank you for getting that guapo from your office to come."

"Ilario? He's here?"

"I just saw him come in."

"Impossible." Julia glanced around the crowd. Not only had he said nothing about coming, but since the day the invitation had gotten slipped under his door, she'd even had the feeling that he was avoiding her. Hadn't he lingered at his car until she was out of sight the last time they had arrived to work at the same time? Hadn't he waited for a second elevator so as not to share the one she was on?

"Are you sure it's him?" Julia said. She raised herself up on her toes. There he was, standing under the jacaranda to the side of the stage. He wore loose-fitting pants and a silk-screen T-shirt. He was alone but he looked at ease.

"Shit!" Julia said.

"What's your problem?" Concepción said.

"I've had too much to drink. I don't want him to see me like this."

"You're hardly drunk," Concepción said. She plucked the beer from Julia's hand. "Go, you're being rude!"

Julia shot her a look. She smoothed her T-shirt down to her hips and took a breath, then made her way over.

"What are you doing here?" she blurted as she walked up to him. Shit. What kind of welcome was that?

But if Ilario was offended, he didn't let it show. He said, "That invitation was pretty funny. I was just in the area, so I thought I'd come and see what kind of party you threw. Of course, I'm still not sure if I was really invited."

Julia blushed fiercely. "I'm sorry about that," she said. "That was my friend Concepción's doing. This really is more her party than it is mine."

Ilario nodded. He looked so different out of his suit. Younger. Not as tall.

"So do you like working at Ostin?" she said. What a stupid question. Of course he liked working there. He was the star.

"It's a good company. Very solid. But a little risk averse, if you ask me. Everything's very by the book."

"Oh, that's what I like about it!" Julia said. "I feel secure there. There are no surprises. And everyone's so nice. I've never worked with people who are so friendly."

"I'd like to make some changes," he said.

Julia hadn't realized he was in a position to make changes. He was a sales associate like her, only in a different sales group. "Like what?" Julia said.

"They need to give the sales staff more flexibility to be creative. I've been floating some ideas by Roger. He's been listening." Roger was the VP of sales. She had met him briefly while interviewing for the job. He was a gruff man in his sixties prone to sudden bursts of frightening laughter. People said he had a short fuse, but Julia had yet to witness his temper.

"Has he made any of the changes you've suggested?" Julia said.

"I'll have more influence when I get the account manager job with Key Accounts. I think I have a good shot at it."

"Oh, you definitely do," Julia said. "Everyone I've talked to says you're the best salesperson in the whole company."

This brought a hint of a smile to Ilario's lips. "Really? They say that?"

"Absolutely! Your record speaks for itself. You're a natural."

His smile grew. "Well," he said, looking into his cup and tilting the remaining ice back and forth, "selling isn't just about personality. It's also about reading what people want. And sometimes what they want has nothing to do with the product you're selling."

"Hmm," Julia said.

"Listen," Ilario said. "If you ever need advice, come talk to me. My door's always open."

With a couple of drinks in her, it was easier to look into Ilario's gray eyes. They seemed softer now in the dappled light that played on his face and shoulders. A jacaranda blossom fell on his shoulder. She reached to pick it off, then noticed that his drink was almost empty. "Let me get you another one of those," Julia said. "What were you drinking?"

"Rum and Coke," he said.

She left him and went to the bar. She was refilling his cup with ice when Ime reappeared, carrying a plastic plate and nibbling on a chicken skewer. "Who's the loner over there?" she said.

"Ilario, from my office."

"I thought you didn't invite any work people," Ime said.

"Concepción invited him."

"Any chance he's in the market for a house?"

"Do you ever stop?"

"Come on, introduce me."

"Not while you're in sales mode."

"I'll be subtle."

"You're never subtle."

"Fine. I'll introduce myself later. Go ahead. Loosen him up first with another drink."

Julia realized she had forgotten what Ilario was drinking. She sniffed the cup but couldn't detect the liquor. She looked up to see Concepción surging toward her.

She clasped her fingers around Julia's arm. "I need to talk to you."

"What is it?" Julia said.

"We have a problem."

"What kind of problem?"

"Señora Alvarez is here."

"Who's Señora Alvarez?"

"My landlady. Julia, you have to talk to her. She just got here and she says we need a permit to have this many people on the property. She's making a big stink and threatening to call the police if we don't make everyone leave."

"I thought you got permission!"

"From my neighbors, yes, but not Señora Alvarez. She doesn't even live in the building. I almost never see her."

"Then what is she doing here?"

"I don't know! She just flew in on her broom and started stirring up trouble. She's had it out for me ever since that time she overheard me calling her a pinche vieja chismosa." She shot a glance at the Pentecostals' balcony. "I bet those fanatics tipped her off. Julia, you have to help me. Everything is going to be ruined. I won't be able to show my face if we have to send everyone home. Talk to her, Julia, calm her down. She hates me, she won't listen to me."

In Concepción's living room, the Pacheco brothers, two of Julia's oldest friends, were trying to persuade Mrs. Alvarez—a narrow, graying woman of about fifty with lingering good looks but no desire to highlight them—to reconsider. But all their charm and flirtation were running against the sharp blade of her personality. She stood with arms folded and lips pursed, rigid in every regard except the loose flesh that hung from the backs of her arms.

"Someone should have checked with me first," she said to the brothers. "If they had, I could have told them that you have to have a permit for this sort of thing."

"Señora, do you remember me?" Julia stepped forward and placed a hand on her shoulder. "We met when I was helping Concepción move in."

Mrs. Alvarez sighed with relief, as though she had at last found a reasonable person to talk to. "Will you please explain to your friend that she needs to have a permit?" she said. "I could be held responsible if anyone gets hurt."

"Señora Alvarez, what do we need to do to get a permit?"

"You can't get one *now,*" she said, throwing up her hands. "It takes weeks to apply for one, and applying doesn't mean you'll get one, and even if you got one doesn't mean I'd approve this many people."

"Señora Alvarez, don't you think maybe this once you could look the other way? Everyone's having a good time. Why don't you stay and enjoy yourself?"

"I know how these parties go," she said. "Things get out of control. People get into fights. Eventually it means trouble."

"I hear what you're saying, I really do. But don't you think you're being just a little harsh? Can't we do anything to change your mind?"

The woman burned Concepción with a look. "For one thing, you can tell your friend that she needs to start paying her rent on time. The only reason I came over here was because she's two months behind and hasn't returned any of my calls."

Concepción looked sheepishly at Julia.

Julia tried to say something more, but Mrs. Alvarez raised her hand. "You have thirty minutes to get everyone out of here. After that I'm going to call the police." She turned and left the room.

"Remedios has won," Concepción said. "I knew it would come to this. I hope she and that old woman and the Pentecostals and everyone else who's working to destroy me are satisfied. I'm done. I'm through. It's over."

"Let's just give her a few minutes to calm down," Julia said. "Maybe if you pay her the rent you owe, that will put her in a better mood."

Concepción brightened. "Oh, Julia, that's a good idea. Maybe that's really all she's upset about. Thank you, Julia, I'll be sure to pay you back, I promise."

Julia stifled her resentment and told Concepción to stay put. She wondered whether it might not be better to let Mrs. Alvarez shut down the party. If Concepción truly felt Remedios had won, perhaps it would put an end to her annual obsession. But this thought passed quickly. She would never hear the end of it if she didn't help Concepción save the party.

In the courtyard, Ime had moved in to talk to Ilario. She handed him her business card and shook his hand.

Julia went out to her car and got her checkbook from the glove compartment. She looked to see if she had enough to cover Concepción's back rent. She hadn't balanced the checkbook in a couple of days, so she did a few quick calculations in her head. She was about to cross back to the courtyard when something shiny down the street caught her attention. A black stretch limousine was pivoting slowly onto the street.

Julia stopped near the vacancy sign in front of Concepción's building and watched as the limo floated into full view. Among the dinged and faded cars parked along the curb, it might as well have been an alien spaceship, so out of place did it look in this part of the Valley. Julia tried to think who among Concepción's friends would rent a limo just to come to a Cinco de Mayo party. She half expected it to drive by without stopping. It didn't. It eased up to the red zone and stopped.

A minute or so went by with no motion from the car. She could not see through the tinted windows, but she could hear voices. She was about to turn away when the back door swung open and a man in a tuxedo shirt with the sleeves rolled up staggered out onto a weedy patch of dry grass.

He appeared to be in his late twenties, and very drunk. Except for the tuxedo shirt, he looked like just the type of guy Concepción would have been attracted to, with shoulder-length hair, dark skin, and elaborate tattoos snaking along both forearms. All that was missing was the chopper and leather jacket to make him a perfect fit for Concepción's tastes. The top button of his shirt was undone, and his tie hung loose around his neck. He had on only one shoe; the other he was carrying in his hand. He steadied himself against the limo as he tried to put it back on.

Two young women's faces appeared in the open door of the car.

"You are so not leaving us here!" one of them, a white girl, yelled. "Frank is going to be furious if we're late!" She was very young with a ruddy, almost sunburned complexion.

The other girl, who might have been Asian, had a long face and a droopy red mouth that rose and fell slowly as she chewed gum. She looked out at the neighborhood with a dazed expression, blinking stupidly against the light. "This doesn't look like Malibu," she said.

"Please come back," the first girl said. "We can still get to Frank's. You promised to take us to his party."

"I said we were going to *a* party," the man said. "I didn't say *which* party. And Frank can kiss, kiss, *kiss* my ass."

He pushed off from the car. The girl continued to shout at him while her friend peered out at the neighborhood. He dismissed them both with a wave of his hand behind him, as though he had just farted and were trying to dispel the odor. Julia knew she had seen that gesture somewhere. She had seen it in a movie. It had been a movie starring Diego Ramirez.

She ran into the courtyard and into Concepción's apartment. She slid to her knees in front of the sofa where Concepción was now reclined in the attitude of an ailing movie queen.

"He's here," Julia said. "He showed up. I don't know how you managed it, but he's out front and he's coming in. C, he's coming *in*!"

"Is it the police?" Concepción said weakly. She plucked a tissue from a box that the youngest Pacheco brother was holding for her.

"That actor that you met at the mall. The Latino. Diego Ramirez."

"Seriously, Julia," Concepción said, "that's a terrible way to try and distract me from my misery. It's actually quite cruel if you think about it—"

She gave a yelp as Julia yanked her off the sofa and pulled her outside. At the front gate Julia stopped and put up her arm to hold Concepción back.

The two girls, skinny as runway models, had ventured out of the limo. The angry blonde wore a shimmering silver strapless dress that pushed two tight round boobs up and forward like a pair of fists looking for a fight. The long-faced Asian girl's dress, white and splashed with green sequins, hung precariously on her slender frame from a single thin strap. Her opium-slow movements and constant blinking made Julia think of a helpless newborn chick.

"Please, Diego," the white girl said. Her voice was now filled with tearful emotion. "There's still time for us to get there. Don't be a brute, be a sweetheart."

The Asian girl was still looking around at the neighborhood. "Are we in the *Valley*?" she said.

"I'm sorry," the actor said. "I can't do this anymore. Frank should be happy that I'm not there. Look at me. What good am I after all I've been through?"

"I think we *are* in the Valley," the Asian girl said with a shudder.

Concepción touched Julia's arm. "It really is him," she whispered. "Diego Ramirez."

The actor approached Julia and Concepción. "Is this the right place?" he said. "I could use a drink. Right now a drink would solve a lot of things."

Concepción stepped forward and put out her hand, and with peculiar, thrilling formality said, "Mr. Ramirez, I'm so pleased that you came. It's such an honor to have you here."

The actor swept the hair out of his eyes and looked at her for several long moments, during which Julia feared she detected a flicker of derision. But the look passed quickly, and he took Concepción's hand and said with all seriousness, "The world is full of shit."

Concepción touched his arm reassuringly. "I think you'll find a minimum of shit here," she said. "We have chicken, drinks, and appetizers. Or maybe you would prefer punch."

Julia did not know why Concepción felt the need to present herself like a waiter announcing menu choices, or why she chose to offer punch when there was none to be had, but she was glad for her friend's ability to rise to the moment. The actor looked past her and up into the sky. "I can't remember the last time I heard mariachis. Did you know my mother was a mariachi singer? That was my introduction to show business, years ago, before shit started falling from the sky."

Concepción took his arm and gently guided him toward the complex. "Won't you come in and meet some of my friends?"

Julia was not offended that Concepción didn't introduce her. She would surely have said something far stupider than anything about punch. She followed in their wake, amazed by Concepción's expert handling of her guest.

"Tell me," the actor said before they entered the courtyard. "Are there any movie producers here?"

"No," Concepción said. "I don't know any producers."

"Any agents? Publicists? Managers?"

"No," Concepción said.

"No Hollywood types?"

"Mr. Ramirez, I seriously doubt you and I know any of the same people."

He turned to her under the archway and took her face in both hands and kissed her forehead. "That is exactly what I was hoping for," he said.

Together they crossed into the courtyard. She led him to the bar to fix him the drink he had asked for. The first long sip he took brought a look of peace to his face. Concepción escorted him through the crowd, pointing out the various features of her building. Julia could no longer hear their words over the music, but whatever Concepción was saying seemed to genuinely interest him. They walked at the leisurely pace of a pair of seniors enjoying an after-dinner stroll.

When they had returned to near where Julia was standing, Diego released Concepción and said, "Do you dance?"

"You have no idea how well, Mr. Ramirez."

He crushed his cup, tossed it into the trash, and followed her to the center of the courtyard. Julia watched as they faced each other and began to move in rhythm to the music. A few people gave him odd glances. Then others began to look and point and whisper.

Ime appeared at Julia's side. She had changed into a handsome chocolate suit with pewter buttons. "I'm on my way. Cover for me with C."

"I don't think she's going to miss you." Julia pointed to the actor. "Do you know who that is?"

"Someone who missed his exit to the prom?"

"You don't recognize him?"

"Should I?"

"That's the actor that Concepción pestered at the mall."

"No. Impossible."

"Anything's possible with Concepción."

Ime shrugged. "All right, if you insist. I'll see you later. Wish me luck." On her way out, she passed Diego's two female friends, who had just walked in. They stood close near the entrance, holding each other as though they had just walked into a house of horrors.

Concepción and Diego danced what looked like a cross between a Jarabe Tapatío and the Hustle. The actor's moves were drunken and uneven but full of expression. Word about the actor's presence was spreading quickly across the dance area. It did not take long before others came to see for themselves. Concepción was aglow, showing off her best dance moves, grabbing his arm now and again as he stumbled, and laughing with him as his dancing became more and more unhinged. The worse the actor's dancing became, the more his audience egged him on, and the more they egged him on, the more he laughed, loudly and freely like a man celebrating an overturned conviction.

Julia found Señora Alvarez at the back of the courtyard, still threatening to call the police if people didn't clear out. Julia took Señora Alvarez's hand and pulled her away. "Señora Alvarez, come with me. I have someone I want you to meet."

The woman gasped at being handled so roughly, but Julia pulled her out to where Concepción and Diego were dancing. She got behind Mrs. Alvarez and gave her a push, leaving her standing right in front of Concepción and the actor.

Concepción stopped dancing for a moment. She looked at Julia. Then she reached for Mrs. Alvarez's hand and introduced her to Diego.

The actor was breathing hard and his shirt was soaked through with perspiration. He took Mrs. Alvarez's hand and shook it. Mrs. Alvarez looked back and forth between him and Concepción a few times, until at last the light of his celebrity overtook her, and she reached out with both hands to touch him, withdrew them quickly, and reached out to touch him again.

She stared as Diego and Concepción started to dance again. Concepción tried to get her to dance with them, but the woman was too overcome to do anything but stand there watching.

Concepción stopped dancing and whispered something into Diego's ear, and he nodded. He looked around him, appraising the size of his audience. Then he took Mrs. Alvarez's hand, tipped her back into his arms, and kissed her.

The crowd erupted in applause and whistling. The kiss was a melodramatic kiss, a Hollywood kiss, a kiss for stage or screen. It had the effect of leaving Mrs. Alvarez clutching her chest.

As though this were the signal that everyone had been waiting for, the other guests, who until now had kept a respectful distance from Concepción and Diego, rushed in to be close to the actor. Gone was any hesitancy to touch him or speak to him. Mrs. Alvarez stood motionless in the dancing, pulsing, driving crowd.

4

Lucite Is Ten Times Stronger Than Glass

All talk among Julia's and Concepción's friends in the days that followed was about the actor. How, people wanted to know, had Concepción enticed someone of such celebrity to attend her party? What merit was there to the allegations that the actor was somehow involved in the disappearance of his ex-wife, Clarissa Mar, the bone-pale actress with the cocaine problem? How far had the police progressed in their investigation? The fact that Julia hadn't heard of Diego's missing ex-wife prior to Marta mentioning it did not deter people from pressing her for her opinion, or ending the conversation more convinced than ever of their own.

Concepción was riding a magnificent wave of euphoria. She called Julia every few hours to recount something the actor had said or done that she had just recalled, as though Julia were her diary for committing each precious detail. "Did you hear how Diego complimented me on my dancing?" she said during one such conversation. "He said he had never met anyone so natural on her feet! He was so friendly. It just proves you can't believe what you read. Can you imagine how Remedios must be eating her heart out? ¡Híjole! It's all gotten back to her by now, I'm sure. This may have to be my last Cinco de Mayo party. I mean, how could I ever outdo myself? I would have to get Madonna or something. I wonder if he knows Madonna." Later, she told about how he had promised to invite her to the premiere of his new movie, a spy thriller that was already being hyped on 3-D billboards throughout the Valley. The ads featured the actor grimacing painfully as he lunged from the window of a fiery building. "It really is amazing, isn't it, Julia? That I could have such a connection with someone so famous? I wonder when he's going to call. He said he would, you know. He must be incredibly busy. I'm sure I'll hear from him. After all, he had such a good time, he said so more than once. I wouldn't doubt if we became close, Julia, very close." Certainly this was wishful thinking on Concepción's part; yet Julia had to admit that, strangely enough, she had witnessed a kind of connection between them, if not the romantic one that Concepción alluded to.

But for all the chatter and awe generated by the actor, the guest who had made the greatest impression on Julia was Ilario. Though their conversation had been short, it still rang in her ears. She was able to recall every word.

It was silly, of course, to read anything into the fact that he had taken her up on her invitation. He had happened to be in the area; there was nothing more to it than that. Still, she wished she hadn't let herself be so distracted by other events. Sometime between Mrs. Alvarez's arrival and her being kissed by the actor, Ilario had slipped away. Julia hoped that she hadn't offended him in some way without knowing it.

One afternoon, after another long, frustrating call with her potential client Mr. Guzman, Julia literally bumped into Ilario as she was rounding the corner outside his office. He smiled at her in the same bright way he had at the party and said, "I didn't get a chance to thank you. The other day was really fun. You throw a good party. I just wish I had been able to stay longer."

"We'll be throwing another one again soon," Julia said, though it wasn't true.

"That's great. Listen, I've got a vendor waiting for me in my office. But we should talk later. There's something I want to ask you."

He said good-bye and continued down the hall. Julia glanced over her shoulder a few seconds later at the same time he did. Smiling, he called back, "By the way, I'm still waiting for that rum and Coke."

Her heart leaped. Prior to the party, they hadn't exchanged more than a couple of sentences. Now he wanted to ask her something. She sat at her desk for several minutes, her heart racing. She looked around for the company policies manual to see what it said about dating among employees. She covered her mouth with both hands and laughed.

A short while later, Ime called to invite her for a drink at Clear, a singles lounge in Studio City where Ime liked to fish for potential clients among the well-heeled after-work crowd from the nearby movie studios. Knowing from experience that socializing with Ime while she was in prospecting mode was a recipe for frustration, Julia had declined Ime's invitations in the past to meet there. But today she was eager to confide in her friend about Ilario. She wanted her advice, too; was she about to make a mistake similar to the one that had ultimately forced her to leave her last job?

At the time, she had been working for about a year as a sales rep for an industrial-lighting manufacturer. What had begun as a mild flirtation with her boss ignited into an all-consuming affair that became the talk of the company. Even now Julia found it hard to pinpoint exactly what she had seen in the slender, balding gringo who had been her manager and who her friends called Mr. Burns, Jr., because he looked like a younger version of the character from *The Simpsons*. She could only say that she had felt a strong sense of security in his arms, an allaying of the anxiety and uncertainty that for her so often characterized work. Amid rumors that Julia was sleeping with him to get ahead, they had agreed to stop seeing each other. But by that time her co-workers' resentments were making her dread coming into work. The situation with Ilario was very different (he wasn't her boss; they worked in separate sales groups). Even so, she wanted Ime's approval.

At the bar, Julia sat on one of the white leather chaise lounges to wait for Ime. After a couple of minutes, Julia realized why the bar was called Clear. Nearly everything in the lounge, from the bar stools to the doors to the lounge tables, was made of transparent Lucite. Julia chuckled to herself at the silliness of it. Just then, Ime appeared in the crowd.

She was wearing a suit that Julia had never seen before, a sienna-colored two-piece with bladelike lapels. She settled in next to Julia and rapped her knuckles on the Lucite cocktail table. "This stuff is ten times stronger than glass," she said, as though this justified something. She shouted for the bartender to send over a couple of drinks, then said, "I can only sell so many more starter houses to boring couples. I need to be thinking bigger. I'm thinking of moving to the other side of the hill."

"But you've built such a great reputation here," Julia said.

Ime dismissed the concern with a wave of her hand. "Commercial properties. That would be more exciting, don't you think?" She patted Julia's knee and laughed. It was wonderful to see Ime in such a good mood. Her life was stressful, and she rarely found time anymore to enjoy herself. In spite of Ime's self-proclaimed self-sufficiency, or perhaps because of it, Julia also worried more about her than about any other friend.

Julia tried to think of a way to bring up Ilario. She was a little embarrassed that she was having such a girlish reaction to him. She folded and unfolded her napkin. But before she could even start, Ime took her by surprise by saying, "Ilario. I've been meaning to talk to you about him. I had a nice little chat with him at the party. He mentioned that he might want to buy a house soon. Don't worry, I didn't press him, he just happened to bring it up when I told him I was a broker. He doesn't think he has enough for a down payment, but I explained that there are all kinds of mortgage options these days. I left it at that, but if he decides to start looking, I want to work with him."

"You gave him your business card, didn't you?"

"Of course. And if he asks, I want you to tell him how committed I am to my clients, how hard I work for them, that sort of thing. You know, if it comes up."

A waitress set down their drinks and a Lucite tray of pretzels. Ime handed her a credit card and took a pretzel, twirling it thoughtfully as she tried to suppress a smile. "There's something else I wanted to ask you, Julia," Ime said. "When I was talking to Ilario, I have to say that I was very impressed by him. He seemed a little self-centered at first, but underneath it all I felt he was genuine, muy simpático. I wouldn't go so far as to say that there was a connection between us, but there was a spark—yes, that's it, a spark. Not that he was flirting with me, exactly. But I've been in sales long enough to know how to read people, and I'm pretty sure he was interested. I've been thinking of asking him out. What would you think if I were to go on a date with him?"

Julia swallowed hard. "A *date*?"

"Oh, I know what you're thinking. I've never had a very positive outlook on men. But recently I've started to wonder, why am I denying myself? And what am I working so hard for if I can't share it with someone?"

Julia set her drink down. Liquid splashed over the rim. She wadded her napkin and dabbed at the spill.

"I didn't want to do anything without checking with you first," Ime said. "I know how you feel about mixing your personal life with work."

The room suddenly felt very hot to Julia. "Ime," she said, "I don't know that that's such a good idea. You see, the thing that I wanted to tell you is . . . well, *I* was thinking about asking Ilario out."

Ime's head popped back a few inches. "What? That's impossible. Just the other day you said . . . you didn't even want him coming to C's party."

"I know," Julia said, "but that was before we talked. At the party he was really friendly to me. And for the first time I got the feeling that . . ."

Ime gave a loud, wooden laugh. "Well, this is really something, isn't it?" She set down her drink and crossed her arms. She smiled tensely.

"I think the best thing," Julia said after a few moments, "is for neither one of us to ask him out."

Ime blinked rapidly.

"Ime," Julia said, "don't you think that's the best thing?"

"I think that's going to be a problem," Ime said.

"How so?"

"Because," Ime said, "I already asked him. He said yes. We have plans for Friday."

"What?! You just said—"

"I know what I said!" Ime said. "I was being polite. I didn't think you'd actually object!"

"So you went ahead and asked him? When?"

"About an hour ago."

"And he said yes?"

"Of course!"

"And he didn't mention me?"

"No." Ime lowered her voice and leaned forward. "Listen, do you really want a repeat of what happened at your last job?"

"This is different."

"Is it? You yourself said you were never again going to date someone you worked with."

"Oh, I see! So you're doing me a *favor* by going out with him."

"Julia," Ime said, the tone of her voice dipping condescendingly. "You've been at Ostin for eight months. If Ilario were interested, don't you think he would have said something by now?"

The silence that followed while Ime waited for her to respond felt like a vice squeezing Julia's head. Finally, she could take the sensation no more. As she stood, her knees knocked the table, tipping both their drinks. She did not stop to clean them up. She headed for the exit. Seeing that the doors, like everything else in the bar, were made of Lucite, she punched through them hard enough that had they been made of glass they surely would have broken.

❧ 5 ❧

Reflections on Chinese
Restaurant Decor

On the drive home, Julia found herself stuck behind a slow-moving Jetta. She was usually very patient on the road, but when she was angry she became a different kind of driver. As the Jetta crept forward—too cautiously for Julia—she whipped past it on the right, firing off a long, satisfying bleat of her horn.

Once inside her apartment, she slammed the door and kicked off her shoes. The left one sailed across the room, banging and scuffing the far living room wall. She went to the kitchen, pulled her "emergency Dos Equis" from the salad bin in the refrigerator, popped the top, and swigged. It wasn't often that she got mad at Ime, but when she did, a beer usually helped to calm her down.

Plopping down on her couch, she wondered how Ime could be so consistently self-absorbed. Putting herself first worked to her advantage in business, but it was often a source of problems for their friendship. Like the time Julia pointed out to her a vintage hand-bag she was bidding for on eBay, only to have Ime show up with it at a party later that week. Or the time Ime booked an Alaskan cruise to celebrate her birthday, but didn't first check to see if Julia could get the time off work (she could) or if their other friends could afford to join them (they couldn't). Julia wasn't sure whom she was more mad at—Ime, for muscling in on Ilario, or herself for not seeing it coming.

As she got down to the bottom of the bottle of Dos Equis, Julia's anger started to subside. What flowed in to fill its space was a twisted mix of guilt and regret, a feeling that made Julia think of someone reaching through her ribs and squeezing hard on some vital, nervy organ. It was hard to stay mad at Ime for very long. After all, she was the closest thing Julia had to a sister.

They had both grown up poor, but the experiences that had brought them the closest had little to do with that. Julia remembered how, when she was sixteen, she fell in love with the stock boy who worked at the AutoZone where she was a cashier. Three months later she was pregnant by him and he'd quit his job and was nowhere to be found. Terrified that her future was about to be destroyed, Julia asked Ime for her help. She didn't want the baby, but knew that her religious parents would never let her have an abortion. Ime had arranged everything, including finding a clinic and getting Julia a fake license that said she was eighteen. She'd stayed by Julia's side throughout, even spending the night in her room for the next two weeks until she was convinced Julia was OK. Later, when the boy reappeared wanting to see Julia again, Ime intervened. She went to his parents. Without giving them Julia's name, she told them what had happened—and warned them to keep their miserable kid away unless they wanted Ime to come back and cut his balls off.

Setting down the Dos Equis bottle, Julia decided she was calm enough to talk to Ime. She reached into her bag for her phone, but it chimed before she could dial. Ime was on the line.

"OK, I won't go out with him," Ime said.

"Seriously? Oh, Ime . . ."

"I'll come up with some kind of excuse why I can't. You know you're more important to me than some guy, right?"

Julia felt a rush of warmth. But guilt also fluttered around the edges of her heart. "I'm so sorry about the way I acted," she said. "I shouldn't have left you there like that."

"Not to worry," Ime said with a laugh that said everything was all right. "I got my business card out to a couple of interesting people after you left. I might just sell another house because of it."

For the next few days, Julia avoided Ilario at the office. She did not want him flirting with her, making her feel awkward. She certainly didn't want to be tempted by his beautiful gray eyes. But a few days later, when she did run into him as he was coming out of the lunchroom, to her surprise he acted neither flirty nor even very happy to see her. He nodded to her awkwardly as he passed but said nothing. She wondered if Ime had told him the real reason she'd canceled their date. Julia had pushed through the door to get out from under his gaze when he said her name.

She stopped with her palm against the door and looked at him. His brow was furrowed deeply. She winced a little as he came toward her. But when he stopped, something softer and sadder crept into his eyes.

"What is it, Ilario?"

"Is your friend OK? I mean . . . Ime, is she all right?"

Someone coming out of the kitchen pulled the door open, making her lose balance. She caught herself and stepped away from the door.

"She's fine," Julia said. "Why do you ask?"

"Well," he said with a heavy sigh, "we were talking at your party . . . and we had plans for Friday. She called and said she wasn't feeling well, and . . . I haven't heard from her since then."

A prickly, guilty sensation ran up Julia's spine. "I think she said

something about not feeling well . . . it might have been that flu
that's been going around. . . ."

"You talked to her today?"

"I think it was . . . a couple days ago . . . only I don't think she
mentioned . . ."

Ilario nodded. His gaze swept the floor at his feet. "I see."

"I'm sure she's been really busy. A lot of her clients are unpredictable, she never knows when she's . . ."

"Well, if you talk to her, could you—"

"Oh, of course I will—"

"Will what?"

"Tell her . . . you know . . ."

"Tell her what?"

"That you asked about her. Right?"

"Right," he said with a nod. "I get it." He turned away. Julia
watched him slowly walk down the hall with his hands in his pockets, his head hung low.

Julia went back to her office. Suddenly she felt terrible that
she'd made such a scene with Ime. Julia wondered if it wasn't *she*
who was being selfish. Ime was right that it would be a mistake to
risk dating someone from work again. And the truth was, Ime was
and always had been more attractive. Though Concepción and her
other friends often insisted to Julia that she was far prettier than
Ime, Julia knew from the way men's glances tended to bounce over
her and land on Ime that Ime had a quality she didn't. Maybe it was
the fact that Ime's eyes were dark and mysterious-looking, whereas
Julia's were brighter and more innocent. Maybe it was the fact that
Ime's features were sharper and more dramatic, whereas Julia's
were rounder and plumper. Whatever the reason, whenever they
were together, it was Ime who got the looks and whistles, even if
she was often in too much of a hurry to notice.

So if Ime wanted to go out with him, and if Ilario preferred Ime, what was the harm in letting them give it a try? Sure, it stung that he was more interested in Ime than her. But what kind of baby was she that she couldn't deal with that?

After mulling over Ilario's reaction for several minutes, Julia called Ime. "Go ahead," she sighed when Ime picked up. "Call Ilario. I can see that he really wants to hear from you."

"Are you sure?" Ime said.

Julia described the conversation they'd just had, how disappointed Ilario looked. "If he's that into you, who am I to stand in your way?"

As Ime thanked her, her voice brightened just as it had when she'd been talking about Ilario at the bar.

"Call him now," Julia said. "It's not pretty. Go ahead, before he falls apart at the seams."

Later that day, Julia walked by Ilario's office to see if Ime had called him. It took only a glance inside to see that his mood had completely changed. He was on the phone, leaning back in his chair with the expansive air of someone boasting about a major sale. Eavesdropping for just a few seconds confirmed what she suspected—he was talking to Ime, making plans for their date. Picturing Ime on the other end of the line, her face brightly lit with laughter, Julia felt good. Sure, Ime had once again gotten what she wanted. But it was worth it knowing Ime was happy. No one she knew deserved happiness more.

About a week later, as Julia was getting ready to meet Ime for their weekly dinner out, her doorbell rang. She went to answer it, and there standing in front of her were Concepción and Marta, hefting a clunky, out-of-date, top-loading VCR.

"We weren't sure you'd be home," Concepción said as she and Marta swept into her apartment.

"I'm on my way out," Julia said. "What are you guys doing here?"

"The Pacheco brothers just gave us a copy of the videotape they made of my party," Concepción said. "We need to connect your VCR to this one to make copies of it for all the doubters who don't believe that Diego Ramirez was really there."

"Who doesn't believe you?" Julia said.

"A lot of people," Concepción said. "Remedios has been telling people I made it up."

"I'll believe what I see on this tape," Marta said. She got to work connecting the VCRs. Concepción went into the kitchen. She came back moments later with a couple of Coronas, a bag of Doritos, a plate of chorizo, and some cold tortillas.

"You know, C, there's something I don't understand," Marta said as she struggled with the cords. "Why do you put yourself through this every Cinco de Mayo? Who cares if Remedios has a party the same day as you?"

"What you have to understand," Julia said, "is that once upon a time C made a mistake that Remedios is still making her pay for."

Marta looked up with interest. Julia glanced at Concepción for permission to tell the rest of the story. Concepción nodded.

"This was back in the day before we started hanging out at the Cantina," Julia said. "Remedios and C and I used to be friends. We used to hang out at the mall. Remedios had a boyfriend, Carlos, who used to flirt with C when Remedios wasn't around. One day, Remedios and Carlos left the mall, but then Carlos came back an hour later without Remedios. He started flirting with C as usual. No one thought much of it—until C showed up at my door the next morning, saying she had slept with Carlos. Well, we all knew it was only a matter of time before Remedios found out. Remedios is really smart and nothing gets by her. It happens that we had all planned to help Remedios paint her apartment that week. C didn't want to go, of course, but we convinced her that it would be best to face her."

"We had all been good friends," Concepción said. "In fact, we used to throw the Cinco de Mayo party together."

"C headed over before the rest of us to talk to her. Let me tell you, we were expecting blood when we got there, or at least paint splattered everywhere."

"Interesting," Marta said. "What happened?"

"Nothing," Julia said. "When C tried to bring it up, Remedios acted like she didn't know what she was talking about. She kept changing the subject until C gave up. We helped her paint. She broke up with Carlos the next day, never called C again, and that was that."

"To this day she acts friendly when I see her," Concepción said, "but she always cuts the conversation short. There's an edge to her. She knows."

"So that's her revenge? To throw a bigger party than you?"

"The party is just her way of reminding me that she hasn't forgotten. It's a game she plays to keep me sweating until she finds the right moment to get back at me. Look at what she did to Claudia Aguilar."

"Who's Claudia Aguilar?" Marta said.

"Claudia and Remedios used to be friends, too. Claudia did something to piss Remedios off—no one quite knows what—but Remedios pretended to forgive her. A few months later they took a trip to Vegas together. On the way back, Remedios kicked Claudia out of the car and drove off—just left her standing there in the middle of the desert. It took Claudia two days to find a way home. She ended up missing an important job interview."

Marta nodded thoughtfully, appearing both fearful and impressed.

Julia went to her bedroom to find her keys, and returned to tell them she was heading out to see Ime and that they should lock the door on their way out. Concepción and Marta, entranced by the image of Diego Ramirez dancing on Julia's TV, didn't respond.

To show that there were no hard feelings and that she really was OK with Ime and Ilario going out, Julia had offered to pay for dinner at the restaurant of Ime's choice. Because Ime's expensive tastes extended to restaurants as well as cars and clothes, it did not surprise Julia that Ime asked her to meet her on the other side of the hill in Hollywood at Chinny-Chin-Chin's, a new Asian fusion restaurant on Sunset that was reported to be popular with celebrities. As Julia carefully managed the twists and turns of Laurel Canyon over the hill, she tried to put herself in a sympathetic frame of mind. Several days had gone by since Ime and Ilario had gone out, and Julia hadn't heard any details, which most likely meant that the date hadn't gone well. Julia could recall hearing of many dates in which Ime had pressed a particular point too hard, resulting in a heated discussion that became an argument that ended the date. Julia admired the way Ime spoke her mind, but her friend had yet to learn that speaking your mind didn't always make for the best impression.

After handing her keys over to the valet, Julia walked into the restaurant and found Ime waiting for her in a booth situated in the middle of the spare, lowly lit room. She edged in across from her, trying not to hit her head on the bizarrely shaped blown-glass lantern that looked like a human heart turned inside out.

"I think I need to move to this side of the hill," Ime said. "This is where all the fun places are. I need a change."

This was not the first time Julia had heard this lament. Ime was never satisfied with her life. But that was also why she was so successful. She was happiest when she was focused on something new. After a minute or two more of filling Julia in on how difficult her clients were and how bored she was selling houses, Ime worked her way around to the topic of her date with Ilario.

"Well," Ime began cautiously, "at first, I wasn't sure we'd have much to talk about, but I think that's because we were both nervous. By the time we got to Capo in Santa Monica—have you been there? I'll have to take you—we were talking all right. Then afterward we went for a walk and then rode the Ferris wheel on Santa Monica Pier."

"So did it go well?" Julia said, not sure how to interpret Ime's neutral description.

"It wasn't bad."

"Are you seeing him again?"

"We'll see if he calls."

"Did he say he would?"

"They usually do."

"Do you *want* to see him again?"

Ime could no longer hold back. A grin emerged on her face, blossoming into an unabashed smile. "Julia, I can't wait to see him again. He's good-looking and smart and has no problem with the fact that I make more money than he does. And when he disagreed, it was *fun* to disagree with him. How many Latino men can you say all those things about?"

"Huh," Julia said. "So you had an OK time."

"It was better than OK. We talked for hours and he was completely respectful. . . . Julia, thank you so much for being such a good friend."

"Oh, sure, sure," Julia said, reaching for her water. She pressed the rim to her mouth, wetting her lips, and put the glass down.

"Really, Julia, he's much nicer than I was expecting. Muy, muy simpático."

"Wow. Well. That's really great," Julia said. "I'm glad it went all right." She opened her menu a second time. The type was too small to focus on. "What should we order? I'm guessing the portions here are small, am I right?"

Ime touched Julia's hand. "Julia, are you sure you're OK with this?"

"With what? You and Ilario? Of course! It's about time you had a date that went well. Now, go ahead, tell me more."

"Well," Ime said a bit thoughtfully, "I like the fact that he has big plans for his future. He's not content to stay in the same place, doing the same thing for very long."

"That is great. Just great, Ime." Julia looked at her menu. "How about the spring rolls here? Have you tried them?"

"I know I shouldn't get too excited after just one date," Ime went on. "Life is so unpredictable. But still . . . No, no, you're absolutely right. I shouldn't be acting like a stupid teenager. OK, enough about that. Let's talk about you. What have you been up to?"

Julia brought the conversation around to her work, her parents, their friends. But every few minutes Ime couldn't help adding something new about Ilario. He looked so good in a suit. He liked to ride horses in the Santa Monica Mountains. His father, a gardener, had cared for the grounds of Bob Hope's estate in Toluca Lake for twenty years. Julia smiled and nodded attentively, torn between wanting to change the subject and trying not to miss a word.

Then Ime mumbled something about waking up in Ilario's bed.

"You slept with him? Already?"

"Not so loud! They can hear you in the kitchen."

"On the first date, Ime? I don't think you've ever done that before!"

"I know," Ime said, "it's not like me. But let's face it, it had been eighteen months, I was overdue, things were going well, and I just figured . . ."

"You just figured! I can't believe what I'm hearing, Ime, I really can't. . . ."

"Since when do you care about things like that?"

"Since when do you sleep with men you barely know?"

"You're always encouraging me to relax and meet more people."

"By relax I mean go on vacation or take a bubble bath. . . . But this . . . Ime, do you think he's going to call you now?"

"I don't see why not. Anyway, I had a good time. And if it means he doesn't call, well, there's not much I can do about that." She grinned again. "His eyes are the same color as my Beemer, Julia. They match perfectly. How do you like that?"

Julia crossed and uncrossed her legs. She picked up her chopsticks and set them down.

"Julia, you said you were OK with this. Are you sure—"

"I said I was OK and I'm OK," she said. She picked up her chopsticks again. She struggled to bring food to her mouth with them, then gave up and switched to a fork. "Concepción is going to flip when she finds out."

"Don't you dare tell her! You know what a gossip she is."

"I'm just watching out for you, that's all," Julia said. "You know how guys are. I don't want you to be disappointed." She swallowed a few bites, then looked around at the interior of the restaurant, fully taking it in. It was modern, cold, and unappealing. There was nothing Chinese about it. Why would someone open a Chinese restaurant and then go out of their way to make it not look Chinese?

∿ 6 ∿

A Poolside Discussion of Love,
Sex, and Murder

So somebody finally nailed her," Concepción said, with disbelief mirroring Julia's. "And by that hot papi, of all people. On the first date, no questions asked. That little puta! Maybe now she'll stop giving me a hard time."

Concepción was referring to the way Ime often criticized her not only for the number and type of men she slept with but also for failing to wait some unspecified proper amount of time before doing so. Ime's self-righteousness was made even more infuriating to Concepción by the martyrlike way she bemoaned how doubly hard it was for a career-minded woman like herself to find quality men who weren't intimidated by her success. Concepción found it bizarre that someone of Ime's looks would deprive herself of something Concepción found essential to her own sanity, which was plenty of good, hot sex. Now, having such a good piece of gossip with which to silence Ime in the future, she eagerly absorbed every detail Julia had to offer over the phone. She even jotted down notes with a pencil, the *scrape-scrape-scrape* of which Julia could hear on the other end of the line.

"This is all good information," Concepción mused. "Did she

make the first move or did he? Was there anything kinky she wouldn't want me to know about?"

Julia ought to have felt guilty that she was talking to Concepción after Ime had asked her not to, but she just couldn't keep the news to herself. "I can't believe she would do something like this," she said. "She can't possibly think he's going to call her now."

"It's a double standard, no doubt about it," Concepción agreed. "But that's life. Oh, speaking of Ime, are you going to her place on Sunday? It's Nina's birthday. Ime's making lunch. I'm bringing the cake."

"Shit. Thanks for reminding me. What a disaster if we'd forgotten again."

No one could explain how it was possible that for the last three years in a row, Julia and her friends had missed Nina's birthday. They had all pledged this year to do something nice for her to make up for last year's rushed, last-minute get-together at Marta's. Not that Nina seemed to mind being overlooked. Each year she accepted the oversight with the same glum resignation that she did most of the facts of her life, assuring her friends that to do anything special would have only embarrassed her. In fact, she was fond of saying, having her birthday forgotten was the best gift she could ask for, since birthdays only reminded her of how, when she was seventeen, the uncle who had raised her admitted that he had long ago lost track of her real date of birth and had replaced it with the date of June 15, since that was the same date his Chihuahua died and was therefore easy to remember.

On Sunday, Julia crisscrossed the wide boulevards of the Valley to Encino, where a few months earlier Ime had bought her latest house. Ime upgraded properties as often as she upgraded cars, with each new purchase bringing her a little farther west into whiter and more upscale Valley neighborhoods. She was now nestled along the rim of the Valley at the base of the Santa Monica Mountains, as far west and south as she could go without leaving the Valley. Marta now referred to Ime as a west Valley girl, as well as a pocha and even a traitor for leaving her northeast Valley roots so far behind (or at least for not bringing her friends with her). Such criticism did not faze Ime. She *was* fazed, however, when one of her neighbors, seeing her for the first time coming out of her new home, mistook her for a housekeeper and asked what her rates were.

Ime's newly constructed three-thousand-square-foot, three-bedroom house with a stucco and masonite exterior sat at the end of a heavily shaded cul-de-sac, with a single high-arched window facing the Santa Monica Mountains. Walking up the front steps, Julia suddenly found herself strangely nervous about seeing her. She rang the bell and Ime came to the door. She gave Julia a queer look. "Why did you ring? You know I always leave the door unlocked when you're coming over."

Julia walked into the bright white living room. She had never seen walls so white. They were almost hard to look at.

"I'm in the kitchen making lunch," Ime said, shaking the hair out of her eyes. "You can help me. But first, boy do I have a story for you about C."

Julia followed her into the kitchen. "What did she do this time?" she said.

Ime sighed. "You know how much she was expecting to hear from Diego Ramirez, right?"

"She thinks they're friends. I know, it's crazy."

"She's been writing letters to him, pleading for him to get in touch with her. But of course he hasn't. So yesterday, she and Marta got the clever idea to pay him a visit in person. They went to Hollywood and bought one of those star maps from a kid on Sunset and went to find his house."

"Please tell me you're kidding, Ime."

"They didn't see him, of course. The security guard at the gate

turned them away, but C kept demanding that she was a close personal friend of Diego's."

"Oh, shit, Ime."

"It gets better. Marta and C decided to come up with an alternate plan, so they drove around while they tried to figure out what
to do next. Well, I guess someone in the neighborhood got suspicious, because the next thing you know, there's a black-and-white
right behind them flashing for them to pull over. They ask C for her
license and registration and all that, and after some back and forth,
the cop decides that something is up, and asks them to get out of
the car so he can search it. And guess what he finds? A little bag of
pot in C's glove compartment."

"¡Ay, que pendeja! What was she thinking?"

"Actually, there were only some seeds and twigs in the bag, so
he just gave them a warning. I'm telling you, Julia, this obsession is
going to get C into some kind of trouble. Do you know she's written
about twenty letters and e-mails to him?"

"No! She's a celebrity stalker."

Ime divided a sandwich diagonally with a knife. "My idea about
changing our phone numbers doesn't sound so bad now, does it?"
She often joked that eventually she and Julia would need to aban-
don Concepción, Nina, and Marta in favor of better friends.

"I'll have a talk with her," Julia said. She began slicing cucumbers rapidly, rattling the cutting board.

"You OK?' Ime said.

"Mmm-hmm." She added the cucumbers to the salad and carried
the bowl out to the patio table.

Marta was already in the pool, swimming slow, steady laps, her
heavy arms and legs crashing against the water with each stroke.
Julia set the salad down on the glass table under the large patio
umbrella. From the pool Marta waved, then emerged in a red, white,
and blue one-piece bathing suit and a rubber bathing cap from

another era, yellowed by age. Water slid off her body, turning the pavement dark around her stubby feet. She tossed off the cap and plucked a couple of times at the elastic around her thighs, creating more sheaths of water. "Órale, Ime, this sure is a nice place," she said. "I'm sure sorry I hassled you for moving out here. You know, you really should come by the bar more often for free drinks." She thrust her wet arm into a canvas bag for a pack of cigarettes. Once a cigarette was lit and dangling from her lips, she patted herself dry and said, "Is that sinvergüenza here yet? Did Ime tell you the trouble she nearly got us into?"

"I hope you can get her to drop this obsession with this actor," Julia said.

"What do you mean?" Marta said. "The whole thing was my idea. I want to meet Diego Ramirez before it's too late. Haven't you been following the news?" She dug through her bag. "There's been a development in Diego's ex-wife's disappearance. They found some of her things. They think there's been some kind of foul play. Here. Look." She unfolded a copy of the Los Angeles Times. She had underlined some key sentences in an article. "Listen to this: 'At the marina, investigators found pieces of the actor's ex-wife's jewelry, namely, links from a bracelet she was believed to be wearing at the time she went missing.'"

Julia leaned over the paper and read. The police had found some of her other possessions as well. Some lace from a blouse she had been wearing. The broken heel of a shoe. The items were being tested in a lab. The police would not say what they hoped the tests would reveal, or whether they thought the actor, the last person known to have seen her, was involved.

Marta then took out a large scrapbook with black pages, a pair of scissors, and a glue stick. She had been saving newspaper clippings about the case.

"Oh my God," Julia said. "You're even more obsessed than C is."

Marta began carefully excising the article. "It's not every day you come so close to meeting a murderer."

"You think he did it?"

She shrugged. "Hollywood fucks people up."

Concepción arrived a short while later, yoo-hooing softly as she came through the house in shorts and clear plastic flip-flops with rainbow sparkles in them, carrying a plastic mesh bag jammed to the breaking point with lotions. She apologized for being late, saying it had taken her nearly an hour to find her bathing suit, and then the Pentecostals had asked her to watch their kids for a few minutes, and so on and so on, she didn't want to bore them with the details, to which Marta said too late. Concepción wiggled out of her shorts, revealing an orange one-piece that was scooped high at the thighs and low at the neck. Instead of joining them at one of the chairs at the table, she dragged a lawn chair up next to them and straddled it, then dug through her bag for a particular tube of lotion, which she applied to her face and arms and legs.

"C," Marta said, "I've told everyone about our little adventure."

"I'm not embarrassed," Concepción said. "It's because you had been smoking that pot that the cop smelled something and searched the car."

"Thank God I *did* smoke it," Marta said, "otherwise there would have been something for him to find. I saved your ass. Speaking of which, haven't I told you not to wear bright colors? Unless hippopotamus street hooker is the look you're going for."

In her sweetest voice Concepción told her to go fuck herself, and then closed her eyes and leaned back in communion with the sun. Marta tried to bring to her attention the clipping she was now carefully pasting in her scrapbook, but Concepción wasn't interested in reading anything that bad-mouthed Diego. She was convinced—as, she said, anybody who looked at the facts would be—that his reputation for being a hotheaded Latino was prejudic-

ing people against him. The bright side of the whole situation was
that it explained why Diego hadn't responded to any of her e-mails
or letters. Clearly he had bigger chicharrones to fry, what with reporters bothering him every minute. No, she wouldn't entertain any
"ugliness," and would someone please change the subject, to, for
instance, Ime and Ilario?

"How is that going, anyway?" she asked Ime.

"It's going well," Ime said. "Ilario and I went out again last night
and were making plans to do something after work on Tuesday."

"Really?" Julia said. "He called you? Even after—"

Ime shot her a look. "Yes, he called me. Why wouldn't he?
We've been having a great time and we seem to be very compatible.
If there's one thing I'm good at, it's reading people. I can tell how
much he likes me. Besides, you should see how good he looks in
my Beemer."

Everyone laughed except Julia. Ime couldn't expect anything
to come of dating him with this kind of attitude.

"Of course," Ime went on, "if I decide to trade up to the 7 Series, then all bets are off. I always coordinate my beaners with my
Beemers."

The others laughed again. Julia sat back and crossed her legs.
She reached over and pulled Marta's scrapbook toward her.

"It's wonderful that you're getting along so well," Concepción
said. "And I think it's so great that you're taking your time getting
to know him. I'm sure that if Ilario is so special, you're not going to
rush anything."

"He's special," Ime said vaguely. "Speaking of special, wait until
you taste these sandwiches. I made them with fresh bread from
the Victoria Market."

"But how long do you think you'll wait?" Concepción said. "I
mean, you want him to respect you. How long should a woman wait
to make sure a guy respects her?"

"It's different for different people," Ime said. "I would never judge anyone for waiting or not waiting."

"No, you'd never do that," Concepción said. "But I'm glad to know that one of us is very principled about that sort of thing. Just out of curiosity, how long *do* you think you're going to wait?"

Ime shot Julia a look. Julia turned a page of Marta's scrapbook. Without taking her eyes off Julia, Ime said, "I've always said that you should do it when the time is right."

"That's such good advice," Concepción said. "When the time is right. I should write that down."

Julia turned another page of Marta's scrapbook.

"Say," Marta said, "isn't there something missing from this birthday party? Like a cake? Like *Nina*?"

"¡Ay, que jodida!" Concepción said.

"You forgot the cake, didn't you?"

"Not just the cake. *Nina.* I told her to meet me outside her place at two."

"You forgot her!"

"I got distracted! Can someone else go get her? I'm all greased up."

"I'll go," Julia said. Ime's eyes were still on her. She was glad for an excuse to get away. But as she started to get up the back gate swung open and Nina appeared. Julia hadn't seen her in several weeks, and she looked no less gloomy for having had that much more time to deal with her breakup with Roberto. Even in the glaring summer sun she looked grim and wintry. Nina closed the gate behind her and joined them at the table, and after everyone had wished her a happy birthday and Concepción had apologized for forgetting to pick her up and Marta had given her a backhanded compliment about her shoes, Nina announced dismally, "Roberto and I are back together."

Julia got up from her chair. "Nina, that's such good news!"

But nothing about Nina's demeanor said it was. She accepted Julia's hug limply, then lowered herself to the edge of a chair. "He was calling me every day and coming by at all hours. Finally I couldn't take it anymore, so I said I'd get back together with him."

"Is that such a good reason to get back together? So he'll stop bothering you?"

Nina shrugged. "I figured I wasn't any happier or unhappier with him or without him, so what's the difference? If it makes him happy to be with me, I guess it's no big deal for me to be with him."

"Are you really so indifferent?" Julia said. "Didn't the two of you used to have fun?" But she realized as she said it that it was Roberto's delight in Nina that she was remembering. She couldn't really remember what Nina had been like with *him*.

"I thought about what all of you said. Roberto really does love me. And I never really cared all that much that he cheated on me."

"Does he still want to marry you?"

"Yes."

"Do you think you might?"

"I don't know."

"There's just one thing I don't get," Concepción said. "If you were never really that upset with him about his cheating on you, why did you break up with him?"

Nina shrugged. She had never been able to give a satisfactory reason. The fact that she still couldn't convinced Julia more than ever that Nina had done the right thing in taking him back, and that she, Julia, had done the right thing in encouraging her.

7

Pages from the Nina Gutiérrez Book of Espionage

The people in Julia's and Ime's lives understood and accepted that their careers often took precedence over spending time with friends. Concepción, Marta, and Nina were used to them rushing off to meet clients and canceling dates with them to attend to unexpected work emergencies. What they didn't know—but what Ime and Julia understood about each other—were the reasons for their being so career-driven. For Julia, her job was a first line of defense against returning to the financially troubled times of her youth. For Ime, it was something quite different.

Around the time of Julia's abortion, Ime had been having problems of her own. Her father, depressed by the closing of the GM plant and unable to find work, turned to the bottle for comfort. Though Julia never saw the severity of his drinking, she saw the pain it caused Ime; she often saw her struggling to hold back tears when she talked about him. To avoid seeing him in such a lost state, Ime began working longer and longer hours at her after-school job doing office work for a plastics company in Van Nuys. The worse her father became, the more she obsessed about work, driving herself harder and harder, taking on more and more responsibility. Her job and eventually her career became her escape. It still was. She had never slowed down. She had never looked back.

A side effect of her industriousness was that she rarely dated. The few men she chose to make time for left her bored by their lack of drive, or they were quickly intimidated by her surplus of it. Now at last she seemed to have found someone who appreciated her for who she was. Yet try as she might, Julia found herself unable to feel truly happy for her. It filled her with shame not to feel like the best friend she so often prided herself on being.

But not feeling like a good friend was no excuse for not behaving like one. After she hadn't seen Ime for a couple of days, Julia called her from work to see if she wanted to meet up for dinner again.

"I'd love to," Ime said, "but I've got plans with Ilario tonight and tomorrow."

"So things are still going well with you two," Julia said.

"Well enough," Ime said. "You know, no major problems yet."

Ime's words were measured, but beneath her steady tone Julia heard hints of optimism, joy.

"Well, that's really good," Julia said. "You deserve this." That much she could be completely sincere about.

During her lunch hour that same day, Julia was pulling up to the drive-through dry cleaner on Sherman Way when Concepción called to tell her to turn on the news. "It's all over the place," she said. "Everything is ruined. *I'm* ruined. I'm never going to get to go to a Hollywood movie premiere."

Julia turned on her radio and skipped through the stations in search of the news while Concepción tearfully did her best to fill her in. Between Concepción and the news on the radio, the story began to take shape:

Police had at last collected enough evidence to charge Diego Ramirez with the murder of his ex-wife, the childhood TV actor, Clarissa Mar. Her body still had not been located, but investigators believed the actor had killed her. Tests conducted on Ms. Mar's personal possessions found near the Long Beach pier south of Los Angeles pointed emphatically to Diego Ramirez. Police would not say what the tests revealed, only that they were more than enough to justify a warrant for Diego's arrest.

Even more shocking announcements followed: Diego Ramirez had fled the country just hours earlier. Passenger records confirmed that he'd been on that morning's Aeromexico flight to Guadalajara. U.S. authorities were working closely with the Mexicans to locate him. The L.A. chief of police, a man Julia remembered seeing ridiculed on TV for his failure to solve several recent high-profile cases, spoke without embarrassment when asked by reporters how Diego could have slipped through his fingers. With steely confidence he said that justice would be served, then praised everyone in his department for their hard work in solving the case.

"I can't believe it," Concepción said. "He's gone. I'm never going to see him again, am I? Do you think this is why he didn't call? It has to be. He didn't want me to get any closer to him. He knew it would only be that much harder to say good-bye."

Julia assured her that this must be the case, though of course she didn't believe it. As the news played on Julia's radio, Concepción speculated as to the actor's whereabouts and intentions. But at no time did the fact that he might have killed someone seem to enter into her thoughts.

"There goes my *dream,*" she lamented.

But Julia knew that Concepción's hopes went far beyond attending a premiere. In coming to her party, Diego had done more than elevate her reputation. Concepción believed he had transformed her life. She longed to return to the source of that transformation, and to be warmed once again by the healing glow of his celebrity.

On her way back to the office, Julia stopped at the Royal Deli on Victory to pick up a sandwich to eat at her desk. She had just been handed her order when her eyes were drawn to a pair of toffee-colored sling backs with flared heels, worn by a smartly dressed woman in line for the register. They were beautiful, expensive-looking shoes, similar to the Via Spigas that Ime loved. Even though Julia could tell just by looking at them that she couldn't afford them, she had to ask the woman where she'd gotten them. She decided to wait for her to finish placing her order before approaching her.

Though she could only partially see the woman's face, she could tell she was attractive. She had a wonderful figure and carried herself with a self-confidence that Julia was able to manage only in the best of circumstances. Feeling inadequate in comparison to this stranger, Julia had quickly begun to reconsider going up to her when the door to the left of Julia opened and a man strode in, placed a hand on the woman's lower back, and kissed her cheek.

It was Ilario. Julia froze. For several seconds she tried to move but couldn't. When her efforts finally translated to motion, she was out the door and across the strip mall parking lot in seconds.

Her heart raced as she got in her car. She wasn't sure what she had just seen, but there was no doubt there had been a kiss. Whether it was innocent or not she hadn't been able to tell. She didn't want to believe that Ilario could be seeing someone besides Ime. Then again, he had slept with Ime on the first date. Who was to say he wasn't just the type of user such behavior would imply? She could have kicked herself for leaving so quickly. Why had she fled? Had she just remained there a little longer, she might have been able to figure out who this woman was. She could have made herself known and then judged from Ilario's reaction whether this was something Ime ought to be concerned about. The kiss had been only a peck on the cheek. But it *was* a kiss. And his hand on her lower back—that was significant.

Struggling to come up with an innocent explanation, Julia drove back to the strip mall. She floated her car through the lot, peering through the deli window. She did not see them. They had already left.

Trying to make sense of what she had seen, Julia took her time returning to her office. When she got there, a message from Mr. Guzman was waiting for her. Her heart jumped. She had completely forgotten that she had made an appointment to speak with him to answer his questions about a service contract with Ostin Security. She had hoped to have his signature by the end of the week.

When she called his office, an annoyed-sounding person who did not identify himself told her that Mr. Guzman had left for vacation and would not be back for at least two weeks.

"Did he say anything about the paperwork I sent him?"

"You'll have to talk to him."

"He didn't say anything?"

"I don't know anything about it. But you might be sure next time to be available when you say you will be. He looked pretty pissed when he left."

Julia sank into her chair. Self-disgust crept over her. How had this happened? How had she let herself be distracted from something so important?

. . .

That evening, Julia's thoughts eventually swung back to Ilario and the woman with the toffee-colored sling backs. She needed to talk to someone before saying anything to Ime. But who? Telling Concepción anything inevitably amounted to making a general news broadcast. Marta could be trusted with a secret in the short term, but she always warned that three months was the maximum length of time she could guarantee secrecy, after which time her rapidly deteriorating memory absolved her of any responsibility for remembering what she had promised to keep secret from whom.

This left Nina. While Nina was Julia's last consideration, this wasn't because she was untrustworthy. If anything, Nina was the most tight-lipped of her friends, and always eager to be of use. It was an unfortunate consequence of her personality, however, that she rarely came to mind as a first choice for, well, anything. Only when other options were ticked off did one consider Nina.

Julia invited her to lunch, and the next day drove by her work to pick her up. Nina worked as a seamstress for Dream Weavers, a company that made and repaired costumes for movies and TV. The business was located north of the railroad tracks in the treeless industrial section of Burbank, among other warehouses in the shadow of the Verdugo Mountains. The Dream Weavers warehouse housed tens of thousands of costumes that moved like ghosts along several miles of elevated electric costume rails. Nina had worked there since high school and now managed five other seamstresses. Nina, never much of a moviegoer, chose the few movies she did see according to whether or not her company's work was likely to appear in the film.

Julia parked behind the warehouse at a safe distance from a stake truck that was unloading enormous bolts of bright yellow fabric. She entered through the back of the building and found Nina coming down the stairs from the office that overlooked the operation. Nina had her wallet in her hand and was ready to go.

As usual, Nina insisted that they go to the Taquería La Esmeralda in nearby Sun Valley. The taquería was an airy, clamorous place with white plastic chairs and tables, high aquamarine walls, and tall brick-arched windows that let in plenty of light. As usual, a line of patrons, many of them workers from the nearby foundries and auto shops, stretched out the door. Fast-working cooks kept the line moving quickly as they whipped together orders of burritos and asada while flames licked up from the grill behind them.

Once they were seated with their food, Nina peeled the wrapper back from her burrito and after sniffing the foil a couple of times, folded it neatly into squares and placed it in her purse. She appeared less depressed than she had at Ime's; or, if she was depressed, her mood had no effect on her appetite, for within a minute she had eaten the better part of her meal. Julia, on the other hand, only picked at her asada as she told Nina about the woman with the toffee-colored shoes. Julia wasn't sure if Nina was listening. But apparently she was, for after chewing thoughtfully for a minute or so, she said, "Maybe she's a friend."

"They looked too friendly to be friends," Julia said.

"Maybe it's someone from an old job."

"How many of your former co-workers do you kiss on the cheek and practically pat on the ass?"

"Maybe it's a sister."

"Ime never said anything about him having a sister."

"Maybe it's his cousin."

"Nina, stop naming random things! Tell me, what should I do? Should I say something to Ime?"

"Well," Nina said between mouthfuls, "you *could* do one of those things."

"Or?"

"You can spy on him."

"Spy? Are you serious?"

"Sure, why not? If he's seeing someone else, he's going to be sure to see her while Ime is out of town at that job thing. While she's gone, you could do some detective work. You could follow him after work and see where he goes. You could go by his house and wait to see if he shows up with her and use a pair of binoculars to look into the house or over the fence into his backyard. You could steal his cell phone and check his phone log and write down the numbers of people he called yesterday and call them and see who answers. You could—"

"All right, Nina, I get it. You've never done anything like that, have you?"

"It's not that hard," Nina said. "People never think to look to see who's behind them in traffic. You can actually follow someone for miles without them knowing it—if you borrow a car so they don't recognize you and keep a couple of car lengths behind them and wear a hat and sunglasses."

Julia stared. "You spied on Roberto?"

"A couple of times."

"To find out if he was cheating on you in TJ?"

"I tailed him to see what he was up to."

"So when he told you, you already knew?"

She nodded.

"And you never said anything?"

"After I saw her, I realized I really didn't care that much. She wasn't much to look at, and when I saw what her life was like, I kind of felt sorry for her."

"Then why did you break up with him when he told you about it?"

The noise of order numbers being called out and dishes clattering filled the air. Nina plucked a napkin from the dispenser and dabbed her lips. "I'm still hungry. You've hardly eaten anything. Is there something else you'd rather have?"

Julia did her best to avoid Ilario at the office the next day. She truly didn't want to believe that what she had seen meant anything. Still, she felt she had to do something. She had pretty much discounted Nina's suggestion of spying, when she overheard Ilario talking to a woman whose voice she didn't recognize. Julia jumped up from her chair and peered out her door. At the end of the hall Ilario was talking to the woman with the toffee-colored sling backs.

She watched as the two of them walked down the hall and disappeared around the corner. She heard the ping of the elevator. She heard the doors open and close, sealing off their conversation. She didn't know what to do. At the very least she ought to follow them out of the building. If she could just see a little more of their body language, she would be better able to judge the situation. So why was she hesitating? The door to the stairwell was right across from her office. She reached for it and raced down the stairwell, her heels clanging on the metal steps. At the bottom she paused at the door and opened it slowly and peered out. Ilario and the woman were crossing the lobby. Once again his hand was on her waist. They stepped out through the glass doors.

Julia counted to five, then hurried to the doors and looked out. Ilario and the woman were crossing the parking area to Ilario's car. Ilario opened the passenger door of his car for the woman. Only it wasn't Ilario's car: It was Ime's. There was no mistaking the bright silver exterior. Julia was the only person Ime ever lent her car to. Now she was lending it to Ilario. Did she have any idea that he was also driving a strange woman around in it? Something definitely wasn't right. Ime deserved an explanation.

She waited until she saw Ilario begin to back out of his parking space before rushing to her car. She got in and circled the perimeter of the lot until she could see Ime's car easing out onto the street. Julia left the lot seconds later and followed until she had Ime's car in sight.

She tried to keep a few cars between herself and Ilario, but a few seconds later the cars ahead of her turned off the road, leaving Ilario in front of her. He came to a stop at a light. She pulled up behind him. She dropped her visor and stretched her neck high to obscure as much of her face as she could. The light turned green and she followed.

About a half mile down Lankershim Boulevard they turned off on Victory in the direction of the Burbank airport. Was she leaving town for a trip, or was she a visitor to L.A.? It looked suspicious either way, this woman departing town only hours before Ime was to get home.

Julia added a little more distance between herself and Ime's car as she followed him down Hollywood Way. Signs for the Burbank airport came into view and the lanes slowed and merged. Julia lost sight of Ilario for a few seconds, but then the silver Beemer came back into view as the road curved toward the terminal. Ilario pulled over to the curb. The short passenger drop-off area was too small for Julia to pull up behind Ilario without being seen, so she eased into the red zone several yards behind him. Ilario got out of Ime's car and popped the trunk while the woman got out on the passenger side. He removed her luggage, set it on the curb, and extended the handle of her suitcase for her. He put his arms around her and hugged her and—

Julia jumped at the sound of a gloved hand knocking at her window. She looked up to see a police office glaring down at her. "Keep it moving," he said. "You can't stop here."

Julia lowered her window just a couple of inches. She nearly whispered, "I'm just waiting for someone. You see, there's no room to park up ahead and—"

"There's plenty of room right there. Come on, let's move unless you want a ticket." He blew his whistle at her and pointed to the white zone behind Ilario. "Come on, I'm not shitting you, move!"

Ilario and the woman were still hugging, swaying slightly from side to side. Julia pulled away from the curb as slowly as she could. She noted again how attractive the woman was, with dark, delicate features and wavy black hair. They were still hugging, still hugging. . . . What kind of hug was it? Was he going to kiss her again? What kind of kiss—

The officer banged his fist on the trunk of her car. "I said *now*."

Shit. Julia shielded her face with her hand so Ilario wouldn't see her. She checked her rearview mirror. The cop was glaring at her. She pressed the gas and swung away from the curb.

And into a passing delivery van.

A metallic shriek tore through the air. She mashed her foot on the brake as the van shoved her car back flush against the curb. The car swayed violently, sloshing the contents of an old coffee cup. Beads of brown liquid flew into the air, spattering her custard-colored jacket and skirt. The van stopped. The cop came trotting up to Julia's window. His red but concerned face peered in at her. A man jumped down from the passenger side of the van and looked in. People along the curb turned and stared.

Ilario was among those looking. He had relinquished his grip on the woman with the toffee-colored sling backs. She was giving him a final good-bye kiss on the cheek as he looked in Julia's direction. Julia covered her face with her hand. Through her fingers she watched. She willed Ilario not to come over. She took a map from her glove compartment and hid her face behind it. He was walking right toward her. Shit. Shit shit shit shit shit shit shit shit shit.

The cop knocked on her window again and asked if she was OK. She told him she was. He told her to get out of the car. The driver of the van peered in at her. He was a big man with black-rimmed glasses and delivery shorts. Giant letters on the van behind him read EMPIRE ELECTRONICS. Julia pressed the map to the side of her face as though applying a bandage to a wound. She pushed her door open. The metal groaned. The cop helped her out. The minivan driver asked if she was OK.

"I'm fine, I'm fine," Julia said. She looked up at the sky. At the van. Ilario, go away, Ilario go away. It was too late.

"Julia, are you all right?" He came up to her and put a hand on her shoulder. She nodded briskly. "Fine, fine."

"Excuse me," the cop said to him, "you need to attend to your car. You can't leave it there. Go back and move it."

"I know her," Ilario said. His hand was like a weight on her shoulder. "We work together."

"What's the matter," the van driver said. He sounded more concerned than angry. "I guess you weren't looking where you were going, huh?"

"Julia, are you all right?" Ilario said.

"I'm fine, I'm fine, really."

"Sir, please go back to your car," the cop said.

"I just want to make sure she's all right."

"I'm really fine," Julia said. "I'll see you back at the office."

"Sir, I'm not telling you again. Your car. Move it. Now."

Ilario looked closely at Julia. His hand came off her shoulder. "All right. I'll see you back there." He went back to his car—Ime's car—but kept turning back to look at her. He kept looking back even as he got into his car. Even as he drove away she could see him watching her in his mirror—silver eyes watching her from a silver car.

Julia and the van driver exchanged insurance information. Julia was grateful to him. He hadn't so much as raised his voice at her. He kept asking if she was all right, if there was anything he could do for her. The force of the impact had gouged a long scar into his van, but he barely took notice of it. He kept looking at Julia's car instead, at the dented door and crumpled front right corner. Julia admitted she'd been distracted. Julia thanked the cop, waved awkwardly to the van driver, and pulled away.

Back at her desk, Julia stared hopelessly at the coffee spots on her jacket, growing more and more disgusted with herself. She could not believe what she had done. What had she really thought she was going to learn? ¡Pendeja! In one day she had missed an important business call, wrecked her car, ruined her suit, and made a fool of herself. Her insides knotted up. These weren't the kinds of choices she made. This wasn't *her.*

How was she going to explain this to Ime? Since when did she not go to her when she had a concern? This was the last time, *absolutely the last time* that she would ever—

"What were you doing at the airport?"

Julia looked up. Ilario was standing in her office doorway. His jacket was off and his arms were crossed and his shirtsleeves were shoved to the elbows. A tie with yellow zigzags blazed on his chest.

"Ilario. Come in, I was just—"

"What were you doing at the airport?"

"I was . . . getting into an accident?"

He didn't laugh. "Seriously, what were you doing there?"

"Well, I was dropping a friend off and—"

"Dropping a friend off?"

"Well, not so much dropping *off.* More like picking up . . . except she didn't show . . . because her flight was late . . . and then I hit that car . . . and then the next thing I knew—"

"Were you following me?"

"Following you? No, of course not! I mean, I was there at the same *time* you were, and you were ahead of me, so I was *following* you. But I wasn't *following* you. . . ."

He kept staring at her. Her throat went dry. She tried to clear it.

He came closer. He pressed his fists against her desktop, driving down at an angle that seemed to make the desk, the room, and everything in it tilt away from her. He wasn't a very tall man, but he seemed tall to her just then.

He said, "The woman you saw me with is my best friend, Lydia. We used to date. Now we're friends. She stays with me when she's here on business. If you had asked, I could have told you."

"I'm *so* sorry," Julia said. "I didn't mean to follow you. I saw you with her and I didn't know who she was and I didn't want Ime getting hurt. I know I should have minded my own business. It was really stupid of me, I just wasn't thinking straight, I only wanted to protect Ime. . . ."

He kept his eyes locked on her for several seconds. His angry yellow tie blazed. Black hair swirled and surged in wild patterns on his forearms. After a few more moments, he took his fists off her desk, leaving a pattern of condensation where his knuckles had met the wood. It evaporated within seconds.

"Can I ask you one more thing?" he said.

She nodded.

"Did Ime put you up to this?"

"No, of course not! She didn't know anything about it. It was me, I just wasn't thinking. I just acted on the spur of the moment. I'm sorry, I really am. . . ."

His eyes mined her for the truth. With a steady calm that was even more unnerving than if he had shouted at her, he said, "Lydia is my friend. Just like Ime is yours. She watches out for me. Just like Ime does for you. But I don't ask Lydia to spy for me. I don't ask her to follow people to airports. I would never ask her to do something like that, and she would never consider doing it."

He turned and left. This time there was no backward glance, no smile, no wink. Only a shake of his head that seemed to say she was the saddest person he had ever met.

Half the air in the room seemed to go out with him. The echo of his words and the lingering residue of his cologne turned her stomach. The zigzag pattern of his tie left an imprint in the air. It burned there before her for the rest of the day, bright and angry and electric.

8

Nina Discerns the Truth

Never before had Ime sounded so angry.

"Do you actually mean to tell me that you followed him to the airport because you thought he was cheating on me?" she said when she called. "Did it ever occur to you that there might be an explanation? Did it occur to you to just call me?" She had returned from her real estate conference and had just talked to Ilario.

"I'm so sorry," Julia said. "I don't even know why I did it. I acted on the spur of the moment, I wasn't—"

"I *met* Lydia," Ime said. "Ilario went out of his way to introduce us. They dated a few years ago, but there's nothing between them."

"I'm sorry, Ime. I just saw them together looking so friendly, and I just assumed—"

"They're friendly because *they're best friends.* Do you know what the worst thing is? Now Ilario thinks I don't trust him. He thinks I send my friends out to spy on him when I'm out of town. My God, we had such an argument about it."

Julia's stomach turned. She hadn't thought she'd be causing a problem for anyone other than herself.

"Ilario and I and Lydia had dinner before I left," Ime went on.

"Was I uncomfortable meeting an ex-girlfriend? Sure. Was I jealous? Of course. But I managed to keep that to myself. Do you know how this makes me look?"

"Ime, believe me, I never meant—"

"You know what I think?" Ime said. "You have a problem with me dating Ilario."

The words were like a jolt to Julia's heart. She clutched at her chest. "Problem? No, Ime, I just—"

"Ever since we started going out, it's been clear you don't approve. What do you dislike so much about Ilario?"

"Dislike? Ime, no, it's nothing like that."

"Do you think I'm not good enough for him? Or . . . is it that *you* still like him?"

The room seemed to rock around Julia. She had to lean against a doorframe to steady herself.

"Ime. Listen. Please. I know what I did was wrong. It was stupid. But you have to know I never meant any harm. I'm not one to interfere."

"You've been acting out at me from the start."

"How can you say that? I'm the one who told you to go ahead and call Ilario."

"You told C I slept with him on the first date right after I told you not to. Why would you do that if you weren't trying to hurt me? Well, I guess it's natural to be jealous when you can't find a man of your own."

The comment was like a boulder tossed into the air. It landed hard on Julia's chest, forcing out a puff of air.

A painful pocket of silence grew between them. Please say you're sorry or you didn't mean that, Julia thought. She listened for some sign of regret on Ime's end. But when Ime spoke again, it was only to say, "I have clients to see. We can talk about this later."

. . .

Julia sat for a long time with the phone in her hand, stunned. Ime could be sharp-tongued, but Julia had never known her to be cruel. Then again, she never would have imagined herself doing something as crazy as following Ilario. Both her and Ime's actions seemed like those of strangers.

It made her dizzy to think of how Ilario must now view her. She wasn't sure what was more upsetting—the fact that her best friend was so angry, or the fact that Ilario was angry *and* thought she was a nutcase.

Later that day she called Nina to ask if she could meet her at the auto-body shop on Vineland so that she could drop her car off and get a ride home. The accident had gouged the left side of her Acura and torn off the left front lights. But more than needing a ride, Julia was desperate for someone to talk to.

Naturally, Nina was happy to see her. She met her at Alliance Auto Body. Once Julia had dropped off her car, Nina drove her home. Julia filled her in on everything that had happened, cringing as she repeated what Ime had said to her. When she had finished relating the whole story, Nina gave her a sidelong look and said, "So you're in love with Ime's boyfriend."

Julia took a gulp of air. "Nina, is it obvious?"

"Well, it seems like you went to a lot of trouble to find out if something was going on with this woman. I know I said you should spy on him, but I never thought you would actually do it."

"Nina, I was just looking out for Ime. Sure, I went overboard, but—"

"And then there's the way you act whenever Ime talks about him. You usually start inspecting your nails, then as soon as the subject changes, you jump back into the conversation."

"Nina, Ime is my friend. Sure, I was attracted to Ilario, and maybe I still am. But I'd never . . ."

"And then there was the time Ime was talking about giving him head and you got this look on your face like someone was sticking a hot poker up your—"

"All right, Nina." Her cheeks sizzled. "I get the point. I mean, maybe it's true. When I told Ime to go out with him I never thought I'd react this way."

Nina nodded thoughtfully. She set her turn signal to make a left on Van Nuys. The directional made an accusatory *tsk-tsk-tsk* sound.

Julia sighed. She'd assumed that whatever feelings she had for Ilario would fade quickly. Now they loomed up around her, frightening her. She looked out on the broad, busy boulevard. Repair shops and strip malls and machine shops floated by. "Nina, can I trust you not to say anything? It'll only make things worse between me and Ime."

Nina nodded again. With this final assurance, Julia revealed to her how hard the last few weeks had been. Only now did she realize how much she had been hurting, how much she had been suppressing. She talked for the length of the ride home. Never would she have thought that she would turn to Nina in confidence. Yet here Nina was, taking in everything she was saying with a knowing tilt of her head that hinted at her own sort of wisdom. It felt safe to tell her. Never before had she trusted her so much. Never had she valued her so much as a friend.

9

U-turn

Four days went by during which Julia did not hear from Ime. Never before had they not made up within hours after having fought. The long silence dug at Julia, carving out a hollow in her soul. Then one day, while she was shaving her legs on the lip of her tub and trying to think of a way to make things up to Ime, Ime called to say she'd overreacted. "You were only trying to help," she said. "I'm sorry about that mean thing I said to you."

"I'm so glad to hear you say that," Julia said. "I've been miserable hoping you'd forgive me."

Ime's voice quavered. "It's just that I really like him, you know? I didn't expect to feel this way. I always figured I'd have my career, my friends, but never . . ."

Julia balanced her plastic razor on the tub's edge and drew her knee to her chest. She'd never heard Ime talk this way. Something within her buckled, giving way to sympathy. "Ime, I promise from here on out I'm going to try and be more supportive. I won't interfere anymore, I swear."

"At least not until I ask you to?"

Julia laughed. "Not until you ask me to."

"It would mean a lot to me if you could apologize to Ilario, too," Ime said. "I'd like it if you could find a way to be friendly with each other."

As far as Julia was concerned, she had already apologized. But she was willing to do so again if it would help things between her and Ime. Not that she was looking forward to it. Ilario's steely calm voice was still echoing unpleasantly in her ears. Nevertheless, she was resolved to clear the air with him once and for all and to put her strange behavior behind her. He'd had enough time by now to cool off. He ought to be ready to forgive her.

The next morning Julia arrived at work feeling tense but optimistic. She went by Ilario's office at eight thirty, but he was on the phone. At nine she went by again, but he was in a meeting with his manager. At nine thirty he was not in his office and at ten he was on the phone again. As vexing as it was to find no opening in which to talk to him, throughout the morning she found herself admiring his energy and the way he applied the full force of his personality to every interaction. Stopping outside his office on her last attempt to speak with him, she listened as he tried to allay a customer who, from the sound of it, had discovered a key clause missing from a contract Ilario sent him. Ilario's intonations rose and fell in an apology that, to Julia's ears, was masculine elegance itself. He spoke in a way that was clear, articulate, and professional, measuring each word to assure the customer that he was understood and appreciated. It was a kind of music. And it must have captivated the client as much as it did Julia, for within minutes she heard Ilario saying, "No, no, no, you have nothing to feel bad about. It's my pleasure to work with *you*."

Standing unseen outside his door, Julia wondered with a pang whether in other circumstances Ilario might not have something to teach her. It was no wonder he was Ostin Security's most successful sales rep. Her admiration for his abilities only fueled her attraction to him, further complicating her already complicated jumble of feelings toward him. Realizing that if she waited much longer she might lose her nerve to talk to him, she took a step into his doorway to make herself known and to wait him out.

He was leaning back in his chair with his tie liberally loosened. He and his client had progressed to some topic that had nothing to do with business and Ilario was laughing freely. Julia was encouraged by his mood. It took several seconds for her to catch his eye. She smiled, hoping this would elicit from him a gesture to come in and have a seat while he finished his call. It didn't. Instead, he furrowed his brow and spun his chair away from her.

Julia found it hard to believe he was still being so harsh. A company sales review meeting was starting in twenty minutes. She preferred to have a private conversation with him, but if he wasn't going to accommodate her, then she was going to have to speak with him at the start of the meeting with other people looking on. This was fine with her. She went back to her office to return a customer call, and then went into the Sierra Room, where all sales group meetings were held.

People were just beginning to gather. As usual, coffee and pastries had been laid out on the bureau under the engraving of the Sierra Nevada mountain range that ran the length of the side wall. Ilario was seated at the front of the room, talking to Roger, the VP of sales. No doubt Ilario was doing everything he could to secure the management job with Key Accounts. Julia ran her fingers along the mahogany bureau as she approached the front of the room. She waited for a break in Ilario and Roger's conversation. The chair next to him was open, so she moved to take it. Just as she reached it, though, Ilario slapped a yellow folder on the seat and said, "That's taken," then continued talking to Roger.

Julia stood for several seconds, not knowing what to do. Flames of humiliation licked up from her collar around her face and neck. Co-workers bustled around her, taking their seats. At a podium another VP tested the sound system by whispering into the microphone. Julia remained in the same spot, feeling more and more foolish. The meeting was called to order and the few remaining people who hadn't taken their seats did so. Julia retreated, taking a seat near the back of the room and off to one side, by the end of the etching where the Sierras dropped off precipitously. Only after the meeting was under way did Ilario remove the yellow folder from the chair, leaving a glaring empty space beside him.

She stared at the back of Ilario's head, which at that moment seemed bigger than all the other heads in the front row. It was confounding that he was being so unreasonable, so unwilling to cut a little slack—for his *girlfriend's best friend*. Julia had been willing to take any opening and he had offered none. She half listened as division heads took turns updating the group on the quarter's figures. She heard talk of projects, targets, challenges, opportunities. Something about an upcoming restructuring, nothing that would lead to positions being eliminated, nothing to cause concern. After a few more minutes, when she thought no one was looking, Julia burned a path out of the room.

"He was awful," she said to Nina when she called that night. "I've done everything I can. Ime can't expect more from me."

"I'd love to talk to you about this," Nina said, "but you've caught me at a bad time. Marta and I are on our way to see *Lovers and Assassins*."

"That Diego Ramirez movie?"

"Why don't you meet us at the theater?" Nina said. "It'll help you get your mind off things."

"You know," Julia said, "that doesn't sound like a bad idea. Get a ticket for me. What time does it start?"

Julia met them a few minutes later under the cursive script neon marquee in Burbank. In the theater, Nina unsnapped the expandable leg pockets of her cargo pants and started handing out roast beef sandwiches and sodas and candy bars.

"I hear there's full frontal in this one," Marta said as the lights dimmed. "Diego shows us his tiliches."

The word "tiliches" sent Nina into a giggling fit. Soda spurted out of her nose. This caused Marta to start giggling as well. They giggled throughout the previews, whispering "tiliches" in each other's ears until the movie started.

Lovers and Assassins turned out to be one of the worst movies Julia had ever seen. Diego Ramirez played a hired killer recruited to assassinate the dictator of an imaginary banana republic, but who unwittingly falls in love with the ruler's rebellious daughter. The indecipherable plot jerked along from Central America to New York to Tibet, and though Julia was no geography expert, she was fairly sure that there was no way to travel those distances in the tiny time frame provided by the story. Even worse than the movie's flaws of logic was the way Ramirez grimaced and poisonously spat his lines, looking as pained when making love to his costar as when leaping from the window of a fiery building. Once, as he was boarding a plane on-screen, Marta shouted, "No wonder you fled the country, Diego. I wouldn't want to be around for the opening of this piece of shit, either!" and the audience rumbled with laughter.

As the credits rolled and they made their way out, Nina said, with something akin to satisfaction, "That was really violent."

"We didn't see much of Diego's tiliches," Marta said, triggering another fit of giggling.

Out in the lobby Marta and Julia perused posters for upcoming movies while Nina went to use the restroom. Julia was drawn to a poster of an upcoming romantic comedy called *Breaking and Entering Hearts.* The poster showed a young blond woman with flushed cheeks climbing through an apartment window where two police officers appeared to be waiting for her. The actress looked a little like one of the girls who had come with Diego to Concepción's party. With a snort, Marta dismissed the movie as just the sort of thing she hated, a romantic story full of whiny women who didn't earn their happy endings. She much preferred stories about adultery and murder. Deaths by cancer were also good.

In the reflection of the poster case, Julia glimpsed two familiar figures walking up from behind. She spun around to see Ime and Ilario approaching arm in arm.

Everyone expressed surprise to see one another. Julia and Ime hugged. Ime introduced Ilario to Marta, who advised them not to waste their money on *Lovers and Assassins,* then, smiling at Ilario, tittered as girlishly as her raspy voice permitted.

The sight of Ime and Ilario together was like a punch in the chest. A gray designer T-shirt splashed with metallic color amplified the silver in Ilario's eyes. Ime had done her makeup in alluring evening tones. They didn't just look good together. They looked like celebrities.

"Of course," Marta was saying to Ilario as she twisted side to side girlishly, "I'm sure even Diego Ramirez would pay good money to have eyes like yours."

"Come on," Ime said to him. "Our movie is about to start."

"We're only missing the previews," Ilario said.

"I don't want to get stuck sitting in the front row."

"The movie's been playing for a month. There will be plenty of seats."

"I hate it when people step all over me after the previews have already started."

"It'll be you stepping on them, not the other way around, honey."

"That's what I love about you," Ime cooed. "Always thinking of others."

"Marta," he said, "it was nice meeting you." To Julia he simply said, "See you tomorrow," and dragged an indifferent gaze across her.

"How fucking hot is he?" Marta said once they were out of earshot. "How lucky Ime is! Look, look at him—look at his butt from here. ¡Híjole! I'm so jealous! Nina, come here, you just missed it. Ime was just here with her boyfriend. Julia, how do you work in the same office with someone that good-looking? It should be against the law to be that good-looking. Julia, invite him over to the Cantina sometime so I can get a closer look. My ex-husband was nice to look at, but I would have dumped his ass for a couple of hours with someone like Ilario!"

"What do you say we head over for a beer?" Nina said.

Marta wasn't done raving about Ilario. She went on for several minutes as they made their way out to the parking lot, delving into more and more graphic detail about what she would do if she had just a few minutes with Ilario and—

"Enough!" Nina said. "We get the point. Come on, let's go. Julia, do you want to meet us at the Cantina?"

"I'm feeling a little funny," Julia said. "You guys better go without me."

"Are you sure?" Nina said. "Just one drink with friends?"

Julia propped up a smile. "Maybe it was something I ate. You guys go, OK?"

She could feel Nina's sympathetic gaze on her as she branched off from them toward her car. Until tonight, it hadn't occurred to her that seeing Ilario and Ime together might pain her. The two of them looking so happy had been like a trapdoor opening under her and plunging her into cold water. Somehow, even while listening to Ime talk about Ilario, the image of the two of them as a *couple* had remained at the borders of her mind. Now it was unavoidable, growing bigger and bigger, taking over her brain like some cartoon tumor.

And the way Ilario had looked at her! As though she were a crazy street person he was afraid to make eye contact with. It was amazing that someone who prided himself on being able to get along with everyone would go out of his way *not* to get along with her. Maybe this was the slap in the face she needed. Ime and Ilario were in love, they were happy, and there was nothing she could do about it. She thanked Ilario. He was doing her a favor. How much easier, after all, to get past your feelings for someone when that person made it clear he despised you. How easy it was to recast what you thought was love—it hadn't been at all!—into something reassuringly hard and cold.

She was also grateful for the feeling of liberation. As she drove home, a light drizzle, unusual for summer, settled on her windshield. She set her wipers and turned on her phone. She had messages. The first one was from Ana, one of the reps in her group: "Julia, I wanted to congratulate you. But why weren't you at the meeting? Everyone was looking for you." Congratulate me for what? Julia thought. What was this *loca* talking about?

The next message was from Monica, a woman in Ilario's group. "Hi, Julia. Why weren't you at the meeting? Well, you really did it. Give me a call so we can talk." About *what?* Julia thought. She kept listening: "Just between you and me, it's about time someone knocked Ilario off his throne. You beat him out in sales for the quarter. And you only started with the company in August!"

Julia replayed the message. She wanted to be sure she understood. The thumping of the wipers matched the thumping in her chest. Was this some sort of joke? Something Ilario had put them up to to try and trick her? She had known her sales were good. Was it possible that without even knowing it she had beaten out all the other reps? Including *Ilario*?

She ran through the facts. Since starting at Ostin Security her main focus was to not repeat any of her past mistakes. It hadn't occurred to her that she might actually be doing *well*. The contracts she was securing had been coming easily enough. A giddy sense of triumph began to overtake her. Was she actually driving home at ten thirty on a Friday night while her friends were out having fun? What was she going to do at home? Cry about the fact that Ilario didn't like her? She pictured herself waiting for the crank-and-grind of her garage gate, then running up to her apartment, dropping her jacket, and stepping out of her shoes. And then what? Dumping herself into a chair? Paying bills? Moping?

Never.

The steady rhythm of the wiper blades seemed to be doing more than clearing rain from the windshield. It seemed to be clearing her thoughts, bringing them into order. Glancing once in the side-view mirror, she swung an illegal U-turn on San Fernando Road and shot south on Van Nuys in the direction of the Cantina. The rain was coming down faster now, but she didn't brake as she curved past the Panorama Theater in Panorama City. The peeling pink and white forties building, long abandoned as a movie house, now served as an evangelical church on the weekends. In lieu of a movie title, the marquee read PARE DE SUFRIR. "Pare de sufrir" is right, Julia thought. Stop your suffering.

A minute later Julia pulled up in front of the Cantina. A car was leaving a space right out front. A car coming in the opposite direction was signaling for it, but Julia pretended not to notice and took the space for herself.

In the bar she shook off the raindrops and made her way through the gathering Friday-night crowd. At the bar Marta was pushing a fresh beer toward Nina. They looked at her as she walked up to them and set her purse on the bar.

"I'm feeling better," she said, as though someone had just accused her of something. In a voice that may or may not have betrayed the manic mix of emotions at work inside her, she said to Marta, "Bring down the Patrón. I just got some good news."

Marta appeared puzzled but nevertheless reached for the top shelf.

"Are you all right?" Nina said.

"I'm fine."

"You looked mad."

"I feel happy."

"What are we celebrating?"

"Do you remember that account manager job I told you about?"

"Yes."

"I want that job. I'm going to ask to be considered for it."

"I thought you said you needed more experience."

"I have experience."

"But doesn't this mean—"

"That I'm going to piss Ilario off in the process? I don't know. But it's time I took Ime's advice. I'm never going to get anywhere if I keep playing everything safe."

"Is that such a good idea? I mean, isn't it going to complicate things? What about your feelings for him?"

Julia dismissed this with a flick of her wrist. "Feelings change."

Just then a guy in a straw vaquero hat and boots and tight jeans came into the bar. He might have been good-looking (it was hard to tell; the bar was dimly lit). He gave Julia the up-and-down as he walked by.

"Do you know him?" Nina said.

"No," Julia said, making herself give the vaquero a smile. The vaquero joined his friends at a table and pointed out Julia to them. A couple of them patted him on the shoulder encouragingly. He nodded at Julia. Julia nodded back.

"You're not acting like yourself," Nina said.

"How should I act?"

"You're worrying me."

"There's nothing to be worried about, Nina." She handed her her bag. "Watch this for me, will you?"

"Where are you going?"

"To talk to him."

"Is he even your type?"

"I think he could be."

"You're going over there by yourself?"

"Sure. If I can make something happen, I'm going to make something happen. Like I said, Nina, tonight's a night to celebrate."

≈ 10 ≈

Ilario Reconsidered

Julia had sex with the vaquero until three in the morning, slept for three hours, then told him he needed to leave. Lying next to her in the knotted sheets, he grabbed his erection and waggled it at her in refusal. She nudged him a couple of times to get him moving, then, only half jokingly, threatened to throw his clothes out into the street.

Grinning slyly, he pulled his skinny body out of bed and drew his underwear up over his pencil legs. Julia's returning sobriety and the piercing morning light were making him look less and less attractive. How had she not noticed the huge gap in his front teeth? He needed to leave before she noticed anything else she didn't like.

From the bathroom he asked her in Spanish if he could shower before he left. Answering him in Spanish she said to go ahead, but to please hurry, because she had places she needed to be. He laughed and told her he thought her pocha accent was adorable. Her doorbell rang and she went to answer it.

Concepción was the only person Julia could think of who would bother her without calling first, and sure enough she was at the door when Julia answered it. Concepción apologized for being out of touch recently, but she had needed time to come to a decision about something, and now that she had, she wanted to share it with Julia. She hoped Julia wasn't going to dissuade her, for her decision was the result of hours of careful thought and soul-searching. Looking back on the enormous success of her party, Concepción said she understood now that God or someone like Him had answered her prayers in a spectacular way by sending her Diego Ramirez, and even if the actor's promise to take her to a movie premiere wasn't going to materialize, she understood that his appearance had been a sign to take action, and now, after turning it over and over in her mind, she was about to do something she never would have dreamed—

"Just tell me what it is!" Julia said. "It's six in the morning and there's a little man behind my eyes poking me with a stick!"

Concepción said, "I'm going to call Remedios and ask her to be my friend again."

Had Concepción said that she was joining the Pentecostal faith or even the military, Julia would have been less surprised. Concepción's rivalry with Remedios, whether real or imagined, had grown to such proportions over the years that it had become an inescapable part of who she was. It was noble-sounding to hear her say she wanted to make peace. It was also one of the worst ideas Julia had ever heard.

"Remedios *hates* you," Julia blurted. "You're only opening yourself up so she can hurt you." Her head was pounding. How much had she drunk last night?

"I don't believe that," Concepción said. "I want her friendship back."

"You've tried to apologize to her."

"I didn't try hard enough. And I can't ignore the fact that we once promised each other to always be friends. Once she sees how sincere I am, she's going to want to try."

"What makes you think—"

"That she'll even listen? Maybe she won't. But at least I'll know I did everything I could."

"Fine," Julia said. "Do what you want. But don't involve me. Remedios is dangerous. Remember what she did to Claudia Aguilar."

"That was a long time ago," Concepción said. "Julia, I'm going to need your help to convince her."

"Are you kidding? No. Never. You should have seen the way she acted when I saw her at the Victoria Market a few weeks ago. It was scary."

"But she's much more likely to agree to see me if she knows that you're going to . . ." Concepción was eyeing something on the floor behind her. Julia turned and looked. One of the vaquero's boots and a pair of wadded socks lay next to the couch. Concepción stepped away from Julia and started to follow the trail of strewn clothes from the night before.

"C, don't! Come back. Don't!" She reached for Concepción's arm, but Concepción shook her off.

"Does this mean what I think it does?" Concepción said.

"Damn it, C, I don't want you to see him."

Concepción followed the sound of running water coming from the bathroom off Julia's bedroom. "Just let me have a peek and I'll go." She pushed the bathroom door open a couple of inches and peered in. "Oooh, that looks pretty nice from what I can see. Julia, I'm happy for you. You needed that; you've been so tense lately."

"That's enough. Now go!"

"Fine. I'll go, but only if you promise to help me convince Remedios—"

"Go!" She shoved at Concepción with both hands to get her out of the bedroom. "Just go. And don't mention my name to Remedios." In the living room she opened the door and pushed her out. She closed it and chained it. She heard the shower shut off. A minute later the vaquero came out and started putting on his clothes from the night before. He came up behind her and nuzzled her shoulder, kissed her neck and cheek. Julia handed him his hat.

"Give me your number." Grinning, he screwed the hat down on his head. He looked better with it on than without it. She had made him keep it on while they were fucking. She could kiss him while he wore the hat.

"You already put my number in your cell phone," she said. "Last night. Remember? I'll call you. OK, thanks. Good-bye."

By Monday, Julia still intended to ask to be considered for the account manager job. As one of Ostin Security's newest sales reps, she knew her chances of getting promoted were slim, but who knew how long it would be before a similar position opened up? This is what Ime would do. This is what Ime would be telling *her* to do if she had never met Ilario.

Julia advised Roger by e-mail that she wanted to be considered for the job, and within seconds he responded that he wanted to see her. Making her way to his office, she pondered the similarities between her situation with Ilario and that with her former boss. In both instances she had mistaken talent for character and arrogance for self-confidence. She had allowed what she thought was love to blind her to opportunity. This time, though, she had broken the pattern. She had seen Ilario for who he was before what she thought was love could lead her into more strange behavior. She was pleased with herself. It was possible to learn from one's mistakes.

With a smile that Julia found greatly reassuring, Roger invited her into his office and asked her why she was applying for the job. Julia began to list strengths and qualifications, and after about a minute, Roger stopped her. "I'm already very familiar with your work," he said. "Obviously, there are other people here with a little more experience, but that by no means rules you out."

"So you think I have a shot at it?" Julia said nervously.

"I wouldn't be sitting here talking to you if I didn't," Roger said.

Given Ilario's popularity, Julia expected any number of people at work to try to dissuade her. But to her surprise, throughout the day, several of her co-workers offered their encouragement. It was Monica, from Ilario's own sales group, however, who surprised her the most. "It's about time someone tried to put Ilario in his place," she said, conspiratorially pulling Julia aside after an impromptu birthday gathering for their receptionist. The hardness in her eyes as she said this shocked Julia. Seeing that she had frightened her, Monica added, "It's just that given the choice between working for you and working for him, I'd take you. If it helps any, he doesn't always follow all the rules when he sets up agreements." Walking away, she gave a meaningful glance over her shoulder at Julia. Look into it, the expression seemed to say.

The fact that Ilario might play fast and loose with rules wasn't something Julia thought she could work to her advantage. It was common for sales associates to bend a rule or two now and then to seal a deal, and just as common for their managers to look the other way. But the exchange with Monica did affect her. On her way out of the office at the end of the day, she wondered whether Ilario's popularity wasn't some sort of illusion. She had thought that anyone with his talent must be universally admired, but she could see now that that wasn't the case. A different Ilario was stepping out from behind the image she had sold herself on.

"Did you want to see me about something last week?" Ilario's voice shot out from across the lot. She turned to see him coming toward her. He was smiling at her for the first time in weeks.

It wasn't a smile she liked the look of. "I want to congratulate you."

Julia stopped beside her car. She didn't want to talk to him. Her head was full of new ideas about him, ideas she needed to sort out.

"Good job on your sales for the quarter," he said.

"Thanks." She searched for her keys.

"And you've only been here for eight months?"

"Ten." Where the hell were her keys?

"Do you think," he said with a skeptical tilt of his head, "that it's a good idea to apply for that account manager job so soon after starting?"

"You have to seize opportunities when they come up."

"You also have to know when what looks like an opportunity is actually a pitfall."

Julia squeezed her keys, now in hand.

"I'm just saying," he said, "I wouldn't want you to create problems for yourself."

"Thanks for the advice," Julia said.

"I'm always ready to help," he said.

"You don't know what a help you've already been."

He turned his hands into guns and squeezed off a couple of imaginary friendly rounds at her. "Just looking out for you." He turned and went to his car.

Julia put her briefcase in her car, slammed the door, put on her sunglasses, and put her car in gear. From opposite directions, she and Ilario reached the south lot exit at the same time. She braked and gestured for him to go ahead of her.

He mouthed the words, "No, after you," and gestured for her to go.

"No, after *you*," she said, and repeated the gesture a little more grandly.

They both sat for several seconds. Inched forward at the same time. Stopped. Finally Julia went ahead, giving the gas an extra punch so that her tires squealed as she sped out.

A couple of hours later, Julia was still feeling good about herself when Concepción called to say that she had contacted Remedios to ask to meet her.

"And she said yes?" Julia said.

"Not only that, she said she was thrilled to hear from me."

"She actually said 'thrilled'?" Julia said.

"Yes."

"Then you're playing a more dangerous game than I thought," Julia said. "Thrilled" was a word Remedios used to use when she was being sarcastic. "Thrilled" worried Julia more than if Remedios had said "Fuck you, I hate you." She could picture a light going on in Remedios's mind, the one right next to the word "retribution."

"I told her you'd be coming with me."

"*Un*tell her."

"I can't. It's all arranged. She really wants to see you."

"Tell her whatever you need to, but I won't be there. I wish you luck. I really do. But this time, you're on your own, C."

She hung up the phone and turned it off and stuffed it down between the cushions of her sofa and put a pillow on top of that. Contacting Remedios would only create more problems than it would solve. And truth be told, Julia had her own reasons for not wanting to see or talk to Remedios.

⪢ 11 ⪡

Sensible Shoes and Sensibility

As much as Remedios might despise Concepción for betraying her, Julia suspected that Remedios resented her as well—not for anything she had done to contribute to that betrayal, but for remaining friends with Concepción rather than her. In their earlier years, Remedios had never been shy about declaring how much she cared for Julia. To anyone who would listen she praised her as her cleverest, most sensible friend. But Remedios—with her enormous eyes, tempestuous hair, and drilling intelligence—had always intimidated Julia. She had a temper, too. One never knew when someone, usually a stranger, would ignite it, creating a scene that would leave Julia rigid with shock and embarrassment. Julia admired her intelligence and assertiveness. But admiration seemed not to make room for affection, at least not that warm rise of feeling that Julia often felt for her other less intelligent, less assertive friends.

Julia's belief that Remedios resented her was confirmed each time Julia ran into her. Rounding the canned-goods aisle at the Victoria Market just a few months earlier, Remedios had met her with a wire-stiff smile that hid neither her indignation nor the dent she was inflicting on the yellow can of El Pato with her thumb. Julia feared that any retribution Remedios might unleash on Concepción would spill over to her as well, and she wanted no part of it.

Concepción continued to leave messages for Julia every few hours, trying to convince her to come. In her enthusiasm, she foresaw only the brightest possible outcome of a reunion: a friendship resurrected and an end to years of unnecessary anxiety. Her messages turned angry and desperate, until at last she threatened never to speak to Julia again if she didn't agree to come with her, adding, "I'm going to send you a check for all the money I owe you. Concepción Santiago de la Vega Smith doesn't end a friendship without paying her debts." The amount of money she owed Julia added up to . . . well, Julia had long lost track. If Concepción's sense of obligation required bringing her debt to zero before ending their friendship, then Julia had nothing to worry about.

It was the state of her friendship with Ime, however, that was most troubling to her. In spite of Ime's words of forgiveness, Julia had barely seen her since the airport incident. Now that she saw Ilario for who he was, she was anxious for her and Ime to get back to their usual routine. She invited Ime to join her at the newly renovated Galleria in Sherman Oaks, where they had spent so many hours together as teenagers. A D.Evine store had just opened there. Ime was sure to want to see the new line of shoes for fall.

But when Ime drove up in her Beemer and Julia jumped in, Ime did not kiss her. She did not launch into exclamations about the real estate market or the stupidity of her clients. She pulled cautiously away from the curb, focusing her attention on the neighborhood street signs—as though she were in an unfamiliar city and needed to be careful not to lose her way. The air-conditioning gave an uncomfortable bite to the air. Julia reached to turn it down, but Ime stopped her. "It took me forever to get the settings the way I like them," she said.

"Ime," Julia said, "you *can't* still be mad about the airport thing."

"What? That? No, of course not. I already told you."

"What then?"

"Hmm?"

"What are you mad about?"

"I'm not mad. Do I seem mad?"

"Something's not right."

"It's nothing."

Julia trained a sharp eye on her. "You're sure?"

"Mmm-hmm."

Ime hummed to the song on the radio, failing to hit most of the notes.

"You *are* mad," Julia said. She pressed down into the leather seat with her knuckles and shifted to face her. "Ime, this isn't fair. You forgave me already. You can't do this."

Ime puffed out her cheeks. "I'm not mad . . . about *that*."

"About what then?"

Ime splayed her fingers out from the wheel, ten crisp red nails. "I promised Ilario I wasn't going to say anything."

"But?"

"But . . . he told me about what you said to him the other day. I think it's terrible the way you talked to him. I don't understand what you have against him, and neither does he."

"Against *him*!" She clasped her hands to her chest. "Am I really hearing this? He said *I* have something against *him*?"

"That's all I'm going to say," Ime said.

"What did he tell you?" Julia said. "Sure, the last time we talked I wasn't exactly *nice*. But you should have heard him, telling me I would 'create problems' for myself if I applied for the same job as him."

Ime snorted. "Ilario wouldn't say something like that."

"Ime, he did! You don't know the way he's been treating me. I'm worse than gum on the bottom of his shoe. There's another side to him you haven't seen."

"Enough, I'm not talking about this anymore. I shouldn't have brought it up. Should I take the freeway? What's faster?"

Julia squeezed her head in her hands. It felt as if it was going to explode.

"Do you really have to go after the same job as him?" Ime said. "It's obvious that he's going to get it. Why are you putting yourself through this?"

"Ime, are you asking me to—"

"I'm not asking anything. I didn't say anything."

Julia bristled. She dug her fingers into the leather seats. She could not believe what she was hearing. How many times over the years had Ime encouraged—no, *demanded*—that Julia never let someone else intimidate her from going after what she wanted? Yet here she was, actually *discouraging* her.

"Why the hell are you taking his side?" Julia said.

"I'm not taking any sides," Ime said. "It was dumb of me to open my mouth. Can we not talk about this and just have a good time?"

"Sure," Julia said. "I'll just pretend you didn't just stab me in the back and everything will be just fine."

She crossed her arms tightly. A few minutes later Ime pulled into the mall garage. There were plenty of open self-park spaces, but Ime pulled up to the valet. She got out, took the ticket from the attendant, then addressed her Beemer: "Be good. Don't talk to any cheap cars while I'm gone."

The renovation of the Sherman Oaks Galleria had left no trace of the mall they had known as teenagers. Gone were the fast-food restaurants and bright, noisy boutiques that had been featured in movies and had drawn teens from across the Southland and beyond. It wasn't a mall at all anymore but a "shopping and business complex," featuring high-end, smartly lit stores and an elegant outdoor promenade. It was disconcerting to Julia that a place that had meant so much to them in their youth could be so totally erased, with no regard for the memories they had created there. Had Ime changed right along with it? Who was this person walking beside her?

Several of Ime's favorite clothing stores had opened in the Galleria. But as they strolled the promenade, Ime disregarded the merchandise in the window displays as not to her taste. Turning a corner, they came upon D.Evine, Ime's favorite shoe store. D.Evine shoes were out of Julia's price range, but Ime owned several pairs. She liked the bold styles and exotic fabrics and leather-wrapped heels. Ordinarily she would have kept Julia waiting while she tried on nearly every pair, but today the selection failed to impress her. She tried on one pair of mules and judged them to be too sensible. When Julia agreed with her, Ime changed her mind, said she liked them, and bought them.

A short while later, Ime sighed heavily and said, "I'm not seeing anything I really like here."

"Maybe we should stop for something to eat," Julia said, thinking that they could iron out their differences over a couple of drinks. "I think I saw a Cheesecake Factory over there."

"No," Ime said, inspecting a watchless wrist. "We should probably go. I have to pick up a key for a condo showing."

Silence hung between them on the way home. Pulling up across from Julia's apartment, Ime said, "Well, that was nice. I'll talk to you later."

Getting out of the car, Julia had the crimped sensation of being at the end of a date that had gone terribly wrong. She was halfway across the street when Ime rolled down her window. "I just thought you'd be willing to make the effort with Ilario," she said. "I mean, given how long we've been friends. I would have thought that would mean something."

She drove off before Julia could respond, leaving her standing in the middle of the blank, wide street.

Julia paced her kitchen. She gave the leg of her kitchen table a sharp kick. Yes, she'd been rude to Ilario, but that was nothing compared to his rudeness to her. There was no way for Ime to understand that. She was in love and was seeing only what she wanted to see. Her phone rang. She answered it, hoping it might be Ime.

It was Nina. Since Julia had confessed everything about Ilario, she had taken to calling Julia almost daily. Julia was glad to have her to talk to about Ime. But before she could tell her what had just happened, Nina was off and running about her night with Roberto. He had taken her to a little Italian restaurant that Concepción had recommended as being romantic but well within Roberto's budget, since it was always important to respect the fact that Roberto made less money than she did. The veal had been a little dry, the asparagus overcooked, and Roberto had asked her to marry him.

"Nina, I knew he would ask you again! What did you tell him?"

"I wanted to know what you thought first."

"You know how I feel about Roberto," she said. "But I can't tell you what to do. Can you see yourself with him?"

"I guess so," Nina said. "Things haven't been bad since I took him back."

"Do you love him?"

"I guess," Nina said. "Sure. I guess there's no reason *not* to marry him."

"Nina, this is a huge decision. How can you be so casual about it?"

"So you think I should wait?"

"Nina, don't put words in my mouth."

"I'm not just asking you. I'm asking everyone. I made a spread-sheet to keep track of what everyone tells me. I made columns for the pros, the cons, for yeses and nos, and for miscellaneous opinions. Should I put you down as a yes or a no? What are the top advantages and disadvantages of marriage? Don't think. Just answer."

Julia pressed her fist to her forehead. Another call was coming through. "Hold on, Nina. Let me get this." She switched lines. It was Marta.

"Marta, hi, how are you? Did you hear the news? Roberto asked Nina—"

"Yes, yes, I heard. That's not what I'm calling about, though. I talked to my nephew Juan, and he said he hasn't heard from you. Do you need me to give him your number so he can call you?"

Julia had no idea what Marta was talking about. "Marta, what do you mean? Juan? Your nephew?"

"Very funny," Marta said. "He'll be happy to hear that you've already forgotten his name. He had a great time with you Friday. I have to say, I was pretty surprised you were interested in him, him being a wetback and all."

Julia dropped to the edge of a chair. "Marta, can you hold on?" She switched back to Nina. "Nina. Listen. Remember that guy I went home with on Friday?"

"Marta's nephew?"

"Shit!"

"What?"

"I didn't know he was Marta's nephew!"

"Of course you did. Marta told you. We all joked about it. How drunk were you that you don't remember something like that?"

"Damn it. Hold on, Nina." She changed lines again. "Marta, hi. Listen, I'm really sorry, but . . . I had a great time with . . . your

nephew. But I don't really think . . . there was much of a connection. To be honest, I really wasn't planning on calling him. . . ."
She bit her lip. "Marta?"

"Oh, that's OK," Marta said. "Never mind, never mind. I just
thought . . . well, he really likes you, that's all. He's been legal since
Reagan, you know that, right? Well, never mind. I'll talk to you
later, eh?"

"OK, thanks, Marta. I'll talk to you later." She switched back.
"Nina, are you still there?"

"Can you help me plan my wedding?" Nina said. "I've never
been in one and I don't know where to start."

"So you're going to marry him?"

"I just decided."

"In the minute I was on the other line with Marta?"

"That was Marta? I wonder if she can get those mariachis that
played at C's party for my reception. Do you know how much they
cost? Do you think Ime would be willing to pitch in to help pay
for it? Should I have a small wedding, or something big and traditional?"

"Nina, hold on again. I think that's Marta calling back. Hello,
Marta?"

"So what exactly is wrong with my nephew that you don't want
to see him again?" Marta said.

"Marta, your nephew is . . . fine. I just didn't feel like we had
much in common—"

"I see, I see. So you decided to lie to him and say that you'd call
him? You don't think he has feelings?"

"Marta, it was just one of those things, I didn't even know he
was your nephew. I mean, I didn't remember, I was really drunk
that night and I—"

"I see, I see. OK, well, I better call him and let him know."

"Marta, I'll call him if you want—"

"No, no," Marta said. "Better that I do it. He's very sensitive, el pobrecito."

Marta was off the line before Julia could say anything else. She tried to get back to Nina, but this time it was Ime who was trying to get through.

"Ime, hi. I'm glad you called. Listen—"

"I'll be quick," Ime said. "I can't stop thinking about how you've been treating Ilario, and I just don't think it's right. It's too stressful to be dating him knowing that you really don't like him. It puts me in a terrible situation. I think maybe we shouldn't talk for a few days. I really want you to like him. But if you can't, then maybe we should take a break. I don't like being in this situation, it's very awkward."

"Ime, you can't seriously—"

"It wasn't until I got home that I realized how upset I really am at you. I just don't see you making an effort. It's not like Ilario has ever done anything to you. It's the smallest thing to ask you to try and get along with him, and if you can't at least pretend to for the sake of our friendship, then I think we should put our friendship on hold."

Julia felt the room go cold. She could barely breathe. What was happening to her friend? To them? She told Ime that maybe they needed to sit down and work things out, but Ime was already off the line. She checked to see if Nina was still there, but she was gone, too.

She tossed her phone and watched it spin across the kitchen tabletop. It stopped near the table's edge. She sat for a long time, Ime's words ringing in her head. She felt as though the walls around her were falling away. Several long minutes went by before her phone rang again. She stared at it, wondering if she should even answer. With each ring the vibration took the phone closer to the edge of the table. She lunged for it just as it was about to go over.

"Hello."

"Julia, hi, it's Roger from the office." Julia sat up. Her heart skipped.

"Hi, Roger. What's going on?"

"I was hoping to tell you this in person, but I'm going out of town tomorrow and thought you should know as soon as possible. We've made a decision about the job. We're not going to be able to offer it to you. I'm really sorry."

"Shit—I mean, shoot! It's going to Ilario, isn't it?"

"He has more experience," Roger said. "You'd be great for the job, but Ilario knows the products really well, and he's been here longer, and . . ."

Julia let out a breath. "That's OK. I understand, Roger." She closed her eyes as Roger went through a speech that she imagined he gave to everyone he turned down for promotion. Maybe it had been too much to expect to move up so quickly at the company. She had really believed she had a chance. It was disappointing, but she wasn't going to let it depress her. It was just a job, and she had learned something about herself in the process and—

"Hold on, Roger," Julia said. "Back up. What did you just say? I sort of wasn't listening. What was that you said? About the restructuring?"

"We've been planning for some time to make some changes," he said. "It's not official, but I guess it's OK to tell you now. We think it's going to create greater efficiencies to merge your group with Key Accounts."

Julia rose from her chair.

"It shouldn't really mean anything for you," Roger said. "You'll keep all your same accounts and the same territory. The only change is that from here on out you'll be reporting directly to the head of Key Accounts."

Julia pressed her fingertips to the edge of the kitchen counter, steadied herself. "The head of Key Accounts?"

"That's right. Ilario will be your boss from here on out. We think it's going to be much more efficient all around. Do you know him well? You're going to find him great to work with, Julia. I'm sure of it."

⤲ 12 ⤲

Anxiety at the
Revolutionary Cantina

The following morning arrived like a flood of wet cement. A stingy gray sky bled a grim measure of light through the blinds as she forced herself out of bed. *Ilario will be your boss. Ilario will be your boss.* The words were still going through her head. And so were Ime's: *I think we should put our friendship on hold.*

As she got ready for work, she wondered what she was going to do. Start looking for another job? The rumors about a restructuring had been circulating for a long time. She just never thought it would lead to this. And she never thought she would have to face a problem like this without Ime on her side.

She came to a standstill at her closet door. What did one wear to a job one had come to dread overnight?

Arriving at the office that morning, she did not stop to assess her appearance in the building's polished surface as she usually did. She went directly to Ilario's office.

"Congratulations," she said to him. She thrust out her hand.

He rose and met her with none of the gloating she had expected. He even seemed a little startled to see her. His Adam's apple rose above the knot of his tie as he shook her hand and said, "Thank you."

"Roger told me we're going to be working together, so I just wanted—"

"I'm going to be making some changes," he said.

All right, she thought. Here it comes. Fire me.

"I'll be meeting with everyone individually later, but as long as you're here, I should tell you. I'm going to take over Guzman myself."

"But I've been working on Guzman for—"

"Months. I know." He tapped a folder on his desk. It was Guzman's file. "This should have been put to bed by now. Technically, Guzman isn't even your territory."

"His main office isn't, but manufacturing is."

Ilario dismissed this with a shrug. "It's a gray area at best."

"Gray area?" Julia said, taking a big step toward his desk. "There's nothing gray about it. I'm *this* close with Guzman." She pinched her fingers together to show how close.

He nodded, but not in a way that indicated he was considering what she said. It was a sad little nod that said: This is just what I expected from you.

"Listen to me," Julia said, her voicing turning dark and a little mean. "I've put hours into this project. If you think I'm going to let you—"

"How long is the probationary period for new employees? A year, isn't it?" He drew a pen from his pen holder and set it on his desk. He gave it a spin.

Julia stared at him for several seconds, biting her lip. Fuck you, she wanted to tell him. Fuck me for ever liking you. And fuck Ime for being fooled by you.

The next words she said came out like dry pieces of gravel. "I guess you're the boss, Ilario. If you think you can close this faster than I can . . . then I guess there's nothing I can do about that."

She broke eye contact and turned and left.

In the women's restroom she went to the mirror and looked at her face. Watched her eyes turning red. Crossed her arms and stood back. Laughed out loud at her reflection. The suit she had put on was black and conservative. She had worn the right thing after all. She had dressed for her own funeral.

She left the office early and called Nina. Since confiding in her about Ilario, she had come to feel closer to her—and a little guilty for all the times she and Ime had treated her like a hopeless renovation project.

When Julia reached her, Nina was full of excitement about marrying Roberto. The consensus among the people she had spoken with was that no one could ask for a better man, and that if she refused him, she would have no one to blame but herself if twenty years from now she found herself living alone in Pacoima in a house full of noisy, shitty parrots. The depth of Roberto's love for Nina, though baffling to some, was undeniable. It filled his every look and gesture. Even Marta, the warning voice against the hazards of matrimony, had said he was Nina's best bet for a secure and happy life, and had told Nina to put a check mark for her in her "yes" column.

"I want your help planning the wedding," Nina said. "I need you to cancel whatever plans you have for Saturday and meet me at Marta's, and don't be late. This is the start of my new life."

Julia couldn't remember a time when Nina had demanded anything. The firmness in her voice was refreshing. Julia was more than happy to help, and told her so. Grateful to have a positive distraction, she stopped by a drugstore on Saturday to pick up some bridal magazines, then headed over to the Cantina. As she was parking on Van Nuys, she noticed Ime pulling into the space behind her. Their eyes met in Julia's mirror. Julia's phone rang.

"I didn't know you were going to be here," Ime said.

"I didn't know you'd be here, either," Julia said.

"Nina didn't tell you?"

"Is it safe to get out of my car or should I keep driving?"

"We should both be here to support Nina."

"I'm stepping out of my car. Hold your fire, I'm unarmed."

Both women got out and locked their cars. Ime's shorter footsteps fell in and out of rhythm with Julia's. "I guess you heard," Julia said.

"Ilario told me. He didn't know anything about being your boss. You should have seen the look on his face."

Julia tipped her face to the sky. "He's taking my best prospect away from me," she said.

"He told me. I know you don't believe this, but he's not doing it to be mean. It's just business."

"It's *not,* Ime. I've worked so hard on that account. Now he's going to take credit for everything I've done."

They stopped for the light at the corner. Ime dug through her handbag as though looking for something, then closed it. "I guess I can talk to him about it, if you want."

"You would do that?"

Ime offered a guilty little shrug. "If you really put all that work into it . . . then you deserve it."

"Seriously?"

She nodded. "I feel bad about the other day. I don't really *not* want to be friends with you. I'm just having a hard time right now. This relationship thing . . . I've never done it before."

"We didn't used to have these kinds of problems, did we?" Julia said.

"It's like we're becoming different people."

"Maybe we have been for a while, but we've been too busy to notice."

The light turned and they stepped into the street. Several seconds went by before Ime said, "We had a fight last night."

Julia looked at her. "You and Ilario?"

Ime waved her hand through the air. "It was nothing serious. Dumb stuff that couples argue about, that's all."

Outside the Cantina they paused and Julia looked at her. "You have changed," she said, and smiled.

Ime smiled back weakly. "Thanks. I guess." She pulled on the door. "After you."

"No, you first."

Marta and Nina were the only people in the bar. Marta was instructing Nina on the proper way to heft a beer keg out of the storage room: "Lift, don't drag. I just recoated the floors. Don't hurt yourself. Don't hurt the floors, either. Be careful. Watch the step behind you. Don't trip on the hoses."

"Why are you making her do that?" Ime said as she tossed her handbag onto a stool. "She's half your size."

"My back hasn't been feeling that well," Marta said.

"Funny how your back goes out when the kegs need to be replaced," Ime said.

"Funny how you come in here and bitch at me and drink my profits," Marta said.

"Don't get your old-lady chones in a bunch," Ime said, edging her ass onto a stool. "Is that keg cold? Don't serve us sudsy leftovers again."

Nina emerged from behind the bar, drawing damp hair away from her face. Marta hooked the keg up to the tap and bled off the top foam while Julia set the bridal magazines on the bar. Nina trumped her by taking about two dozen magazines from her satchel.

Each magazine was bursting at the borders with Post-it notes. "I have a few ideas," she said.

Julia and Ime exchanged worried looks.

"Let's choose a color theme," Nina said. "I read that that's the first step in creating a feel for the wedding. Since I'm partially color-blind, I'll have to rely on you."

"You're color-blind?" Ime said.

"How did we not know that?" Julia said.

With a chuckle, Marta said, "Maybe that was Carmen Diaz's problem. She had a December wedding, too, and made her bridesmaids wear red dresses with white trim that made them look like Santa's helpers and—"

Nina smacked the bar top with a magazine, making everyone jump. "Are we talking about Carmen Diaz's wedding or mine? Are we going to sit here all day gossiping about people we barely know, or are we going to plan my fucking wedding?"

Eyebrows popped. "Nina," Ime said. "I think Marta was just trying to—"

"Can everyone just *concentrate*?" Nina said, her voice trembling. "There doesn't need to be so much *chatter*." She turned a page of her magazine with a snap and jabbed her finger at a picture, wrinkling the page. "What do you think of this? How would you feel about wearing this? What color is this, anyway?"

For the next hour Marta and Ime and Julia answered questions only when asked, and exchanged curious glances as Nina checked off items on her list with a pencil clenched so tightly that eventually the lead snapped. Mumbling that the pencil was a worthless piece of shit, she went to find a pen in Marta's office, then to the restroom.

"What the hell has gotten into her?" Marta said.

"Who told her she could grow a spine overnight?" Ime said.

"She's kind of going overboard with her ideas, too, don't you think? I mean a full mariachi band? Releasing doves into the air?"

"Who does she think is going to pay for all of that?" Marta said. "Us?"

"This is obviously stressful for her," Julia said. "I think we should go along with what she says for now. We can convince her to scale things back later."

"Fine," Marta said. "I'll bite my tongue. But as soon as this is all over, she's getting a big fat kick in the ass from me."

Nina came out of the restroom. "Marta, why do you insist on buying that cheap toilet paper? And why haven't you fixed the lighting in there? Is it because you don't want the customers to see the cockroaches? Because I'm pretty sure one just scurried over my shoe."

"That's it," Marta said, jumping up. "I'm kicking her ass right now."

"Marta, stop," Julia said. "Nina, what's bothering you? We've never seen you like this before."

"I don't know what you mean," Nina said, pressing her finger-tips to her chest mockingly. "Isn't this what people do when they get married? How are you supposed to act when everything in your life is about to change? Why don't you tell me how I should be act-ing? How did you act when you got married? Oh, wait, that's right, you've never been married before, have you? Well, when you do, be sure to let me know and I'll be sure to come to you for your excel-lent advice—"

"Nina, please calm down," Julia said. "If you're not ready—"

"Of course I'm ready. Don't I *look* ready? Hasn't everyone been telling me for years that I should marry Roberto? Doesn't every-body think he's perfect for me? Isn't that what everyone says? Well, isn't it? *Isn't it?*"

Everyone had taken a step back from Nina. Her face was red

and her eyes were wide and she was clutching a Paper Mate in her fist. Julia took her arm gently and guided her to a stool. "OK, Nina, OK. Everything will be all right. Breathe, Nina. Breathe."

Nina looked from Ime to Julia to Marta as she got her breathing under control. Marta pushed another beer toward her and stood back as though expecting Nina to self-combust.

"Nina," Ime said, "you don't have to decide everything today. Don't rush this if you're not sure."

"I am sure," Nina said, sipping from the mug. This seemed to calm her. "I don't know why I'm reacting like this. I didn't know it was all going to be this hard."

"I tell you what," Julia said. "We've made some good progress here today. We can always finish up another time. Why don't we play some canasta or something? Would you be up for that?"

Everyone agreed that this was an excellent idea. Marta produced cards from her apron pocket and ushered everyone over to their usual table. The suggestion of canasta was a good one, for within minutes Nina's normal pallor returned. She lay down the majority of melds. She was within three cards of going out when a burst of laughter drew everyone's attention to the front of the bar.

Concepción had just walked in wearing knee pants and a sleeveless top. Her purple dance bag was slung over her shoulder and sunglasses were turned up on top of her head. Her hair was pulled back and she was beaming. Her arrival was a surprise. Even more surprising was the person she had brought with her. On her arm, smiling as though she were Concepción's oldest and dearest companion, was her onetime friend and longtime rival, Remedios Salazar.

Dark-eyed and nearly six feet tall, Remedios cut as imposing a figure as any of the gun-toting Mexican revolutionaries in the photos on the wall behind her. The hard, wide angles of her face gave her a fearless look. Her hair was still a wiry explosion of black. Her smile was broad and intense, as though it had gotten stuck at the midpoint between joy and hostility. Her eyes sucked in the details of the Cantina, and when she opened her mouth, a thunderous laugh flooded the room.

"Julia! Ime! It's been such a long time! Where have you been hiding?"

Remedios came forward, pulling Concepción along like some kind of accessory. "You guys look wonderful," she gushed. "I'm jealous, you haven't changed. I can't believe it's been so many years. You'd never guess it from looking at you."

"We were just in the neighborhood," Concepción said, "and I was saying to Remedios—"

"Julia, you're as lovely as ever," Remedios said, locking eyes with her. With an audible gasp, she added, "How did we fall so completely out of touch? How, how how, how, *how*?" She detached Concepción from her arm and gave Julia a hug. She held her for several long seconds, pressing the air out of her. Over Remedios's shoulder, Julia widened her eyes questioningly at Ime.

Remedios released Julia. Concepción introduced her to Marta and Nina. Nina held her cards close to her face.

Marta offered to pour them a couple of beers.

"That sounds great," Concepción said, reaching for a chair. "It's a little early, but I guess there's no harm in—"

"I'm sorry, we can't," Remedios said. "C and I have a lot planned for today. We've been so busy doing things ever since we reconnected." Still looking at Julia, she said, "C told me you guys were going to be here, so I said we had to stop by to say hello."

"You wouldn't believe the fun Remedios and I have been having," Concepción said. "To think so many years went by and we never—"

"Julia." Remedios's smile was still stretched tight. "I understand you work for that company that makes security systems."

"She's doing great at her new job," Concepción said. "She's been there only for a few months and already—"

"That's wonderful," Remedios said. "We'll definitely have to get together and talk. We need to catch up. You won't believe this, but I was thinking about you—and you, too, Ime—just minutes before C called."

"Isn't that amazing?" Concepción said. "Doesn't that say we were meant to be friends? And look at the top Rem bought me. Isn't it special?"

"Something special for someone special," Remedios said.

"I'm so glad we're friends again." Concepción reattached herself to Remedios's elbow.

"I'm so glad you called," Remedios said, still looking at Julia.

"I'm glad you found it in you to forgive me."

"What kind of person would I be if I couldn't?" Remedios said. "Silly, the things we do when we're kids." She gave a satisfied sigh. "All right, C, we'd better get a move on. We have a million things to do. Ime, Julia, it was great seeing you. It was nice meeting you, Marta, Nina."

For the last few minutes Nina had been intently reordering her three remaining cards. From time to time she would glance over them to take in Remedios.

"Nice meeting you," Nina said almost inaudibly.

"Julia, I'm serious about us getting together," Remedios said. "I won't take no for an answer, understand?"

Remedios and Concepción left the Cantina. Through the window Ime and Julia watched them walk down the street.

"That's the strangest thing I've ever seen," Ime said. "The two of them going around like sisters after all this time. Look at them. Now they're holding hands!"

"Remedios must want something," Julia said.

"Poor Concepción, what's she getting herself into?" Ime said.

"And did you see the way Remedios kept looking at you? I'd check your brake lines."

Nina contributed nothing to the conversation. She continued to stare at her cards as the other women speculated about Remedios. The pulse in her neck hammered at hummingbird speed—as though someone had just walked into the bar, pointed a gun at her, and demanded that she choose between her money and her life.

~ 13 ~

Out of the Valley

When Julia returned to work on Monday, Ilario asked her to join him for a one-on-one meeting in his office. Assuming that taking Guzman from her was only the first in a series of steps to make her life miserable, she braced herself for more bad news.

The first thing she noticed as she came into his office was that he had begun boxing up his files to move to the new office she presumed came with his new position. On top of a box beside his desk a silver photo frame glinted in the light of his high-powered desk lamp. It contained the same photo she had been looking at just before Ilario had caught her snooping in his office, the one of the woman people said was his ex-fiancée. Only now did she make the connection: The woman in the picture and the woman with the toffee-colored sling backs were one and the same.

She sat down and Ilario began to talk about the advantages of merging the two sales groups that he would now be overseeing. He told her he intended to treat his staff like family, always placing their needs above his own. Whatever zeal Ilario might have employed in delivering these remarks to other people in the group appeared to be diminishing, for after another minute or two, his words trailed off and he smoothed his tie and said, "I've decided to let you keep Guzman."

She shifted in her chair. "You did?"

"Yes, well . . ." He reordered three pieces of paper on his desk to no apparent purpose. "I hadn't quite realized how . . . there were certain things I hadn't taken into account. If you want to keep on working on Guzman, that would be great."

He noticed Julia watching his hands. With what appeared to be some effort, he brought them to rest by hooking his thumbs under the table. So Ime really had talked to him. Julia hadn't really been sure she would. But she'd kept her word.

"That's great," she said.

"I thought you'd think so," he said.

"Mr. Guzman will be happy, too. I don't think he'd like it if I were to suddenly—"

"There's one thing, though," he said. It was his turn to shift in his chair. "When you go up north to see him next week, I'm going with you."

"Going with me?"

"Guzman's could be huge for this company. I think it's important that I be there to make sure that nothing—to make sure that Ostin Security is well-represented."

She knew what this meant. He didn't trust her.

"It's not that I don't trust you," he said. "It's just that Guzman is big and growing fast. I want to make sure we start off on the best possible footing."

"All right," Julia said.

"Good."

"Good."

He drummed his eight visible fingers on the desk as though trying to think of something. "Oh, wait." He ran a finger down one of the sheets of paper in front of him. "Do you have any questions for me?"

The question she most wanted to ask she kept to herself: How did Ime convince you to let me keep Guzman? It was obvious he was embarrassed to be retracting his decision. Julia felt a surge of optimism. Ime had stood up for her. There was hope for their friendship after all.

"Superchicana to the rescue," she said.

"What?" Ilario said.

"Nothing," Julia said. "No, I don't have any questions."

In the summers the Valley became a frying pan, cooking the suburban single-family homes and apartments with temperatures stretching to the triple digits. Air conditioners ran nonstop under a tight lid of smog. Had Ilario not insisted on accompanying her to see Mr. Guzman, she would have welcomed the trip to Oakland as an escape from the oppressive heat.

The day they were to fly together, Julia met Ilario at the airport. As they boarded the plane, Ilario seemed as relieved as Julia to discover that their seats were not next to each other. From across the aisle and three rows back, Julia watched Ilario study the account history she had prepared for him about Mr. Guzman's company. Mr. Guzman was a short, bald, nervous man with tense eyes and a sharp, unpredictable stab of a laugh. She called him the Mexican Jumping Bean because the last time she had been to see him, he had spent the meeting popping up from his chair and jumping from topic to topic. Julia had been trying to secure his signature on a two-year agreement, but time and time again, Guzman would ask to revisit some issue she thought had long been settled. Nevertheless, she had been certain that he was nearly ready to sign; she had envisioned applause from her co-workers for landing such a big account. Now, with Ilario involved, there was no guarantee that she would get the credit if she did land it. And she had a pretty good idea who would get the blame if she didn't.

Once off the plane, she and Ilario hurried through the terminal and onto the car-rental shuttle. A car was waiting for them at the rental agency. Ilario signed for it and got behind the wheel. Not until DO NOT BACK UP: SEVERE TIRE DAMAGE slid past them on their way out did he ask Julia whether she minded him driving.

Midafternoon traffic near the airport was light, and the day was bright and cool. The air, even filtered through the car, was fresher and cleaner than the air in the Valley even on the best of days. Julia had expected a tense, awkward drive. But Ilario's focus was entirely on the challenge presented by Guzman. "Is he the sole decision maker, or is he relying on procurement and facilities?"

"He decides everything without much input from other people," Julia said. "I think that's part of the problem."

"Did the last agreement you wrote up stipulate upgrades if his company grows faster than expected?"

"It did. But it doesn't seem like that's a big selling point for him."

Julia didn't know if Ilario was asking these things for his own edification or to test her, but the exchange put her in a ready frame of mind, and she was able for the time being to forget her dislike of the man sitting next to her.

"We have the best product at the best price with the best terms. So why isn't he signing?"

"His reasons keep changing," Julia said. "First it was the length of the service terms. I changed those. Then it became the terms of upgrades. I did what I could. Then it was the payment terms. I did what I could there, too, but payment terms are nonnegotiable for first-timers. I went as high as Roger to get him an exemption, but Roger said no."

Ilario's eyes scanned the horizon in ways that had nothing to do with the traffic. "It's not really about any of those things, then, is it?"

Julia shrugged. "I guess not."

"Something's paralyzing him."

Julia watched him as he worked away at the problem. She had a feeling that he was about to reveal the key to getting Mr. Guzman's business. Just what she needed—for Ilario to show her that the answer had been right in front of her all along. She closed her eyes.

But Ilario said nothing else. When Julia opened her eyes, she noticed him pawing awkwardly at the steering wheel with one hand.

"Are you all right?" she said.

"Fine. Of course. Why?"

"Nothing."

But as they came within a few blocks of their destination, she heard his breathing change. He began to fidget with the corner of his shirt collar. She had always pictured Ilario striding toward every interaction with the same confidence bordering on arrogance that he wore like a second skin around the office. Yet here was something else, a different Ilario.

He saw her watching him. "What?"

"Nothing," she said, and looked out her window.

Mr. Guzman's offices resided on the second floor of a two-story building that was shaped like a horseshoe and embraced a forecourt with a giant stone sphere fountain that emitted water at a trickle. As they approached the main entrance, Ilario regained his composure, his personality swelling back to familiar proportions.

After a short wait in the reception area, Mr. Guzman greeted them with a gleaming smile and a gleaming forehead, shaking their hands so vigorously that Julia feared her watch clasp would come undone. On their way to his office, Ilario remarked on the baseball diamond pattern on his green and gold tie and asked whether he thought Miguel Tejada was going to be re-signed for the coming season.

"Nope!" Mr. Guzman said, popping a couple of inches off the ground. "And they're going to slide Mark Ellis in as shortstop, and boom! No problem! Tejada? Who needs him?"

Seamlessly, Ilario folded the topic of baseball around the subject of Mr. Guzman's business, and by the time Mr. Guzman bade them to sit down in his office the two men were talking as though they had known each other for some time.

Mr. Guzman's office was even smaller than Julia's, with a desk pushed to one wall to provide just enough room for Mr. Guzman to squeeze by to get to his chair. Julia admired him as a modest man with little interest in flaunting his success. Once coffee had been offered and declined, Ilario began to review all of Mr. Guzman's self-stated needs as Julia had outlined them, bringing his attention to a few changes that he believed would work to the advantage of Guzman Industries. Although much of the subject matter was familiar to Mr. Guzman, something about Ilario's manner and enthusiasm made it sound fresh and promising, producing in Mr. Guzman's eyes a light Julia had never seen before, and in herself a slow leak of envy. Ilario's energetic but measured gestures as he spoke and his instinct for emphasizing just the right words, and even the way the overhead light highlighted the few premature flecks of gray in his hair, all worked to his advantage, making him . . . well, *shimmer*. He was a warm wave of energy and possibility. Anyone, anyone at all, would have been drawn in, would have found it impossible to—

"Hmm? Yes, yes," Julia said in answer to something Ilario had just asked her. "Here, let me show you how I've outlined the terms. Let me get that, I have it right here. . . ."

She and Ilario went through the terms of the agreement. But once again, Mr. Guzman began to question the payment terms. The last time Julia had spoken to him he had appeared ready to accept them, but now he said he wasn't comfortable paying for two years of service in advance just to get a discount. Other companies didn't have that requirement. Other companies were more flexible. It was a lot to ask a first-time customer to lay down that kind of money, and, well, Mr. Guzman just didn't know, he just didn't know. He shook his head. He bit his nails. He bounced in his seat and sighed and furrowed his brow. Julia and Ilario explained once again the reasoning behind the payment terms. They listened to his concerns. They sympathized.

"I don't know," Mr. Guzman said over and over, sounding like a nervous game-show contestant being egged on to risk all his winnings on one final question, one final spin of the wheel. "I just don't know, I just don't know. . . ."

Ilario remained composed, but in his eyes Julia saw his anticipation pressing forward, willing Mr. Guzman to a decision. But Mr. Guzman continued to deliberate. Julia knew from experience that they were losing him. At any moment the light would go out of his eyes and he would push back his chair and with a heavy sigh say that he wasn't ready to make a decision. Then it would be weeks before Julia heard from him again, and another visit would need to be planned. The opportunity was slipping away. Julia could think of nothing to do or say to save it.

Mr. Guzman retreated into thought. No one said anything for a long while. Just as Mr. Guzman started to give his telltale sigh, Ilario leaned forward and said, "Mr. Guzman, it's clear there's only one way to get your business. If we have to adjust the payment terms for you, then that's what we're going to do."

Julia jerked a look at Ilario. The slightest twitch of his fingertips signaled her not to say anything. Assuming a tone of defeat,
he said, "We have no choice, Julia. Mr. Guzman has made himself
clear. Ostin is going to have to make an exception in his case."

They waited. Ilario had called Mr. Guzman's bluff. He looked
back and forth from Ilario to Julia. "You're really willing to do
that?" he said.

"We'll draw up a side letter. So long as you're willing to keep the
arrangement between us, I think we can move ahead."

The smile that crossed Mr. Guzman's face at that moment
was so broad, and the look in his eyes so bright, that for a moment
Julia thought he was going to jump up and kiss Ilario. His right
hand shot out and clasped Ilario's. The handshake seemed to go
on forever, as though some electric current were surging between
them, preventing them from letting go. When Mr. Guzman's attention finally floated back to Julia, his smile was a shadow of the one
he had given Ilario, his handshake an afterthought.

"Wonderful," Mr. Guzman said, swinging his attention back to
Ilario as though he were some sort of hero. "Wonderful."

Julia clutched her briefcase handle as she strode down the corridor from Mr. Guzman's suites, trying to keep up with Ilario. "What
was that?" she said. "What did we just agree to?"

"That was a sale," Ilario said. "Our first big deal of the quarter.
Good work on the agreement, by the way. I'm surprised how many
bells and whistles were in it."

"You told him we'd change the payment terms. That's the one
thing we *can't* do."

"Can't we?" Ilario said. "We just did. And we made him very
happy in the process."

"Roger's never going to approve it," Julia said. "We can't make those kinds of promises."

"We can and we did, and how about lowering your voice until we're out of the building?"

"So you just promise whatever you feel like and assume you'll get your way? That's how you do business?"

"Again with the voice," Ilario said as they stopped at the elevator. "We can talk about this when we're outside." He knuckled the down button.

"You just did the one thing we're never supposed to do, which is to draw up a side letter. This is my account, Ilario. I'm the one who's going to get called on it."

"Look," Ilario said, facing her. "I happen to know—I'm not saying *how* I know, but trust me, I know—that in about four months that stupid policy is going to be history. Everyone at Ostin knows it's a pain in the ass and has to go. But the higher-ups want to wait until Roger retires to do anything about it rather than have a fight with him now. So I used my discretion." Ilario punched the call button with his fist. "What's wrong with this thing?" He headed for the stairs. Julia went after him.

"I don't know what you know or don't know," she said. Her voice echoed in the stairwell as she followed him down. "All I know is that my ass is on the line. I'm going to Roger."

"Why would you want to do that? Don't you want the commission?"

"I don't care about the money. I care about my reputation."

The first-floor door opened on the glazed concrete lobby. They passed through it and out to the forecourt. The sphere fountain was now gushing.

"You made me look like an idiot," she said.

He screwed up his face. *"What?"*

"I've been telling Guzman for six months that there's no way around the payment terms, and then you come along and completely undermine me."

"Yes, you've seen through my plan. Forget that we just made a sale with a company that in two or three years could be one of our biggest customers. My *real* plan was to make you look bad."

"You *did* make me look bad."

"I don't think you need help—" His face reddened even before the words were out. They were in the parking lot now. They stopped on opposite sides of the rental car and faced each other. Julia swallowed hard and fought the tug of tears. He unlocked the doors and got in. She got in, too, and buckled up.

A flat silence leaned on the next few seconds as Ilario got back on the road. Julia hugged her briefcase. She did not look at Ilario and he did not look at her. She waited until he was going up the on-ramp before she said, "I can't work for somebody who doesn't know how to follow the rules."

He gave a short laugh. "Meaning what? You're quitting?"

"I'm taking another job. With another company."

He shook his head. "No, you're not. Where?"

"It doesn't matter. I applied for a job and they made me an offer a couple of days ago. I haven't given them an answer, but now I think I'd better take it."

He looked at her. "You're serious? You're not. There's no job. I would have . . . heard something."

From Ime? She wanted to tell him: I don't tell Ime everything. Not anymore.

"Seriously," he said. "What company?"

"I'll tell you when it's official. I'll give you my resignation."

He shook his head. "No, I don't believe it."

She wanted to say: Believe it. I'm leaving. I can't take this. I can't take you.

"It's not Halcyon Systems, is it?"

She looked out her window.

"Shit, it is, isn't it. It's Halcyon. Shit."

She didn't want to continue the lie, but it was already rolling and she couldn't stop it. "I promised them my answer by Wednesday."

Ilario made a strange sound through his teeth. When she looked back, he was pulling at his tie, loosening it. She didn't see why any of this should bother him. He ought to be happy.

He said nothing for about a minute. He shook his head. "There's no job," he said. "You're not leaving."

At the Ramada they checked in at the same time but with different registration agents. When they were done, Ilario asked her if she wanted the keys to the rental car. He was having dinner with his ex-fiancée, Lydia, who lived in the area. She was coming by to pick him up, so he didn't need the car. She told him she didn't need it, either. She just wanted to eat and go to bed early. When the elevator door opened, he let her enter first, then said he had forgotten something at the desk and let the door close.

In her room she threw open one of the sliding doors to the balcony and sank into a chair, breathing as if for the first time that day. What an idiot she was to lie about a job offer. Now she was either going to have to quit or admit to being a liar. She thought about how disappointed Ime would be. How had she let this happen? How had she ended up again in a work situation that was unbearable?

As depressing as these thoughts were, something else began to nag at her: Maybe she just wasn't meant for this level of success. Maybe she wasn't even the kind of person who knew what to do with success when she got it. Maybe Ime was right. Maybe she couldn't see opportunity when it was in front of her.

A few minutes later, after a quick, hot shower, she sat down with her PDA to calculate how much she would be losing on the Guzman commission by quitting. It was a lot. And as a recurring commission, it would have added nicely to her sense of security. But she couldn't think about that now. She got dressed and went down to the hotel restaurant.

There were two restaurants to choose from. One was a small, cheap diner with a flashing apple pie over the arched entrance. The other was more expensive and dimly lit with candles on white tablecloths. Ordinarily, she would have saved the company a few dollars by eating at the diner. But tonight she chose the more expensive one. She would order the priciest item on the menu and expense it to Ostin. She would order a full bottle of wine, even though she didn't like wine.

The restaurant was mostly empty. A waitress slid a menu toward her and floated away. Julia looked at the wine list. She knew nothing about wine and there were no prices listed to tell her what was good. Out of the corner of her eye she saw Ilario making a straight line toward her across the polished marble floor of the restaurant.

"All right," he said, "maybe you do have a job offer. But you can't seriously be thinking about taking it."

She held her menu in front of her as though blocking a hockey shot.

He said, "Why would you want to leave Ostin when you've just made a huge sale?"

Julia stared at him. Why was he still going on about this? Was this some kind of joke? But he looked dead serious. A hint of panic escaped from the corners of his eyes.

He said, "All right, here's the deal. Can I be up-front?"

The waitress glanced at her from a distance, but Julia shook her head that she needed more time.

"The deal is this," Ilario said. "I can't afford to lose three people in my first month as manager."

Julia raised an eyebrow at him. She thought: bullshit. "What do you mean? Who's leaving?"

He leaned toward her, the pressure of his forearm creating ridges in the tablecloth. "Monica gave me her resignation this morning."

"Monica," she said.

He sighed. "Things between us have been"—he gave a vague wave—"not good for a long time."

"Who else? You said 'three people.'"

"Banyon is going back to school. At the end of the summer."

Banyon was a sales assistant who had been promoted to sales associate at about the same time Julia had come on board. Julia had forgotten he was leaving. He hadn't liked Ilario much, either. He and Monica had been close.

Ilario smoothed the tablecloth where he had creased it. "My sales force is being decimated. I won't make my numbers. It'll take months to rebuild a sales team."

"So what are you saying?" Julia said. "You want me to stay?"

"I can't afford to lose another salesperson."

"I don't know what I can do about that."

"You said you haven't accepted the job yet."

"You've helped me make up my mind."

"Then what do you want?"

She looked at him, uncomprehending.

"Tell me what it is you *want.* If you stay, you keep the commission for Guzman. What else to keep you?"

She couldn't believe what she was hearing. She wanted to laugh. In her mind she was already laughing.

"I can't give you a raise, but this commission and your last bonus should set you up pretty nicely for the year. And if you have another quarter like the last one, I can make sure that your end-of-the-year bonus is . . . special."

Something about the word "special" made Julia laugh out loud. She didn't know what was funny about it. It just sounded wrong coming from Ilario. He frowned at her. But she couldn't stop laughing. She laughed until she had to wipe away a tear. "Oh, God. Oh, God."

"Great. It's funny. I'm glad." He pushed away from the table. "You ought to at least consider what I'm saying. I'm willing to do anything reasonable to keep you. Most people would see that as an opportunity."

The comment struck Julia hard. She watched him walk away. This time it was she who struck out after him. She got up from her table.

"I just want to know one thing," she said, pulling on his shoulder as she caught up to him. "I just have one question."

He stopped and faced her. "OK. What?"

"Why do you hate me so much? It can't be because I was in your office that one time, or because you thought I was spying on you. There has to be something else. Why don't you tell me what it is?"

Ilario's cheeks changed color several times. His expression seemed to retreat into itself. He looked at once much older and much younger—as though her words had knocked something out of him or insulted him in some deep way. For the briefest moment, the look on his face was so . . . fragile . . . that she regretted her words without knowing why she should regret them.

His gaze traveled over her in short, sad ticks. She had the sense that he was mentally rearranging the features of her face, trying to create some new composite of her that better matched the person who had asked him that question. When he at last spoke, his words were almost inaudible: "'Hate' is a strong word," he said, and turned away in a manner that appeared so boyishly sad that as he disappeared from sight, some of the light in the room seemed to follow him out in sympathy.

Julia drank most of the bottle of wine and returned to her room. She took some Advil in anticipation of the headache that was sure to come, then stepped out onto the balcony. Fog pouring in from the bay was beginning to consume most of the view, including the towers of Oakland International Airport. The air turned biting cold. She closed the sliding balcony window and went to bed even though it was still light out. She slept the dreamless, inoffensive sleep she always slept in hotel rooms.

⪜ 14 ⪝

The Truth About Salazar of Salazar & Salazar

Sitting next to each other on the return flight, Julia and Ilario clung to fragments of conversation and turned the pages of in-flight magazines that could not possibly have interested them. They met each other's eyes only reluctantly, less a result of animosity, it seemed to Julia, than a lingering sense of embarrassment—as though, unavoidably and regrettably, they had seen each other naked the previous day, and now were burdened with information neither of them knew how to process.

When their plane landed in Burbank, the cabin depressurized with what sounded like a massive sigh of relief. They wasted no time pushing their way off the plane. Unbeknownst to either of them, they had parked only a couple of spaces away from each other in the overnight garage. They unlocked their cars and looked at one another a final time.

Ilario said, "Whatever you decide about the job . . . good luck. I mean, whatever is best for you, that's what you should do."

Hearing what sounded like goodwill in Ilario's voice made Julia dizzy with the foolishness of her lie. Burning bright red, she got into her car quickly and drove off.

. . .

The moment she got home she called Nina. She hated to burden her with another problem, but she could think of no one else to whom she could admit what she had done.

"Nina," Julia said. "I need to talk to you. I've done an incredibly stupid—"

"I've been trying to get ahold of you since Wednesday," Nina said, sounding more energized than Julia had heard her in months. "Roberto wants a smaller wedding, so we're going to need to scale things back. I guess I went a little overboard with my ideas. Why didn't you guys stop me when I was getting so crazy?"

"Nina, I've just had the most horrible couple of days. I don't know why I keep doing such stupid things. Can you come over later?" Julia heard a burst of laughter in the background. "Nina, where are you? It sounds like you're at a party."

"I'm with C and Marta and Remedios," Nina said. "We're on our way back from Tijuana. Remedios insisted that C invite us, so we all loaded up the car for the day on Wednesday, but it turned into an overnight thing."

"*What?* You just spent three days in TJ? With *Remedios*?"

"Julia, she's been just wonderful Her uncle has a house in the Colonia Obregón, so we all stayed there and went out dancing every night. We're just crossing back into San Ysidro. Who knew Remedios could be so fun?"

Julia sat down. She was baffled. "How did you get the time off from work? Who's watching the Cantina for Marta?"

But evidently Marta had snatched the phone out of Nina's hands, because it was she who answered: "The Cantina can take care of itself for once. Julia, I have to tell you, Remedios is the most wonderful person I've ever met. Why did you hide her for so long? You should be ashamed, Julia. She's wonderful. We had clams on the beach at night and a cop came and told us to put out the fire but C convinced him to stay and drink with us and then she went home with him. Remedios has been paying for everything. She's so generous and sweet and I think I love her."

"Marta . . . has anyone heard from Ime?"

"Ime," Marta said with dry contempt, "is too good for TJ. If you ask me, you're becoming too much like her. Your job has become more important to you than we are."

"Marta, are you drunk?" Julia said.

"I'm not drunk," Marta said, though it was clear that she was. "I'm in love. I'm in love with Remedios. I'm drunk with love for Remedios. Remedios is my new friend. Did you hear me, Rem? You're my new friend and I love you! Love love love love love love love love—"

"Marta, put Nina back on the line. I really need to—"

"Love love love love love love—"

The line went silent. Julia turned the phone upward in her lap and stared at it. What alternate universe had she just returned to, in which Remedios had worked her way into her group of friends and was admired by them? What did Remedios think she was doing? And why did Julia suddenly feel so terribly, terribly alone?

When Concepción called Julia that night, she was no less enthusiastic about Remedios than Nina and Marta had been. "You really need to call her, Julia. She wants to see you. You don't know what a good time you missed. I'm telling you, she's not the same person."

If Remedios wanted to satisfy a grudge, infiltrating Concepción's friends did seem like an elaborate way to go about doing it. Still, Julia had to believe that Remedios wanted *something*. "Don't you think it's a little strange that she would want to spend so much time with you so suddenly?"

"You're being stubborn and ridiculous," Concepción said. "She's one of us now."

"I didn't know we were a club. I didn't know we were voting in members."

"Now you're just being a fregona for the sake of it," Concepción said. "What are you going to do, avoid her forever?"

That was exactly what Julia had planned to do. But Concepción had a point. If Remedios was determined to force her way into their lives, there was nothing Julia could do about it. "I'm not promising I'll call," Julia said, "but I'll think about it. Maybe if I talk to her, I can get a sense of what she wants."

"That's wonderful," Concepción said. "You're not going to regret it. You're making the right decision." With a sigh, Julia took down Remedios's number. Maybe she would call in a few days when she was in a better mood. But she was off the line no more than a couple of minutes before Remedios called *her*.

Remedios trilled with the same enthusiasm with which she'd praised Julia at the Cantina. "Julia, I just talked to C. I'm so happy you've agreed to get together with me! How does Monday for lunch sound? I could come by and get you or you could come over to my work."

Julia felt a cold wave go through her. "Remedios, I didn't . . . I was only saying to C that—"

"It's going to be so great to see you," Remedios said. "I've already checked and we really don't work that far away from each other, so it'll be easy. We can start having lunch together all the time. Won't that be great?"

"Remedios, I don't know about tomorrow. I mean, maybe the next time you and C get together we could all—"

"Nonsense," Remedios said. "I've had plenty of time to catch up with C. It's *you* I want to see now."

Julia thought she heard a slightly sinister edge in these last words, but Remedios gave her no opportunity to question her meaning.

"So I'll hear from you Monday, right, Julia? Just give me a call when you're on your way over. I'm so glad C convinced you. We're going to have such a good time, I'm sure of it."

The more Julia thought about the lie she had told Ilario, the more certain she was that to continue the lie would cause her greater problems in the long run. She wasn't sure what she dreaded more—facing Remedios, or admitting the truth to Ilario. Deciding that it was best to get these things over as quickly as possible, she arranged to see Remedios for lunch on the same day she planned to come clean with Ilario.

She saw Ilario coming out of the kitchen with a mug of coffee when she arrived. She strode up to him in her best imitation of a self-confident woman. "Can we talk? I have something to tell you."

He paused and leaned a shoulder against the hallway. It was just as well he didn't ask her into his office to talk. The sooner she got this over with, the better. She took a deep breath and let out with: "What I said to you yesterday about the job wasn't true. You were right. Of course you were right. I was angry. I made it up. It was stupid. I'm sorry."

She braced herself for fireworks. Scorn. Contempt. Instead, what crossed his face at the moment was . . . a meandering look of hurt. He nodded thoughtfully, then said, "So what does this mean?"

"I think it's better if I find something else. We're too different in how we approach sales. It shouldn't take me long. Anyway, I wanted you to know the truth."

Ilario looked down into his cup. Something there seemed to disappoint him. "All right, well . . . can you give me at least a month's notice? I know that's not required, but—"

"Absolutely," Julia said. "You have my word. And please don't give me the commission on Guzman. I don't want to be accused of taking it and running."

She turned and left, telling herself that a month was a small thing to promise in exchange for not being yelled at.

Just after noon, Julia drove out to the address Remedios had given her. Her heart wobbled as she approached the machine shop, Salazar & Salazar Metalworks, located down an alley off of Van Nuys Boulevard in the industrial section of the city. Julia had learned from Concepción that Remedios managed the business for her older brother Victor, who had inherited it years earlier from their father but whose sloppy management and feeble business sense had nearly driven the shop into bankruptcy. Remedios had agreed to take over Victor's finances until the business was solvent again, but, disgusted by her brother's ineptitude, she had muscled her way into every other aspect of the business, from pricing and purchasing to maintenance and repair. Since then the shop had earned the reputation as one of the best in the Valley.

Seeing no sign of Remedios or anyone else in the outer office, Julia cautiously followed the sound of machinery out onto the shop floor. All around her machines whirred and thundered at ear-splitting pitch. Some of the machinists stared at her as she followed the perimeter of the floor. She felt awkward being there in a suit. They must have thought she was some sort of inspector come to cause trouble. The noise from the machines made her swallow hard. She remembered hearing stories about men losing fingers and whole hands in machines just like these.

Julia found Remedios standing near a C-shaped machine, shouting at a small, red-faced man with a backward yellow baseball cap and work goggles that looked too big for his small face. He was screaming back at her and waving his arms like an angry insect. But as soon as Remedios saw Julia, she abandoned him completely. She swept across the floor and pulled Julia into her arms. "Look at you," she said. "How fantastic you look." She threw a glance around the high arched ceiling. "What do you think of my little shop? You have to admit, I've become quite a success in my own way, haven't I?"

Julia smiled uncomfortably. The machinist in the baseball cap was still shouting at Remedios, but she ignored him as she took Julia's arm and led her toward the office entrance. "Don't worry about him," Remedios said. "He needs time to cool off. He keeps coming into work late and then complaining because I don't give him enough hours. I've tried to fire him three times, but Victor keeps hiring him back because he feels sorry for him."

"Remedios," Julia said, looking down at her watch, "I don't have a lot of time, so maybe we could—"

"That's fine, that's fine!" Remedios said. "I can't really leave for long, either. That's how it is running this business. Why don't we get something off Mamacita's truck and eat in the back? They serve the best machaca con papas you've ever tasted. Seriously, you're going to shit yourself."

Julia hadn't noticed a catering truck when she drove up, but following Remedios out to the front, she saw one there, parked with two wheels on the curb so as not to block the alley. Remedios pushed her way up to the window and ordered machaca con papas for two with tortillas, a Coke for Julia, and a grape Fanta for herself. Then she led Julia back to what she called "the dining area," a tarp-covered plot behind the building with a few workbenches for tables and plastic chairs weighted down with rocks. The Santa Ana winds whipped and cracked the tarp awning overhead as Remedios pulled a chair out for Julia.

She dusted it off. "Be careful not to get your nice suit dirty. Ay,

Dios, anyone can tell at a glance that things are going well for you."
She spread a napkin out, opened Julia's Styrofoam container, and
popped her drink for her. "Do you need anything else? Do you need
some Tapatío or chile or anything?" She rubbed her big palms together vigorously. "Look at the two of us sitting here having lunch.
Who knew that when C called so much good would come of it?"

Julia knew that the longer she waited, the harder it would be to
extract the truth from Remedios about what she wanted. She
cleared her throat and started off with, "Rem, I wanted to ask you
something. When C called you after all this time—"

"Oh, sure," Remedios laughed, "I was skeptical. But she was so
sweet on the phone, and I could tell all she wanted was to be
friends again. How could I refuse? Well, we've been having the best
time ever since."

Julia began to peel back the foil from her plate but stopped. She
put her hands flat on the table. "I guess that's what I don't understand. If I remember right, the two of you were never really that
close to begin with. And then after what happened with her and
Carlos—"

"C has changed so much," Remedios said. "I have to believe
you've had something to do with that. You were always such a good
influence. No one was ever more sensible than you. That's one thing
I always admired about you. Whether you intended it or not, I
think it's rubbed off on C. I can tell, I really can."

Julia had never known how to respond to Remedios's compliments, and once again she felt herself getting tangled in sticky
strands of awkwardness. "Rem . . . why did you want to see me? Why
did you ask me here?"

Remedios gave a look that was pure surprise. "What do you
mean? Did I ask you here? I don't think I did. It was you who called
me, wasn't it? Was there something *you* wanted to ask *me*, Julia?"

"No . . . I just mean . . . I thought that we should talk."

Remedios's smile was a thin line. "Isn't that what we're doing? Talking? Like old friends?" She peeled back the foil from her machaca, releasing a thin, vaporous veil.

Julia shifted in her chair. Overhead the tarp cracked harder in the wind. "I just really feel like there's something we need to clear up. Ever since what happened with you and C—"

"Mmm, doesn't this smell wonderful?" Remedios said. She inhaled appreciatively.

"I've had the feeling for a long time that you've held something against me—"

"Try it with the chile," Remedios said. "It's even better that way. Mix it in with the potatoes. By the way, that friend of yours, Nina—she's the funniest thing. She had me laughing all the way down and back from TJ. Did she tell you we went? Julia, you really should have been there."

"I just want to know what it is. If I ever did something to offend you or hurt you, I want you to tell me. Why were you so mean to me the last time I saw you?"

Remedios sighed. She leaned back from her plate, wiping her lips with a napkin. "Really, Julia, do we need to go over the past like this?"

"I want to know. I need to."

"How can you be so sure I was mad at you?"

"I could feel it when I saw you at the Victoria Market."

"I don't shop at the Victoria Market."

"I saw you there a couple of months ago."

"I was probably in a bad mood that day."

"It wasn't a mood, it was me."

"Please eat your machaca," Remedios said. "It's getting cold. Stop being so stubborn."

But Julia didn't move. She sat with her arms crossed. She didn't take her eyes off Remedios. Remedios had a couple more bites of food. Julia hadn't touched her lunch, and she wasn't going to. Not until Remedios had answered her. Not until she had an answer that she could believe.

It seemed like an eternity before Remedios finally dropped her tortilla on her plate and said, "You really want an answer? Fine." She took a huge swig of her grape soda and swished it around in her mouth like mouthwash before swallowing. Then she swung her chair to Julia's side of the table. She scooted close to Julia. "Here's your reason." She cupped a large hand behind Julia's neck and pulled her face close and kissed her.

The kiss was so sudden—and Julia's surprise so complete—that Julia didn't even resist as Remedios's tongue drove between her lips and past her gums and teeth and into her mouth. It hunted there for what seemed like several seconds, probing about like a burglar ransacking a room. Then, not finding what it was looking for, it retreated.

"That's why," she said. "That's always been why. I never wanted to admit it, but there's your reason." She moved her chair back to the other side of the table and continued with her lunch.

"Rem, I'm not . . . I didn't know that you were . . . but personally . . . I'm not . . . I've never been . . ."

Remedios waved away the suggestion. "I know you're not. But when I was younger, I kind of always hoped. Maybe even now I was hoping a little, who knows?"

Julia tasted grape soda. In her mouth. On her lips. "Have you always been—"

"A lesbian? Oh, sure. It just took me forever to figure out that that's why I couldn't keep a woman as a friend. I kept falling for them and then getting pissed off when they didn't give me what I wanted." When Julia said nothing, Remedios went on. "I met this girl a couple years back. All of a sudden everything started to make sense. I finally understood why I cared so much that you didn't stay friends with me. It was because I wanted something more than friendship—"

"Rem, I never meant to make you think—"

"I know, I know. It wasn't you. It was me. When C called, I thought, OK, here's my chance to make it up to you. C wants my forgiveness? Fine, she can have it. After all, it turns out she did me a favor sleeping with Carlos. But it wasn't C that I wanted to see again. You're the one I regretted fucking things up with."

Julia's mind was firing. Everything about Remedios's past behavior now seemed to fall precisely into place. Remedios anticipated Julia's next thought before she uttered it.

"Don't worry, Julia. It's not like I have feelings for you now. At least not big ones. There are plenty of other women out there. And to be honest"—she gave a little laugh and a wink—"I exaggerated a little earlier. You're not *quite* as good-looking as you were back when we were friends. And women who wear suits never did that much for me."

A thoughtful silence followed as everything Julia thought she understood about Remedios shifted to accommodate these new facts. It was not an awkward silence. Suddenly the whole situation struck Julia as very funny.

"Why are you smiling?" Remedios said, eyeing her suspiciously.

Julia reached across and touched her hand to reassure her. "Nothing," she said. "Nothing at all." Then, swayed by Remedios's admission, she decided to make one of her own. "Rem, I think the reason I was never able to stay friends with you . . . was that I was always intimidated by you."

Remedios demonstrated no surprise at this. Rather, she sighed deeply, as though such a scenario was all too common in her experience. "Yes, I always sort of thought so," she said.

A few more seconds went by before Julia suddenly sat straight up. "Oh, no. What about C? Have you told her?"

"That I like women? Not yet."

"Are you going to?"

"Sure, eventually."

"When? How?"

"I don't know. Soon."

Julia shook her head. She suddenly felt nervous. "Shit, she's not going to handle this well. She's not going to handle this well at all."

"You don't think so?" Remedios raised her Fanta to her mouth.

"She's going to flip out. I mean, she's really, *really* going to flip out."

Remedios pressed the can to her lips, but this did little to disguise the wicked smile taking shape there. "Isn't she, though?" Remedios said. "Isn't she?"

In the Sierra Room

At work the next day, Julia received an e-mail from Remedios, letting her know how much she had enjoyed seeing her again and asking her to hold off on saying anything to Concepción about her being gay until she'd had a chance to tell her herself. Julia was glad she had agreed to meet her, for knowing about Remedios's lesbianism explained a number of things. For one, it explained the excessive praise Remedios had always heaped on her, praise that had always embarrassed Julia deeply. For another, it explained why Remedios was so bitter toward her in the aftermath of the loss of their friendship, which Julia had never viewed as especially deep. It even seemed to explain how Remedios, after so many years of claiming to hate Concepción, could agree to be friends with her again; coming to terms with her sexuality had put a generous spin on her outlook on life, making possible once impossible things. As Julia thought about their conversation, she realized that she felt incredibly flattered. As far as she knew, no woman had ever had feelings for her, and while she hoped that Remedios was beyond such feelings now, she could not ignore the curious swelling of her ego that accompanied the revelation.

How Concepción would react to the news that Remedios was gay, however, was another matter. Concepción had always exhibited an extreme and unnatural fear of women who loved women. While she argued that she had nothing against lesbians to speak of, the thought of two women touching each other sexually was enough to give her what she called "los creepy-jeebies," and the thought of a woman touching *her* sexually—an impulse she believed must necessarily reside in any lesbian who laid eyes on her—was enough to trigger in her a debilitating fit of anxiety. Julia had begun to compose a response to Remedios asking her to be gentle when her thoughts were interrupted by the sound of yelling.

It was coming from down the hall, two angry voices pitched high in argument, growing louder as they drew closer. She recognized one of them as Ilario's. He was defending himself against an onslaught of ugly, accusatory language, the likes of which Julia had never before heard in an office environment. The other voice sounded like Roger's.

"I knew it was a fucking mistake to promote you," he was saying. "I didn't make you a manager for you to pull this kind of bullshit behind my back!"

"Roger, you can't expect me to be effective if I don't have—"

"You have all the fucking resources you need! Policies aren't for you to fuck around with. They're there for a reason! We're screwed if even one of our other customers finds out."

"Roger, we both know that somebody needs to revisit that policy."

"*You're* not going to revisit it. Don't tell me how to do my job!"

The window of Julia's office that looked out onto the hall trembled as they swept past her office. A flash of something green went by with them. She heard the door to the Sierra Room open and then slam shut. She stepped out into the hall. Other people in other offices did the same. Worried glances ricocheted from door to door. The men's voices, muted but loud, grew hotter in the conference room. Then the sound of something hitting a wall and an enormous crash. Then silence.

When Roger reappeared a minute later, he looked utterly calm. "So if you could do that, I'd really appreciate it," he said as though he had just requested that Ilario make some copies for him. "I'm glad we understand each other." He smoothed his tie and gave Julia a slight nod as he passed her, then whistled as he disappeared around a corner.

Julia watched for movement from the Sierra Room. A black silence oozed from the door. Ilario didn't come out. Hearing her heart beating in her ears, she went to the door of the room and peered in.

Ilario's back was to her. His hands were locked behind his head in the manner of a cruise-ship passenger enjoying the view from a deck. He must have seen her reflection in some surface in the room, because he said in a cheery voice, "Come on in. It's a party. Just you and me so far, but so what?"

When he turned to look at her, there was nothing cheery in his face. His expression was like a dark bruise. The damp heat of conflict still lingered in the air. With his toe he pushed a chair toward her, but she didn't take it. Then she saw the cause of the crash she had heard and let out a gasp. During the argument someone— she assumed Roger—had thrown something at the wall, causing the wall-length etching of the Sierra Nevadas to come down. "Oh my God," Julia said.

"He found out about Guzman," Ilario said. He gave her a bent smile. His face radiated darkness. "Someone tipped him off."

For a moment she thought he was going to accuse her, but he added, "Guzman called to ask a question about the agreement. I wasn't here and somehow he got transferred to Roger and spilled everything about the side letter."

She put her hands on the back of the chair he had pushed out for her. "So what does this mean?"

"Nothing. Guzman's happy. Roger's pissed, but he'll get over it. We win." He dismissed Roger with a wave in the general direction of his office. "He retires in four months. Fuck him. Don't sweat it."

The word "sweat" caused Julia to glance at the perspiration marks on the underarms of Ilario's shirt. He brought his arms down. On the chair beside him was a copy of the Guzman agreement. He strummed the pages with his thumb, patted it protectively. She turned to leave, but he stopped her with: "So what's happening with the job search?"

It was the first time since she had lied about having a job offer that he'd mentioned it. A genuine curiosity held his words aloft. He gave another little push at the chair with his toe. She lowered herself cautiously to the side edge of it. She was surprised by her own honesty when she said, "No progress. I only just started looking, though."

He shook his head as he considered this. She noticed his tie. It was kelly green. It was this that had caught her eye as he and Roger swept by her door. The color looked out of place—hopelessly optimistic. He stopped strumming the pages. "Things are tough right now."

"They are."

"I mean"—he stirred the air with his hand—"around here. Everything. This place."

She nodded. "Change is like that."

"Yeah," he said. "I guess it is."

She rose from the chair.

"I'll see if I can do anything," he said.

"What?"

"If I hear anything. Jobs. You know."

"Why would you want to do that?"

"I don't know. I will, though. If you really want to leave."

"I do."

This time she was as far as the door when he said, "Remind me again why you want to leave?"

The question caught her like a hook. She looked back. She was about to say something, but once again she was distracted by his tie.

"That's new."

He looked down. "This?" He turned the end of the tie up and looked at it.

"You never wear green."

"You don't like it?"

"Red or yellow is better for you."

"This was a gift."

"From Ime?"

"How'd you know?"

"She likes that color."

He studied it. "I'm not sure I like it."

"But it was a gift."

"Right."

"So what can you do?"

"Exactly." He let the tie drop but still stared down at it. "What can you do?"

During the course of the following week, several more arguments erupted between Ilario and Roger behind closed doors. Though Julia couldn't tell exactly what they were arguing about, each argument seemed to be the result of Ilario overstepping his bounds or refusing to adhere to policies he thought were outdated. Julia was amazed that two people who previously had seemed to get along so well would now be unable to see eye to eye on almost anything.

And she was fascinated that Ilario wouldn't or couldn't keep a low profile until Roger's retirement. Then one day, while she was washing her hands in the restroom, she overheard the following conversation between two of her co-workers:

"Once you get on Roger's bad side, that's it. Remember how he treated Bettina when she lost the Universal account?"

"I don't think Ilario's ever been on Roger's good side."

"Then why did he promote him?"

"Politics. Other people were afraid Ilario would go somewhere else if they didn't reward him with manager."

"Roger's retiring, right?"

"He's having second thoughts."

"Then Ilario's in for a rough ride."

They walked out of the room. Their words stayed in the air, mixing with the sound of pipes knocking in the walls. Julia looked at herself in the mirror. She wanted to take satisfaction in Ilario's situation, but she couldn't, at least not completely. For one thing, it seemed unfair that Roger should treat him so roughly for one mistake. For another, it was hard to take pleasure in someone else's work problems when she had so many of her own. She didn't know what Ilario's job meant to him, but she knew what hers did to her. Taking care of herself now had to be her first priority.

Julia washed her hands a second time. No sooner had she walked out the door than she found herself face to face with Roger.

"Can I talk to you?" he said. "In the Sierra Room. Five minutes."

Julia felt the air tighten around her skin. She had been wondering whether Roger would eventually call her to task as well for the Guzman situation. It had been Ilario's call, but it was her account. In her office she pulled the Guzman file, then quickly jotted down a few points in her defense on a notepad.

In the Sierra Room, the etching had been hung back on the wall. There was no sign that any confrontation had taken place there. If anything, the room and chairs in it were more orderly than usual. For some reason, Julia found this reassuring.

"So, Julia," Roger began as they settled in. "How are you handling things since the transition?" He was not wearing a jacket today. This, too, she found reassuring.

"Fine," Julia said. Trying not to appear as though she were reading from her notepad, she said, "Roger, I just wanted to say, about the Guzman situation—"

He waved off her comment. "I've already given Ilario an earful about that. He put you in a shitty position. There wasn't much you could do."

"I realize I probably should have said something, but . . ."

He cocked an eyebrow in a way that said, Do you really want to go into it? She folded the top sheet of her notepad up and creased it at the middle.

Roger brought his fingertips together in front of his face. "Julia, do you have everything you need to do your job? Are there any obstacles I should be aware of?"

"Obstacles. Well . . . Roger, I guess I don't know what you mean."

"Let me ask the question this way. Is there anything I should be aware of, or any problems I can help fix that would help you do your job better?"

"Problems . . . do you mean with Ilario?"

"Ilario, or"—he turned his palms up—"whoever."

As he waited for an answer, his palms remained extended. They seemed to be offering her something . . . and requesting something as well.

"Well, Roger, that's a hard question to answer. I mean, it's been a learning curve figuring out how to work with each other . . ."

What exactly do you want to know? she thought. That Ilario is a terrible boss? That Guzman isn't the only account he's played fast and loose with? That she felt she needed to look for another job because of him? The temptation to tell him everything was huge; a flurry of words inside her waiting to be aired. But she couldn't do it. She thought of Ime, finally standing up for her with Ilario, convincing him to let her keep the Guzman account. She'd probably had to fight him hard, and she'd done it for the sake of their friendship. Julia believed that she and Ime were on the verge of repairing the rift between them. Telling Roger everything about Ilario would jeopardize that.

"Roger, things are fine with him. Since the trip to Oakland, things have been . . . better."

Roger nodded thoughtfully. "All right, then," he said. "That's all I need to know." He started to get up. "If you need me for anything at all, you know I'm always available. You won't hesitate. Understood?"

"Understood."

"We want to keep you happy, Julia," he said. Then, as they made their way out of the Sierra Room, "I understand that Ilario is dating a friend of yours."

Julia took a breath. She was surprised—not just that he knew this, but that he would bring it up.

"Yes," Julia said. "My best friend, Imelda. Why do you ask, Roger?"

"No reason," he said with a smile. "Just making conversation."

For the rest of the afternoon Julia pondered Roger's words. His mention of Ime gave her the eerie feeling that he knew more about her situation than he was letting on—not just about the tensions between her and Ilario, but perhaps even about the way she had once felt for her new boss. But that was impossible. There was no way he could have that kind of insight, especially given that she had hardly spoken to him before the day she applied for the account manager job. Even so, the feeling that he understood more than she wanted him to was strong. It stayed with her for several hours. Then, at the end of the workday, she opened her pay stub. It included the commission for the Guzman account.

She went to find Ilario.

"I told you I couldn't accept this," she said. She shoved the pay stub out for him to see.

"Your paycheck?"

"The commission. I don't feel right taking it when I know I'm leaving."

"I'll have to do a ton of paperwork to rescind it. Do you really want to do that to me?"

"Why did you give it to me in the first place when I told you not to?"

"I don't know, maybe I thought you deserved it?"

"You're trying to get me to stay."

"I'm not doing anything. Commissions are generated automatically."

"You should have stopped it."

"Please, just take it," he said. "You'd be doing me a favor. It belongs to you, you earned it, no one is going to think anything less of you if later you decide—" His eyes slid off her and into the hallway behind her.

A voice behind Julia said, "Do you want me to wait somewhere else?"

"Lydia." Ilario jockeyed around his desk and past Julia.

Julia turned to see him hugging his ex-fiancée. He lifted Lydia off the ground. Julia took a step back.

"You're early," Ilario said.

"It's my worst character flaw."

"I'm ready."

"I'm not interrupting? That looked important."

"Julia, this is Lydia. Lydia, this is Julia."

Lydia extended her hand. "I'm sorry to break up your meeting. I'm never in the right place at the right time." She touched Ilario's cheek affectionately. "Right, Ilario?"

Julia mumbled that it was nice to meet her, then tried to get by, but Lydia blocked her. "Julia. How do I know that name? Ilario, have you told me about her? He's always telling me such stories about the people who work here. Are you one of the crazy ones?"

Julia could see Ilario's face turning red. Hers was, too.

"Yes, she is," Ilario said, reaching for his jacket. "Everyone here is. You need to be getting along."

"It was nice meeting you," Lydia said to her. Ilario ushered her out of the room and down the corridor, placing his hand on her lower back as he had done each time before. Yet in spite of these intimacies, Julia was fairly sure he had been telling the truth when he'd said they were just friends. Friends with a past, but just friends.

As Ilario and Lydia reached the end of the hall, Ilario leaned toward her and whispered something in her ear. This caused Lydia to look back at Julia with wide eyes. Julia twisted away quickly. She felt her face turning even redder. She could only imagine what Ilario had told Lydia about her. She could only imagine what he was telling her now.

⇜ 16 ⇝

Shopping at the Camarillo
Premium Outlets

The Labor Day weekend arrived like a blessing—three days in which to forget about work and indulge in the company of friends. If there was ever a reason for keeping her job and her personal life separate, it was this: It ensured that she could always escape completely from one into the other.

In years past, Julia and her friends, at Concepción's urging, had taken the Long Beach ferry to Catalina Island for the weekend. But this year Marta, claiming that she could not afford to leave the Cantina unattended during a holiday, overrode her. It was decided instead to spend the day shopping at the factory outlets in Camarillo. Julia assumed that Ime would be joining them. But the night before they were to get together, Nina called to say she had spoken to Ime, who had decided to take a trip with Ilario to Vegas. Julia was instantly disappointed. She was eager for any opportunity to continue to repair the damage that had been done to their friendship.

Everyone agreed to meet at Nina's at nine. But at about eight thirty Concepción called to say that she was on her way over to Julia's. Several cups of coffee and an antihistamine had left her feeling too agitated to sit around waiting. When Julia went downstairs to meet her, Concepción was sitting at the wheel of her boxy orange Tercel hatchback with the rust-colored racing stripe, gnawing her lip and staring into space. Behind her in the backseat, Marta was dozing soundly, her bare feet propped up on a laundry basket and her plump brown arms folded over her chest. Julia got in carefully with a mug of coffee she had brought with her and buckled up. She asked Concepción if anything was wrong.

"Hmm? What? No, nothing. I'm fine." Concepción took a deep breath and pulled away from the curb. "I could use a cigarette, though." She nodded at the glove compartment. "Could you check for me? I think Marta left some in there."

Julia found a soft pack of Winstons. She pried out the last remaining smoke. Concepción took it, cracked her window, lit up, and pulled hard and deep.

"C, what's going on?" Julia said.

Concepción bit hard on her lower lip, fighting tears. "Life is crazy, Julia. Just when you think things are coming together, something comes along and throws everything off." She cranked her window down another couple of inches and knocked out some ash.

Julia shifted in her seat to face her. She brought both hands around her coffee cup. "Does this have anything to do with Remedios?"

Concepción looked at her. "How did you know?"

"Just a feeling."

"Oh, Julia, it's so terrible. I was talking to Clarita Montes, who knows everything about everybody. I happened to mention that I was friends with Remedios again. She seemed surprised by that, which I was expecting. But as I was explaining everything to her, she got this really weird look on her face. I asked her what was wrong, but she wouldn't tell me. So I kept at her, and finally she told me something she had heard. About Remedios. She said it wasn't something she could confirm, but she was pretty sure. . . . Julia, it's just so . . . I'm friends with Remedios again and I don't think I can bear . . ."

"C, I think I might already know what you're talking about."

Concepción glanced Julia's way. "Really?"

"She mentioned it."

"So it's true?"

"I think it is, C."

Tears leaped from Concepción's eyes. "Oh, Julia, isn't it awful? Who ever would have guessed? Remedios, of all people. And now I'm friends with her. I'm friends with a *lesbian*." She made a choking sound and covered her mouth.

"Oh, come *on,* C. You can't really have a problem with this."

"I can't be friends with someone like that, Julia. It's such a perversion, the church says so. And it's just a matter of time before she tries something."

Julia let out a groan. "C, when have you ever paid any attention to what the church says? And she's not going to *try* anything. And even if she did, are you really so helpless that you couldn't handle the situation?"

"I don't have to accept this," Concepción said. "I never would have contacted her if I had known. Nobody can make me be friends with someone like that."

Julia thumped her head against the passenger window. She was in no mood to cater to Concepción's irrational fears. She held the Winston pack to her eye to see if she had missed a cigarette. It was empty. She sipped her coffee.

A few seconds later, Concepción's phone rang. Concepción glanced to see who it was. With a shriek she threw the phone in the glove compartment and slammed it shut and covered her mouth.

"That was her?" Julia said.

"Don't answer it!"

"You're ignoring her calls?"

"I can't talk to her!"

"You have to!"

"I can't. I wouldn't know what to say, Julia. You were right when you said that contacting her was a mistake. I really, really should have listened to you."

Julia would happily have admitted to being wrong about Remedios if it would make Concepción come to her senses. But she was in no mood to fight her. She was contemplating asking Concepción to take her back home, when Marta started to come to behind her with much grumbling and stretching. Marta explained that she'd been at the Cantina late the night before and hadn't gotten more than a couple of hours of sleep before this loca showed up at her door, demanding her company, for what reason she had no idea. What she needed now was a strong cup of coffee—preferably with some Baileys in it—her feet were killing her, and who was going to offer to give her a foot rub to make up for this awful inconvenience? As for Remedios being a lesbian, she had her doubts, since the lesbians who sometimes dropped by the Cantina were the worst tippers, whereas Remedios had already proved herself to be generous to a fault.

"Just look at this nice turquoise ring she bought me in TJ," Marta said, snaking her arm through the space between the front seats.

Ignoring her, Concepción said, "What will people think if I'm seen with her?"

"You should be so lucky as to have people associate you with Remedios," Marta said, admiring her ring at arm's length. "Anyway, sleeping with the same sex is very fashionable in Hollywood." She began listing the names of actresses who were rumored to be lesbians.

"Mexicans just aren't supposed to be that way," Concepción said.

"Well, I have news for you," Marta said. "I'm a lesbian, too. I like to lick pussy."

"Shut up," Concepción said. "You've never done anything like that."

"Maybe not," Marta said, still admiring her ring, "but that doesn't mean I wouldn't try it. I'm willing to try anything since my divorce." She started digging through the backseat pocket. "Do you have any pot back here, C?"

"You warned me not to trust Remedios," Concepción said to Julia. "You were right. This was all part of her plan."

"What plan?" Marta said. "To get back at you by sleeping with women? You really are stupid. Did I say that out loud? Well, it's nothing you haven't heard." Once she had emptied the backseat pocket of its contents, she started sifting through Concepción's laundry.

"C, you've done a great thing making peace with Remedios," Julia said.

"Seriously, don't offend Remedios now," Marta said. "Lesbians can be touchy. Did you know her brother just installed a hot tub? She promised to invite us over when he's not there. Don't fuck that up. Call her back. Be nice to her."

Just as they were getting to Nina's house, Marta excavated Concepción's pot from her box of laundry detergent. She gleefully waggled the bag next to Concepción's ear, sprinkling soap flakes.

Concepción parked in front of Nina's small wood-frame house. It sat next to the railroad tracks that divided Pacoima and much of the rest of the northeast part of the Valley. She had inherited the house from her uncle years earlier. She had painted it inside and out with shockingly bright colors. Julia and her friends had thought they were being clever by calling it "Nina's cartoon house," but later learned that that was what most of the people in the neighborhood called it, too.

From somewhere within the house, Nina shouted for them to come in. When they did, they were met not by Nina but by Nina's wedding dress, displayed to full advantage on a tailor's dummy in the middle of the living room. Nina had undone the side seams to take the dress in, but even partially disassembled, the gown, a strapless design of creamy charmeuse with sumptuous embroidery, was breathtaking. The dress was more modern than anything Julia thought Nina would have chosen for herself. The women circled it, viewing it from every angle and expressing their approval in hushed, appreciative gasps.

Nina appeared in the kitchen doorway. Her hair was pulled back from her face, her cheeks were ruddy, and she was smiling. Bouncing on the balls of her feet, she asked them whether they liked the dress. Everyone said they did. But why, Julia asked, hadn't she consulted with any of them first? Nina explained that there had been no need to go dress shopping. The dress had called out to her, not from a store, but from one of the many yard sales that peppered her Pacoima neighborhood. She had found it lying in an open box on a front lawn between a broken 8-track tape player and a stack of *Hustler* magazines, but she had known the moment she lifted it out of the box that with a few changes, the dress would be perfect for her.

"But it looks brand-new," Concepción said.

Marta marveled at the quality of the dress, then clutched her heart and staggered when Nina said that she had paid only twenty dollars for it. Why, Marta wondered, would anyone sell such a fine dress at such a cheap price—unless, of course, the dress was somehow cursed, doomed to bring unnatural ruin to anyone who wore it. She had heard about such things. She had read books.

"The dress is beautiful," Concepción said, "but we should get going to avoid traffic."

"We need to wait for Remedios," Nina said.

"What? Who? Remedios? You invited her?"

"She asked us to be sure to call her the next time we hit the outlets, remember?" Nina stood back from her handiwork. "What would you think if I added some mother-of-pearl or some rhinestones . . . here, here, and here?"

"She's on her way here?" Concepción said.

"She's a couple minutes away."

Concepción excused herself to use Nina's bathroom.

Marta picked up a bridal magazine and sank into the cushions of Nina's couch. Smiling, she started turning pages.

Remedios came through the door moments later, apologizing profusely for keeping everyone waiting. Marta answered that if there was anyone worth waiting for it was her. Remedios tilted up her sunglasses and surveyed the room with a slow turn. She told Nina that her house was about the cutest thing she had ever seen. She ran her hands over the furniture and the drapes and looked at the pictures on her wall. Not until Nina brought her attention to the dress did Remedios give a gasp—less of appreciation, it seemed to Julia, than of embarrassment at having overlooked it. After examining it from several angles, she nodded and murmured approvingly, though with slightly less approval than she had given the furniture and the drapes.

When Concepción came back into the room, any anxiety that remained in her face was no more than could be attributed to too much coffee.

"I've been trying to reach you since the day before yesterday," Remedios said, and rubbed Concepción's shoulder affectionately. "Why haven't you been answering your phone?"

Concepción looked at Julia, then said, "I think there's something wrong with it?"

"She has problems with her phone all the time," Marta said. "Sometimes I can't get through to her for days. It leaves me heartbroken not to be able to hear her sweet, beautiful voice."

Remedios held Concepción at arm's length and drilled her with a look. "Just as long as you're not avoiding me." Then she laughed thunderously and pulled Concepción into a hug. "I'm kidding, I'm kidding."

Once Remedios had released her, Concepción said, "We'll need to take two cars, so I'll drive and—"

"I can fit five," Remedios said brightly. "We'll take my car."

"Yes, we'll take Remedios's car," Marta said, and stuck her tongue out at Concepción when Remedios wasn't looking.

Remedios and Nina walked ahead. Concepción reached for Marta. "Marta, what did you do with that pot? Light one up for me. Now. Hurry."

On their way out to Remedios's car, Marta rushed ahead of the others, practically body-checking Nina in order to sit up front with Remedios. Julia and Concepción and Nina piled into the back with Julia in the middle. For the next few minutes, Marta had nothing but praise for Remedios. She loved her car (it was stylish and practical), her hair (practical), and even the way she drove (she commanded the road). Marta delivered these compliments with a girlish lilt and lots of high-pitched laughter. Everything Remedios said struck her as witty, and several times she said, "Oh, Rem, that's just the funniest thing," and pressed Remedios's shoulder coyly.

Julia marveled at how, almost overnight, Remedios had gained such acceptance from her friends. Even Nina, who had seemed terrified of her the day she appeared at the Cantina, now treated her with the casual regard of a longtime friend. While Julia no longer believed Remedios intended anything sinister, it still struck her as peculiar that she had chosen to devote so much time to them. Where were her other friends? What did they think?

Concepción sat slumped next to her window with a flat, lifeless expression. When Remedios asked her if anything was wrong, Marta interjected, saying that Concepción was disappointed not to be going to Catalina this year.

"Really?" Remedios said, looking for her in the mirror. "I never thought it was all that special. What is it you like so much about it, C?"

"Buffalo," Marta answered for her, referring to the free-roaming bison that were one of the island's attractions. "Concepción loves the buffalo. She's crazy about them."

Because they were getting an early start, traffic on the 101 was light, and within a few minutes they were traversing the rolling brown hills out of the Valley and into Ventura County. Next to Julia, Nina started to make a happy, squeaky sound. She drummed her knees a few times with her fists. She bounced up and down on her seat.

"Shit," Concepción said, "I've never seen you so excited about shopping."

"It's not that," Nina said. "It's something else. I'll tell you later."

Marta looked back. "No fair keeping secrets."

"I can't say anything yet." She looked at her watch. "Later today. I promise."

Remedios proclaimed that this was entirely unfair, and that Nina was being cruel by mentioning anything at all. Since it was Remedios's car, her rules applied, and her rules stipulated no secrets. But Nina only shook her head in refusal. She squeezed her lips together. She pounded her knees harder.

The outlet stores were just opening when they arrived. Already hundreds of other cars were pouring into the lot, people like them, trying to beat the crowds and the heat that had been forecast. The Camarillo Premium Outlets had long been one of Ime's favorite places because of the high-end stores like Saks and Barneys that made up the vast shopping center. Julia wondered if Ime was doing any shopping in Vegas. And if so, was she also thinking of her?

Once out of Remedios's car, Marta led the charge though the mall. She was in search of a new pair of sandals to replace the tattered chanclas she was wearing. She rushed ahead through the archways of the putty-colored arcade and into an Easy Spirit that was advertising items up to 80 percent off. In the store, Julia steered Concepción out of earshot while Marta took Remedios and went in search of a salesperson. Nina followed close behind.

"I'm really proud of you," Julia whispered to Concepción. "You're doing great."

"I keep picturing the sex," Concepción said. "Does that mean I have lesbian tendencies?"

"I think it's a good step that you can even think about it," Julia said.

Concepción shook her hands in front of her and hopped from foot to foot like an athlete getting psyched up. "I'm going to try not to let it bother me. It's not a big deal, right? It's not. It's not."

They found Marta seated at the back of the store with her feet extended in front of her while an irritated salesgirl helped her by putting a pair of leather sandals on Marta's feet. All around her were boxes of sandals that Marta had already rejected. "What do you think of these, Rem? Do these make my feet look not so fat?"

Remedios told her she liked the sandals and thought that Marta's feet looked fine in them.

Marta stood up and tromped around in them. "You really think so? They are awfully nice, aren't they? Oh, but look." She considered the tag on the box lid. "Even with the discount they're expensive. Should I pay this much for a pair of sandals, Rem?"

Remedios said she thought they were reasonably priced.

"Do you think so? Hmm, I don't know." She turned her foot this way and that, considering. "If only the Cantina weren't doing so badly, Rem . . . of course, my birthday is coming up. I could always use that as an excuse to splurge. . . ."

Remedios asked her if she wanted to look around for something less expensive.

"We could," Marta sighed. "Then again, these are the last pair in my size. . . ."

Looking a little dejected, Marta left the store without the shoes. Outside, Remedios said that she thought five women shopping together was a recipe for frustration, and suggested that they break up into two groups. "C, you come with me, and Marta can go with Julia and Nina. We'll meet back here under this archway in two hours."

"OK, Rem," Marta said. "I'll catch up with you later."

Remedios linked arms with Concepción. Concepción looked back in a way that reminded Julia of a child being led away from her mother on the first day of school.

"What's the matter with C?" Nina said as she and Julia and Marta strolled. "She's hardly said a word all morning."

"Don't tell her," Marta said. "Not until she tells us what *her* big secret is."

"I told you, I *am* going to tell you. Just not yet."

Julia said, "I don't know if Remedios wants everyone to know—"

"Remedios is a leg licker," Marta said. "A tortillera. She likes the scissor action, if you know what I mean." With her middle and index fingers she made two pairs of scissors and started bumping the cruxes together.

"Really?" Nina said. "Remedios dates women?"

"C's having a hard time dealing with it," Julia said.

"Well, what a thing to find out," Nina said.

"You have a problem with it, too?"

"Oh . . . I don't know." Nina looked fearfully from Marta to Julia. "Maybe not. I mean . . . should I?" She was bright red.

"Lesbians are everywhere," Marta said. "Get with the times." She pushed her sunglasses up the ridge of her nose and started snapping her fingers and shimmying to the jazzy music piping up from speakers hidden in the landscaping.

"Just don't say anything yet, OK?" Julia said.

Marta added her scissor bumping to her little dance. A family passed nearby. The parents stared. Marta intensified the scissor bumping for their benefit. They moved to block their children from her.

A few minutes later Julia and Nina stopped to use the restroom.

"So Remedios is gay," Nina said, approaching the mirror and peering at herself. "Does it bother me? No. No, I don't think it does." She turned one cheek then the other to the mirror, as though the true answer resided in her complexion.

When all the women met up again under the archway, Concepción was carrying a Kenneth Cole bag. Julia was relieved to see that she was in better spirits than before, her face no longer showing signs of strain about Remedios.

Concepción suggested that maybe it was time for lunch, and everyone agreed. Rather than eat at the mall's cheap food court, Remedios suggested finding a nicer restaurant in town. They all said this was a wonderful idea. Except for Nina. For several minutes she'd been looking at her watch. On the tenth or twelfth look, Concepción snapped, "Nina, why do you keep doing that? Why don't you just tell us what this secret of yours is?"

"Well," Nina drawled, "I promised I wouldn't say anything until one o'clock. It's only twelve thirty. If you could just wait a little longer, then I won't be breaking my—"

"Tell us!" Concepción said.

Nina's face lit up with nervous excitement, just as it had when they had first questioned her. "All right, I guess I can tell you now. You're not going to believe it. OK, ready? Here goes: In twenty minutes . . . Ime and Ilario . . . are going to be . . . *man and wife*."

The bubble of silence that followed was charged with disbelief.

"*What?*" Concepción said. "They're getting *married*? You have got to be kidding."

But Nina did not look as though she was kidding at all. She gave a squeal of delight and shook her fists at her sides. "They went to Vegas to elope. Ime didn't want anyone to know until it was final. She's completely in love. In twenty minutes she'll be Mrs. Ilario Ortega." And then, standing a little taller, as though this were the very best part, "I'm the only one Ime told. I'm the only one she trusted to keep their secret."

≈ 17 ≈

The Truth Emerges

S he did *what*?" Concepción said. She kept repeating the question, even as Nina tried to explain.

"Ime didn't want to make a big fuss. You know how impatient she is. She's in love and she knows Ilario is right for her. She figured, why wait?"

"But we're her *friends*," Julia said. "Doesn't that count for something?"

No one seemed to have an answer for this. In their shock the women had settled into folding chairs on Remedios's garden-facing back porch. She had been excited to show them the little fixer-upper Craftsman house she had bought through the success of her machine shop, but so far no one had been able to talk about anything other than Ime.

"It just goes to show what I've always said," Marta said. "To Ime we're just nacas of the lowest sort."

"I guess she wasn't joking all those times she said she wanted to get rid of us as friends," Concepción said.

"You're not being fair," Nina said. "You don't have all the facts. Maybe she'll have a real wedding later that we can all go to."

"Can anyone tell us anything about this guy she's marrying?"

Everyone turned to Julia. "Why are you looking at me?" she asked.

"You're her best friend," Concepción said. "She tells you everything. You must have known something." She squinted at Julia, mining for some missing truth.

"I told you, I don't know a thing. I never talk to Ilario about anything other than business, and Ime and I haven't been . . ." She felt herself choking up. She got up to go to the restroom.

As she went into Remedios's house, she heard Concepción say, "Nina, are you *sure* she told you they were going to Vegas 'para casarnos'? Not 'para descansarnos'?"

Julia went to the bathroom and shut the door. Never could she have foreseen something like this. Was Ime pregnant? Even if she were, she wouldn't have let it rush her into marriage. Julia could picture Ime deciding that marriage was what she wanted, in the way she decided that she had to have a 5 Series or the newest Chanel suit, and then applying every practical pressure to make it happen. What Julia *couldn't* picture was Ilario agreeing to go along with anything so . . . *radical*. He was a risk-taker, but he wasn't impulsive. Above all, he just didn't seem like a man . . . *in love*. But whether it was a smart decision or not was beside the point. For Ime not to have involved her after so many years of friendship—to have told Nina everything and her nothing—that was the real blow. She felt it through her whole body. The world around her seemed to be shuddering from the impact.

There was a knock. Julia cracked the door and Remedios peered in. "I forgot to tell you, the toilet won't flush unless . . . Julia, what's the matter?"

Julia began to cry. She stood back and Remedios came in and shut the door behind her. "Julia, what is it?" She dropped the seat cover so Julia could sit down, then spun some paper off the roll. "Here. Take this."

"How could she do this, Rem? We've been friends since we were *seven*. Then after one little misunderstanding . . . to not even call to tell me . . ."

Remedios pressed her hip into the sharp edge of the tile sink and crossed her arms. The bathroom was small and cramped and the light was harsh. "What's going on with the two of you? You used to do everything together."

"Rem, things are so screwed up. One day everything was fine, then Ilario came along."

"And broke your heart?"

"What?! No. I mean . . . what did Nina tell you?"

"Nothing that I couldn't figure out right now looking at you. Is Ime the only one you're crying about?"

Julia shook her head. "This is the thing I always disliked about you," she said. "You're much too insightful for anybody's good."

"Then you're not going to like me saying this, either. You're expecting too much of Ime. She's always been a spoiled little brat."

"Rem, that's not fair—"

"Yes, it is. She's gotten what she's asked for. Why? Because she never asks, she takes. It only bothers you now because now it's you she's treating this way."

"I've done everything she's asked, Rem. *Everything*." She wadded the tissue in her fist. She was angry now. This was better than the empty shock. "I can't think of anything—*anything*—that would have kept me from sharing something that important with her. Tell me honestly, Rem. Wouldn't you be insulted if someone you were close to fell out of your life and . . ."

Remedios had only to raise an eyebrow to point out the irony.

"Well . . . anyway," Julia said, "I'm always the one who has to fix things. Not this time. If this is how she wants things, then that's how they'll be."

Such a statement would have been the cue for any of Julia's other friends to contradict her, to assure her that with time things would right themselves. But Remedios wasn't one of Julia's other friends. She only gave a dry little shrug. "If you guys patch things up, great. But if that doesn't happen, I'm not going to cry with you about it."

Remedios's seeming indifference calmed Julia more than any of her other friends' reassurances could have. She dried her tears and took in the room and its decor for the first time, ready to change the subject with some sort of compliment about Remedios's new home. But the bathroom was all peeling gilt wallpaper and ugly pumpkin-colored fixtures.

Remedios gave a knowing roll of her eyes. "I know. This room is a disaster."

To Julia, September in the Valley was always a melancholy time of year. In the mornings the Verdugo Mountains cast long, low shadows that seemed intended as an impediment to her day. While this time of summer usually marked the start of more comfortable temperatures, she still preferred the longer, hotter, brighter months of July and August. Those were the months that she and Ime usually took a trip together, just the two of them, without the company of any of their other friends. The realization that the summer was already on the decline and they had not seen each other for most of the last two months fed her sadness. With each hour that she did not hear from Ime, the more heavily the realization weighed on her: Their friendship as it had once existed was over. Ime was a married woman. Julia did not know where she would fit into her life, or in what capacity Ime would ever want her in it again.

The holiday came to an end without word from her. But at 10:45 on Monday night, after Julia was already in bed and beginning to think about the workweek ahead, her phone rang. It was a number she didn't recognize, but she still hoped that it might be Ime. It wasn't. A man's voice came on the line.

"Julia, I'm sorry to be calling you so late."

"Ilario?"

"I hate to bother you on your holiday. I need to talk to you."

"I'll have time in the morning—"

"I need to talk to you now. About Ime."

Julia sat up. "What's going on? I heard you guys got married."

He gave a deep, troubled sigh. "We didn't get married. I just dropped her off at her house. I need to talk to you, Julia. I think your friend has just about lost her mind."

Julia swung her legs out of bed. "Ilario, what's wrong with Ime?"

"Can we talk in person? I can come by your place if that's easier. You're the only person I know who knows Ime. I don't know what to do."

Julia gave him her address and directions. She pulled on her clothes and started picking up around the apartment. Ilario must have already been in the neighborhood, because within minutes there was a knock.

A burst of warm air followed him in. His features flickered back and forth between aggravation and confusion. She asked him if he wanted to sit down. He paced the room in short bursts.

He said, "So we planned this trip to Vegas a couple of weeks ago, right? It was going to be our first trip together. Things between us had been going pretty well. You know, a couple of arguments here or there. But nothing out of the ordinary. About as good as anyone can expect after four months. After we had made the reservations, we started joking—*joking*—about how funny it would be if we got married while we were in Vegas. Wouldn't our friends think we were crazy? I thought it was funny, and she thought it was funny. As the trip came up we kept joking about it more and more—*joking.* About how we were going to get married at one of those places where Elvis does the ceremony, and how we were going to come back and shock all our friends who never thought either of us would ever get married. The joke went on like that—you know, *un chiste,* just kidding around, right?"

Julia felt behind her for a chair. She started to lower herself into it.

"So there we were in Vegas, out to dinner on our second night, having a nice time, laughing like we usually do."

"Oh, no," Julia said.

"And what does Ime do? That's right, she proposes. She tells me that it's obvious that we're right for each other and she doesn't see any point in drawing things out, and if I'm ready and willing, she's ready to get married the next day. She was *serious.* She actually thought *we were going to get married.*"

"Oh my God, oh my God, oh my God."

"How could she possibly think that?" Ilario said. "How could she have thought that I was going to say yes?"

"Oh, God, Ilario. What did you say to her?"

"What did I say? Well, let's see. I thought she had to be joking. So that's what I said: 'Ime, you have to be joking. Tell me this is how you like to joke with your boyfriends. Because I'm getting worried, fast. And by the way, where are the exits in this place?'"

"Oh, God, poor Ime."

"Poor *Ime?* Poor *Ime?*"

"I mean . . . oh, Ilario, I don't know what I mean. What happened? What did she say?"

He rubbed his hands together. "This is where it gets good. She said that if I wasn't serious about her, I shouldn't have given her the impression that I wanted to marry her. Then she got all strange and quiet and hard and . . . crazy. She wouldn't say a word to me. Can you believe that? Can you?"

He stopped pacing. He sat down and dropped his face into his hands. Julia moved from her chair. Cautiously, she sat down a few feet away from him on the couch. "Ilario, I know this is hard to understand, but sometimes Ime gets . . . ideas. She assumes that other people are going to see things the same way she does. She's always talking about how good she is at reading people, but sometimes—"

"You should have seen the look on her face. Like I had to be crazy not wanting to marry her. Like it would have been the most natural thing in the world to do."

Julia felt an odd twist of sympathy for both Ime and Ilario. She could picture it happening just as Ilario described, could see the logic Ime had been following. For her, it made a certain kind of sense. This was how Ime lived her life. She pointed her car at the desired destination and pressed down as hard as she could on the gas.

"She hardly talked to me for the rest of the trip. It was terrible. I don't know what she's thinking or what she expects me to do."

If Julia understood Ime, she knew she had done the only thing she could think of to hide her humiliation—shut down the engine and locked the doors. If only she had talked to Julia first. Julia thought: Sure, I rely on you a lot, Ime. But you rely on me, too. If only you had told me what you were planning, I could have helped you avoid all of this. I could have told you what not to do. . . .

"I can't believe I'm sitting here telling you this," Ilario said.

"Ilario, I'm sure she's home right now crying and hating herself for being so stupid. She probably wants to find a way to talk to you, but she doesn't know how."

These words seemed to have no effect on Ilario. He was in as much a state of shock as Julia had been in when she'd thought they'd gotten married. It was a while before he lifted his face. Its expression was a question mark for which she had no answers. All she could think to add was, "You have to understand that Ime has almost no dating experience. She's never even had a serious boy-friend."

The look that came over Ilario made her wish she hadn't said this. She could see from his expression that Ime had painted a very different picture of herself.

"Is she going to do something crazy if I dump her?" he said. "Should I be worried?"

Julia drew one foot under her leg. "Is that what you're thinking of doing?"

"I don't know. I don't know if I can be with someone who thinks she can just . . ."

"Ilario, before you do anything, let me talk to her. Let me see if I can . . . well, I don't know what I can do, but let me talk to her. Maybe I can help in some way."

Ilario drew his palms down both sides of his face. He rose slowly and stuffed his hands in his pockets. "I hope so. Because I can't talk to her right now."

At the door, he thanked her. He said he hadn't realized it was so late. "Your boss shouldn't be bothering you with something like this. I just thought I was going to lose my mind." His apology was warm and sincere. She remembered how, at Concepción's party, he had offered to give her advice about work anytime she needed it. She had felt a connection to him at that moment. She felt some-thing like that now. He was about to leave, but he stopped and looked at her. A regret of a different kind seemed to be working in his face. "I think I might have been wrong about some things . . . about you," he said. "I think I might have been . . . unfair."

Julia did not take his words to be an apology. They were strung together too tentatively to be mistaken for anything so concrete. Instead, they seemed to hint at something that was only just occurring to him, some thought that would need more consideration. It was more of a suggestion of an apology yet to come, one that might materialize should further consideration justify it. As apologies went, it wasn't much. But it was more than Julia had expected.

All of Julia's attempts to reach Ime the next day went straight to her voice mail. When she called Ime's agency, they told her she had gone out with a client for lunch. Rather than leave another message, she went by Ime's house later in the day. She wasn't there. Julia knew where she kept her spare house key. She found it in its usual place, hidden in the porch lamp cover. It was hot from the bulb that constantly burned there, and she tossed it from palm to palm until it was cool enough to grasp. She had once been free to use it anytime, to come and go as she pleased, to borrow whatever she wanted of Ime's without asking, just as Ime had always been free to do with her. She hesitated only for a second to let herself in.

Inside, Ime's house was clean and neat and in order. For some reason, this reassured her that Ime was all right. She called for her, but there was no answer. She went upstairs and looked around. She didn't know what she was looking for, but the sight of old photos of the two of them from past years on Catalina Island also reassured her. Julia always thought of Ime as being taller than her. But every photo confirmed that Julia was the taller of the two. Looking through the other bedrooms, which Ime used mostly for storage, she found nothing to cause her any alarm, though what such a thing would be she wasn't sure. She heard a sound and went downstairs.

Ime was just getting home and was closing the door behind her. Julia stopped. Ime had her mail between her teeth and was struggling under the weight of two huge bags of oranges that strained from each hand. She spat out the mail onto a table near the door and swung the door shut with her foot, then turned and saw Julia standing at the middle of the staircase.

"What were you thinking?" Julia said.

"What are you doing here?"

"Why didn't you talk to me first?"

"Do I have to run everything by you?"

"Don't you wish you had this time?"

They stood facing each other. It was like a standoff in an old Western. Ime held tight to her bags of oranges with small fists. There must have been a hundred oranges in the two bags, straining the plastic mesh to capacity. Julia had no idea what Ime could need with so many oranges. She imagined a party, a hundred guests holding tropical drinks with orange slices, noise, frivolity. Goings-on to which she was not invited, guests and friends to whom she had never been introduced or even told about. She imagined that letting herself in had been a mistake. That Ime's life was going on without her. That there had been no need to come, that there was nothing Julia could offer her in the way of solace or advice or help. That it was Julia who had come here needing something.

But it was only a matter of seconds before pain seeped into Ime's face, and Julia knew she had done the right thing in coming. Ime set the oranges down and pressed her fingers to her mouth. Tears flooded her eyes. She ran, childlike, to Julia.

"It was terrible, terrible," Ime said. "What have I done? What have I done?"

Julia opened her arms and took her in and absorbed her powerful sobs. "Tell me everything," she said. "Tell me everything."

≈ 18 ≈

Julia Makes a Save

Things had happened more or less as Julia suspected. Misreading Ilario, Ime had hit him with a hard sell; then, humiliated by his rejection, she had retreated into a cold, hard shell.

"I was so stupid," she said, plucking at a bit of loose piping on her couch. "If I had just laughed it off like I was joking, we could have moved right past it."

Julia knew she ought to say: Go to him, apologize, explain that you were hurt. But some piece of Ime's story wasn't sitting right.

"I understand you love him," Julia said. "But why marriage? Why now? That's the part that doesn't sound like you."

Ime turned her face to the high living room window. In the falling light, the ridgeline of the Santa Monica Mountains appeared soft and gray, like a pile of ash rising above neighbors' rooftops. Ime said, "Ilario makes me happy. Even if he *was* joking about marriage, I thought there was something serious behind it. With Lydia moving to town, I thought it would be as good a time as any, but I hadn't considered—"

"Hold on," Julia said. "Lydia is moving here?"

With a regretful shake of her head, Ime said, "A couple of weeks

ago Ilario told me she was being transferred to L.A. He promised to
help her find a place and get settled in, and I—"

"You got jealous," Julia said.

Ime hung her head.

"Even though you were the one who told me there was nothing
between them."

"It was easy to accept that they were just friends when she lived
four hundred miles away," Ime said. "But to find out that she's moving here, and then to see how excited Ilario was about it—"

"So all of a sudden she became a threat. And you panicked. You
tried to make sure that Ilario was yours. . . . Ime, that's so crazy!"

"I know!" Ime said. "And I'm sorry I was so mean to you. You
were right and I should have listened."

"No! I was wrong about her. *You* were right."

Humiliation, guilt, and fear fought one another for a place on
Ime's face. Humiliation seemed to be prevailing.

"They're *just friends*," Julia said. "Isn't that why we haven't
been talking?"

"Do you know why they broke up?" Ime said. "Because work
kept taking them to different cities. There was no fighting or hating or anything. Just distance. And now there's none. Yet they still
have this thing, this . . . spark. You don't understand."

Julia did understand. She had seen that spark. Any woman
would have been concerned about it. But she also believed Ilario
now. She couldn't say why, but she believed him.

Ime braced herself with both hands on the sofa cushions. "What
did he say? Does he hate me? Does he never want to see me again?"

"He didn't say that. But he needs some answers. You need to
tell him how you feel about Lydia."

"He'll think I'm crazy."

"But he might understand jealous-crazy. Crazy-crazy isn't going to fly."

"Then tell me what I should say," Ime said. "I'll listen to you. I can't lose him—I love him so much."

Julia didn't know what to say to her. Her own feelings toward Ilario were too snarled by recent events and her opinion of him too uncertain for her to comfortably offer advice. It rankled her to be in such a position after the way Ime had treated her. She looked out again at the mountains. They were almost indistinguishable now from the charcoal sky behind them. Only a wire-thin line separated earth from clouds.

Moments later, the power went out. The room went dark and the air conditioner clicked off.

"Shit," Ime sighed. "Is it just us?"

Julia went to the door and looked out. Lights were out throughout the cul-de-sac. An eerie quiet settled on the neighborhood, broken only by the far-off howling of a dog. "It's everybody," Julia said.

Ime went into the kitchen and came back with a flashlight and a portable radio. Julia held the flashlight while Ime played with the dial looking for news. A voice came through: A rolling blackout had sunk part of Los Angeles, including most of the Valley, into darkness.

Without power to run the air, Ime's house quickly began to heat up. Ime went around opening windows. From the front door, Julia could see Ime's neighbors doing the same. Ime began to grumble about how there had to be a way to keep all the air conditioners running at the same time during the summers. Julia, however, was glad for the distraction. Looking out at the night, she imagined that people all across the Valley must be opening their windows and doors just as Ime was, cursing the utility company or the weather or life in general in the hot, hot Valley. She imagined them wondering out loud how long it would be before things returned to normal, how long it would be before they got relief.

. . .

Ime promised three things to convince Ilario that she deserved another chance: to never again mention marriage unless he mentioned it first; to "back up" to where things stood before they'd begun planning their trip to Vegas; and to help Lydia find an apartment, proving to him and to herself that she could conquer her feelings of jealousy.

"Thank you so much," Ime told Julia once she had given her the good news. "I wouldn't have known what to say if it weren't for you. And whatever you said to Ilario—thank you for that, too."

Julia didn't remember advising Ime to say any of the things she'd said. Nor did she say anything to Ilario to influence him. Ordinarily, Julia would have basked in Ime's gratitude regardless. But this time Ime's words of thanks only caused Julia a scraping discomfort.

Because Julia was out on sales calls for the next few days, she did not see Ilario again until the third-quarter sales review. The meeting was just getting under way as she walked into the Sierra Room, giving her only enough time to wave to him from across the room before sitting down. In the days since he had come by her apartment, he had begun to grow a beard and mustache. The look was striking. As he went up to the podium a few minutes later to give his group's update, Julia wondered how Ime was reacting to it. Whereas Julia thought facial hair was sexy, especially on a Latino, Ime disliked it intensely. "Shaving is one of the few things that separate men from dogs," she'd been known to say. To Julia, though, there was nothing like the anticipation of a first kiss from a man with facial hair, that moment of discovering whether the hair was soft or bristly. Ilario's beard was especially handsome, dark and even and neatly trimmed, accentuating the fullness of his lips as he shaped his words.

"I just want everyone to know what a great job Julia is doing," Ilario said.

Julia looked left and right. There were no other Julias. Ilario was looking at her.

"Julia's been doing the work of three people," he said. "Thanks to her, our numbers are up again. Her hard work and talent are examples for everyone."

A brief wave of applause worked its way through the room. Julia stood up, then back down quickly. She fanned herself with a notepad. She pulled her skirt taut to her knees.

When the meeting was over, she went to talk to Ilario.

"You didn't have to do that," she said.

"I wanted to."

"I'm still looking for other work," she said.

"I just thought people should know how hard you've been working."

"Just as long as you know I'm still looking."

"I know. And I'm sorry if I embarrassed you."

"You didn't."

"Good." He flexed a yellow folder between his hands. "Listen, I really never got to thank you—"

"You don't have to—"

"For backing me up."

"Oh. Wait. What?"

"With Roger the other day. He told me he talked to you. I guess you told him . . . nothing too terrible about me."

"So you two have worked things out?" she said.

His folder creaked as he shaped it into a tube—a subtle strangling motion. "Not exactly."

Across the room Roger was joking with some of the sales managers, his face red from exertion. Even in a good mood he cut an intimidating figure. People gave him as much space when he was jolly as they did when he was in a rage.

Ilario said, "Listen, I also wanted to thank you—"

"You don't have to."

"I shouldn't have come by the other night."

"We both care about Ime."

"We do," he said.

There seemed to be nothing else to say, so they went back to watching Roger. Julia felt bad about the way Roger had been treating Ilario. She didn't approve of the side agreement Ilario had made with Guzman, but she had seen Roger forgive people for much worse.

Ilario's cell phone sounded. She heard him say Ime's name as he sidestepped through the crowd and out of the room with the phone pressed to his ear. She walked over to the juice and coffee bar for some tea. When she turned back, she saw Ilario's yellow folder sitting on a chair near the door. She picked it up and went to his office to return it to him, but his door was closed and his blinds were down. She looked inside the folder. It contained his presentation outline. Halfway down the page a handwritten note read:

Julia: Exceptional. <u>Say</u> so.

The words floated up to her. They signified nothing more than a reminder to praise her. Something in her shifted and buckled. She didn't know why these words should mean more to her than those he had spoken in front of her co-workers. But they did.

The next day, walking into the Ostin offices, Julia was met by several of her co-workers huddled near the reception desk. Their stunned expressions as they turned and looked made her drop every thought of Ilario.

"What's wrong?" she said, slowing her step and feeling hairs rise on the back of her neck.

"It's Roger," Anne said. Anne was Roger's part-time assistant. She looked as though she had been crying. "He was in an accident last night at Magic Mountain. He was there with his family and he got thrown from the car of a roller coaster."

"What? How is that possible? How is he?"

"His seat harness failed and he slid out of the ride. He broke nearly every bone in his body."

Julia remembered hearing something on the news the previous night about the accident, but they hadn't said a name.

"My God," Julia said. "How horrible. Where is he?"

"They transferred him over to Valley Presbyterian. He's in critical care. He was in surgery for six hours. He's going to make it, but he's really banged up."

"He's completely conscious," someone else said in a way that sounded a little disappointed.

"I can't believe it," Julia said. "You hear about things like this all the time, but you never think—"

"Julia, can I talk to you for a minute?" Ilario had just come up behind Julia. His eyes shook nervously in his head. He looked as pale as if he had personally witnessed the accident.

"This is just amazing," Julia said. "Terrible . . ."

"It is," Ilario said as he ushered her away from the group. "It's awful. I know this is going to sound insensitive, but we've got another problem. Roger and I were supposed to meet with the facilities director at Fizonic today."

"The manufacturing company? Can't you reschedule it?"

"No. We can't cancel this one, it's too important." He ran his fingers through his hair, something she'd never seen him do before. "They're expecting to meet with me in an hour. But I'm going to need your help."

"What do you need me for?"

"Anne has a summary I put together for Roger. Ask her to make a copy of it for you. I'll explain everything once we're on our way. I'm really sorry to do this to you."

Julia's pulse quickened. Fizonic was one of Ostin Security's biggest customers. She was ready to help out in any way she could. She hadn't heard anything about a meeting, but it sounded important.

"Come by my office when you're ready," Ilario said. "A lot is riding on this."

Fizonic Industries was an industrial manufacturing conglomerate with headquarters in El Segundo near the L.A. airport. Ilario had acquired Fizonic's business during his first year with Ostin Security, and since then it had flourished into one of the company's most lucrative accounts. Now, as Julia looked through Ilario's notes on the drive down, the reason for that day's visit became shockingly clear. Ostin was on the verge of losing the account. At the core of the customer's dissatisfaction was a promise Ilario had made that a new systems upgrade with expanded capabilities would be available for installation before its official release date, in time for the opening of a new plant in Nevada. Fizonic's facilities director had agreed to an expanded contract based on Ilario's assurances that the product would be ready in time. The new facility was opening in two weeks. The new system wasn't ready. It had yet to even be tested.

"I can't believe this," Julia said, turning the pages faster. "*This* is what Roger's been so upset with you about, isn't it?"

Ilario pawed the steering wheel uncomfortably. "Our software

people seemed like they were ahead of schedule. I knew if I could
get Fizonic the upgraded product in time, they'd sign on to a longer
agreement. But then we fell behind by a month, then another. . . ."

"And you didn't say anything to Roger until *after* you got
promoted . . . only by that time . . ." Julia was still reading. After
weeks of complaining to Ilario, the facilities director had gone over
his head to Roger. Roger was supposed to meet with her today to
try and resolve the situation.

"This is terrible," Julia said, shaking her head. "Do they know
Roger's not coming?"

"They know."

"How are you going to handle this?"

Ilario appealed to her with a look that was at once urgent and
pathetic. Julia had the sensation of a rope tightening around her
waist.

"I want you to lead this meeting," Ilario said.

"A company I know nothing about?"

"Everything you need to know is there in front of you."

"This person is expecting someone with the authority to *do*
something!"

"What they want is a face other than mine to look at. You can
calm the situation down enough to buy us some time—"

"There *is* no time left to buy. Ilario, they want to talk to Roger,
not another sales rep."

His Adam's apple peeked over his collar as he looked at her.
"They don't know who you are."

She stared back. "What are you saying?"

"We'll say you're standing in for him. If they ask about your
title, we'll tell them you're our specialist in charge of . . . principal
customer relations."

"You can't make up a position that doesn't exist!"

"I can deputize you."

"Deputize me? *Deputize me?*" She pressed the file to her mouth and made a strange sound, something between a laugh and a bark.

"Nobody wants to lose this account, Julia. Even Roger would back me up in this situation. All you need to do is follow my lead for a minute, then take over. Use your judgment. I'll take responsibility for everything you say."

"Oh, you will? Well, in that case, sure, let me go in there and lie my ass off to save yours. It makes me feel so secure to know that you're going to 'take responsibility' for everything."

"Come on," Ilario said. "You're looking to leave Ostin anyway, right? You've got nothing to lose if this doesn't work. And if it does . . . you become the company hero."

"No," she said. "I'm not lying. It's how you got in this mess in the first place. I'll support you, but no deception."

Ilario parked outside Fizonic's headquarters. A fat, low-flying jet wobbled above them in the sky, looking as though it would land right on them. It passed overhead, a blast of heat and noise. Ilario shouted, "If it helps at all, I think she's gay."

"Who's gay?" Julia said.

"The facilities director, Mimi. One of their distributors told me."

"And just what am I supposed to do with that?" Julia said. "Show cleavage?"

"I don't know," Ilario said. "I'm just thinking out loud."

Julia followed him into the building. "I can't believe I'm doing this," she said.

Julia's first impression of Fizonic's facilities director was that she was too young to hold such an important title with such a large firm. With her eager smile and highlighted blond hair gathered in a scrunchie, she might have been mistaken for an Agoura High cheerleader who had been held back a couple of years. But a couple pumps of her powerful handshake and the hard, unexpected smell of cigarette smoke wafting off her clothes quickly did much to dispel the notion that she was soft or inexperienced. "In a nutshell," she said as they settled into a meeting room no bigger than Julia's office, "I'm fucked in orifices I didn't even know I had."

As she leaned back in her chair, her face caught the light from the flourescent bulbs overhead in a way that was not flattering. Smoke and worry lines appeared around her eyes and lips, making her appear at once both tired and angry. Julia felt guilty for the position Ilario had put her in.

"So, let's hear it," she said. "How are we, and by 'we' I mean 'you,' going to get our plant covered in two weeks?"

Mimi trained her gaze on Julia. Julia sensed that this was less because she thought she was someone important and more because she was sick of dealing with Ilario. Julia had no intention of lying to this woman about who she was. But she was willing to do whatever she could to help the situation, not for Ilario, but for all the people at Ostin who would be affected if the account was lost.

"I'm so sorry that there was so much miscommunication," Julia said, flicking a crumb of a glance at Ilario. "We want you to know that we're going to do everything we can to make sure—"

Mimi squeezed the ridge of her nose with her thumb and forefinger. "I need solutions," she said. "I need to go to my VP in two hours with *something*."

Julia could feel Ilario urging her on with his eyes. She could see fear peeking out from behind Mimi's hard eyes, too. The poor woman's job was probably on the line.

All right, Julia thought. Let's see if this flies.

She flipped the file over so that the Ostin logo was facedown and folded her hands on top of it. "What if we do this. Let's install the upgraded system at the plant now and use it as our testing site. We'll send a team to oversee the testing. You'll have the product right away and our best people right there on site to answer your questions and train your people. We'll stay as long as we need to to make sure everything is running to your satisfaction."

Mimi's chair creaked as she twisted left and right. "That sounds expensive," she said.

"Fizonic doesn't pay anything until the upgrade is officially released."

"And if that's not for another two months?"

"You get the benefit of a free system until then."

"That would really be doing you a big favor."

"We'd be doing each other a favor. If you're satisfied with the way things go, Fizonic can become a future testing site for all our products."

Mimi gazed at her thoughtfully, her chin tucked deep into her neck. She clicked a plastic pen methodically. She nodded a couple of times. Julia felt as though she had cracked open a window of possibility. Mimi's nodding was like a breeze blowing through it.

"One more thing," Julia said. "As of today, you won't be working with Ilario anymore. I'll be taking care of all your needs. If you'll let me." She kept her eyes on Mimi. Ilario said nothing. He wasn't in a position to.

Mimi leaned forward. She narrowed her eyes questioningly. "Tell me again. Who are you with the company?"

Julia looked at Ilario, then back at Mimi. "I'm just a sales rep," she said. "But I'm a good one. Everything I've offered will need to be cleared. But I think our VPs will go for it. I can get you something in writing by morning."

Taking Ilario's silence as an OK to continue, she sketched out for Mimi a rough timetable of action items. Mimi peppered her with questions and she answered them honestly. Maybe Ilario was right that she had nothing to lose by lying. But she also had nothing to lose by being honest.

She was in the middle of explaining to Mimi how the installation would take place when the woman cut her off. "Draw up the details and e-mail me a draft and I'll run it by my VP."

The walk back to the car was brisk and tense. Julia braced herself for Ilario's worst.

"That was brilliant," he said.

"It's only brilliant if the other veeps go for it."

"I'll make sure they do."

Julia said nothing, kept walking. Her pulse was still racing from the meeting.

"Fuck you for putting me in a position like that," she said.

"You enjoyed it. You were alive like I've never seen you before."

Sure, she had enjoyed it. She was still high from the thrill of it. But she wasn't going to let Ilario see that.

He laughed. "And taking me off the account was masterful."

In Ilario's car, Julia fumed in her seat. "How could you let something like this *happen*?"

"It was a calculated risk," he said innocently.

She cocked her head back and stared. "Doesn't your job *mean* anything to you?"

"What is that supposed to mean?"

"Your job isn't a dice game," Julia said. "You can't take chances when other people depend on you."

"What makes you think that they aren't depending on me to *take* chances?"

"That makes no sense!"

"Sure it does. Rules and policies are fine, but sometimes you have to bend them for the greater good."

"You and Ime are so perfect for each other."

"What does that mean?" He drew into himself as though Julia had insulted him. Julia hadn't intended to.

"It just means you think alike. You're well-suited. That's all I meant."

"Anyway," Ilario said, still looking a little hurt, "I've done well with the way I do business."

Julia felt her face turning red. "Obviously you don't know what it's like to be fired from a job. Or to go months without finding work."

"Are you kidding? I've been out of work plenty of times."

"Have you ever almost been evicted from your home?" Julia threw back. "Or had to line up with the homeless people to make sure you got something to eat that day?"

The words were out before she could stop herself. Sweat gathered at her neck. Why had she said this? After her father had lost his job, there had been a whole month when they'd needed that kind of charity. It was something she rarely mentioned.

Ilario was quiet for the next several minutes. He seemed to be reevaluating something, taking in something that he found both enlightening and troubling. When he spoke again, he sounded apologetic. "I guess we look at things differently," he said. "And I guess sometimes . . . I do overpromise things."

Julia wondered if Ilario's overpromising hadn't led to the incident between him and Ime in Vegas. Until now she hadn't considered that it had been anyone's fault but Ime's. But she could easily imagine him saying things to Ime that would have led her to assume he wanted marriage.

It was a while before he said, "The 405's going to be a mess. Do you mind if I take the 10 to the 110 to the 5?"

· · ·

Julia stayed late at the office that evening getting approvals from
the VPs and putting together a formal proposal for Fizonic. The
next morning, she e-mailed it to Mimi. Mimi e-mailed back requesting changes. Julia made them, then e-mailed again. Within
an hour, Mimi responded saying that she had run the agreement
by her VP, and to please send a copy for signature. Julia forwarded
the e-mail string to Ilario. He appeared seconds later.

"You did it," he said.

"Nothing's signed yet."

"It will be."

"We don't know that."

Without asking, he came into the room and unfolded himself
into a chair. "You're not really going to look for another job now,
are you?"

"I can't stay here."

"Roger's going to want you to. You're responsible for Fizonic
now."

"I'll do what I can for them until I find something else," she
said. "I'll make sure it's a smooth transition."

"You saved this account," he said, jumping to his feet. "Don't
you realize what that's worth?"

Julia stood up. It was late, she had been up since six, she wanted
to go home.

He intercepted her at the door. "Just listen," he said. "Roger
might retire, or he might not. Either way, if he comes back and I've
lost my best salesperson, there's no hope for me. If you're out, then
I'm out."

"I understand that, but—"

"Tell me what it's going to take to get you to stay."

"We've talked about this."

"We haven't talked about options. You convinced Mimi to stick
with us. Now it's my job to convince you. The possibilities are wide

open." He pressed her with his gaze. "Fizonic becomes yours if you stay. You get a recurring commission. I'll also give you one other big account. Take your pick. Gordon Industries. Laraline."

"Those are major accounts."

"You can handle them."

Looking into his eyes, she saw not desperation but a sparkling earnestness that was touching. Yes, he was trying to save his own skin. But he also really believed that they could work together. He had come to *like* working with her.

"Ilario," she said, placing her hand on her heart, suddenly not angry at all. "You still don't get it. It's not about the money or the accounts. It's about us. It's about how you do business. About what's OK and not OK."

"But if I say I'll change? What would you say then? Would you stay?"

Julia stepped to the south-facing window and looked out over the parking area toward the Burbank airport. One jet was descending. Another had just taken off. How she would have liked to believe that he could change. That old patterns could easily be broken. That Ilario wasn't telling her, as he did with so many people in his business and life, what she wanted to hear.

He came up beside her. "I take responsibility for all the problems we've had," he said. "But today showed us both how well we can work together. Give me one last chance to make this work. We'll do things your way. By the book. By the rules. Just let me make things right."

In the window's reflection she could see him looking not out at the view but at her. Circles of condensation were forming on the window where their fingertips met the glass. She smelled his cologne. She felt the warmth of his determination. She hated the fact that after all this time she was still attracted to him. She hated the fact that she almost, almost believed him.

⚍ 19 ⚍

A Very Special Visitor

A week went by, during which Julia and Ime spoke by phone but did not see each other in person, adding to Julia's feelings that something fundamental had changed between them. So it was a complete surprise when Ime showed up at Julia's door on a Wednesday night, much in the manner that Ilario had after their trip to Vegas, her features similarly splintered by distress.

"I can't take her anymore" was Ime's only greeting as she swept in. "She's too fucking perfect. She's beautiful and educated and she gets D.Evine shoes at a thirty percent discount. How am I supposed to compete with that?" She handed Julia a bottle of premium imported tequila decorated with a red silk bow, and then wrangled her arms out of her jacket. "I'm talking about Lydia," she said in response to Julia's confused look.

"Ah," Julia said. "So she's here."

"I've spent the last two days with her and Ilario looking at apartments." She made room for herself on the couch next to a pile of unfolded towels that Julia had just taken out of the dryer. She took the bottle back from Julia, uncapped it, and took a sip, making Julia realize that the tequila was not a gift from Ime to her but from one of Ime's clients to Ime. "I know this looks bad," she said, giving the bottle a tight little nod. "But I've just spent the afternoon with—are you ready for this?—Miss Latina San Fernando Valley 1996. Can you believe that? She's a fucking *beauty queen*."

Julia sat down on the other side of the laundry pile. "Former beauty queen," Julia said. "And I didn't think she was that pretty."

"That's nice of you," Ime said gravely, "but we both know it's bullshit. Not only does she turn heads everywhere she goes, but she's also thoughtful and sweet, and . . . so fucking . . . *Mexican*. So connected to her roots, you know? Everything is *latinismo* this, and *chicanismo* that. Her great-great-uncle was some famous Mexican general or something."

"Really?" Julia said. "Which one?"

"How should I know?" Ime said. "I don't know anything about that stuff. To her I must seem like the world's biggest *pocha*."

"You are a *pocha*," Julia said, pushing some towels toward Ime in the hopes that she would help her with the folding. "We both are. What of it? We're third-generation. What does she expect, that you're going to speak flawless Spanish and know all about Mexican history?"

"The thing is, she's not a snob about it. If she were, at least I could despise her for that. There's no satisfaction in hating her for just being better than me." She offered Julia the bottle, but Julia declined. Tilting her head back on the couch, Ime let out a great sigh. "So, go ahead. Tell me what an idiot I am."

"For offering to help her find an apartment? That was pretty stupid."

"Now tell me that there's really nothing between her and Ilario."

"I've told you before. I still believe it."

Ime drew a towel from the pile and smoothed it over her lap. "Let me ask you this. How would you feel about coming with me and Lydia and Ilario to the Auto Show?"

"What?! Ime, that's *our* thing. It's always just you and me."

"I know, I'm really sorry. The subject came up and the next thing I knew I had agreed to go with them. Of course, now I want to shoot myself." She examined the corner of one of Julia's bath towels. "If you come it will be so much easier for me. You can distract me from her perfection."

"With the blinding glow of my *im*perfections?"

"You know what I mean."

"No. I made a fool of myself following her to the airport, remember?"

"And I asked Ilario to marry me after four months."

Julia smiled. She imagined they both rated high in terms of foolishness.

"You don't have to look like you're enjoying my predicament so much," Ime said.

"I'm not. I was just thinking . . ."

"About?"

"We haven't done this in a long time."

"Done what?"

"This." She made a sweeping motion that included the tequila, the laundry, the room.

"So that means you'll come?"

"No."

"Cabrona." She wadded the towel and threw it back on the pile. "If you won't do it for me, do it for Ilario. He'd like to have you there."

"Now you're just saying random things."

"No, I mean it. He hasn't shut up about how you saved that account."

"Really?" Julia said.

"Of course. You'd think you saved the whole company from collapsing, the way he's been going on."

Julia straightened a bit. She smoothed a crease in the towel over her knee.

"So, you're going to tell him something soon, aren't you? About whether you're staying long-term?"

"What do you think I should do?" Julia said.

Ime made a face. "You want *my* advice?"

"Sure. You know him. Do you think Ilario can follow through on his promises?" She moved a stack of three folded still-warm towels from her lap to the coffee table.

"All I know," Ime said, "is that he's on the edge of his seat waiting to hear from you. I'm pretty sure he'll deliver. And if he doesn't . . . he has me to deal with."

She went on to tell Julia other things Ilario had said about her: that he had been an idiot not to recognize Julia's strengths sooner; that he'd never worked with someone he respected more. Julia nodded and listened, enjoying the warmth rising up from the towels as she folded one after another after another.

A few days later, at an in-house software training session, Julia happened to glance toward the glass door of the conference room. The door had been left ajar, angled in such a way that she could see Ilario reflected in it. He was seated behind her and to her left, and he was looking at her. Unaware that she could see him, he kept watching her for some time. What struck Julia most was the *way* he was looking at her. Gone was the scorn he had once reserved exclusively for her. He seemed to be appraising her with new eyes. He'd told Ime he appreciated her, and in that moment, seeing him looking at her in this new way, it seemed to Julia—if it were possible to draw such a conclusion from a look mirrored in glass—that his opinion of her truly matched his words.

She caught him during the break. "I think we can do this," she said. "If you really mean what you said. About following the rules. Then I'll stay." Even as she spoke, she had the breathless sensation of taking a step off a tall building. She searched his face nervously for some assurance that she was making the right decision. He seemed to be in a state of suspension that matched her own. Then color washed through his face.

"We'll make this work," he said.

"I'm holding you to everything you promised."

Julia could feel his desire to do or say something more. She sensed it pressing against the inside of his skin, trying to convey to her the fullness of his gratitude.

He hugged her. It was a blocky, clunky, awkward hug, so awkward that they both had to laugh at how badly it was executed. This was not the first time she had heard Ilario laugh, but it was the first time she could remember the two of them laughing together. The sparkle in his eye relit her optimism. It burned quick and bright for the rest of the day.

As Julia was leaving the office a few hours later, Concepción called to ask if Julia could drop by that night to look at some invitation samples for Nina's wedding.

"I thought I was responsible for the invitations," Julia said.

Nervously, Concepción responded, "Oh, I know that, but I saw a card shop on Lankershim and something told me to pull over and I saw these and decided to bring them. What time can you get here?"

"Does it have to be today?" Julia said.

"Nina's here and she says it has to be tonight. She's been very touchy and I think she'll be very upset if you don't come over."

Something about the treble of Concepción's voice warned her that she didn't really want to see her about invitations. "Is something wrong?" Julia said. "Did something bad finally happen between you and Remedios?"

"Of course not!" Concepción said. "Why would you say that? Promise me you'll come over, OK?"

With a reluctant sigh, Julia agreed to drop by. She was off the phone for no more than a few seconds before it rang again. It was Ime this time. Her voice was pitched to a new level of desperation.

"I think Ilario is planning to break up with me," she said. "I just got off the phone with him. He was really abrupt. There's definitely something wrong."

"Did you guys fight or something?" Julia said.

"Nothing like that," Ime said. "But there's something he's not telling me."

"Something that has to do with Lydia, right?"

"He's told me he's been working late this entire week. We haven't gotten together in days. What else is he doing if he's not seeing Lydia?"

"Would it make you feel any better if I told you that he really *has* been working late? He's been taking care of the details of this Fizonic thing. He must have told you about it. Last night I was at the office until eight thirty and he was there the whole time. Alone. Without Lydia."

"Really? It's just that there's something in his voice. Do you think you could—"

"No."

"You don't even know what I'm going to ask."

"You're going to ask me to spy on him."

"Not spy, just keep an eye out . . . let me know if you notice anything unusual. Is that so much to ask?"

"After what we went through after the airport thing? Yes, it is. Don't put me in the middle of anything. Listen, I'm pulling up in front of C's place. I have to go. You have nothing to worry about. Call Ilario and talk to him."

She made a U-turn in order to park on the side of the street closest to Concepción's building. As she did so, the sweep of her headlights captured two pairs of wide, frightened eyes. Concepción, in a pink terry robe and slippers, and Nina, in a denim shirt and baggy white pants, were waiting for her on the curb. The streetlight above them hummed with electricity, casting them in an eerie light reminiscent of old monster movies.

"Thank God you're here," Concepción said, practically pulling Julia out of her car. "I don't really have any invitations for you to look at. I just said that to get you here."

"You never know who might be listening in on your phone," Nina added.

Julia locked her car. "You two look like you've been visited by La Llorona. What the hell is going on?"

"It's better if you see for yourself," Concepción said.

"Keep your voices down," Nina said. "We don't want to attract attention."

Julia followed Concepción and Nina. Nina kept hushing Concepción to be quiet and Concepción kept telling her not to hush her. Concepción placed her palm against her apartment door and said, "You have to swear to God, Jesus, the pope, and all the saints that you won't tell anyone what I'm about to show you."

Julia pushed past her and into the living room. The room was dark. She reached for the Medusa lamp near the room and turned it up. The outline of someone sleeping on the couch appeared before her. The figure was covered head to toe with a blanket and was snoring loudly. Marta was the only person she knew who snored.

"What's wrong with her?" Julia said. "Is she OK?"

Concepción and Nina looked at each other. Concepción carefully peeled back the top of the blanket to reveal not Marta but a man with a shaved head and a beard. The smell of rum and sweat rising from his body made her take a step back. "Oh my God," Julia said.

"That was my reaction," Nina said.

"It's not possible."

"Tell *him* that," Concepción said.

Julia trained one of the heads of the Medusa lamp at the body. Diego Ramirez, the famous actor and fugitive, was sleeping on Concepción's couch. Dreams stormed behind his eyelids.

"I can't believe this," Julia said. "How did he get back into the country? What's he doing *here*?"

"I told you before," Concepción said proudly, "that he and I share a connection. It makes perfect sense that he would turn to me."

"But why? Did he just show up here? Aren't the police looking for him?"

"I think he came back to clear his name," Concepción said. "Obviously he can't turn himself in. There's no way someone who always plays the hot-tempered Latin in the movies could get a fair trial."

"That's insane," Julia said. The body heaved and rumbled. "He showed up here expecting you to hide him?"

"He must have run out of options," Concepción said. "He didn't give me a lot of details, but it sounds like he snuck back over the border. I'm sure he had a plan, like in that movie where he played the guy who was framed for killing the vice president."

Julia reached for her phone.

"What are you doing?" Concepción said.

"What do you think I'm doing?"

"You can't call the police!"

"You can't hide a murderer!" Julia said.

At the word "murderer" the actor stirred on the couch. His breathing became shallow and he curled into the fetal position.

"Let's go in the kitchen," Concepción said. "I don't want to wake him."

"C, you can't do this," Julia said when they were in the other room. "Do you realize how much trouble you could be in?"

"Julia's right," Nina hissed at her. "What does he really think he's going to accomplish by hiding here?"

"We haven't talked about that," Concepción said. "As soon as he's sober and awake . . ."

Julia sat at the table and put her head down. "My day was going so well," she mumbled.

There was a rustling sound behind her. Julia jerked up, expecting to see the actor. It was Marta. She was hugging a bag of groceries.

"They didn't have any fresh cinnamon at the Victoria Market," Marta said, "so I'm going to have to use the bottled stuff."

"What is she doing here?" Julia said.

"I had to call her," Concepción said. "She didn't get to meet Diego at my party."

"So that's him on the couch?" Marta said. "How long do you think before he wakes up? But it doesn't matter, I'll stay all night if I need to. I'm not letting this opportunity go by. Diego Ramirez. Can you believe our luck?"

"Who else did you call?" Julia said.

"Just us," Concepción said.

"You should call Remedios," Marta said.

"Remedios won't come," Concepción said.

"You're right," Marta said. "If it was Salma Hayek or Sharon Stone it would be different. Anybody with a vagina." She set down her bag, then started looking in Concepción's cupboards for pots.

"What are you doing?" Julia said.

"Making capirotada," Marta said. "It's Diego's favorite dish from when he was a kid. He said so on *Cristina*."

"Listen, everybody. You have a man *wanted by the police* in the other room."

"A murderer," Marta said with a joyful clap of her hands. "We're a part of history. It almost makes me wish I'd had kids so that I could have grandkids I could tell this story to."

"Sure, it's exciting that he's here, but you're going to be in a huge amount of trouble if you don't call the police this very minute."

"'This very minute,'" Marta mimicked, sticking her hip out and shaking a wooden spoon in the air with each word. "Do you really want to be known as the person who turned Diego Ramirez over to the police?"

"She'd turn over the pope if he showed up," Concepción said.

"The pope isn't a murderer," Nina said.

"The pope has plenty of blood on his hands," Marta said.

"Diego is innocent," Concepción said. "I don't want to hear another word about that. There's a logical explanation, and when he gets sober he's going to explain it all and we're going to help him in whatever way we can."

"Our story is worth more if he did kill her," Marta said.

Julia turned to Concepción. "Why did you ask me to come here?" she said. "Why did you want to involve me in something you knew I wouldn't approve of?"

"I never know what you're going to approve of," Concepción said. "I just thought as my friend you ought to know what was going on. I thought you would want to participate."

Julia looked around the room at the other women. Concepción and Marta suddenly seemed alien to her. Only Nina, her eyes wide and her hands trembling, seemed to grasp the seriousness of the situation.

The actor appeared at the kitchen door. He was wearing one of Concepción's terry robes. It hung slightly open on him, revealing a slice of boxers with a tomato-and-chili-pepper pattern. He held tight to the doorframe as though he were on a rocking ship. His complexion was darker than it had been at the party, and his eyes were even darker than that. He was like a sliver of night stealing its way in from the other room. Concepción and Marta swarmed toward him.

"Are you OK?" Concepción said. "Did you sleep all right? Did we wake you?"

Diego looked around with excruciating concern. "Who are all these people?"

"We're all your friends and we're going to help you," Concepción said. "This is Marta, and you might remember Julia and Nina from my party."

Nina backed a few steps away from him. Marta, however, approached him critically, as though he were a curious and slightly dangerous biological specimen. She used her spoon to retract the loose fold of his robe to better assess him. "Hmm," she said, looking at the others with mild disappointment, "he's not really what I expected. I guess given all that he's been through we can't exactly expect him to shine, and the drinking doesn't help, either."

"Don't insult my guest," Concepción said. "Don't listen to her, Diego. And just so you know, you're welcome to stay here as long as you need to."

Diego molded his head in his hands as though it were a mound of falling dough. "Why did you invite all these people?" He winced at the sound of his own voice.

"Oh, don't worry," Concepción said. "They just wanted to meet you. They're not going to tell anyone you're here. We're here to help."

Still appearing disoriented, the actor took in the details of the bright kitchen. He reached for a chair and sat down at the table. "What have I done? What am I doing here? Oh, fuck . . ."

With a laugh, Concepción said, "Don't you remember? You came here because you knew you'd be safe. You asked me to hide you."

Diego looked doubtful that he had made any such request. Nina pushed a glass of water toward him, then stood back.

"He needs to turn himself in," Julia said, "before he gets any of us in trouble."

"Tell us what you've been doing," Marta said. "Have you been in Mexico all this time? How did you sneak back? Did you shave your head so that no one would recognize you?"

These questions seemed to be too much all at once for Diego. He looked from Julia to Marta to Concepción. "Your friend is right," he said. "It's not a good idea for me to stay. I don't know what I was thinking in coming here."

"That's silly," said Concepción. "You're not going anywhere until you get some rest and food. None of us are going to let on that you're here." He looked in confusion as Concepción touched his hand and looked deep into his eyes. "You and I have a connection, don't we, Diego? I've always said so. I've always felt it."

Before Concepción could indulge further in her scene, Julia took her arm and pulled her into the living room. "Do you know how insane you're being?"

Concepción met her eyes with a powerful stare. "You don't have to be a part of this if you don't want to. I only asked you here because I didn't want to leave you out. Go if you want to, but you're not going to ruin this opportunity for me."

"*What* opportunity? You have a fugitive in your kitchen. I'm not seeing the 'opportunity' in any of this."

Concepción held her face inches from Julia's. "The only way I'm going to find the answer to that question is if I let him stay. If you don't understand that, you should go. But I'm telling you, Julia, don't you *dare* tell anyone about this."

They stared at each other for a long time. Concepción refused to back down. Julia had never seen such determination in her.

"Fine," Julia said. "Do what you have to. But this time I'm not going to be there to bail you out when things go wrong. Don't waste your time leaving me messages when all of this blows up in your face."

To keep Concepción from seeing the tears forming in her eyes, Julia strode into the kitchen and got her bag. Diego looked up as she came into the room, but she cut her eyes away from him. To no one in particular she said, "I'm leaving. I don't know anything. You didn't see me and I didn't see you. I was never here. Do you hear me? *Never.*"

She punched her way through the swinging door and into the living room, clipping Concepción's shoulder as she went by. She walked out to her car, hoping no one was noticing her. She drove. Concepción. Marta. Nina. She needed to get as far away from them as possible. She needed to think about what being friends with them really meant.

❧ 20 ❧

An Unexpected Opportunity

You seem distracted," Ilario said. He went heavy with the salt on his steak and eggs. He had called Julia the night before and asked her to meet him for breakfast at Harry's Diner on San Fernando Road to do account reviews.

"I'm sorry," Julia said. "I've got stuff on my mind, nothing you'd want to hear about."

Ilario put the shaker down with a twist. He raised an eyebrow at her. "Try me."

She shook her head. She'd never discussed anything personal with Ilario, and though the opening he was giving her now was tempting, she couldn't involve him. She stared down at her Belgian waffles. They were saturated with syrup. A heavy gob of butter floated helplessly in one of the square wells. "I'm sorry," she said, sensing his disappointment. "It's something my friends did. Something stupid. I shouldn't talk about it."

He jabbed a chunk of steak with his fork. "You're loyal," he said firmly. "There's nothing wrong with that." He broke the yolk of one of his eggs and dipped the piece of meat into it. His gaze crossed hers awkwardly as he chewed. When he was done, he said, "Come with me and Ime and Lydia to the Auto Show."

"The three of you? I'd be in the way."

"Not true. And it would be easier for Ime if you were there."

These were nearly the same words Ime had used. It was strange hearing them from Ilario. "Easier?"

"Ime's been having a hard time getting used to Lydia. If you were there . . . I think she'd have a better time."

"I followed Lydia to the airport," Julia said.

"So?"

"I must seem so stupid to her."

"She doesn't know about that."

"You didn't tell her?"

"If I did, I doubt she remembers. And if she does, she's much too . . ."

Too what? Julia thought. She remembered the last time she had seen Ilario and Lydia together. She remembered the way they had been looking at her and talking. What else had they been talking about, if not her, if not *that*?

"At least think about it," Ilario said. "It would help get your mind off . . . whatever's happening with your friends. Plus, I think you'd like Lydia. I know she'll like you."

For the rest of the morning, Julia couldn't concentrate. She found herself jumping at noises. Every time the phone rang, her heart raced. Nothing good could come of what Concepción and Marta had done. She was desperate for news about them, but didn't dare call them. She wanted no record that she had talked to them, that she was involved in any way in their schemes.

After several hours of worrying and getting almost no work done, she couldn't take it anymore. She called Nina. At least Nina seemed to understand the danger Concepción and Marta had gotten them-selves into. It felt safest to talk to her. She was the one person who might be able to get them to come to their senses.

"They both have it in their heads that so long as Diego turns out to be innocent, nothing bad will happen to them," Nina said.

"That's crazy. How long do they think they can hide him?"

"Marta thinks the longer they keep him, the better the story they'll have to sell."

Nina's use of the word "keep" pulled an already tight knot in Julia's chest tighter. She pictured Marta and Concepción holding Diego like a prisoner, making him do their bidding, making him act out their favorite scenes from their movies, threatening to go to the police if he didn't do as they said.

"I wish I knew more," Nina said, "but I don't think I can afford to have any more contact with them. I don't want a jailhouse wed-ding."

"Are you coming with us to visit Roger?" Anne said, popping her head into Julia's office. It was a Thursday morning. Julia was just settling in for the day. Again distracted, her nerves frayed, she'd forgotten that a couple of sales groups were going over to Valley Presbyterian on Vanowen. Julia's eyes were tired. She had woken from a bad dream about Concepción at 3 A.M. and hadn't been able to get back to sleep.

"You should come with us," Anne said. "I know Roger would love to have a visit from you."

It had actually been Julia's idea to visit him in the first place. She was in no mood to go now, but it would look strange if she didn't. She told Anne she would need to meet the rest of the group there in order to leave promptly for a customer visit.

"By the way," Anne said, "I don't know if you've heard, but

Roger's decided not to retire. He's coming back as soon as the doctors say it's OK."

Julia felt a pang of sympathy for Ilario. Although he had been working under the assumption that Roger might return, the certainty that he was coming back was sure to be a blow to him. On her way out to her morning appointment, she went to look for him to see how he was taking the news, but he wasn't in his office, and no one seemed to be sure whether he had come in yet.

Later that morning, Julia arrived at Valley Presbyterian to find Anne and several other co-workers already gathered around Roger's bed, listening to him tell about his roller-coaster accident. Delighting in his audience's awe, he described with peculiar relish how, on a bend near the end of the ride, his harness had popped up over his head at the moment of greatest centrifugal force, sending him careening out of the side of the car and forty feet below to what he had been sure would be his death. Dense shrubbery in the park's landscaping had broken his fall, but not sufficiently to prevent twenty-eight broken bones, a concussion, a ruptured spleen, and a punctured lung. None of these traumas, however, had diminished the forcefulness of his personality. Julia's co-workers stood at the usual safe, respectable, and slightly fearful distance demanded by his presence. Even the flowers that people had brought for him seemed to incline in such a way as to give him the room he needed.

The group stayed with Roger for only about fifteen minutes before Anne looked at her watch, signaling that she needed to return to work. Roger thanked everyone for coming and promised to return to the office as soon as he felt up to it, regardless of what his doctors advised.

Julia was glad the visit was short. She was too agitated to keep smiling and making small talk. She placed a card she had brought next to his bed and squeezed his right forearm, the only part of his body besides his badly scratched face that was exposed to light, and the only limb that hadn't broken in multiple places. She was relieved to be on her way out, but then Roger said, "Julia, could you give a cripple a couple more minutes?"

Julia watched nervously as the door closed behind the last person leaving. "Sure, Roger. What is it?"

"There's something I want to run by you. Something I didn't think should wait until I got back to the office."

Julia reached behind her for a chair and pulled it up to Roger's bedside. With some difficulty, he turned his head to look at her. "I heard a rumor around the office that you were starting to look for another job."

"Well, I was, Roger. But I'm not now. You see, at the time—"

He made a dismissive gesture with his good hand. "I don't need explanations. I think I can guess why you weren't happy at Ostin. Now that I've decided not to retire, I wanted you to know I'll be making a few changes. One of them involves you."

Oh, no, Julia thought. Here it comes. Brace yourself for the worst.

"I don't want you repeating this to anyone. If you do, well, I can't be responsible for what happens. It's in your best interest to not be looking for another job right now. Because I'm planning on having you take over Ilario's position."

She heard the words, but they didn't connect. They floated loosely in front of her, not meaning anything. "Roger . . . what do you mean 'take over Ilario's position'? Do you mean . . . are there accounts of his . . . you want me to take over?"

"No, Julia. I mean his *job*. I want you in it. Let me put it another way. Ilario's out. I'm promoting you to account manager for Key Accounts."

Julia stared. She wasn't sure if he was making some sort of a joke.

"Don't worry, Julia, it's not the morphine talking. I've had plenty of time to think in this damn place, and that's one thing I've spent a lot of time thinking about. I'm coming back to Ostin, and I'm making you head of Ilario's group. Ilario's unpredictable. He's an excellent salesperson, but his follow-through, his management style . . . terrible. I helped to found this company, and there are certain standards I expect. You're still green, but you meet those standards."

"My God, Roger . . . I don't know what to say."

"Just say you'll stick around long enough for me to get back. Normally, I wouldn't have said anything, but when I heard you were looking, I got a little panicky that we were going to lose you, so I thought I'd better let you know. You will stay now, won't you?"

Something hot and intense pulsed behind Julia's eyes. "Roger, I . . . if you're really sure this is what you want . . . but there's just one thing. What's going to happen with—"

"Ilario? I don't think he'll make too much noise when he sees his severance pay. But I don't want to make the transition until I'm back." He coughed, rattling the bed frame. "I think you're the future of sales at Ostin."

Julia nodded. Her head was spinning. Her brain was seizing up with the dry, strange smell of the room.

Roger grunted. "This isn't quite the reaction I was expecting."

"Oh, Roger, I'm sorry. It's been such a strange couple of days and . . . I'm just so distracted with . . . this is the last thing I was expecting—"

"Just say you're interested in the job," Roger said.

Julia nodded. "Roger, I appreciate all of this. You don't know how much. But you should probably know that in the last few weeks, Ilario really has been—"

Roger's crooked smile brought Julia to a stop. It seemed to ask, Do you really want to defend him when I'm making you this kind of offer?

"Never mind," Julia said. Struggling to sound a little more grateful, she said, "Thank you, Roger. This means a lot to me. You won't be disappointed."

"I like to create opportunities for people who deserve them," he said, fluttering sleepily. "Yes, you're the future of Ostin Security."

With that, he dismissed her with a twitchy wave of his hand over the bedrail and drifted off to sleep.

When Julia got back to her office, a stonelike feeling pulled her down into her chair. She ought to have been thrilled with Roger's decision, but she mostly felt sick and dizzy. She ought not to have come back to the office. She was beyond any ability to do work. How was she going to face Ilario? Or Ime? What was going to happen to Concepción and Marta? Her problems spun and clashed in her head.

Ilario looked in, startling her.

"What?" she snapped.

His expression was pinched and uneasy. "I heard you saw Roger today."

"I did."

"I heard he asked you to stay behind. What was that about?"

"He wanted to thank me for helping out with Fizonic."

"Yeah? He didn't say anything else?"

"You should have been there with the rest of us, Ilario," she said, standing up and reaching for her coat. "Then I wouldn't have to give you the play-by-play." She pressed the back of her hand to her forehead. "I'm sorry, Ilario. It's not you. I think I'm coming down with something. I might not be in tomorrow. I don't want to spread this around."

⁓ 21 ⁓

Hydrotechnics at the L.A. Auto Show

Julia stood in the South Hall lobby of the Los Angeles Convention Center, waiting for Ilario and Ime and Lydia to appear in the crowd pouring in for the L.A. Auto Show. Ilario had urged her again to join them, and in a moment of weakness she had said yes, thinking it would be easy to cancel at the last minute. It hadn't been. Both Ilario and Ime had been so pleased to know she would be there that she feared their reaction should she back out.

She was regretting the decision now. The thought of spending the day with Ilario knowing she'd soon be given his job gave her a seasick feeling. It didn't help that for the last few weeks they had been getting along so well; or that, as far as she could tell, he had been fulfilling his promise to her to conduct his job honestly, playing by the rules, surpassing her every expectation. The thought of what was about to happen to him made her heart ache. How much easier it would have been to enjoy the prospect of her own advancement had she still been able to view him as a jerk.

She caught sight of Ilario and Ime and Lydia waving to her from near one of the tall white pillars that supported the soaring glass-and-metal atrium. Ilario bounded ahead of Ime and Lydia. Shadows cast by the metal crosshatching overhead danced over him, making him seem younger and more energetic than ever. "You really came," he said. His eyes glinted with pleasure. "Why didn't you let us pick you up?"

Julia offered only a faint smile as an answer. She had insisted to Ime that they arrive separately so that she could break away early to do some work she had brought home for the weekend. She didn't want to spend more time with Ilario than she needed to.

Seeing how pleased Ilario looked to see her made her wish all the more that she hadn't come. How was she going to act natural knowing what she knew?

Julia magnified her smile for Lydia as Ilario reintroduced the two women. Julia had forgotten how beautiful Lydia was. The diffuse winter sunlight streaming down through the glass only made her more so. A fitted sweater and pencil skirt gave full advantage to her figure, and a pair of kitten-heel sling backs amplified her beauty-queen stature. Like Ime, she dressed impeccably; unlike Ime, she wore her clothes effortlessly, as if her DNA had provided the pattern from which they had been fashioned.

"Ilario told me about how you saved him at the company," she said, giving Julia a hug that felt surprisingly natural coming from someone she'd met only once before. "I told him he needs to make sure he doesn't lose you."

Over Lydia's shoulder Julia caught Ime mimicking Lydia. Meeting Julia's eye, Ime dropped her sneer and came forward with a too-sweet smile. "Julia is always rescuing people," Ime said. "She's like a superhero."

Lydia regarded Julia appreciatively. She may have been beauty-queen beautiful, but her smile was warm, genuine, and inviting. Ilario had told the truth—either Lydia hadn't connected her to the airport incident or she was just too generous to let it prejudice her.

Reassured, Julia said, "There's something I have to ask you. Your shoes. Where do you get them? I love them so much."

Lydia extended her narrow leg to better display the leather sling back with cream stitching that spilled across the toe like icing. "I'm a regional sales manager for D.Evine."

"You're kidding! Those are Ime's favorite shoes."

"You can both come by one of my stores sometime and pick something out from the new line," Lydia said.

"Don't tease me."

"About something as important as shoes?"

"You know just the thing to say to make friends," Julia said.

"I can use all the friends I can get."

"You grew up here. You must already have friends in L.A."

"Making friends has never come easily to me," Lydia said.

Ime watched on with a pinched smile. Ilario took her arm and suggested that they get tickets.

"Honey," Ime said, "why don't you take Lydia with you so I can talk to Julia for a second, OK?"

Ilario kissed her, then walked off with Lydia. Ime waited until they were all the way across the atrium before she dropped her smile and said to Julia, "Do you see what I'm up against? Miss Latina San Fernando Valley, with her fake laugh and her fake chi-chis?"

Julia looked back. "They're fake?"

"Oh, they're fake all right," Ime said, "like everything else about her. What was the bullshit about not being able to make friends? I'm sure she has plenty of friends—the male kind. And she spreads it for them every night."

"What's gotten into you? What happened to 'Lydia is so thought-ful and sweet?'"

"I'm sorry, I know I'm not being rational. But having her around is driving me crazy."

"I didn't come here so you could have someone to talk dirt about her to," Julia said sharply.

"I'm sorry," she said. "It's just so hard to be compared to her. Can you blame me if I start to look for flaws?"

"I'm sorry you don't like the situation," Julia said, "but you created it, so you're going to have to stick it out for a couple of hours. Then you can explain to Ilario that she makes you uncomfortable and you don't want to spend time with her anymore."

"No way. I'm going to prove that I can be just as charming and generous as she is. She's not getting any more points on me than she already has."

Julia sighed. "Points. That's what this is about. Competition."

When Ilario and Lydia returned with the tickets, Ime led the way up the escalator to the second-level exhibition hall. Throngs of people circulated among the dazzling displays of new cars and new car technology. The Auto Show had long been a tradition for Ime and Julia. At the age of sixteen, after lying to their parents that they were going to a church bazaar, they had taken the bus downtown to see the show. From the moment they walked in, Ime had been mesmerized by so much metal and glass, by the slogans promising speed and luxury and happiness. It was there that she had become infected with a hunger for the flawless design and status of German cars. She had spent the next eight months working overtime at the AutoZone to save enough money to buy a used Mercedes 450SEL, then another six months hiding it from her father, who would have grounded her for buying a foreign car.

Today, not even the most elaborate displays were enough to hold Ime's attention. As they toured the hall, Ime could not stop watching Lydia and Ilario. Jealousy radiated off her skin like a fever each time Lydia and Ilario laughed at the same joke. But Julia was more confident than ever that any romantic inclination between the former couple was a thing of the past. Theirs was an intimacy of friendship too natural to be hiding secret feelings.

At an exhibit of new Porsches, Ime climbed the terraced platform to pose against a cherry red Boxter. "Ilario, how do you think I would look driving this?"

"I think you'd be dangerous in a sports car," Ilario said.

"You mean *more* dangerous, don't you?" she said, giving him an exaggerated, lashy wink.

"It wouldn't be very practical for driving around clients," Ilario said.

"Practical?" With a girlish laugh, she draped herself on the car's hood. "Oh, Ilario, there's so much about me you have yet to learn."

He came up the steps and extended his hand to her. She pushed off from the car and danced out of his reach. "I live in the sun. I should have a convertible."

"If you like the Boxter," Lydia said, "you should look at the Nissan Z. It has the same horsepower but it's cheaper."

"I don't go for cheap," Ime said.

Julia stepped between them. "How do you know so much about cars?" Julia asked Lydia.

"Her father owns a dealership in Riverside," Ilario said.

"And my brothers are all mechanics," Lydia said. "All they talk about is cars."

"She can fix a carburetor," Ilario said.

"A beauty queen who can fix cars," Ime said. "Imagine that."

"Our fathers used to work at the GM plant," Julia said.

"The one in Van Nuys?" Lydia said.

"You remember that?"

"Of course. A lot of people lost their jobs."

"My father was one of them," Julia said. "He worked for GM for thirteen years."

"I hope he got a pension or something," Lydia said.

"He hadn't worked there long enough to qualify."

"It looks like you turned out all right."

"You know who else is good with cars?" Ime said. "Lesbians."

Everyone looked at her. She stepped down from the exhibit, turning her back to their stares.

As they moved on to another display, Julia guided Ime away from Ilario and Lydia and held her back a short distance. "That does it," she said. "I can't stand the way you're behaving. It's disgusting."

"What are you talking about? I just—"

"I'm telling you right now that if you make one more crack to Lydia, I'm leaving."

"You wouldn't do that, you—"

"I will," Julia said. "I'm not putting up with this. You're embarrassing everybody, but mostly yourself."

Ime screwed up her face like a spoiled child. "All right. Fine. But you don't know how hard this is for me."

A few minutes later, when Julia had a moment to talk privately to Ilario, she said, "I'm sorry about Ime. She's in a strange mood."

"It's OK," he said. "She gets that way around Lydia. I thought this was a good idea."

"Ime really does want to prove to you she's not jealous."

"I think mostly she needs to prove it to herself. I didn't want to take that away from her."

Ilario's insight and willingness to accommodate Ime's flaws surprised Julia. It moved her, too. There was a tenderness in the way he looked at Ime, as well as a sadness, as though he wished he could help her in some way.

"Thank you for coming," Ilario said. "It helps."

"It's nothing," she said.

"It's something," he said. "You're a good friend to her. I don't think many people would go to the trouble."

Julia felt herself blushing under his gaze. They paused near a huge three-dimensional cutaway model of a car transmission that towered above them. Lit from within, the model pulsed with red and white light as the gears turned slowly.

"Thank you for everything you've done for me at work," he said. "I'm happy with the way things are working out."

She nodded. "Things have gotten better." The transmission gears slowed, then reversed direction.

"I don't think we understood each other before. But we make a good team, don't you think?"

"Sure. Sure." She scanned the crowd for Ime.

"I guess it's OK to tell you now . . . I've been trying to get a higher year-end bonus approved for you. I mentioned it to Roger, and he said it was fine. He wants me to work with you as closely as possible—"

"That's great, Ilario. Thank you. But you know what? Let's not talk about work right now, OK?" She pushed ahead and caught up with Ime and sank her fingers into her friend's arm.

"What's wrong?" Ime said.

"Nothing," Julia said. "Slow down, that's all."

For the next hour or so, the two friends stayed in close proximity like a couple of objects locked in orbit, each eclipsing the other from the person she least wanted to be near. Just as Julia was beginning to feel that she had met her obligation to Ime by coming, a voice over the PA system announced that the makers of BMW were about to debut the new 7 Series in the West Hall of the convention center.

"This is it," Ime said, newly energized. "This is what I came here for. We can't miss this." Without regard for whether anyone else was interested in seeing the car, she led the way out of the

South Hall and through the concourse. The 7 Series was Ime's last step on the BMW ladder, the one that was still out of her reach; she hoped to have one within the next two years. The air around her seemed electrified as they approached the exhibit area.

They did not find the usual silk-draped car waiting to be unveiled, however. Instead, hovering about thirty feet in the air in the center of the room like a magician's trick was a ring of metal tubing emitting a downward curtain of water. A similarly shaped receptacle on the floor caught the pouring water, completing a circular fountain of sheer water that filled the hall with a rushing noise. A nearby boy of about seven or eight wearing a Lakers jersey reached out, breaking the continuous flow of water with his fingers.

Moments later a dramatic flourish of music overpowered the sound of rushing water, and all the lights in the hall except those that lit the fountain dimmed. A woman's sultry voice came over the speakers:

"Ladies and gentlemen, the makers of the ultimate driving machine bring you the sublime culmination of all things BMW: Performance. Luxury. Technology. Style. The blending of precision with passion. Without further ado: the BMW 745i."

With another flourish of music, the curtain of water broke in a line and began to recede, revealing a high dais. No car was visible at first, but as the gap in the water grew, there arose from the center of the platform a shimmering dark red sedan. Seconds later the water cut off completely and the remaining curtain of water vanished, exposing the car from every angle. It completed three rotations on the dais while the announcer detailed some of its features. Then the music cut out, and the car (driverless as far as Julia could see) fired its engine and rolled to the edge of the platform, where a hydraulic ramp had risen to meet it. The car took the ramp up to the higher main stage at the back of the room, where a light display showered it in color. Ime, hanging on Ilario's arm, melted into a dreamy calm as video screens at the back of the stage lit up with images of the sedan's features.

When the presentation was over, Ilario whispered something in Ime's ear, eliciting from her a look of appreciation. She then gave a backward glance at Lydia that was full of guilt.

"That really was a nice car," Lydia said to Ime as they began to move again. "I'll go with you to take it for a test drive as soon as it's available, if you want."

Ime shifted to Ilario's other side, closer to Lydia. "That would be nice," she said. "I know a dealer in Glendale. He's a friend and he'll even let me borrow a car overnight."

A short while later, Julia said to Ime, quietly so as not to be overheard, "What just happened?"

"What do you mean?" Ime said.

"All of a sudden you're being nice."

"I'm always nice."

"I mean to Lydia. What did Ilario say to you?"

"He said I'm the girl for him and I have nothing to worry about. Lydia has nothing over me. Maybe I need to give her a chance, Julia."

"Well, I'm glad to see the change," Julia said.

Fifteen minutes later, they found themselves in the restroom. Ime said, "Thank you for being here, Julia. I should have saved today for just you and me. The Auto Show has always been *our* thing."

"You're in a relationship now," Julia said. "I have to expect things to change. I've been resisting that." She thought, We'll see how you feel when your boyfriend gets fired and I get his job.

Just then, the door opened and Lydia came in. Ime gave Julia a look that said, Watch this and be amazed.

She walked up to Lydia and said, "Lydia, I want to apologize to you. You really are a nice woman, and if I haven't been as nice to you as I should be, it's only because I'm jealous."

Warmth flowed into Lydia's face. "You don't know how much that means to me," she said. She reached out and hugged Ime. Ime submitted to the hug, rolling her eyes at Julia. Nevertheless, she was clearly pleased with Lydia's reaction.

"All right, all right," Ime said. "That's enough girl stuff. Go pee or whatever it is you came in here to do."

Julia and Ime went out. Julia said, "I'm impressed. That was quite a turnaround."

"Just doing what I have to do to keep my man," she said, and cracked her knuckles.

After another hour of exploring the convention center, Julia started to say that she needed to get going. But before she could finish, an announcer came back over the speakers to say that another BMW would be debuted in a few minutes at the same location as before.

"I want to see it," Lydia said. "I bet Ime does, too."

"It wouldn't kill us," Ime said. "Let's see if we can get closer this time."

With a sigh, Ilario and Julia agreed, and they all trekked back to the staging area in the West Hall. They moved through the crowd and right up to the display area.

"This is perfect," Ime said. She pushed her hand through the waterfall just as they had seen the child in the Lakers jersey do.

"Where's the water coming from?" Julia said. "And what's holding the whole thing up? It can't just be floating there."

"I know how this works," Lydia said. "Somewhere behind the water there's a pipe supporting the whole structure and supplying water to it at the same time. You just can't see it because it's on the inside, behind the waterfall."

"How about that?" Ime said. "You're a beauty queen, a mechanic, *and* an engineer. I'm so impressed."

Incredibly, Ime's voice was free of sarcasm. Everyone laughed. Moments later, as Lydia was asking Julia about places to shop in the Valley, Ilario's phone went off. He turned it up in his palm with an annoyed look. "I have to take this," he said. "It's Roger." With a finger in one ear, he walked away to answer the call.

Once again the presentation began. This time the fountain peeled back to reveal a bright yellow sports car. Again there was applause as the presentation ended, and again the wall of water returned. The women looked around for Ilario.

"I don't see him," Lydia said. "Let's wait here so he can find us."

"So tell me," Julia said, trying to keep the conversation going, "how is it being back in L.A.? It must be very different from the Bay Area."

"It is," Lydia said, "but it feels like home."

"Where are you living now?"

"I found her the cutest apartment in Studio City," Ime volunteered. "It's got a balcony and a pool and an underground garage. It's about halfway between you and me, Julia."

"Actually," Lydia said, "I don't think I'm going to be taking the apartment after all."

"But it's so cute!" Ime said. "And you said it was exactly what you were looking for."

"It really is nice," Lydia said, "but a few things have changed for me since we talked, and I'm not so sure renting is such a good idea anymore."

"But you already signed the lease," Ime said. "I was there."

"I know," Lydia said, placing a hand over her heart as though experiencing physical pain there. "I don't like losing my deposit. And believe me, I really, really appreciate all your help in finding it. But after talking it over with Ilario—"

"Ilario?" Ime said. "What does Ilario have to do with this?"

"Well," Lydia said, "nothing, except that we were talking this morning, and I realized that it might make more sense for me to buy a place."

"Well, I can help you with that," Ime said. "You just tell me what you're looking for, and I can get on it right away. And of course I won't charge you anything for my services since you and Ilario are so close."

"And when I decide to do it, you'll be the first person I'll call."

"When you decide? What do you mean, 'when'?"

"Well, I just mean that since I'm new to my job, Ilario and I thought it might be a good idea for me to save some money in order to be able to buy. . . . So, we were talking, and we thought it might work for me to stay with him for a few months, until I have enough of a financial cushion to be able to afford . . ."

Ime's lips barely moved. "A financial cushion . . ."

"Right," Lydia said.

"A financial cushion," Ime said.

"So that I can save enough for the down payment."

"Save enough for the down payment," Ime said.

A few seconds ticked by, during which the sounds of passersby filled the air.

"You mean to tell me," Ime said, with unusual calm, "that you and Ilario . . . without telling me . . ."

"Ime, take a look at this," Julia said, trying to draw her attention to another display. But Ime didn't look at her. She kept her eyes screwed tight on Lydia.

"Imelda," Lydia said, "we only started talking about it this morning. . . ."

"This morning you both decided . . ."

"Nothing is decided. We were only talking."

"You were talking this morning. . . ."

"I'm sure Ilario was going to tell you just as soon as . . ."

"Just as soon as . . ."

"As soon as, well, I guess later today. You'd have to ask him. Like I said, nothing is definite . . . and I wouldn't consider moving in with him if you had any sort of problem. . . ."

"But you already gave up your deposit. . . ."

"Well, yes, but I . . ."

Ime continued to grip Lydia in her sights. Her look was dark and steady and metallic. Then Ime reached out and pushed her.

It wasn't much of a push—just the slightest application of her fingertips against Lydia's collarbone. But there was no mistaking that it was a push. Lydia's face scrambled with confusion. "What did you just do?" she said.

"I pushed you," Ime said.

"Why?"

"I don't know."

"All right," Julia said, reaching for Ime's elbow. "That's enough, let's—"

"I don't like being touched," Lydia said.

"I didn't like touching you," Ime said.

"Then please don't do that again," Lydia said.

Ime kept staring at her. Lydia, whose gaze had been flickering with fear and uncertainty, now returned Ime's look with a steady one of her own. Julia heard herself saying something about how they should all go and look for Ilario, but neither woman paid attention to her. Then Ime reached out and pushed Lydia again.

Again it wasn't much of a push. This time, though, it carried enough force to require Lydia to take a step back to keep her balance. But because Lydia was already standing with her calves just inches from the back of the base of the fountain, the step she took was not enough to allow her to keep her balance, and she fell backward through the curtain of water.

She went through as gracefully as anyone falling through a wall of water probably could have. With a gasp, Julia reached out to try and grab her, but she wasn't fast enough. The water sliced Lydia like a giant blade as she disappeared through it. "Oh my God! Lydia!" Julia said.

Several other people who had been standing nearby rushed forward to help, but Lydia had completely fallen through to the other side. Through the water Julia could see her outline as she got to her feet.

"Lydia, are you OK?" Julia looked around. "Somebody, get somebody to turn this off!"

Lydia's voice came from the other side. "I'm fine," she said, "fine, fine, fine. Get out of the way, I'm jumping through."

Everyone stood back. On the count of three, she lunged through, this time with her heels in her hands.

She emerged damp but not at all soaked as Julia had expected. With perfect calm, Lydia shook her shoes in the air, then put them back on. She tossed her hair. As though a splash in a fountain were just the thing she had been wanting, she let out a spirited laugh. Several onlookers laughed with her in relief. If it was possible for anyone to have fallen through a fountain and emerged looking more dignified, Julia wouldn't have known how to accomplish it.

Lydia did not look at Ime. She brushed off a man's offer of a handkerchief. "I'm fine, I'm fine. I'm really not that wet, see?" The man's eyes grazed her breasts as she removed the damp sweater she had been wearing to reveal a T-shirt underneath.

By now, something akin to regret was creeping onto Ime's face. Ime moved toward Lydia, but Lydia turned her back to her just as Ilario came up.

"What in the world just happened?" he said. "My God, are you all right?"

"I'm fine," she said breezily. Then, to Julia's amazement, she added, "I'm so stupid, I must have slipped."

Ime's face was beginning to soften with worry. Still, Lydia did not look at her. She looked at Julia instead as she said, "These shoes. What was I thinking coming in heels?"

Ime said nothing. Once Ilario was convinced that Lydia was all right, he came around to Ime's side. She clung to him. Julia judged that it was to protect herself more from Julia than from Lydia. For Lydia showed no signs of anger. It was Julia who was livid. Livid and brimming with disgust and done, done at least for now, with Ime.

They made their way out and through the concourse and back to the parking garage. Ime offered nothing in the way of conversation. Julia refused to look at her. But when, a minute or two later, Julia's gaze crossed hers by accident, there was a look of fear in Ime's eyes that said—as clearly as if she were speaking in Julia's ear—that she was sorry. And that she knew she was in the deepest, deepest sort of shit.

≈ 22 ≈

An Honest Deception

"Has anyone said anything to you about Roger's plans for when he gets back?" Ilario asked.

Julia did not look up from her computer. She had been keeping her door closed to avoid Ilario, but today had inadvertently left it ajar. She stared at her screen and typed quickly to appear busy. This didn't deter Ilario from coming in and unraveling in a chair.

"Plans?" Julia said. "What kind of plans?" Nonsense words spilled across her screen.

"I'm not sure. I was asking Russ in finance whether Roger called in to ask about next year's budget, and he got this look on his face like he knew something. Did Roger say anything to you when you saw him?"

"Roger? No. Why would he say anything to me? I'm just a sales rep."

"I don't know. I thought it was weird he didn't ask me about it."

"You saw him?"

"I went by the hospital the day after you did."

Julia typed: *Please stop talking, please leave, please don't ask anything else. . . .*

Ilario dismissed the subject with a wave of his hand. He pushed off from the chair. "He's probably cutting my budget and wanted to avoid an argument."

That's what you think . . . if you knew what's coming . . . why did Roger put me in this position. . . .

"Lydia's coming by for lunch. Do you want to join us? She liked meeting you. She said—"

"Ilario, not now, please. I need to finish these visit reports."

He drummed his fingers on his rib cage. "OK. Some other time." With his hand on the door he looked back and said, "Don't work so hard. You're making me look bad."

Julia focused on her screen. "Close the door for me, OK?" It clicked shut. She reached for her phone.

"Nina, when do you get off work? I need to see you. I can't go on like this."

"If keeping the truth from him is so hard," Nina said, "maybe you should call in sick for a few days." She and Julia were in Nina's car on their way to the Northridge Fashion Center to look at brides-maid dresses. Nina had been looking for several weeks and still hadn't found anything she liked.

"I wish I could," Julia said, "but I can only be out of the office for so long. And there's a lot I need to brush up on before Roger gets back. I feel so . . . dishonest." She dug her fingernail under a rivet on the handbag in her lap. "I know it sounds stupid, but I feel like I owe something to Ilario."

"A big 'muchísimas gracias, cabrón' is what you owe him," Nina said. "He practically handed you his job."

This was true. Ilario had no one to blame but himself. Even so, the situation felt unfair to her. "I guess," Julia said.

Nina cut her a harsh look. "Don't tell me you feel sorry for him after everything he's done. Remember, this is the job you wanted so badly a few months ago. Now it's sitting right in front of you and all you have to do is keep your damn mouth shut. Really, Julia, even you can manage that."

In spite of Nina's harsh words, Julia was glad she was there. Who would have guessed that she would come to rely so heavily on her for friendship and advice? Who could have predicted that after knowing Nina for so many years, she would now emerge as her smartest, most reasonable, and most valued friend?

"It sounds easy enough," Julia said after a couple of minutes went by, "but Ilario already suspects something. He's going to keep pressing me to find out if I know anything."

"Then you're going to have to say you don't."

"I'm a terrible liar."

"Then don't lie."

"What do you mean?"

"Do what I do. When somebody asks you a question, answer it with something that's true but doesn't really answer the question. Let's say someone asks you, 'Did you steal a twenty from my purse?' Don't say yes or no. Say something like, 'Funny that you mention it. I noticed Susana buying her lunch with a twenty.'"

"That's terrible," Julia said.

"It works," Nina said.

"Where do you pick up these things?"

"Around."

"You actually do that?"

"When I need to."

"Have you ever done that with me?"

Nina looked her in the eye. "I've never stolen from you, Julia, not ever. There. See how well that works?"

· · ·

Just past the railroad tracks, the Northridge Fashion Center appeared on the left on Tampa. The mall was composed of an array of ugly, gray, jammed-together buildings that from the outside promised little in the way of natural light or uplifting design. Nina joined the crush of cars into the parking garage, winding up several levels in search of a space. The Northridge quake in the nineties had reduced the garage to a twenty-foot pile of rubble. Even now the building brought to Julia's mind the image of people being crushed to death, though no one had been killed in the early morning collapse. The garage had been rebuilt the following year to current safety standards, but the thought of such destruction still made Julia nervous every time she went into it.

Once they had parked, they made their way out and past the front entrance of the Robinsons-May and toward the bridal boutique. As they looked through the samples, Nina mused, "I'm thinking of asking Remedios to be in my wedding."

"Really?!" Julia said.

"You think it's a bad idea?"

"Not at all. I think she'd love to be asked. What made you consider her?"

Nina drew a length of skirt into her hands from one of the bridesmaid racks and caressed. "It's weird. I know I hardly know her, but I feel like I've known her for a long time. Does that make sense?"

Julia wasn't sure that it did. As much as she had come to like and appreciate Remedios in recent months—as much as she believed Remedios had changed for the better—Julia felt she had only begun to scratch the surface of her character. "Some things about her are still kind of mysterious to me," she offered.

"You mean like how she could do what she did to Claudia Aguilar?"

"I wasn't thinking of that specifically. But yes, I guess so."

Nina let the fabric fall away and continued down the rack. She pulled each dress out a few inches before releasing it. "I don't think it's so hard to understand," she said. "It's easier to destroy a friendship than try and repair it. The more badly people perceive you, the more power you have." She let go of another dress and looked at her fingertips, as though the fabric had left some sort of residue. "Whether she admits it or not, I think what she did to Claudia is the one thing she wishes she could undo."

How Nina had garnered such insights about Remedios, Julia didn't know, but she was impressed by them. They carried the weight of truth. "I think it's terrific that you're asking her," Julia said. "And I think it's terrific you guys are becoming such good friends."

Nina made a face as she stood back and regarded a rack of dresses that were mostly frills and ruffles. "None of these would really look good on Remedios, would they?"

"I guess she would be pretty hard to dress," Julia said. "But it's your wedding; you shouldn't let that influence your choice."

"Oh, I don't agree," Nina said. "If I'm going to include her, the least I can do is make sure she doesn't look ridiculous."

The visit to the boutique produced nothing in the way of a decision about Nina's bridesmaid dresses. After about another hour of wandering the mall, Nina wondered out loud whether it might not be better to wait until she had Remedios's commitment to be in the wedding before continuing to look. She reasoned that Remedios would be much more likely to agree to be in the wedding party if she had some say in what she would be wearing. Julia said she thought this was a good idea, so rather than continue to shop, Nina bought Julia lunch at the food court and then drove her home.

No sooner had she dropped Julia off than Julia again began to feel oppressed by thoughts about Ilario. It saddened her that she could find no pleasure in the prospect of moving up into her first management position. She wondered whether once she was promoted, the joy that she ought to be experiencing now would pour in to fill the space that sadness now occupied. Or would Ime's reaction to finding out that she had taken her boyfriend's job (Ilario would certainly portray her as scheming for his position) ruin any hope of joy?

As she climbed the stairs to her apartment—heavily, as though gravity were working extrahard that day—a stranger in an ugly mustard-colored jacket passed her in the opposite direction. Not recognizing him, she paused at the top of the steps and looked back. At the same moment, he looked up at her from the bottom of the steps.

"Can I help you with something?" Julia said.

"Are you Julia Juárez?" He pronounced her first name with a hard "J."

"I'm Julia," she said, pronouncing the "J" softly, the way she preferred.

He bounded up the stairs toward her, causing her to instinctively take a couple of steps back. As he reached the top landing, he produced a badge from his breast pocket. "I'm Detective Dan Piper, LAPD." He regarded her in a way that was friendly and professional, but only for a couple of seconds. "Do you have a few minutes to answer a couple of questions?"

"About what?" Julia said, gripping the stair railing.

"About Diego Ramirez."

Julia had the brief sensation of thousands of insect feet scurrying over her skin. When the sensation vanished, she was left with the feeling that the walls around her were at once expanding and becoming very bright. "Diego Ramirez?"

"The actor," he said, meeting her at eye level. In one deft movement, he slipped the badge back into his pocket and produced in its place one of Concepción's Cinco de Mayo green card invitations. "I understand you were one of the hosts of this party. Did you talk to Diego Ramirez that day?"

"I saw him, but I didn't talk to him. At least, I don't remember saying anything to him. He didn't say anything to me." Light pulsed behind her eyes. She gripped the rail more tightly. "Can I ask why you're asking?" She noticed that the corduroy of his jacket had been worn flat and shiny in places. For some reason this bothered her intensely. She wondered if it was a tactic of detectives to intentionally wear things that they knew would irritate other people.

"I'm working on the case of his missing ex-wife. Maybe you've heard about it."

"No," Julia said, having no idea where that answer came from. Who hadn't heard about it? "I mean, yes, I've heard about it. I think. I don't watch the news much."

"You might have heard that he fled the country. He might still be out of the country, or he might not be." Without taking his eyes from Julia, he folded the invitation and expertly returned it to his jacket pocket. His eyes made her very uneasy. Was she supposed to look at them or follow the invitation as it made its way back to his pocket?

He said, "We're asking people who spoke with him in the weeks before he fled the country." He nodded in the direction of her apartment. "Would it be possible to chat inside?"

"Like I said, I didn't talk to him," Julia said.

"I'd still like to talk to you," he said, resurrecting his friendly, professional smile.

Julia nodded and dug out her key and led him to her door. It took her several seconds to get the door open. Her face flamed hot as she struggled with the key.

Inside, she turned on the lights. The apartment was too warm and she noticed a strange, sweet smell. She left the door ajar and pushed open a window. She heard herself offer him a seat, which he took. She heard herself offer him something to drink, which he declined. Why did everything coming out of her mouth sound like the words of a guilty person?

"Who invited Mr. Ramirez to your party?" the detective said.

Julia explained how Concepción had approached the actor at the mall.

"Was that the first time your friend Concepción had ever met him?"

"Yes."

"Had anyone else at your party ever met him before?"

"No."

"Do you have any thoughts about why he would come to a party of people he didn't know?"

Julia had her theories about how the actor, plagued by problems she could not understand, had been in search of solace, of something that would remind him of a more innocent time in his life. But she sensed these were not the kinds of answers the detective was looking for. "He just showed up. He was drunk, and he was with these two other women. I think one of them was a model or an actress or something. They didn't want to be there. They had somewhere else to go."

"Did you overhear anything he said while he was at your party?"

"I remember him saying something about someone named Frank. They were going to see him. But they stopped at Concepción's party instead."

"Did you talk to either of the girls?"

"No."

"Did you overhear them say anything to each other?"

"Just that they were mad that Diego had brought them."

"How long did they stay at the party?"

"I don't know. I left around six and they were still there."

"Do you know where I might find this person?" He removed the invitation again and made an impression with his thumbnail next to Concepción's name.

"I guess at her apartment."

"I'd like to talk to her. She wasn't there when I went by. If you speak with her, let her know I'm trying to reach her."

Julia nodded. "I'm sure I'll be hearing from her soon."

"We know that she sent several letters and e-mails to Ramirez's manager between the time of her party and Ramirez's disappearance."

The detective seemed to expect Julia to say something in response to this. When she said nothing, he produced his friendly, professional smile a third time and handed her his card. "Have her call us. The sooner the better."

At the door, Julia watched as he made his way down the stairs and out of sight.

Her thoughts raced. Whether or not to call Concepción. She had said she wouldn't get involved. She had warned Concepción not to expect help from her. But who could have guessed that the police would show up at *her* door? She could tell Concepción the police wanted to talk to her and that would be all. She could hang up before Concepción told her anything she didn't want to know. Or would she only be helping her avoid the police? She paced. Felt her fear combusting into anger. She had never been so angry with

Concepción. She heard a sound coming from the bedroom, went down the hall, and saw that the door was closed. She never closed it. She heard voices. She approached quietly, listening. Moved her face closer to the door. The door snapped open and Concepción's face appeared, making Julia jump and let out a squeal.

"Is he gone?" Concepción hissed. She peered out from a crack in the door.

"What are you doing here?"

"We let ourselves in! That detective guy came snooping around my apartment when I wasn't there, so we came here as soon as we could." Opening the door a little wider revealed that she was not alone. With her were Marta and Diego Ramirez.

"You brought him here?"

"We had nowhere else to go," Concepción said. "The Pentecostals were starting to suspect something, and then that detective came around. We couldn't take him to Marta's because her relatives are always dropping by."

"So you came here! Well, obviously you can't hide him here."

"But this is the perfect place," Marta said. "The police have already been here, so they probably won't come here again for a while."

"Oh, well, in *that* case," Julia said, "go ahead, move him in! I can sleep on the couch and he can have my bedroom." She swung toward Diego, who was watching with wide, worried eyes. "Diego, what would you like for breakfast? I'm happy to cook for you as well. Do you need any laundry washed? Is there anything else I can do for you?"

Diego tried to say something, but Marta cut him off. "We'll do the washing and cooking. Just let us stay here until things cool off. You can stay at my place. We'll rotate him back to C's place in a few days."

Julia pressed her hands to the sides of her face. She was still holding her house keys. She pressed them into her cheek. Diego sat perched on the edge of her bed with an uncertain look, as though considering bolting. He looked a bit drunk, too. It was then that Julia recognized the smell she had noticed upon walking in. Rum. She stormed to the kitchen and the others trailed behind her. The cabinets above her stove were wide open. Liquor bottles formed a glass skyline on her kitchen table.

Julia pressed her keys even harder against her face. "This isn't happening. I'm not standing in my own kitchen with a fugitive."

"Can I say something?" Diego said.

"No," Marta said. "We told you we'd take care of everything, and that's what we're doing." She poured an inch of rum and pushed the glass toward him. In Spanish she said, "He's nice to look at, but he's not bright. Don't worry, he can't understand me. Believe it or not, Mr. Latin Stallion's Spanish is awful, so as long as we talk fast, he has no idea what we're saying."

Julia took the glass away from Diego and the rum from Marta and angrily poured the contents out in the sink. "The cantina's closed. You don't have to go home, but you can't stay here."

Concepción said, "Diego thinks he knows what happened to his ex-wife. But the police aren't going to believe him, and he needs to prove it himself. But obviously he can't be seen, so we have to do what we can to help him."

"What we really need to do is get into that director's house to show he was sleeping with her and had reason to kill her," Marta said.

"Or have her killed," Concepción said.

Julia put two fingers in her mouth and with a stamp of her foot gave a sharp whistle. "Is *anybody* listening to me? This is not a safe house, and I want all of you out of here."

"Listen," Diego tried again, "you've all been really wonderful, but if your friend doesn't want me here—"

"Please, Diego," Marta said with an exasperated sigh, "let us do the thinking."

"I've heard enough," Julia said. "You're pushing me to the edge."

"Now listen," Concepción said. "This is *the best place for him*."

"Either go and take him with you or I'm calling the police."

"Fine. Here. Go ahead." Concepción held out her cell phone.

"Hold on," Marta said, "don't get crazy."

"Yeah," Diego said, "there's no reason to—"

"Go ahead and call," Concepción said. "If you really think what we're doing is so terrible, then go ahead. That detective probably hasn't gotten far. He can come over right now and arrest Diego. Well? What are you waiting for?"

Julia trembled with anger. She had never before felt such fury. The kitchen light flickered a couple of times as though responding to her rage.

"Well?" Concepción said.

Julia hooked her bag off the counter with a sweep of her arm.

Marta scrambled to her feet. "Where are you going?"

Julia shot through the living room.

"You better not do anything stupid," Marta called after her.

No, Julia thought, I would *never* do anything stupid. She opened the apartment door and slammed through the screen door with her shoulder. Her vision narrowed as she stormed down the hall.

"So this means he can stay here?" Concepción called out.

She flew down the steps, past the spot where the detective had stopped to talk to her, and down to the parking garage. One of her neighbors said something to her, but she kept walking.

In her car she shook with anger. She jammed the steering wheel a couple of times with her knee, shaking the car. She cracked open her phone and dialed Nina as she shot out of the garage. "Nina," she said into her voice mail, "call me when you get this. I need a place to stay tonight. Call me. Please."

She drove for nearly an hour, trying to control her anger enough to figure out what to do. To her surprise, she found herself wanting to call Ilario. But it was foolish to think about involving him.

She tried Nina again instead. While she waited for her return call, she swung from the 5 to the 101 to the 405, carving out a giant triangle within the Valley. She decided she couldn't wait for Nina. She had a key to her house. She left her another message saying that she was going to let herself in, then stopped at a liquor store, bought a six-pack, and walked out without counting the change. She arrived at Nina's house a few minutes later and let herself in.

In Nina's kitchen she found a glass and poured a beer for herself, then went to the living room. Nina's wedding dress still stood in the middle of the room on the tailor's dummy. The charmeuse glistened with rhinestones that had not been there before. The finished dress struck her as beautiful and innocent and wonderful. She could imagine Nina walking down the aisle in the dress, and handsome Roberto turning to look at her. The picture was enough to bring tears to Julia's eyes. It was an image that she needed at that moment more than she could describe, an image of beauty and joy and hope.

She reached out to touch the dress. A shuffling sound from the back of the house made her withdraw her hand. She heard footsteps and realized she was not alone. A sound like a man clearing his throat came from a back room. Shit. She had walked into Nina's house while Nina and Roberto were together, making love. That's why Nina hadn't been answering. What an idiot she was!

She stood frozen, uncertain whether to leave the glass on the side table and sneak out, or take it back to the kitchen and erase any signs that she had been there.

Nina's voice rolled down the long, narrow hall. "Julia, is that you?"

"Nina, I'm so sorry. I let myself in. I called to say I was coming over. I should have waited, I didn't think . . ."

She noticed a pair of boots lined up against the wall . . .

"I called you, but you didn't answer and . . ."

A pair of brocade-belted jeans collapsed in a pile . . .

"I need a place to stay, but I can always . . ."

A discarded sweatshirt turned inside out . . .

"I'll call you tomorrow and explain everything. I'm sorry, I . . ."

Passing the mouth of the hall, she saw down to the far end of the house. Nina was peering out at her from the bedroom with a sheet wrapped around her petite frame. Her hair was mussed and her face was pink with confusion. Then, a second later, another figure appeared behind her—tall, dark, and equally naked. Remedios Salazar stared down the hallway at Julia with a look that was as hostile as it was confused.

"Nina, I'm sorry, I didn't . . ."

"It's OK," Nina said, struggling to keep herself covered. "We were just . . . I was just . . ."

"I better go," Julia said. "I didn't realize—"

"No, don't go. Stay. What are you doing here?"

"I shouldn't have . . . I was just . . . Concepción and Marta . . ."

Nina flowed down the hall, gripping her sheet. "Julia, are you all right?"

"I'm feeling . . . I think I'm going to . . . I should go. . . ."

"Please, sit down. You look—"

"I should go, I really should—"

Go, she thought. I should really go. But the effort to do so did not translate into motion. She felt light and heavy at the same time. She wondered if this was what it was like to be on the verge of fainting. And that was her last thought before the room and everything around her went inescapably black.

≈ 23 ≈

A Body Surfaces

I'm not a lesbian," Nina said once Julia had come to. According to Nina she'd been out for only a few seconds. Remedios was gone now, having left at Nina's insistence. "I'm really, really not a dyke," Nina said.

"Then how did it happen?" Julia said, riding up more comfortably on Nina's couch and taking the glass of water Nina was offering her. She remembered Remedios's grape Fanta kiss.

Nina slumped next to her and hung her arms between her knees. "I'm not sure. I asked her to come over so I could ask her in person if she wanted to be in my wedding. She said she didn't and I said why not and then it turned into this big argument and the next thing I knew I was kissing her."

"*You* kissed *her?*"

Nina tried to retract her words, but only got tangled up in them. Julia set the water glass down and reached for the beer she had poured earlier. It was warm but it still tasted good.

"You're not going to say anything to anyone, are you?" Nina said. "I don't exactly know why I did it. It was just one of those things. I guess I was just trying to convince her to be in the wedding so I kissed her."

"Nina, it looked like you were doing more than kissing."

"No, no, no. I know what it looked like, but we were just . . . I'm marrying Roberto. I was being stupid. I wanted her to be a bridesmaid and . . ." A realization fell over her like a shadow. "Julia, thank God you came when you did. Who knows what more might have happened. You saved me, you really did."

The idea of having "saved" Nina gave Julia little comfort. As she took another sip of beer, the reason for her coming flooded back to her. She knocked her head against the sofa back. "Shit."

"Oh, no," Nina said. "Was I bad? Have I ruined everything?"

"It's not that. C and Marta . . . they've really done it this time." Hardly believing her own words, she related to Nina everything that had happened prior to her coming to see her.

"Unbelievable," Nina said, jumping at the change of subject. "Unacceptable. They've gone too far."

"I tried to stand up to C, but you know how she is. She actually thinks—"

"I'm going to talk to her."

"Don't get involved," Julia said.

"But it's not fair to you."

"Nina, there's nothing to do right now. Just let me stay here until I have a chance to think this through."

"You can stay," Nina said. "But I'm not letting them do this to you." With exaggerated urgency, she began to put on her socks and shoes. Julia intuited that the real reason behind her determination had nothing to do with protecting her—and everything to do with hiding her embarrassment at being caught with Remedios. "I'm going to take care of everything," she said.

Julia did not try to stop her. When she returned an hour later, her face was painted with remorse and failure. Concepción and

Marta had refused to listen to her. They had, however, given her fifteen minutes to pack a bag of clothes and toiletries for Julia. "I wasn't sure what you needed, so I grabbed a suit and packed as much as I could fit in here," she said, rolling the overnight bag toward Julia on the hardwood floor.

That night, after insisting for the tenth or eleventh time that she was not a lesbian, Nina told Julia she was welcome to sleep with her in her bedroom, adding, "Nothing will happen, I swear." Julia joined her in the bedroom, but after an hour of tossing and turning, moved to the sofa so as not to keep Nina awake any longer.

Before she knew it, morning light was seeping through the curtains. At seven o'clock Julia rose to face a day of client visits. She drank as much coffee as she could stand, then left a note for Nina thanking her for letting her stay and telling her she would call her later.

Outside, Santa Ana winds were shaking the tops of trees, stirring up dust and leaves and making Julia's eyes feel crisp. She removed a brown palm frond from the hood of her car. More fronds and stems littered the street. They crunched under her tires as she pulled out.

At work she parked, then leaned into a harsh wind as she crossed the parking lot to the building. Before going to her office, she stopped at the restroom to drag a comb through her wind-tangled hair. As she was coming out, she ran into Ilario.

"Did you get that e-mail I forwarded you? Guzman has questions about program options."

"I just got in. I'll look at it in a second."

"How are you coming with the projections for next quarter?"

"I'll have them tomorrow. I'm out on calls starting at ten."

"Did you set up a time to update the rest of the group about the SFA training?"

"I sent the e-mail out yesterday."

"OK. Well. It sounds like you're on top of everything."

"I am. Thanks."

She brushed past him—but not before noticing the dusky strain of worry running through his face. He knows, she thought. He knows *something*. It's only a matter of time before he pieces it all together. If only I were a better actor. If only I knew how to *lie*.

She felt him watching her as she walked away. She went into her office and closed her door and kept it closed until it was time to leave for her first call of the day.

He must have been waiting for her to come out in order to talk to her, for he appeared within seconds of her opening her door. Miraculously, her cell phone rang, giving her an excuse to turn and walk away from him.

"How are you holding up?" Nina said.

"Good," Julia said. She walked out of the building. The sun slammed hard on her shoulders. The sky was clear—no haze or pollution to soften the sun's blow. She felt around for her sunglasses.

"Then I guess you haven't heard the news."

"No more talk about C or Marta," Julia said.

"I mean *the* news. It's on TV. They found Diego's ex-wife's body."

Julia slipped into her car and reached to turn on the air. "Tell me—what happened?"

"Some guy was walking along the beach in Long Beach and his dog sniffed out the body. It was washed up near one of the piers. They won't say for sure that it's her because she's so decomposed, but from everything they're saying, it looks like it's her."

The ground in front of Julia wavered as she pulled out of her space. Light flickered behind her eyes. "My God."

"I know."

"It makes everything seem . . ."

"So much more serious?" Nina offered.

"That's it." An actual body. A real murder. Traffic thinned unexpectedly, as if to accommodate this new information. "Is it possible that this will make C come to her senses? I mean, there's a *body*."

"I already thought of that."

"You talked to her?"

"She's not budging. She still thinks it's her duty to protect him, whatever that means. But Marta's in a panic."

"You talked to her, too?"

"She's starting to sweat. It's hitting her that this isn't a game."

"I hope you're right. Maybe she can make C see the light. . . . Hold on. That's her. Nina, let me take this." She switched to the incoming call. "Marta?"

"What have I gotten myself into?" Marta panted. "He did it. They found her body. I've been helping to hide a *murderer*."

"Marta, you don't know how happy I am to hear you say that."

"Sure, I *said* I thought he did it. But I guess I didn't really believe it until now. He killed her! I'll bet he strangled her, too. He was probably high on drugs and he *squeeeeeeezed* the life out of her."

"Where are you?" Julia said. "Where's C?"

"I'm on the 5," Marta said. "I'm not spending another minute with him or C. I was never there, do you hear me? Hiding him was C's idea. She . . . blackmailed me into doing it. I can say that, can't I? They can't blame me if she forced me to help her, right?"

"Is he still at my place?" Julia said. "Is C with him?"

"I'm such an idiot. Why did I listen to her? I'm a successful businesswoman. People depend on me. I have—oh my God, oh my God. Shit. Fuck. Oh my God . . ."

"What?" Julia said. "What's going on?"

"There's a cop behind me. He wants me to pull over. I'm really screwed, Julia. This is the end of me. Everything I've ever worked for is about to . . . No, no, he's going around me. Oh, thank God, he's going around me! What have I done, what have I done?"

"Marta, you're the only person that C might listen to. Where is she?"

"She's at the studio. She's teaching classes all day. I want nothing to do with her."

"So Diego's at my place? Alone?"

"I think so. I'm not going back there. Who knows what he's capable of? You were right, Julia. Let's call the police."

"No," Julia said, signaling a left in time for the freeway. "Not yet. What time is C's last class?"

"She works until six, then again from eight until eleven. What are you going to do?"

"I'm not sure. I'll call you later. Don't talk to C or anyone else."

Several seconds went by before the call alert reminded her that Nina was still holding. "Shit. Nina. I'm sorry."

"What did Marta say?"

"You were right. She's coming to her senses."

"What are you going to go?"

"C's at work. Diego's alone. I'm going to try and reason with him."

"That could be dangerous."

"Nina, I'm supposed to be promoted in two weeks. I can't let anything screw that up."

Julia called ahead to her first appointment. Faking a bad cold, she rescheduled it for later in the week. She turned up her radio and combed through the airwaves in search of more information about the body. By the time she reached her exit, the police were confirming that it was that of Diego's ex-wife.

She pulled in her garage. She did not know what she was going to do, but she had to do something. She turned off the radio and waited for the throbbing in her head to ease, then got out and took a tire iron from the back of her car for protection.

At her door she heard the dampened sounds of music coming from within. Touching the door, she could feel the *thump-thump-thump* of the bass. But upon letting herself in, she discovered that the vibration was traveling down the wall from a neighbor's apartment, not hers. Her apartment was quiet. The lights were off and the blinds were drawn. She prayed that the actor was gone. Moving closer to the bedroom, she heard the sound of news leaking from the tiny six-inch TV she kept by her bed but never used. She cracked the door.

Diego sat on the edge of Julia's bed, looking down at the TV tilted up in his lap. The blue and gray TV light splashed his face and the walls of the room in watery patterns. As she pushed the door open a little farther and said his name, he regarded her as though she were only half visible. "She's gone," he said. "She's really gone."

Coming up the stairs to her apartment, Julia had been preparing urgent, angry words. She had planned to insist, demand, threaten. But the sight of the actor looking so lost washed away her intentions. She heard herself say, "Did you do it? Did you kill her?"

The question seemed to come from some other person, from some other room. It was not the sort of thing she would have thought she wanted an answer to. But hearing the question asked, she realized she did want to know. A curiosity she didn't know she had flooded in through some small opening in her chest, pushing out her other concerns.

"Did you?" she said. "Tell me."

He looked back down at the TV, cradling it as though it were the very corpse of the woman he had once loved. The actor looked too stunned to be dangerous. Julia placed the tire iron on her dresser and came closer.

"I was bad to her when we were together," he said. Julia remembered Marta relating rumors about how tumultuous their marriage had been, about drug abuse and alcohol and fights and arrests. He said, "I pulled her into the scene, into the shit. She'd be alive today if . . ."

"Who is Frank?" Julia said, feeling her heart race faster.

"Frank is my business manager. He was a great friend, too. We grew up together."

"And?"

Diego turned his head to hide the tears that came flooding into his eyes. When he looked at her again, his expression was marbled with pain, horror.

"He helped me kill Clarissa."

Fear traveled over Julia's skin. "How?"

In barely a whisper, Diego said, "Frank knew people. People he could call to get rid of her. I was drunk when I told him to make her disappear. At the last minute I changed my mind. Couldn't go through with it. I'd loved her once, for God's sake. I tried to stop it. I thought I had. But three weeks later she disappeared. It was Frank. He wanted her gone more than I did."

"Why?" she said.

"She was threatening to bring me down. With things she knew and could prove. She was threatening to kill my career if I didn't start paying more. She'd been doing it to me for years. Frank was sick of it. His livelihood depended on me. I brought him with me and made him my manager. He didn't want to go back."

"Go back?"

"To the way things were before. To being broke. As long as he had me, he never had to worry. Clarissa threatened that. He knew people who could get rid of her."

"But you tried to stop it," Julia said.

"That doesn't matter," Diego said. "He made sure all evidence pointed to me in case I ever said anything. The body wasn't supposed to show up. Now everything implicates me."

Julia understood now why Diego had turned to Concepción. Only an obsessed fan could offer him what he most needed—unconditional acceptance and faith in his goodness as a person. Looking at Julia now, his eyes shimmered with the need to be understood.

"You're a good person," Julia said.

"I would never hurt her," he said.

"I know you wouldn't."

"You believe me?"

"I believe you."

"I thought I had stopped it."

"I know you did. But unfortunately, you can't stay here anymore."

"What am I going to do?"

"Maybe you can still prove that it wasn't you. That you had a change of heart and it was your manager. But you can't do it from here. You've involved my friends enough. You have to leave."

Diego seemed to emerge from his dazed state. Julia glanced at the tire iron. He noticed her do this and said, "You don't need that." He clicked off the TV. "I'm sorry I caused you problems."

"I promise I won't call the police if you go now," Julia lied. "But you have to leave and not tell anyone you were here. You owe that to C and Marta after all they've done for you."

He nodded and whispered, "Thank you."

She didn't know what he was thanking her for. Even so, she said, "You're welcome."

"Good-bye."

"Good-bye."

She walked him to the door. He took a baseball cap—his? Concepción's?—from a hook on the wall and pulled it down low over his face. She watched until he had turned down the corridor and out of sight.

She closed the door, chained it, and picked up the phone. She dialed information and asked to be connected to the police.

"I understand you're still looking for Diego Ramirez, the movie star," she said. "I know where you can find him if you hurry." She spoke quickly as she described her neighborhood, then hung up.

She reached for the remote to turn on the living room TV. Only then did she realize how hard she was shaking.

☞ 24 ☜

Security Measures

When Concepción returned to Julia's apartment that night, she discovered that her key no longer fit the lock. From inside, Julia listened as she began pounding on the door and yelling, "Marta, are you in there? Why won't my key work? Is anyone in there? What's going on?"

Julia came to the door. "It's me, C. I can't let you in. I changed the locks. Diego's not here."

As far as Julia was concerned, her friendship with Concepción was over. There was no room for doubt or sorrow. Now was the time to protect herself.

Evidently, Concepción had not yet heard that the actor had been arrested, whereas for the last hour Julia and Nina and Marta had been watching events unfold on TV. Nearly every station was airing footage of the actor being led in handcuffs up the steps of the Beverly Hills Police Department. Hours earlier squad cars had swarmed a strip mall not far from Julia's house. There they had found Diego making a call from a pay phone, and he had surrendered at gunpoint without incident. The chief of police was expected to make a statement. No mention had yet been made about Julia's call.

Marta broke away from the TV to join Julia at the door. "Go away, C! It's all over. Go home and turn on the news."

Concepción pounded harder. "What do you mean it's all over? Where is he? What did you do?"

"I can't believe you pulled me into such a thing," Marta said. "We could have been killed!"

"C," Julia said, "I'm not letting you in. Please go home."

"I left some of my things in there," Concepción said. "Let me in so I can get my dance bag at least."

"I'll send it to you," Julia said. "Go home."

A dead silence ensued. Julia pressed her eye to the peephole. She did not see Concepción. She cracked the door and peered out. No sign of her. She hadn't expected getting rid of her to be that easy. She relocked the door and she and Marta rejoined Nina. Moments later a rattling sound somewhere else in the apartment made everyone start. The women rushed to the bedroom and into the bathroom, where the sound was coming from. Concepción was climbing headfirst through the tiny sliding window above the tub.

"C, stop. Enough."

"I'm stuck," Concepción said. "Pull me through."

"Go back the way you came," Marta said.

"I'm hurting myself," Concepción said. "Pull me through."

"We don't want any more of your schemes," Marta said.

"Maybe we should help her," Nina said.

"No," Marta said. "What an embarrassment—her big fat nalgas on display for the whole neighborhood."

"How did you get up this high?" Julia said.

"I moved the trash bin under the window and balanced a ladder on top of that."

"Well, you can go back down the way you came up."

"I can't. I'm not kidding. I'm going to hurt myself."

Marta stepped over the lip of the tub and unhooked Julia's shower massage from its cradle. She pointed it at Concepción's face.

"Don't you dare!" Concepción screamed.

"I swear I will. On three," Marta said, and reached for the faucet handle.

Concepción's face turned purple. After a few seconds, she managed to wiggle back out the way she had come. Julia and Marta looked out.

"We'll talk some other time, C," Julia said.

Marta aimed out the window and gave Concepción a couple of squirts for good measure, and cackled.

Back in the living room, Nina and Julia went back to surfing the channels while Marta made popcorn in the kitchen. Several reporters were filing stories from the very strip mall from which Diego had been taken. Behind one reporter, curious spectators looked on through the window of a donut shop, waving at the camera. Then the news switched to live coverage of the chief of police. He boasted to reporters that through diligence and perseverance they had caught their man. The only mention he made of the call that had tipped them off was when he referred to "information that came to us at a crucial moment." From the kitchen Marta groused that it was entirely unfair that the pointy-faced little police chief should take credit for doing next to nothing. Nina's phone rang. Julia could make out Remedios's loud voice on the other end of the line as Nina took the call.

"I told you, there's nothing to talk about," Nina said. "I was nervous about getting married and I made a mistake."

"What mistake?" Marta said, returning to the living room with a huge bowl of popcorn. "Who's she talking to?"

"No. No. I'm not going to do that. It didn't mean anything. It was my fault for starting something."

Marta cut the TV volume. "What didn't mean anything? What's she talking about?"

Nina shifted so her back was to Marta. "No. No. No. I won't."

"That sounds like Remedios," Marta said. "What's going on?"

Nina stood and made her way toward Julia's bedroom. Marta scooped her popcorn bowl into her arms and followed. Nina closed the bedroom door and locked it from the inside. Marta thumped it a couple of times before pressing her ear to the door.

"Give her some privacy," Julia said. "They just have something they need to—"

"Shhh!" Marta said. She flailed an arm, straining to listen. "Something . . . about the wedding . . . cheating . . . doesn't want . . . Roberto to find out . . ."

About a minute later the door popped open. "She's being ridiculous," Nina said, storming out of the room. "She wants to talk, but I don't see what there is to talk about. It was a mistake, end of story. I can't believe I wanted her in my wedding."

"Wait . . . A mistake . . . Did you guys . . . You had sex with her, didn't you?"

"Hardly anything happened," Nina said. "Technically you can't call it sex."

"*Something* happened," Marta said.

"I'm *not* a lesbian," Nina said.

"You *did* sleep with her!" She turned her chair to face Nina. Through a mouthful of popcorn, she said, "What was it like?"

"It was nothing," Nina said, "but Roberto can't know."

"Oh," Marta said, "Roberto would forgive you in a second. He loves you so much it's ridiculous. You could probably get away with a lot more than a little lesbian love on the side if you wanted." She licked butter and chile powder from her fingers. "You're so lucky."

Nina was pacing. "You don't think she'll try and make problems for me, do you, Julia?"

Julia had no idea. She found the whole thing so hard to imag-ine. Not because it involved two women, but because . . . well, Nina and Remedios together just didn't make sense. "I don't think you have to worry," Julia said. "But if you want I can—"

"No. Don't stir up anything. If nobody says anything, maybe she'll drop the subject. I'm getting married."

"Did she use her tongue on you?" Marta said. "I mean, down there? My husband used to do that before we got married. After that—no more trips south of the equator."

Nina dropped like a stone into a chair and turned the volume back up. Minutes ticked by. Nina stared at the TV as though it were a mortal enemy. Then she launched out of her chair and left the apartment, letting the front door slam shut behind her.

In the days that followed, with the actor at last out of her home and out of her friends' lives, the reality of what was about to transpire at work rushed in to fill the part of Julia's mind previously devoted to worrying about Concepción and Marta. She was on her way to work one day when she was struck by the image of herself sitting in Ilario's office, directing his sales staff, taking his customers' phone calls. Only slightly more than a year ago she had wondered whether she would ever recover from the mistakes she'd made at her last job. How had so much confidence been placed in her so quickly?

That day at the office, she took advantage of the fact that Ilario was out. She began reviewing sales histories for some of the ac-counts belonging to sales associates she would soon be overseeing. But the more she worked, the jumpier she became, fearing that Ilario might suddenly appear.

A short while later, when Roger called her from home to let her know that he'd be returning to the office in a week, it was a huge relief to be able to say to him, "Roger, this is harder than I thought it was going to be. Ilario is getting suspicious that something is up."

Roger sighed in a way that was at once thoughtful and pained. "I didn't realize what an awkward position I'd be putting you in. I wouldn't have said anything if it weren't for the fact that I needed to make sure you didn't take another job."

"I know," Julia said. "But this feels strange. It feels . . . dishonest."

Roger considered for a few seconds, then said, "What if I were to send you to the SFA training in San Diego? I'll tell Ilario that I want an additional sales person trained as a backup. By the time you get back, I'll be in the office again and I can run interference for you."

Julia breathed. "Roger, that's a great idea. Thank you for understanding."

He told her that he would do everything he could to make the transition easier for her. He reminded her that he had faith in her abilities.

"Is Ilario there?"

"He's out today."

"I'll call him and let him know I'm sending you to the training. Take the rest of the day off if you want to."

Once she was off the phone, she got ready to leave for the day. She was closing her office door when Monique, one of the sales associates she would soon be managing, approached her and, regarding her slyly, said, "I guess I should start being nice to you, Julia."

Julia tightened her grip on her door handle. She pictured the news of her promotion spreading like a gasoline fire across the floor. "Why?" Julia said. "What are you talking about?"

Monique leaned in confidentially. "I really liked the sweet ones you made last year, the ones with the pineapple in them." Then, conspiratorially: "What do I have to do to get you to sneak me an extra batch?"

Julia breathed and felt the door handle slip from her grasp. Monique was referring to a promise Julia had made in passing to some of her co-workers a few weeks earlier—to make tamales for the company holiday party. She had made them the year before and people had raved about them for weeks afterward. With this year's party approaching, people had begun hinting that they hoped she would make them again.

"I don't want to make more work for you," Monique said, "but my kids love them. I'd be happy to pay you for them."

"Sure," Julia said. "Please don't say anything, though. If people know I'm making extras for you . . ."

Monique smiled and locked her lips with an invisible key, then bounced away.

"I told you last year was the last time," Marta said when Julia asked her later that day if she would help her make the tamales.

Julia held her cell phone to her ear with one hand while she packed an overnight bag for her trip to San Diego with the other.

"I'll give you my recipe, but I'm not slaving in a kitchen for ten hours to help you look good at the office."

"I can't do it by myself," Julia said. "They come out terrible when I make them."

"That's because you don't have the soul of a Mexican. You're too pocha. It's a curse when it comes to tamales."

"Which is why I need you."

"My tamale-making days ended with my divorce. Last year was an exception because I felt sorry for you."

"Fine. Maybe Ime will help me."

Marta chortled. "Good luck. She's the worst cook ever. Plus, she seemed awfully depressed the last time I saw her. You don't want that kind of negativity getting into the tamales."

"Depressed? About what?"

"I don't know. She never gives me details. I rely on you for that. Call her."

As soon as she was off the line with Marta, she did, reluctantly. Although she and Ime had been in touch sporadically since the Auto Show, Julia had been keeping their conversations short and had put off seeing her in person until Ilario was fired. She thought Ime would blame her less for not saying anything if she could claim fewer opportunities in which to have done so. Guilt played its part, too. During their few brief phone conversations, it snaked around her, squeezing the air out of her lungs, making natural conversation impossible.

When Ime answered, she sounded even more depressed than Marta had described. Her voice sounded as though it were coming through layers of glass.

"You need to speak up," Julia said. "I can barely hear you."

"I'm sorry, I have a little bit of a cold," Ime said.

To Julia it sounded far worse than a cold. "Is everything all right?"

"I think this is it," Ime said. "I think Ilario is really going to break up with me."

"Why do you say that? Did you do something?"

"I pushed his stupid ex-girlfriend through a waterfall. Isn't that enough?"

Julia zipped her overnight bag shut and moved it to the floor before sitting down on her bed. "Ime, you've thought he was going to break up with you before and—"

"No. This time something is different. Lydia must have told him about what I did at the Auto Show. I spent the day with him yesterday and he didn't smile once. He's been like that for days. I think it's over, Julia."

Julia hooked a finger through one of the rosette eyes of her crocheted bedcover. She ventured, "Couldn't it just be that something at work is bothering him?"

"That's what he said when I asked him," Ime said.

"Did he say what, specifically?"

"No," Ime said. "Not really. I don't remember, really."

"Did he say anything about . . . me going to San Diego?"

"No," Ime said. "Why? I mean, what does that matter?"

"No, nothing," Julia said. "It doesn't."

"I can tell something is up," Ime said. "Everything is different all of a sudden. I stayed over last night, but when I woke up he was already out of bed and dressed. He always waits for me to get up and shower first."

He knows, Julia thought. Ilario knows. He had seen the change in her behavior, and Roger's sending her to San Diego was probably adding to his suspicions. How much he knew, she wasn't sure. Things were turning bad for him, he knew that much.

"Listen," Julia said, "things at work have been kind of . . . strange recently. If he says that something at work is bothering him, I think you should believe him. I don't think he's making that up."

"Really?" Ime said. "What's going on there? He won't tell me. What would affect him this way?"

"It's kind of complicated to explain," Julia said.

"He did say something about that boss of his coming back to the office. He's not looking forward to that."

"Everyone's a little nervous about him coming back," Julia said. "Anyway, if Ilario says it's about work, I wouldn't doubt him."

"I hope you're right," Ime said. "But . . . I still have this feeling.

I've had it ever since Lydia got here, and it's not just because I'm jealous of her. It just feels like it's the end, you know? Like it's the end and there's nothing I can do to keep it from coming."

The defeat in Ime's voice was so uncharacteristic that it made Julia want to reach through the phone and touch her. She wanted to tell her that contrary to everything she was thinking, Ilario was going to be turning to her soon for her support, not turning away. She wanted to explain everything and ask her to forgive her for what was about to happen. It wasn't my idea, it just happened, please, please don't blame me. But under the circumstances, there was little she could say—little she could offer beyond reassurances so vague she was embarrassed to hear herself utter them.

Once off the phone, Julia took her bag down to her car and got on the road. Although San Diego was only 130 miles away, the drive nearly always took about three hours, with traffic giving her more time than she wanted in which to anticipate how Ime and Ilario would react to the news. She imagined the two of them turning to each other in solace, the bond between them strengthening, pushing Julia further away. As she drove, Julia practiced what she would say. To herself she offered the only words she could think of that were of any comfort: This will all be over soon. This will all be over soon. This will all be over soon. This will all be over soon.

≈ 25 ≈

Merry Christmas, Good-bye,
I'll Miss You

Julia completed her training in San Diego and returned to the office in time to join the rest of the sales staff in welcoming Roger back to work. In the Sierra Room a spread of bagels, gourmet pastries, and coffee had been laid out in his honor. Roger appeared in particularly high spirits as he once again recounted his roller-coaster accident. He seemed to delight in the horror he elicited from his listeners, and offered more and more gruesome details of waking up in the emergency room to find bones breaking through flesh. He drew nervous laughter by joking that he was sorry to disappoint everyone at Ostin Security by not only surviving but recovering so quickly. Julia looked around for Ilario but didn't see him. Was it possible that in her absence Roger had already let him go? That question was answered when Monique told her that Roger had sent him out to see a customer who, as far as Julia recalled, was not due for a visit. A glance from Roger confirmed what she was thinking—true to his word, he was keeping Ilario out of her way.

After a few minutes, she went to her desk and booted up her computer to discover that Ilario had e-mailed her from a remote location. The e-mail was tagged with an "urgent" icon, a tiny red flag waving above the subject line. She opened and read the e-mail:

> I need to talk to you about something in person. I'll be back in the office at 5. Will you still be there???

The three question marks hinted at a growing desperation. She was not ready to face Ilario. She looked at her watch. It was 9:30. She closed the e-mail, but the red flag kept flickering. She erased the message. At 4:30, she turned off her computer and headed out. She was pulling out of the company lot just as Ilario pulled in. It was too late to pretend she hadn't seen him. Traversing a speed bump in opposite directions, they gave each other friendly waves, but she could not mistake Ilario's look of bewilderment and . . . agony. There was no other word for it. It dragged across her heart like a shard of glass, exposing a throbbing guilt the likes of which she had never experienced before.

She tried calling Nina but got no answer. She needed a distraction, and the only one that came to mind was to shop for the ingredients for the tamales she had promised for the company holiday party. She drove to the Victoria Market in San Fernando, the same Mexican goods store her mother and her friends' mothers used to shop at when Julia was a girl. Entering the store, her nose began to twitch at the charred, smoky smell of ancho chiles drying on lines above the register. The same gray-haired old woman who had once helped her mother greeted her with a nod and a smile. The woman's hands and face were now as tough and crinkled as the drying chiles above her head. Julia placed her order for the masa and husks, asked the woman if she knew of a carnicería that had good pork, then thanked her and headed out to her car. It was then that she saw Roberto, Nina's fiancé, coming out of the hardware store across the street.

She jangled her keys overhead. "Roberto! Over here! How are you?"

As he turned to look, Roberto's face lit up. He crossed the street, grinning widely through his dense beard. He gave Julia a great crushing hug. An affable, burly man, Roberto never failed to elicit in Julia a flutter of pleasure on seeing him. Because he worked nights as a security guard and sometimes during the day doing odd repair jobs, Julia rarely got to see him. Today he was an especially bright spot in her day.

"How great to run into you," she said, brushing what appeared to be wood drill shavings from his gray flannel shirt. "Look at you . . . always working. I hope you and Nina are going to take a real honeymoon. Have you talked about it?"

With a roll of his eyes he said, "We'll see what we can afford after I finish fixing up Nina's place. Did she tell you that I'm moving in with her after we get married? She wants me to fix a few things before I do. Today I'm putting up a door on the bedroom." He opened a plastic bag to show her the hinges he'd just bought. "Why now all of a sudden she wants a door on her bedroom I can't tell you. But I love her, so what am I going to do?" He glanced at the storefront of the Victoria Market. "Are you making tamales again this year?"

She told him she was. He patted his belly, which had grown out a bit farther over his belt since the last time she had seen him. "I better stay away from them this year," he said. "Nina says she doesn't want me looking like a pansón in our wedding pictures. I have to thank you, by the way, Julia."

"Me? What for?"

"For convincing Nina to marry me."

"I didn't convince her," Julia said.

"You did," Roberto said. "She looks up to you and listens to you. You've always been on my side, Julia. I never knew I could be this happy, and it's thanks to you."

As much as Julia would have loved to bask in Roberto's gratitude, she was unable to shake the image of Nina and Remedios
standing naked in the very doorframe Roberto was now charged
with repairing. Only now, as she gazed upon Roberto's happiness,
did she see how truly reckless Nina had been. By the time she finished talking to Roberto, she was quite angry with Nina. But it was
Remedios she called as soon as Roberto had said good-bye and was
out of sight.

Remedios agreed to come over on Sunday and help Julia make the
tamales. Julia hoped to casually extract from her a promise to
keep what had happened between her and Nina to herself. But
no sooner had she come through the door than Remedios let loose
with: "Can you believe that little friend of yours really thinks I'm
going to stay quiet like nothing happened between us?" She tore
off her sweatshirt and rolled her shirtsleeves to the elbows. Julia
invited her into the kitchen, where she had set out bags of corn
husks for cleaning. As they sat down across from each other, Remedios said, "She has a lot of nerve acting like it was nothing after
the way she threw herself at me."

It was hard for Julia to envision Nina "throwing" herself at anyone, but Remedios did not appear to be in a mood to be contra-
dicted. Julia pushed a stack of leaves toward her. Remedios began
ripping out fistfuls of reddish fibers. "It wasn't like she had never
done this before, either," Remedios said. "She dived right in, if you
know what I mean. She didn't need lessons."

Troubled by the picture Remedios was painting, Julia ventured,
"Nina does strange things sometimes when she's under stress."

"Maybe it was stress, maybe it wasn't," Remedios said. She
arched her long back and grimaced. "I think I hurt my spine. I
swear, Julia, she was like a pit bull on a tenderloin."

As hard as it was to picture Nina as a ravenous sexual beast, Julia saw no reason to doubt Remedios's version of events. After a minute or two, Julia said, "Rem, I hope you understand how important this wedding is to Nina."

Remedios stopped stripping husks and stared. "What are you saying?"

"Nothing, just—"

"You think I would do something to hurt her?"

"No, no, I just—"

"After all this time, Julia, haven't I proved to you that I've changed? You actually think I would . . . what? Go to Roberto and tell him his fiancée likes to throw herself at skirt? Do you really think so little of me? Still?"

"That's not what I'm saying," Julia said, hoping her backpedaling didn't seem too desperate. "I'm just saying that I hope you don't think . . . given what happened between you and Nina . . . that there's any possibility that the two of you might . . . you know . . ."

"You think I'm *interested* in her? In *Nina*?" Remedios gave a laugh so high and sharp it made Julia jump. "Oh, Julia, please tell me you're not serious. No offense to Nina, but do you think she's the best I can do?"

"Well, fine," Julia said, blushing. "I didn't know. But if you're not interested in her, there's no harm in forgetting about what happened."

Remedios went back to stripping leaves. "Fine," she said after a couple of minutes. "If it's really important to you, I'm willing not to say anything. But"—she eyed her intently down the blade of a husk—"if anyone asks me anything, I can't lie. Don't ask, don't tell, that will be my policy."

Julia nodded and thanked her, adding, "It might sound silly to you, but right now Nina's wedding is the one thing I have to look forward to that isn't . . . complicated. I need that right now, Rem. It might sound selfish, but I really do."

Remedios dismissed this with a grunt. The rustling sound of the husks filled the space between them. When the pile became too high to support any more husks, Remedios gathered them in her arms and stood them upright in a paper bag next to her chair. "Me and Nina," she muttered. "The idea of it."

On Monday, Roger pulled Julia aside and told her that he appreciated how hard she had been working, and if she felt she needed a day off, Wednesday would be a good day. From the look he gave her, she gathered that he intended to let Ilario go that day, and that it would be best for everyone if she were not there. She thanked him and he nodded knowingly before disappearing down the corridor.

Her stomach made a fast, hard turn. The walls of her office seemed to brace themselves for what was coming. Tomorrow, Tuesday, she would be out of the office on customer visits. That meant that today was the last time she would see him.

The realization fell on her like a weight. Where was the relief that ought to have come with knowing he would be gone soon? The tightening in her stomach inched up into her chest. She looked at her watch. If she slipped out a few minutes early, she could avoid Ilario altogether. That would be the smart thing to do.

It would have been. But the thought of leaving without some final word was unbearable to her. She needed to say *something* to him. But what could she say? Good-bye? Thanks for everything? I'm sorry? Of course not. There were not words she could offer, nothing that could have any meaning. Even so, moments later she found herself standing in his office doorway as she had so many times before, awkwardly waiting for him to look up and notice her.

"Yes?" he said. "Do you want something?" He was poring over figures of some sort, his brow furrowed and his left hand tensing around a red pen. She had never noticed before that he was left-handed. It was a strange thing to notice now.

"It's nothing," she said. "I can see you're busy—"

He snapped the pen down irritably. "No. Please. You're here. What?"

"I'm sorry I didn't answer your e-mail the other day. I meant to, but I got distracted, and by the time I remembered . . ." Why was she bringing this up? What was the point?

"If it had been important," he said with a hostile shift in his chair, "I would have reminded you. It wasn't."

"Good. Good," she said.

"That's all?"

"I just wanted you to know . . ."

"What?"

"I wrote up a summary of what I learned in San Diego."

"E-mail it to me."

"It's on its way. Also, Ilario, I just . . ."

"Yes?"

"I know things have been . . . that I've been inaccessible recently. I have a friend that's been having problems, and I've been distracted and . . . I'm sorry about that."

"You're sorry. Fine. Got it."

He continued to look down at his work. He did not seem to be looking at it so much as glaring through it—through the paper, through his desk, through his shoes, through the floor. Julia had the impression that at any moment the paper on his desk might suddenly ignite from the heat of his gaze. But behind his anger she saw something else at work as well. She saw it leaking out from the soft corners of his eyes, his mouth. It was pain. The same pain she had seen when they had driven past each other in the parking lot a few days earlier. It encouraged her to go on with, "Before I left I just wanted—"

"Julia," he said. "I have a lot of work to do. I'm sure you can see that. I'm going to be here late enough as it is, so if you don't mind . . ." The sharpness in his voice failed to hold. His words choked off, absorbed by some other, greater emotion. It was then that Julia realized how much she was going to miss him. They had come so far in the last few weeks. Somehow, miraculously, they had gotten past their biggest differences. They had learned from each other, and had even come to understand each other at little. I'll miss you. That was what she had come to tell him. I'll miss you. But under the circumstances, there was no way to say anything of the sort.

"Merry Christmas," she said.

Without raising his head, he aimed an upward glance at her. "It's barely December," he said.

"I know. Just . . . Merry Christmas."

She went back to her office. She turned off her computer and lights and left the room. Merry Christmas. She hoped it meant something. She hoped it was enough.

A drink with Nina was in order. As if telepathically aware of Julia's desire for company, Nina called within the minute. But cocktails were not on her agenda. "I just came from the Cantina," she said. "I think Marta's in some kind of trouble."

Julia was trying to make a left-hand turn against a hostile stream of rush-hour traffic. As she was distracted by Nina's call, the light turned red, leaving her stuck in the intersection with horns blaring at her. She inched her way forward until someone in oncoming traffic let her through. "What kind of trouble?" Julia said. "Wait. Do I really want to know? Do I need to know?"

"I don't know much," Nina said. "I went by to pick her up for her fitting, but she wasn't there. One of the bartenders told me the police had just called her and asked her to come down to the station, so she took off."

"No," Julia said. "Tell me it's not true. What else did he say?"

"That's all I know," Nina said. "She wouldn't tell him anything else. But she was furious when she left. Do you think it has something to do with Diego?"

"Of course that's what I think! Didn't I say she and C were going to get in trouble? I can't let this be my problem."

"But it could be anyway," Nina said. "You let him stay a couple of nights at your place, didn't you?"

"No. No, no, no, no, no. He didn't stay at my place." She pushed the truth out of her mind. Why couldn't she deny it? People denied things all the time and got away with doing so. Why not her? Why not just this once? "Damn it!" she said. "Now of all times! Why?"

"Hold on," Nina said. "That's Marta. Let me see what's going on."

Julia bit her lip and waited. She wasn't going to let her anger get the better of her. How weak she had been not to stand up to Concepción! Now she was paying for it. Or she would be soon. But why Marta? Surely Concepción was the person they wanted to talk to.

Nina came back on the line. "She wants me to meet her at the Van Nuys station," she said. "She said something about bail money and needing me to bring a credit card."

"Bail money!" Julia said.

"That's all she would tell me," Nina said. "She sounded angry. Do you want to meet me there?"

Julia swung a hard U in the direction of Van Nuys. She zipped by strip mall after strip mall on Victory. At Sylmar, she cut left into the dense civic center area and parked in a structure that looked like a triple-layer cake.

Nina was waiting for her at the bottom of the steps in front of the elevated police station. "I'm afraid to go up," Nina said. "What if they arrest us, too?"

"We hardly did anything," Julia said. "They couldn't possibly care about us."

"What if Marta is ratting us out right now?" Nina said. "We could be walking into a trap."

Julia cast a worried look up the steps. "Do you think . . . ? No, no, we're just being paranoid. Come on." But as Julia climbed the steps, her heart started to race. She took the hard right at the top of the stairs and went in through the glass doors.

The station was nothing like what she had expected. In her imagination it had been alive with prostitutes spitting and swearing and gang members struggling in handcuffs. But the station could not have been more orderly. Two sergeants at the front desk worked on paperwork while a plastic radio leaked a thin stream of jazz. Julia was about to ask one of the men for help when Marta's voice made Julia and Nina turn.

"I'm sorry to drag you here," she said, rising from one of the waiting-room chairs. "Nina, I'll be able to write you a check as soon as I do another bank drop."

"What's going on?" Nina said as she handed over her credit card.

"It's my nephew, Juan," Marta said.

"Your *nephew*?"

"That's right. He started dating this girl a few weeks ago, but it didn't work out. He left some of his stuff at her place and tried to get in while she wasn't there. Someone thought he was breaking in and called the police. It's all a big misunderstanding."

Julia and Nina looked at each other.

"You didn't think that *I* did something, did you?" Marta said.

"No, no. We were just worried, that's all," Julia said.

Once Marta had taken care of the bail, Julia held open the station door for her and Nina. She was about to follow them out when a commotion caused her—against her better judgment—to look back. At the end of a long, thin corridor that ran past the front desk to the back of the station, she glimpsed one of the very prostitutes she had expected to see when she had walked in, a woman in a halter top and knee pants and heels being guided down the hall by police officers.

"You guys," Julia said. "Come back. You need to see this."

Marta and Nina stepped back. They followed Julia's gaze down the corridor to where the prostitute was demanding that the officers let her go. "I didn't do anything wrong!" Julia heard her say. "You weren't there. You don't know anything about it!"

A few seconds later the prostitute caught Julia and Marta and Nina looking at her. She stopped struggling and stared at them. But she was not a prostitute at all. With her hair in disarray and her hands cuffed behind her back, Concepción looked at them with wide, desperate, pleading eyes.

26

Tamales, Interrupted

We're fucked," Marta said. "Fucked, fucked, fucked, fucked, fucked, fucked, fucked, fucked, fucked." Her hands trembled as she tried to shake out a cigarette. At the station the police had refused to give any information about Concepción, so after posting bail for Marta's nephew, the women had gone into the first restaurant they had come to on Victory to wait for word from Concepción. The restaurant, a seedy little place with torn vinyl seating and dingy windows, made Julia feel all the more as though she and her friends had crossed over to the dark side of the law.

"We don't know anything yet," Nina said, folding and unfolding one corner of a grease-spotted paper menu. The triangular piece tore off in her hand. "This might not even have anything to do with Diego Ramirez."

"Of course it does!" Marta barked. "Concepción's in there right now ratting me out. Do you think she's going to take the fall alone? No. She's going to want company. That's us. That's *me*."

"Please, just take it easy," Julia said, trying to disguise her own panic. "There's nothing we can do but wait for more information."

"If we leave now," Marta said, "we can be at my sister's in TJ by nightfall. She can put us up until this blows over. At the very least, we should coordinate our stories. We can say that Diego threatened to kill Concepción if we didn't help him."

"What's the worst that can happen if we tell the truth?" Nina said.

"What's the worst that can happen if we tell Roberto about your lesbian love affair?" Marta said. "No, I'm not throwing away everything I've worked for because of that stupid C." Ignoring the nonsmoking regulations, she lit up and sucked hard, then added, "Ordinarily, the cops wouldn't care about a bunch of beaners hiding one of their own, but this is a celebrity situation. The more people they can take down, the better they look." She expelled a stream of smoke. "Fucking asshole shithead pigs."

When the waitress came by, Marta concealed her cigarette under the table and asked for a beer. Julia and Nina asked for coffees and a campechana to share. The waitress listlessly waved her hand through the smoky air, then scratched out the order. When she was gone, Marta brought her cigarette back into view. "I'll wait as long as it takes to finish my beer and three cigarettes. If we don't hear anything, I'm putting one of my bartenders in charge of the Cantina and jumping on the 405."

She managed a couple more puffs before everyone jumped at the sound of Julia's cell phone. She answered and heard Remedios say, "Are you aware that stupid puta you call a friend just got arrested?"

"She called you?" Julia said. "What did she say?" Julia angled her phone off her ear so Marta and Nina could hear.

"She wants me to come get her at the Van Nuys station. I don't have time for this, Julia. I'm behind on sending out invoices for the shop. You can get her, can't you?"

"Rem, I'm sorry she bothered you. We're sort of not talking right now. What else did she say?"

"She won't tell me what she did, but they're letting her go on bail and she's got an arraignment or something like that tomorrow. Are you going to get her or not?"

"I think it would be best if you did," Julia said. "Things are complicated with us right now. I can explain more later, now's not a good time to talk."

Silence ensued on Remedios's end, punctuated by bursts of grinding from the machine shop. "Fine," she said at last, "but you owe me. By the way, C says to tell you she needs the dance bag she left at your place back as soon as possible."

"You can come for it this weekend. I don't want her in my apartment. And Rem, one more favor, please. When you see her, get as much information as you can. I need to know if she's gotten anyone else in trouble, or just herself."

Reluctantly, Remedios said she'd try. "I didn't sign up for this kind of crap when I agreed to start hanging out with you putas again."

As Julia got off the phone, Marta climbed over Nina and out of the booth. "That's it. I'm gone. Good luck. We never met."

At home that night, Julia kept her phone close by as she waited for more news. The fact that Concepción had called Remedios and no one else probably meant that she had told the police everything, implicating them all. But so far the police hadn't contacted anyone but Concepción. If they'd wanted to talk to her or Marta, surely they would have done so by now. That had to be a good sign. But as the evening hours stretched on with no word from Concepción or Remedios, Julia grew more agitated, not less.

At ten o'clock, she turned on the news to see if there was any more mention of Diego. As a story about the holiday shopping season played out, Julia remembered what Remedios had said about

Concepción wanting to get her dance bag. It was strange that she would care about such a thing at a time like this. Julia remembered her climbing through her bathroom window to get it.

In a flash of heat and worry, Julia went into the bedroom and found the dance bag in her bedroom closet. In the time it had been sitting there Julia had given it little thought. Now two round vents on the side of the bag seemed like menacing eyes. She swept up the bag, put it on the bed, and unzipped it. She started removing Concepción's things. Makeup. Salsa shoes. Hair scrunchies. Tampons. A package of broken taco shells. What did she think she was going to find? Please let there be nothing out of the ordinary. Loose change, safety pins, birth control pills. Good. A movie stub, nail files, a wash cloth. Good, good, good. Nothing strange, nothing to worry about. She refilled the bag. Her body lightened with relief.

Her phone again. This time it was Ime.

"Ime. Hi. I hate to tell you what's been happening. Maybe you've already heard about C. . . . Ime? Are you there?" She heard only the *tick-click-tick* of a bad connection.

When Ime's voice came through, it sounded flat and metallic: "Ilario broke up with me."

Julia gasped. "How? When?"

"He met me after work to tell me. Didn't I tell you it was coming? I just wish it had been sooner. The waiting was the hardest part." She laughed bitterly. "You sound more surprised than I am."

Julia was. But what had she really known? She had barely spoken to Ilario since finding out she was going to be promoted. "What did he say?"

"That he loved me, but couldn't give me what I needed. What does that mean, Julia? It doesn't mean anything. And it's not the real reason."

"What then?"

"Lydia."

"No!"

"It's true."

"He said so?"

"More or less. I asked him if there was somebody else. He didn't say yes . . . but he didn't deny it, either. He didn't deny it, Julia."

Julia sat on the edge of the bed. She had been fully convinced that there was nothing between Ilario and Lydia. How could she have been so wrong? She recalled Ilario's recent mood, his aura of pain. It took on a different light now. This was what he had been struggling with. She remembered his e-mail saying that he needed to talk to her. Maybe all he had wanted was advice about Ime. He had turned to Julia for help before and she had given it. This time she had ignored him. This was the result.

"I don't know what to say," Julia said. "Do you want me to talk to him?" It was a stupid thing to offer, but the words came out before she could stop herself.

"No," Ime said. "I can't make him love me. He loves Lydia." Then, with the finality of a hammer driving a nail into a plank: "It's over."

Julia wondered how Ime would feel now if she knew what was about to happen to Ilario at work. Would it satisfy her sense of justice? Or would she still take Ilario's side over hers?

"Do you want me to come over?" Julia asked.

"No," Ime said.

"Do you want to come over here?"

"No. Just stay on the phone with me. Talk about something else. What were you going to tell me about C?"

Not wanting to give Ime anything more to worry about, Julia gave a murky version of how Concepción had hidden the actor. She made no mention of Concepción's arrest. As Julia talked, part of her mind tried to solve the puzzle of how she had so misread Ilario and Lydia. How could Ilario have fooled everyone completely? Was he really capable of that kind of deception?

Ime began to sob.

"Ime, are you sure you don't want me to come over?" Julia said.

"Well, I . . ."

A knock at the front door distracted Julia. "Shit. Ime, hold on. Somebody's here." She made her way to the door and pressed her eye to the peephole. On the other side, Detective Piper stood scratching his frowning face with the corner of a folded piece of paper.

He was flanked by two officers of about Marta's nephew's age, one of them Latino-looking, the other a tall, pasty blond. The detective wore the same mustard-yellow jacket he had sported before.

"Shit."

Ime drew in snot. "Who is it?"

"That thing I told you about C. It's a little more complicated than I made out. The police picked her up today, and now there's a detective at my door."

"What do they want with you?" Ime wasn't crying anymore.

"I can't explain now."

"You're worrying me. I'm coming over."

"No! Don't. Just keep your phone on. I'll call you."

She peered out. The detective's face was set in a hard block. What was the worst that could happen if she didn't answer? She watched his lips move as he conferred with the officers. She didn't have to answer. They would go away, they couldn't wait forever. He struck the door again with his fist. She yanked the door open.

"Detective. Hi. How can I help you?" Her words sounded sickly sweet and desperate. The detective did not smile. His eyes were already probing her living room as he unfolded the paper in his

hand with a gentle snap. "Search warrant," he said. "Officers Gómez, Gardiner. Can we?"

He barely gave Julia a chance to glance at the warrant before
crossing her threshold. Officers Gómez and Gardiner, by contrast,
smiled at her and diligently wiped their feet on the mat before entering. A nod of the detective's head was their go-ahead to begin
searching. They did a quick survey of the living room without
touching anything before the detective, with another nod of his
head, directed them to search the back of the apartment. He mumbled that he would join them in a minute. His gaze continued to
sweep the living room. Then he produced a small notepad and
began to write in quick, hard strokes.

"What's this all about?" Julia squeaked. She could barely believe how fake she sounded. Heat and shame burned her face.
She felt as though everything she knew about Diego and Concepción was written on her skin. The detective massaged his temple
with the eraser end of his pencil. His silence was unbearable.

Julia said, "I know you must be here about Diego Ramirez. I
tried to get my friend Concepción to call you. She's so stubborn!
You've talked to her by now, haven't you? Whatever she's telling
you, it's probably not the full truth. Please, I can tell you everything that happened. Just ask me, I'm happy to cooperate. Ask me
anything."

A faintly derisive smile crossed his lips. Did he think it was
funny that she was so eager to finger Concepción? Well, she was
tired. Tired, tired, tired of protecting her. She was going to tell the
truth. All the detective had to do was ask. Ask me, she thought. Ask
me anything.

The first time they had met, the detective had at least made a
passing effort to appear friendly. Now he was a hard surface as he
said, "How long did Diego Ramirez stay here?"

"Two days," Julia said.

"How did he end up here?"

"Concepción brought him."

"Why did she bring him here?"

"She was worried that the police were going to go by her place."

"And you told her it was OK for her to bring him here."

"No. She just showed up with him. She has a key. She and our friend Marta brought him over when I wasn't here. He was already here, hiding in the bedroom, the day you came by, only I didn't know it, I swear."

"And you agreed to keep him here?"

"I didn't. I begged them to get him out of here or to call the police, but they wouldn't listen."

"Why didn't *you* call the police?"

"I did eventually. But I didn't leave a name. I was scared. I didn't know what would happen."

"Did you and Diego talk much? Was he friendly with you?"

"I wasn't here at the same time he was here. I left. I went to stay at my friend Nina's. She can tell you. I didn't want anything to do with Diego or Concepción or Marta. This was all Concepción's doing. When I finally came to my senses, I called the police."

Each answer Julia gave felt like a step farther away from trouble, so she spoke honestly and openly. She told him about how she had come back to the apartment to find Diego alone. She told him everything she could remember him saying. "That was the only conversation I ever had with him," she said. "It didn't last more than a couple of minutes."

The detective nodded—approvingly, Julia thought. She sensed that she was telling him what he wanted to hear, and that he believed her. He didn't want to arrest her, he only wanted answers. Answers and whatever the officers were looking for in her bedroom. If she were in any serious sort of trouble, he would have told her by now.

After a couple more minutes of questioning, he directed her to follow him as he joined Gómez and Gardiner.

They were in the bedroom now. From the doorway she watched as they sorted through her belongings with gloved hands. They don't mean any harm to me, she thought. They're just looking for facts, for clues. There was nothing for them to find.

Or was there? Julia hadn't searched the apartment carefully since Diego had left it. What if he'd left something there, some piece of evidence that would make Julia look as though this was all her idea? Her brain started to thud. Gómez went to her closet and started running his hands between her dresses. Gardiner opened a dresser drawer and plucked through her underwear. Julia felt ill. She had nothing to hide, but she hated seeing them handle her things, the things that would touch her skin. She was going to have to wash everything.

"Is there something in particular you're looking for?" Julia said, a little more angrily than she would have liked.

"It's all on the warrant," the detective said without offering to show it to her again. Crouching down, he pulled back the dust ruffle and peered under Julia's bed.

"I haven't vacuumed in a while."

Gómez placed Concepción's dance bag on the bed and with gloved hands began going through it.

"There's nothing in there you'll care about," Julia said.

"Is it yours?" the detective said.

"It's Concepción's." Then, in a tone that was perhaps too chummy too fast, "What's up with her, anyway? She's something, isn't she? I bet you guys had your hands full with her."

Detective Piper asked Gómez to take Julia to the living room and wait there until he and Gardiner were done searching. With a friendly smile, Gómez led her out of the bedroom. Julia asked him if she could use the bathroom. He did a quick search of the room, then let her go in. She shut the door and locked it and called Marta. "They're here," Julia said when Marta picked up. "The cops."

"Fuck," Marta said. "Shit. Damn."

"I don't think we have anything to worry about. They asked me a bunch of questions, but I don't think they care about me—or you."

"What did they ask you?"

"Everything. And I told them everything."

"You did *what*?"

"I had to. And I don't think they care that you or I knew anything."

"Then what are they doing there?" Marta said.

"They're getting information. They're looking for something. C must have told them they could find something here. Maybe something that belongs to Diego."

"I don't know what that could be," Marta said.

"Me, either. I've already been through C's things. I didn't find anything besides her usual stuff."

"Did they say anything about me?"

"No. I don't think they care anything about us. You didn't let Diego stay at your place, so I doubt they're going to want to talk to you."

"I still think leaving is the best thing to do."

"Stay put," Julia said. "I'll call you as soon as they leave."

Julia got off the line, flushed the toilet, and splashed some water on her face. She looked in the mirror. What a wreck. Nervous and guilty-looking, no doubt about it. What was she really guilty of, after all, besides trying to protect her friends? She ran a comb through her hair, then opened the door and went out.

Instead of going into the living room with Gómez, she invited him into the kitchen. "I was going to put on some tamales," she said to him. "Is that all right? Would you like some?"

He told her it was fine if she wanted to put some on, but he wasn't allowed to have any. Good. He was letting her steam tamales. He wouldn't do that if they planned to arrest her. Gómez turned a chair out from the table, sat down, and crossed his legs. Julia opened her freezer. It was loaded top to bottom with bags of the tamales she and Remedios had made. She hadn't really intended to heat tamales at all, but she desperately needed something to do with her hands. She set a pot of water to boil. It felt good to keep busy. She set some tamales on the steamer insert and turned up the burner. Flames licked up the sides of the pot. She gave Gómez a smile. He looked like such a boy to her, inexperienced, with big cheeks and black fuzz struggling to form a mustache above his lip. Nothing to be afraid of. She turned to put the tamale bag back in the freezer. That was when she noticed Ilario standing at her front door.

One of the officers had left the door ajar, and either Ilario or a breeze had pushed it all the way open. He stood watching her. The pain of recent days had pushed its way up into his eyes, concentrating there in dusky pools. Fluorescent lights flickering in the courtyard behind him gave him the aura of a restless ghost.

Gómez rose from his chair.

"It's my boss from work," Julia said to him. She closed the freezer door and stepped out into the living room. Gómez followed.

"Ilario," Julia said, "what are you doing here?"

Ilario's eyes went from Julia to Gómez, then back. "Is everything all right? Why are there police here?"

"I'm fine," Julia said, coming farther into the room. "They're here about my friend Concepción. She's been having problems with the law. They're looking for something she might have left here. I'm just waiting for them to finish up."

Ilario took in Gómez critically for a few seconds before saying to Julia, "I'm sorry I didn't call. There's something I need to talk to you about. Is there any way we can talk in private?"

"I'm sorry," Gómez said. "I can't let you go anywhere until we're done." His voice suddenly sounded strong and authoritative. Julia would have thought this would be enough to make Ilario decide to come back later, but he appeared determined to speak to her.

Julia turned her back to Gómez. She took Ilario's sleeve and pulled him to the far side of the room, away from Gómez, and in a low voice said, "Ilario, obviously this is a bad time."

"I'll only take a minute," he said.

"I'm sorry about what happened with you and Ime, I really am, but I can't be getting involved."

"That's not what I came here to talk to you about," he said. From the nervous way his eyes moved, it was clear that he had something important to say. Julia had things to say to him, too. Had the officer not been standing a few feet away, she might have demanded answers from Ilario on behalf of Ime. How could anyone have deceived her the way he had?

"I need to talk to you about how things have been at work," Ilario said. "You've been avoiding me. We need to talk about why."

Julia couldn't believe it. The police were searching her apartment, he had just broken up with Ime, and he wanted to talk about how things were at *work*?

"Ever since Lydia moved to L.A., I've been thinking about things," he said. "She's always been like a compass to me. You know we were engaged once. If it weren't for her moving here, I wouldn't have started to see things the way I have recently."

"Fine, Ilario. You've found Lydia. I'm happy for you. But aside from the fact that this isn't the time, you don't owe me any explanations. Be with Lydia, that's fine with me. It's not going to affect us at work."

"Is everything all right there?" Gómez said.

"Yes, yes, it's fine," Julia said. To Ilario she said, "Let's talk about this some other time, OK?" She tried to guide him to the door, but he didn't move.

"You don't understand what I'm trying to say, do you?" he said.

Whatever Ilario was trying to unburden himself of, Julia wanted no part of it. She tried to get by him, but he blocked her. She felt him trying to impart some truth to her with his eyes. Gómez was watching with interest. Julia could tell that Ilario wanted to say something more, but the officer's presence was preventing him. Then, rather than say anything at all, he kissed her.

He kissed her suddenly, in a way that made Julia think of a man thrusting his entire personal worth on a single spot on a gaming table. Julia was so stunned she hardly had time to resist before his lips and teeth ground uncomfortably into hers, splintering her thoughts. She shoved against his chest, freeing herself. "Ilario . . . what . . . are . . . you . . . *thinking*?"

Ilario's face flamed with embarrassment. He started toward her again, but Gómez muscled his way between him and Julia. "I think the two of you can finish this conversation some other time, don't you think?"

Julia stood back. The room swam. Ilario looked at her expectantly. His features appeared on the verge of fracturing depending on what she said or did next. She saw now with dizzying clarity how completely she had misconstrued his mood in recent days. It had had nothing to with the prospect of being fired. It had had nothing to do with being treated badly by Roger or the state of his relationship with Ime. Something else had been distracting him, building within him, eating away at him. As Julia began to understand that she was the reason for the changes she had seen in him, she felt a quiet quaking of her heart. It started gently, then gathered strength, reopening splinter fissures within her that she had long thought healed.

She took a step, reclosing the space between them by half. But before she could ask him what he really meant to say, Detective Piper and Officer Gardiner emerged from the back of the apartment.

Their faces were screened with an intense solemnity, but it was a forced kind of seriousness. Beneath it surged an unmistakable current of excitement.

"Ms. Juarez," the detective said, "we found this under your mattress."

Gardiner daintily, almost girlishly, held up a plastic evidence bag by its corner. The bag contained a shiny black revolver.

Ilario's gaze swung back and forth between the detective and Gardiner. "What's going on? Why are they . . ."

"You've never seen this gun before now?" Detective Piper said.

"What . . . no . . . no, I haven't," Julia said.

"Julia, what is that?" Ilario said. "Why are they . . ." He tried to come forward again, but Gómez again blocked him easily.

"Do you know what kind of gun this is?" Detective Piper said, taking the bag from Gómez and rolling it over in his hand. "It's a .38 Special. Circa 1930, from the looks of it."

"I don't know what that is," Julia said. "Where did you . . ."

Again Ilario tried to move forward. He tried to explain that he worked with Julia and knew her and that there had to be some kind of mistake. But the cops were not interested in anything he had to say and they would not let him near Julia.

"You've never seen this before now?" Detective Piper said to Julia. "Is that what you're saying?"

"I haven't," Julia said. "I don't know anything about that. Concepción didn't . . ."

"It looks just like the revolver that's missing from Diego Ramirez's gun collection," Detective Piper said. "The same one he used to kill his ex-wife."

"He didn't," Julia said. "He said he was framed. He said that his manager . . ."

The detective gave a knowing little laugh. "Yeah. Right." He handed the gun back to Gómez, then told Julia that she was being arrested for concealing evidence and being an accessory after the fact in a murder.

The room began to flood with strange colors as the detective read her her rights, a staccato spray of meaningless words. She did not say anything as the detective placed handcuffs on her, their heft and pressure and coolness strangely comforting. She interjected nothing as Ilario's bewilderment grew, as he began to demand an explanation, telling them again that he worked with Julia, that he knew her well, that there had to be a mistake. She did not say anything about the tamales she had set to steam in the kitchen, the scent of which was only now beginning to reach them tauntingly. She did not resist as they escorted her to the door. Instead, she watched Ilario. She watched his confusion and distress. She watched his eyes and his hands. She searched for any sign of what she believed anyone in his situation ought to be thinking—that he had made a terrible mistake in coming; that in his eagerness he had acted too soon and too recklessly; that he wished he could retract his actions and his words.

27

Accessory After the Fact

The more Julia talked, the more unbelievable her story sounded to her own ears. She understood why the police thought she was more involved than she was. Still, she hated them for not believing her. What was Concepción telling them, and why hadn't she explained to them that Julia knew nothing about the gun? After a few more minutes, Julia realized with a creeping horror that she had made a huge mistake in talking without a lawyer. She told the detective that she didn't want to answer any more questions. To her surprise, he abruptly agreed to let her call someone to make bail for her.

Using the greasy phone the detective provided, she called Ime, the person who had always come to her rescue in the past, but there was no answer. She tried a couple more times, only to get her voice mail. Only then did it occur to her that Remedios might be a better person to call. Despite the fact that she was likely to yell at Julia for waking her, she felt confident that Remedios would jump to her aid.

The irritation in Remedios's voice when she answered was superficial. Beneath it Julia heard an eagerness to be of use. "I had a feeling I'd be hearing from you," Remedios said. "I'll take care of bail and pick you up on Sylmar behind the station."

When she arrived about an hour later, Julia burst into tears. After a long hug, Remedios said, "You don't deserve this, Julia."

"Did you talk to Ime or something?" Julia said. "How did you know I was going to be calling?"

"I didn't need to talk to her. I heard your name on the news last night."

"No! Oh, God, please say it's not so."

"I'm sorry, but it's true. I was flipping through the channels when I heard your name. Of course they didn't pronounce it right, but I knew it was you. One reporter even did a story from in front of your building. He was interviewing your neighbors and asking them if they had seen Diego Ramirez." A restrained pride infected her voice. "So you were hiding the gun he used to kill his ex?"

"No! I didn't know anything about it. God, this is the worst thing that's ever happened to me, Rem, and I really didn't even do anything!" She felt her stomach flip.

It must have been apparent that she felt sick, because Remedios said, "If you're going to throw up, do it now. I just had my car detailed."

On the drive home, Remedios sped through the empty streets, gunning for the yellow lights. "The first thing we need to do," she said, "is get you a lawyer. I've already been looking into it. My last girlfriend married a snob huera attorney who ought to be able to help you. I swore I would never speak to my bitch ex-girlfriend again, but given the circumstances, I called her. She feels guilty and she owes me, so we should take advantage."

"Oh, God, Remedios, that would be wonderful. I really need help. I don't even know what I'm supposed to do next."

"I've already set up an appointment for you to talk to her tomorrow morning."

"Seriously? My God, Rem, thank you. You don't know how much that means to me. I knew you were the right person to call."

"Well, just don't make a habit of it," Remedios said. "Don't worry, don't worry, we'll figure out what to do together, OK?"

Julia conceded with silence. It was a relief to have Remedios take charge. From her smile it was clear that she was deriving enormous pleasure from being able to help. Julia had no idea if she could afford a lawyer. But now wasn't the time to bring up the subject. She was too grateful to have Remedios's help and company.

"Rem," Julia said, "what station was it that you heard my name on?"

"Pretty much all of them," Remedios said.

"All of L.A. knows?"

Remedios cast a sympathetic glance in her direction. "Pobrecita," she said. "This is a national story. I nearly shit my chones when John Quiñones said your name."

When Julia got home, she was overcome with the desire to put her head down. She did not think she had ever felt so tired. Her mind was swirling with thoughts and fears, but her body felt as though someone had poured lead into her veins. But checking her messages, she realized it would be a mistake to go to sleep now, for her voice mail was full of messages from reporters and TV people wanting to know if she was the same Julia Juarez whose name had been floated by the police. She imagined people showing up at her door in the morning wanting to talk to her. She imagined being pursued by cameras as she tried to get to her car. Did things like that really happen to people outside of the movies? She wasn't sure. She didn't want to find out.

Her head throbbing painfully, she dialed Nina and kept redialing until Nina answered. "I'm sorry to wake you," she said. "I need a place to stay again."

Julia got to Nina's house at about 3 A.M. Nina came to the door with a great tuft of hair jutting out from the side of her head as though she had just emerged sideways from a wind tunnel. With eyes barely open and lips sticking together, she mumbled something about the late hour and toilet paper being on sale at Ralph's. Julia apologized for waking her. "OK, OK," Nina said as she shuffled like a zombie back to her room. "We'll talk in the morning. Ralph's. Crest. Three for $4.99 plus tax."

Julia settled in on Nina's couch. Sleeping turned out to be harder than expected. Not only was Julia's mind racing with the events of the day, but also Nina's couch felt much harder than the last time she had slept on it. She wondered if Nina had replaced the cushions in anticipation of her new life with Roberto. Julia closed her eyes and tried to sleep. In her head faces swirled and voices competed. She could still hear the detective badgering her with questions, and Ime lamenting her breakup, and Remedios directing her as to what to do. But strangely, Ilario's voice rang louder than these other voices. And his was the last voice she heard as she slipped over the ledge into sleep.

When Julia awoke a few hours later the first thing she did was check her voice mail to see if Ime had called during the night. What she found instead, mixed in with various messages from reporters, were several messages from Ilario. He had gone by the police station the night before hoping to see her, but the police had refused to give him any information. He had waited there until one in the morning before giving up and returning home. He wanted to know if there was anything he could do to help her. He was sorry, deeply sorry, for impulsively showing up at her place. There was much more they needed to talk about, though he realized that now wasn't the time. "I hope you'll call me," he said. "Let me know you're all right."

Ilario was right. Now wasn't the time. The idea that he loved her—if he really did, if this wasn't some kind of delusion he had created to distract himself from bigger problems of work and a deteriorating relationship with Ime—was too much to even consider. Julia had far more pressing things to worry about. She got dressed and ready for her appointment with Remedios's ex-girlfriend's girlfriend.

In her law offices in Burbank, Brenda—a stout, amiable woman of about thirty-five with thick white hair—greeted Julia warmly. Julia felt immediately reassured by her calm, steady voice, and by the warm, soft colors of her office. "Go ahead," she told Julia. "Tell me everything the way it happened."

Julia talked. By the time she was done, she felt as hopelessly depleted as she had after hours of questioning by the detective. Again she found herself fighting back tears. But Brenda's next words recharged Julia with hope: "You have a lot working in your favor."

"I do? What?"

"You have people who can corroborate that you weren't at your apartment at the same time Diego was. You had almost no prior contact with him. You've never been in trouble with the law before. I'm willing to bet the DA agrees to substantially reduced charges."

"Reduced charges?" Julia said. "What does that mean?"

"It could mean a number of things. He might drop the accessory charge if you'll plead to the concealment charge, or vice versa. He might reduce one or both charges to a misdemeanor. Most likely, you'd be looking at a suspended sentence or a fine or both."

"Seriously?" Julia said, sitting forward in her chair. "I might just have to pay a fine?"

"The DA's office isn't going to want a trial. They'll plea bargain. They always do in cases like this."

"That would be wonderful," Julia said. "You can really make that happen?"

"Like I said, it's pretty standard. On the other hand . . ."

"On the other hand? No, no, no. I like *this* hand."

"The fact that there's a celebrity involved could change things a bit."

"How? How could it change things?"

Brenda shrugged and twisted left and right a couple of times in her chair. "I'm not sure. I've never dealt with a case involving a celebrity of this stature before. It could put a different spin on things."

"Please," Julia said. "Do whatever you have to. I'm happy to pay a fine. I don't even care how much it is. I can't be a felon. I don't want to go to jail."

Brenda's features softened sympathetically. "I doubt you'll spend any time in jail. In the meantime, it would help if your friend came clean about the gun you say she hid. It's working against you. It would do you a world of good if she fessed up."

Julia left Brenda's office buoyed by what she had learned. The attorney's fees were going to be a strain, but she was grateful for the hope she had just been given. A fine. She could deal with that. A suspended sentence. That seemed fair. On her way out of the building, she stopped in the lobby, dialed Concepción, got her voice mail. "Call me," she said, trying to sound as nonthreatening as possible. "We're both in trouble and I think we can help each other."

Julia's sense of relief lasted through the rest of the day and the following day. But by Thursday, the thought of facing her co-workers began to weigh on her. She prayed that no one at the office would believe that the Julia Juarez they worked with could possibly be the same Julia Juarez who had helped a murderer. She hoped Ilario hadn't had a chance to say anything to anyone about what he had witnessed before Roger had fired him the next day.

Thursday morning, trying to appear as calm as possible, she walked into the building and nodded and said hello to some of her co-workers as she passed them. They smiled and nodded back. She detected nothing unusual in the way they regarded her. Maybe, just maybe, no one had made the connection. And if someone had . . . well, she could laugh, couldn't she? *Me, hiding a fugitive? That's so funny! Yes, I heard that name on the news, too. Everyone's been calling me asking about it. . . .*

She made it to her office and sat down. Her racing heart slowed a bit. Thank God she had kept her personal life separate from the office as well as she had. But she had not so much as booted up her computer when Roger poked his head in. "Can I see you in my office?"

Her heart sped up again. She nodded and said she would be there, then grabbed a notepad and a pen. She passed Ilario's old office, vacant now, the lights turned off. The sight of the dark room was so jarring that she nearly stumbled. Ilario was really gone. She suddenly felt exposed to danger. Only now did she feel how much of a buffer Ilario had been, absorbing Roger's anger.

She knocked at Roger's door and went in, then pulled up a chair across from him. "Is everything all right, Julia?" he said. Every crease and furrow in his face conveyed concern.

"Yes," Julia said. "Fine . . . I mean . . . I guess you heard the news. It's not going to affect anything here, Roger. It's a big misunderstanding. I met with a lawyer on Tuesday. Everything's going to be fine."

"So you have a lawyer," Roger said. "I'm glad to hear it. Is he good?"

"She," Julia said. "Yes, I think so. I mean, I've never needed a lawyer for anything, but I think she knows what she's doing."

"Good, good," Roger said with exaggerated relief. "I have a couple of names I could pass on to you, but it sounds like you have things under control."

"I do," Julia said, a little relieved. "I do."

"Good, good, good. If there's anything I can do, you'll let me know, won't you?"

"Thanks, Roger. I'm just hoping it will all be taken care of before too many people find out."

"I'll be completely discreet," Roger said.

"Thank you. And Roger . . . I'm really looking forward to starting in the management job."

Roger shifted in his chair. He cleared his throat. "I did want to talk to you about that," he said.

"You did?"

He nodded. "I'm thinking that, given your current situation, we should hold off a bit. I don't want you taking on that level of responsibility while you have this . . . other thing to take care of."

"Roger, that's not necessary. I can really handle this. The job, this situation, everything."

"It's important," he said, "that I think about what's best for the company."

"I care about what's best for the company, too," she said. "Roger, I'm telling you, this isn't a problem. It's a temporary thing, it'll all be cleared up—"

"I know, I know. I'm sure everything will be fine. But let's not go down that path until we're both sure, hmm? Then, at that point, we can talk again and . . . see where things are."

"See where things are? But Roger, I thought . . ."

He threw up a stiff smile. It was like a gate closing off the one avenue she needed to get to. "We'll talk, Julia. Good luck . . . with everything."

He turned his attention to his computer. Julia stood for several seconds before moving to the door. She stopped and looked back. "By the way," she said. "How did things go with Ilario on Wednesday?"

Still smiling unnaturally, he looked up at her and said, "It's funny you should mention it. Ilario ended up quitting Wednesday morning."

"He did?"

"He did. Isn't that something? So it turns out there was no need for anything . . . unpleasant." His smile was rigid. She nodded, then turned and left the room.

She imagined his smile floating off his face and following her down the hall. It followed her all the way to the women's restroom, where she made a hard right through the door and went into a stall and bent down. Every muscle in her body felt as though it were cramping. She heaved up a small bit of coffee, the only thing she had consumed that morning. It splattered against the side of the bowl. It was only a modicum of brown liquid, but the sound she made could have been mistaken for that of someone surrendering a portion of her soul.

. . .

Later that day, Julia called Ime again. She felt bad that she had turned so completely to Remedios rather than her for help. But for the third time since her arrest, there was no answer. A different kind of worry began to work its way into her heart.

⫷ 28 ⫸

Permission

The morning of her arraignment, Julia tried to reach Ime again, but still there was no answer. She left her another message. "If you're embarrassed by me, I can understand that," Julia said. "If you're depressed about Ilario, I understand that, too. But Ime, I need you. If there's any way you can come to the arraignment, it would mean so much to me. It's at ten at the courthouse."

She did not hear back. Waiting for Brenda on the civic center plaza, Julia grew dizzy and panicky. She had never before stood before a judge, not even for jury duty. She did not know what to expect. The monstrous metal-and-glass courthouse reigning at the south side of the plaza filled her with dread. The forecast had been for clear skies, but the windows of the courthouse reflected only steel gray clouds.

Brenda appeared across the plaza about five minutes later. At that distance, with her Armani man's suit and her stiff brush of white hair, she was indistinguishable from a middle-aged gentleman. Only when she was a few feet away did the feminine features of her face work their way into view. She squeezed Julia's

shoulder firmly. "Today is easy. You don't have to do or say anything. We'll enter a not-guilty plea and be out of there in five or
ten minutes."

"What about the DA?" Julia said. "Did you talk to him? What
about getting the charges reduced?"

"I've been talking to one of his deputies. I should hear something from him today about a plea bargain. Trust me, everything's
going to be fine. Let's just focus on the task at hand, OK?" She re-
shaped the dimple of her tie. "Ready?"

The arraignment concluded as quickly as Brenda had predicted.
The judge accepted the not-guilty plea, paperwork was signed, and
minutes later Julia and Brenda emerged on the plaza. "That wasn't
so bad, was it?" Brenda said. "We'll talk again tomorrow. Go back
to your life, try to forget about this. Let me handle everything.
You're in good hands."

On the plaza in front of the courthouse, Julia thanked Brenda
and said good-bye. She hadn't understood everything the judge
had said to Brenda or everything Brenda had said to the judge, but
Brenda's assurances that a plea bargain was in the works offered
her some relief. Julia looked up at the sky. In the few minutes they
had been inside, the sun had licked through the cloud layer in
several places. It felt good on her back and shoulders. She turned
to go back to her car, and saw Ime standing in the middle of the
plaza.

Julia bounced a couple of times and waved. Ime did not wave
back or call out to Julia. She remained still, like a statue that
had been erected there. She was wearing jeans and a T-shirt and
a Dodgers cap. Julia could not remember the last time she had
seen her dressed so casually. She was not even wearing makeup.

Stripped of color and chic, she appeared at once exposed and re-solved.

As Julia walked up to her, Ime said, "I got your message."

"The arraignment's over."

"I'm sorry C caused you so much trouble."

"Remedios put me in touch with a lawyer. Things are looking as good as I could hope for."

"That's good," Ime said.

A breeze picked up at their backs as they began to walk. Julia filled Ime in on all the details of her arrest and about how Concep-ción had hidden the actor and the gun in her apartment. She told her that she was wise to have kept her distance, lucky that she hadn't gotten caught up in Concepción's schemes. But Julia was hardly listening to her own words as she spoke. She was waiting for Ime to give her a sign that their old intimacy still remained, to of-fer some opening through which she could touch what they'd once had as friends. But Ime, absorbed with concerns of her own, seemed to be only half listening to Julia. After a couple of minutes, Julia's words trailed off like a wisp of sadness. Ime, turning her face up to the sun as if to draw strength from it, said, "That night the police were at your place, I was worried about you."

"Ime, I'm sorry about this whole mess—"

"Please," she said. Her eyelids fluttered. She came to a stop and said, "After I talked to you, I was worried. I didn't know what was happening. It sounded like you were in trouble. I waited for you to call back, and when you didn't, I got in my car and drove over to make sure you were OK. And I saw Ilario's car parked out in front of your building."

The breeze picked up around them, flipping Ime's hair and cre-ating ripples in her loose T-shirt. As if spurred on by the wind, Ime resumed walking.

"I couldn't understand why he would be there," she said. "My head was spinning. I sat in my car trying to understand. Why would Ilario be at my best friend's apartment after he had just broken up with me? It didn't make any sense. I thought maybe it wasn't really his car, but when I went to check I could see his briefcase in the backseat and the tie I had given him next to it. I went back to my car and sat there, trying to make sense of things, and trying to figure out what to do. Then I saw the police come out with you. And then I saw Ilario come out. He didn't see me. I sat in my car, just watching. The police drove away with you, but I stayed where I was. I waited for Ilario to get in his car and drive away, but he didn't. He just stood there on the sidewalk, looking in the direction of your building. I was watching him and he was looking at your building. Just looking and looking. He stayed like that for the longest time, Julia. The longest time."

"Ime, you have to know that I never, ever did anything or encouraged anything. I don't know what Ilario thinks, but—"

Ime stopped and faced her. Their walk had taken them beyond the plaza and onto Van Nuys Boulevard, into the hum and hustle of pedestrians and traffic. Ignoring the shoppers trying to get around them, Ime looked at Julia. Her eyes shimmered with expectation. "Do you love him, Julia?"

Julia's heart thundered. The sound of a bus blaring its horn as it swept by saved her from having to answer the question right away. Did she love Ilario? Certainly not in the crazed way she had when Ime had first been dating him, if such a thing could really be called love. But over time, as respect and appreciation had sprung up between them, so had a mutual affection, one that did not blind them to each other's flaws but accommodated them. So yes, she loved Ilario, or at least knew that love was possible. But there was no way to say any of this to Ime. For the sake of their friendship she said the only thing she felt she could.

"No, Ime."

Ime nodded. She seemed less convinced by Julia's response than resigned to it. Continuing down the street at the same cautious pace as before, she said, "I have something I have to confess to you."

"You can tell me anything," Julia said.

At a bus stop, Ime paused and pressed her backside against one of the tilting plastic seats. The bus that had swept by them had pulled over and absorbed all the passengers that had been waiting there. It was just driving away now, leaving the stop empty except for Julia and Ime. Ime gripped the seat on either side and looked up at the sky at a steep angle. "When Ilario showed up at C's Cinco de Mayo party, he was asking about you. About where you were from and what you were like. Anybody could have seen that he was there to see you. I don't remember everything I said, but I made it clear to him that you weren't interested in him. I made sure by the time he left he was interested in me instead."

"Why . . . would you do that?"

"I wasn't trying to be a bitch, I swear. I thought I was protecting you."

"From Ilario?"

"From yourself. You had just come off that whole office romance mess at your old job. It looked like you were going to repeat the same kind of mistake. I didn't want to see you creating problems for yourself at work again. That's what I thought I was doing, anyway. I thought I was doing you a favor."

It took a few seconds for Julia to pluck Ime's words from the loud traffic noise and make sense of them. "Ime, I don't understand. You could have told me this earlier."

"Maybe I should have," Ime said. "You have every right to be mad."

Julia hardly knew how she felt. It was a confusing thing to hear. But she knew that their friendship was more important than any betrayal involving a man. She said, "Whatever happened, happened. And anyway, if you think about it, if anything had started up between us, it *would* have been a disaster the moment Ilario became my boss."

"What about the fact that he loves you?"

The question was like a fast breeze blowing through Julia. Until now she had not looked directly at the question of whether Ilario really was in love with her, or whether he had simply confused his appreciation of her with something more than what it was. But Ime's words were like a spotlight on the truth. Ilario had been in love with her, and it had tormented him.

But as far as Julia was concerned, pursuing anything with Ilario was as impossible as it had always been. It didn't matter that Ime had done what she had done. They had been friends for too long for Julia to let something like this come between them. Friends had to be able to forgive each other. So it was not hard for Julia to say, "First Ilario liked me, then he started treating me terribly, now he loves me? What am I supposed to make of that, Ime?"

Ime hunched forward and rocked. "It's my fault he treated you badly." Another bus swung up noisily to the curb, discharging passengers. Ime waited until the bus had pulled away before she added, "I told him about how you slept with your old boss."

"Ime!"

"I told him you did it to get ahead," Ime said.

"What?" Ime's words were like bullets. "Why, Ime? Why would you tell him that?"

Ime said nothing. She shook her head. Julia couldn't tell if this indicated regret or uncertainty. But she understood now. This was why Ilario had been so cold to her when he and Ime had first been dating. This was the picture he'd had of her and had held on to for so long.

Julia was at a loss for something to say. She felt the urge to sit down. But there were only two seats at the bus stop, and the one Ime wasn't sitting in was broken. A searing pain passed through her, a hot crackling sorrow unlike anything she'd experienced before. She hugged herself as tears spilled over.

"Ime . . . Ime . . ."

"On some level I knew Ilario still liked you," Ime went on without looking at Julia. "I guess I wanted to make sure that nothing between you ever developed."

Julia looked out at the street. She had always known that Ime, being in love, might not defend her against Ilario as strongly as she would have wanted. But this was new.

"I think you should talk to Ilario," Ime said.

"Damn it, Ime, are you trying to test me? Is that what this is?"

I hate you right now, Ime. I really do. But I'm not letting go of you. Your friendship. I need it. I'm not ready to . . .

The muscles in Ime's face twitched. Julia stepped in front of her, casting a shadow directly over her. Ime would not look at her.

"What, Ime?" Julia said.

The strain in her face increased.

"What is it, Ime?"

Ime still would not look at her.

"Ime, what are you telling me? That whether I get together with Ilario or not, you and I can't be friends?"

Ime rocked herself harder. Her face blazed with shame, frustration. "You should know me by now," she said. "You should know me."

With that she pushed off from her seat in a way that made it clear that Julia was not to follow. Another bus swept up, stirring dust and paper. Passengers poured off. Through the crowd Julia watched until Ime was out of sight, swallowed up by people and distance. Maybe Julia didn't know her. Or maybe she had changed and Julia hadn't noticed. Maybe she had been blind all along. This much Julia did know: There was no point in going after Ime. Her heart grew heavier and heavier. The ache was unbearable.

~ 29 ~

An Office Visit

The next day, Brenda called to tell Julia that the deputy DA
had agreed to reduce the charges against her to a single
count of obstruction of justice, a misdemeanor. While the charge
carried a potential jail penalty, Brenda assured Julia that no judge
in his right mind would actually make her serve time given her
clean record and the unusual circumstances of her case. "We can
ask to have your arrest record wiped clean in exchange for community service," she said.

Julia was so relieved, she welled up with tears. She thanked
Brenda several times. She wanted to reach through the phone and
hug her.

"Save the tears for when you see my bill," Brenda said with an
unconvincing laugh. "I'll be in touch."

Julia floated through the next few hours as though a physical weight
had been lifted from her body. It did not take long, however, for
relief to give way to bewilderment. Over and over in her head she
ran through her and Ime's conversation on the plaza, trying to

process what had happened. She could not accept that their friendship was over. The idea that Ime didn't think she could stay friends with her because of Ilario weighed on her far more than any of the things she claimed to have told him. But it wasn't only thoughts of Ime that weighed on her. She began to think more and more about Ilario as well.

Since the night of her arrest, she had pushed all consideration of him to the outer reaches of her mind. But now, with the charges against her nearly resolved, and her world cleaved by what Ime had admitted to, the messages he had left her came flooding back. In one of them, he had explained how Lydia, noticing at the Auto Show that he was far more animated when talking to Julia than to Ime, had called him on his feelings for Julia. From that moment his feelings had only continued to grow. There had been no point in saying anything to Julia, of course. He doubted she would risk her career by getting involved with him, and he knew she was too loyal to Ime to hurt her. But when rumor touched his ear that he was about to be fired, half his reasons for keeping his feelings to himself had disappeared. This had been enough to convince him to take the risk and come by her place and speak to her.

As Julia played this and other messages from him back in her mind, the possibility of being with Ilario began to take shape in her heart, adding to her confusion. She was amazed at how much she wanted to speak to him. But she couldn't. She and Ime had been friends for far too long. No matter how angry Julia might become with her, they were still friends as far as she was concerned.

At the end of the week, Brenda called again to give Julia her next court date. "Did you ever talk to your friend Concepción?" Brenda said. "It would be really nice if she could come clean before we talk to the judge. If we got something in writing to show you had nothing to do with the gun, it would help with the sentencing."

A withering dread had kept Julia from calling her, but she realized now that she could not put it off any longer. Harnessing her anger for strength, she made her way during her lunch hour one day to the dance studio where Concepción normally taught Latin dance classes, mostly to Anglo housewives and their reluctant husbands.

Located on the second level of a severely weathered strip mall, the east-facing studio hovered above a nail salon and a fabric store. From the parking area Julia could see the dancers practicing what looked like a rumba or a samba. Climbing the outside steps up to the studio, Julia heard Concepción applauding her students as she cut the music and brought the class to an end. Julia waited outside the door as middle-aged couples poured out of the studio. When the last pair had left, Julia stepped into the doorway. Concepción was crouched in front of the CD player, removing a disc, a towel draped around her neck. Seeing Julia's reflection in the mirrors, she jerked upright. She covered her mouth, then ran toward Julia, her dancing heels *click-click*ing across the floor.

Julia tensed. Concepción stopped just short of hugging her. "Julia, I've been meaning to call you, I really have. How are you? I talked to Remedios and she said—"

"How could you, C?" Julia said. "Do you know the trouble you've caused me? I actually could have gone to jail because of you. Why haven't you told the police I wasn't involved?"

Concepción's entire body seemed to contract with shame. "I *want* to," she said, "but my lawyers aren't letting me say anything. They said the more I talk, the more likely I am to dig a hole for myself that I can't get out of. Julia, I'm so sorry. I have to listen to what they say, otherwise—"

"Back up a minute," Julia said. She gave a cartoonish waggle of her head. "Did you say *lawyers*?"

Concepción nodded. Sheepishly, she lifted a corner of the towel that hung around her neck to her mouth and bit it.

"How can you have *lawyers*?" Julia said. Concepción took a step back for each step Julia advanced. "Where are you getting the money for even *one* lawyer?" Julia had come intending to hire Brenda to represent Concepción in exchange for Concepción agreeing to tell the full truth. Now she was talking about *lawyers*? "How many law*yers* do you have?" Julia said.

Like a little girl being asked her age, Concepción bit her lip and raised three fingers.

"What?!" Julia said with a stomp of her foot. "How is that possible?"

"Well . . . I let Diego's people know that I was in trouble. Diego found out and asked his lawyers to help me. They're from the same firm that's defending him. He felt really bad for getting me into this, so he got me the very best, and . . ."

"The very best? The very *best*?" Spittle flew from Julia's lips. "You have a multimillion-dollar law firm representing you courtesy of Diego Ramirez?"

Julia advanced another step forward and Concepción took another step back. "Do you want me to talk to them?" she said. "Maybe I can get them to represent you, too. I don't know if Diego would pay for that, but I can ask him. He'd probably understand. Julia, these are really good lawyers. They've come up with all kinds of reasons why it's not really my fault that Diego stayed with me, things that I never would have thought of, and—"

"I don't want to hear what they're telling you," Julia said. "What I want is for you to come clean about everything. I want everything out in the open. I want all of my friends and everyone I work with to know that this was all your idea. I want them all to know that I didn't hide a murder weapon. Why did you do it, C? I still don't understand."

"You know I didn't mean to get you into trouble," Concepción said. "Diego asked me to hold on to the gun until he could find a way to prove that his manager framed him. Julia, I wish I could say that, but the lawyers—"

"Forget about the lawyers! You don't have to listen to them!" Trying to feed the guilt she could see seeping into Concepción's face, Julia said, "I know it's a tough situation, C. But I hope you'll give some serious thought to what's right. I hope all the years we've been friends means something to you."

She turned to walk away. She was at the door when Concepción said her name. Julia looked back. "What, C?"

"I heard them mention you on the news the other day."

"So?"

"Have you talked to any reporters?"

"No."

"Have reporters been by your place?"

"I don't know. I've been staying with Nina."

"Oh."

"Why do you ask?"

"Well . . . why do you think they want to talk to you but not me?"

"I don't know. Maybe because of the gun. Or because I was the last person to see Diego." She shrugged. "Either way, I guess they think I have a better story."

Julia was scheduled for a one thirty appointment, but putting on her work face at that moment was the last thing she felt like doing, so she drove aimlessly, nursing her anger. It was not only Concepción she was angry with. She had left several messages for Ime and still had not heard back. One thirty came and went. Were it not for the fact that she had left her jacket with Nina's house key in her office, she would have skipped out on work for the rest of the day. Instead she went back to the office and strode into the building, ready to square off with anyone who decided to confront her. But the person waiting for her in the reception area was the last person she thought she would ever see again.

Lydia rose from one of the two plush chairs angled off the far wall. "I know I should have called first," she said. "I wasn't sure if you'd call me back. I want to talk to you about Ilario."

Julia considered the obvious excuse: She was late for a meeting and couldn't talk. But instead she heard herself say, "Fine. Not here. My office."

She led Lydia down the corridor, past the office that had once been Ilario's. It was still vacant, dark. Passing it still made her uneasy. The open door was like a question impatiently demanding an answer.

"I'm sorry to hear about all the problems you've had with the police," Lydia said as Julia brought her into her office.

"It's all just about worked out," Julia said. "I'm facing a misdemeanor that probably won't amount to much." Why was she telling her this? It was none of her business. She closed her door and moved around to the far side of her desk. "I'm sure you didn't come here to talk to me about that." She pulled her skirt taut as she sat down and folded her hands. In spite of always having been warmly inclined toward Lydia, Julia felt the need to protect herself by appearing as professional as possible. "Did Ilario send you?"

"Yes and no," Lydia said. "He asked me to talk to you. I told him no. But for some reason at the last minute I decided to come. I don't know why. He doesn't know I'm here."

In her simple navy suit, Lydia looked stunning in an entirely different way than the other times Julia had seen her. The suit said she had arrived, and having done so, was not overly impressed by the surroundings. It was no wonder Ime hated her so. She was everything Ime aspired to be but hadn't quite achieved.

"I've never seen Ilario like this before," Lydia said. "I've known him for eight years, but I've never seen him this unhappy."

"I'm sorry about that," Julia said. "I don't know what to say. I mean, I'm sorry if he misconstrued anything I said, but—"

"That isn't all. He told me that the day before he quit that he did something he's never done before. He was in a sales meeting with a client that he'd been working on for almost a year. Finally the client said he'd sign on with Ilario if Ilario promised to discount his renewal rate. Ilario could easily have stretched the truth to him like I know he's done many times before to close the deal. But he didn't. The next day the client signed with another company instead."

"You mean . . ."

"He said he was picturing you there sitting with him. He was thinking about what you would have wanted him to do. Roger used it as an excuse to pressure him out." Lydia stepped closer to Julia's desk. "In all the years I've known Ilario, I've never seen him sacrifice a sale, much less a career, because of a woman. He loves you, Julia."

There was something at once accusatory and expectant in her look, as though she both held Julia responsible for making Ilario feel this way and saw it as Julia's obligation to do something about it.

"And has Ilario been looking for work?" Julia said, trying to get off the subject of love. The lump in her throat barely let her get the words out.

"He's already got a job offer. Spectral Lasers had been recruiting him when he found out he was going to be let go."

"Oh," Julia said. "He always lands on his feet, doesn't he?"

"Not always," Lydia said, and Julia could tell they were back on the subject of love.

Julia swallowed. She could not believe how close to the surface her emotions were. She squeezed a pencil in her hand.

Lydia said, "Ilario says he's been calling. He's not sure if he should keep trying."

"He shouldn't," Julia managed. "You must know that, Lydia. I mean . . . you must know that."

Lydia nodded. She folded her hands in her lap and looked down at them. Then she surprised Julia by simply saying, "You're right. I'm sorry. I shouldn't have come."

She was about to turn away when her gaze connected with something on Julia's desk. It was a photograph of Julia and Ime from when they were younger. She picked it up. "It says a lot about you that you're so loyal to Ime," she said. "It's one of the things Ilario says he likes so much about you." A faint smile hinted that the disappointment was as much hers as Ilario's. She set the picture down and was gone.

"Have you ever heard of such a thing?" Julia said. She paced while Nina positioned a rhinestone onto the front of her wedding dress. Nina looked uncertain. Whether about the rhinestone or Julia's story, Julia couldn't tell. "Who interferes like that?" Julia said.

Nina pulled a nearby standing lamp closer to where she sat on the couch. "Sometimes you do," she said.

"She doesn't know anything about me."

"She knows what Ilario told her. She knows what she saw."

"What did she think I was going to do, pour my heart out to her?"

"I thought you liked her," Nina said. She narrowed her eyes as she tried to thread a needle.

"Doesn't Ime count for anything? Does she think I can just for-get everything about her and go to Ilario?"

"Damn it!"

"What?"

"I jabbed myself."

"Let me help you."

Nina jerked her hand away irritably. "I can do it." She got up off the couch and disappeared into the kitchen. She came back with her finger in a Band-Aid.

Julia continued. "No matter how Ime may have hurt me, I can't do that to her. I still have to think about all the things she did for me. She stood by me all those years. Even if I never see her again, that has to count for something, it has to mean—"

"Stop," Nina said. She pushed her needle into her tomato cush-ion. "Just stop. *Please.*"

"I know this must be boring, but—"

"What's boring," Nina said, "is the way you always make ex-cuses for Ime like she's some queen with her own special set of standards."

"Nina, where's this coming from? What are you—"

"I'm talking about the fact that no matter what selfish things Ime does, you always forgive her even before she's figured out that she's done something wrong."

"I haven't forgiven her. But that doesn't mean I should shut the door on her, does it? You're not being fair. Ime may have screwed up, but she's our friend, she—"

"Is she?" Nina asked. She tossed the pincushion into her sewing kit and slapped the lid shut. "I mean, has she been? Maybe she was in the past, but was she being a friend when she decided to go out with Ilario even though she knew you liked him? Was she being a friend when she let Ilario think that you screwed your old boss in order to get ahead? Was she being a friend when she spent months not talking to you even though you had apologized a hundred times?" Nina tossed the sewing kit on the medical supply table that held the rest of her sewing supplies and swung it out of her way. "Where has she even *been* for the last year? We barely see her, and then it's only so she can show off whatever new car or suit or house she's just bought."

Julia stared. She had had no idea Nina felt this way. "Nina, maybe that's how you see her. But you have to understand that she and I go much further back. Whatever she may have done to me, there's still so much that I owe her. If it weren't for her—"

"Stop," Nina said, throwing up her hands. "Stop, stop, stop, stop, *stop*." She pulled at her hair. "How many times have you said, 'If it weren't for Ime?' 'If it weren't for Ime, I never would have gotten that first job.' 'If it weren't for Ime, I wouldn't be where I am now.' 'If it weren't for Ime, I wouldn't have discovered my potential.' Let me ask you something, Julia. Do you really think that if you had never met Ime, you wouldn't be doing just as well as you are right now? That if it weren't for Ime, you wouldn't have gotten out of the old neighborhood? That if it weren't for Ime, you wouldn't have been able to decide whether or not to have an abortion or found a way to help your parents or any of a million other things? Has it ever occurred to you that the life you're living is because of your choices and not because of Ime?"

Julia reached for something to say. The spray of Nina's anger was disorienting. Her words stuck—painful, gleaming shards of truth. Julia tried to respond, but Nina kept rolling.

"You act like Ime saved you from some terrible life, and I think you believe that. But for the last year it's been the rest of us who've been there for you. Even C, as fucked up as she is. Sure, she totally screwed up with the whole Diego Ramirez thing. But she only wanted to include you because she thought it was exciting and she wanted to share it with you. Can you say the same thing about Ime? What has she done except think about herself?"

Julia wagged her head and waved her hands.

"Look," Nina said, "I'm not saying Ime *wanted* to hurt you. But we all know how she is. Ime looks out for Ime."

"So what are you telling me?" Julia said. "That I should go running to Ilario and forget about Ime?"

Nina sat next to Julia on the couch. "I have no idea what you should do. But maybe it's time you stopped giving Ime credit for everything that's ever gone right in your life. And started giving yourself—and us—a little more."

Nina's words kept Julia awake that night and stayed with her the following day. That Nina felt the way she did had shaken her, loosening within her some new understanding about herself and how she was living her life. She could not have described exactly what that understanding was, but it was growing, creating within her a heady mix of hope and fear. The sensation grew throughout the day. On returning to the office in the afternoon after lunch with a customer, she was feeling so peculiar and outside herself that rather than make the customer calls she had planned, she instead began to type at her computer. She typed cautiously at first, then a little faster, then even faster. The words came flying from some new place within her, words she would never have thought she would type under circumstances such as these.

The next thing she knew, she had written her letter of resignation. She stared at the screen, dazed by what she had done. As if to test herself, she printed out the letter. As if to test herself further, she took the document from the printer and signed it with a bold flourish that was not at all the way she usually signed things. And as if to test herself even further, she walked down the hall and rounded the corner. She took the stairs up to Roger's office. The next thing she knew, she was handing the letter to him.

He looked down at it grimly. "Are you sure you want to do this?" he asked.

Julia reiterated some of the things she had said in the letter. That she truly appreciated everything Roger had done. That she thought it was best for everyone involved if she were to go. That without Ilario there, she didn't feel comfortable continuing in her position. She made no mention of the promise Roger had made and then rescinded; or the fact that more than once he had promised to keep something she had said confidential, only to tell it to Ilario later; or the fact that she really, truly believed that he had made a mistake firing Ilario. As critical as these thoughts were to her decision to leave, she made no mention of them. Encouraged by the look of shock on his face, she came around to his side of the desk, intending to shake his hand. Instead, she hugged him. She did not know why she did it. It just felt like the right thing to do.

Moments later, as she took the items from her desk, she thought of Ilario. She felt an unexpected sensation of solidarity with him. He had made terrible mistakes, but he had been wronged. She thought, too, of how her grandparents had risked everything they had and knew to come to this country to build a life. What a strange thought for a pocha such as her! She was thinking of a man and woman she had never met and had only the vaguest remembrance of from photographs. She imagined them nevertheless, vividly, risking everything they had, fearful yet determined. She drew strength from the thought of them and others like them, their compatriots, their compadres and comadres, crossing a border into an unknown world. What was Julia going to do? She had no idea. She did not know how she was going to pay her rent beyond a couple of months or how she was going to help pay for Nina's wedding or how she was going to pay for an attorney that already she could not afford. She was probably making the most foolish decision of her entire life. But if that was the case, why did it feel so right? Why did she feel exhilarated?

⌒ 30 ⌒

December Wedding

Julia and Nina were coming out of Discount Bridal in downtown San Fernando when Julia told Nina what she had done. She expected Nina to react with dismay. She did not expect her to say, "Maybe I should postpone my wedding."

"Are you crazy?" Julia said as they stepped into the flow of weekend shoppers along the sidewalk. "Why would you?"

"I always pictured my friends being happy when I got married," she said.

"We *are* happy. We're happy for *you*."

Nina gave a dejected sigh. "You're unemployed, Ime and you aren't talking, C and you are having all of your legal problems, and my maid of honor is hiding somewhere south of the border. What kind of circumstances are these for a wedding?"

"Nina, if you wait for us to solve all our problems, you might never get married. Are you having second thoughts?"

"No, of course not. I just wonder if it's not bad luck to have a wedding when—"

"Look at it this way," Julia said. "We're absorbing all the bad stuff for you so that your wedding will be perfect."

. . .

As confident as Julia felt that she had done the right and necessary thing in quitting her job, there was no ignoring that she needed to find work right away. So that night, after Nina had gone to spend the night with Roberto, Julia began searching for sales rep jobs online. She had been at it for a couple of hours when she received an e-mail from Ilario.

The sight of his name embedded in a longer account name was like an electrical charge to her chest. A light pulsed behind her eyes. She opened the e-mail.

In it Ilario said he had continued to listen for Julia's name in the news, but hadn't heard anything recently. He hoped this meant that her legal problems were at an end. He had talked to Lydia, who had told him about their conversation. He wanted Julia to know his feelings hadn't changed. Julia pictured him sitting in front of his computer, waiting for a response. This image, more than his words, choked her. She wanted to call him. She *ought* to. Ime had made it clear she didn't want to talk to her. She was even having her agency screen her calls. So what was preventing Julia from calling him? She ought to do it. She really ought to. . . .

For the last couple of minutes Julia had been aware of Nina's phone ringing. Someone had been dialing, hanging up, and redialing. Fearing it might be an emergency, she went to answer it.

"Nina," the voice said. "Is that you?"

"Is this Roberto? Roberto, it's me, Julia."

"Where's Nina?" he said. "I've been calling her cell phone but she won't answer."

"She left here a couple hours ago. She's not with you?"

"No, she's not. I wanted to ask her if there was room to add a couple of people from my work to the wedding reception."

"She left here around eight," Julia said. "I thought she was going . . ." Julia felt herself teetering on the brink of saying too much. Instead, she lied, "Actually, Roberto, I don't know. She may have told me . . . but I wasn't listening."

A strange silence followed.

"Roberto?"

"This is the second time this week she's turned off her phone and I haven't been able to get her," he said.

"Roberto, people turn their phones off all the time and forget to turn them back on. I'm sure she's fine."

"OK." Roberto sighed. "If you hear from her . . ."

"I'll tell her to call you."

Off the line, she deleted Ilario's message—and intrusion on more serious things—and powered down the computer.

That night, Julia slept fitfully. At about five in the morning, she heard Nina come in through the back door. Julia got out of bed and met her coming through her laundry room.

"You're up early," Nina said.

"Put some coffee on," Julia said. "We need to talk."

"Don't look at me like that," Nina said as she served up chorizo and eggs for herself and Julia in the kitchen. The pan had been too hot when she had thrown in the ingredients. Smoke still lingered in the air. "I know it can't happen again. It won't."

"You lied to me."

"No. I *was* on my way to Roberto's, just like I said. But I felt like I needed to clear the air with Remedios. So I called her and she said to stop by and . . ."

"Nina, if you're gay, you better say so. Because in less than a week—"

"I'm not gay," Nina said. "I keep telling you. It's something that just happens with Remedios. She's . . . persuasive." She brought the plates of eggs and chorizo with tortillas folded on the side to the table. Her expression bubbled with shame and frustration. "What do you expect me to do?" she said. "If I could undo it, I would. I can't ruin everything with Roberto because of this. If I were gay it would be one thing. I just wanted to try something different. Don't forget, Roberto cheated on me, too."

"*Years* ago. Not a week before your wedding. Nina, how many times?"

"How many times what?"

"How many times have you and Remedios been together?"

"Twice," Nina said. "The first time and this time."

"Roberto said there have been other times he hasn't been able to reach you."

"Three times," Nina said, "but the third time hardly counted. Not all of our clothes came off . . . four times if you count when we took a bath together. You can hardly count taking a bath as anything."

Julia dragged her fingers down the sides of her face. "Oh, Nina. Are you sure you should be getting married right now?"

Nina's face became a knot of resistance. "I'll tell you what I told Remedios. Nothing more is going to happen. It's done. I'm marrying Roberto. And just because you're jealous is no reason to try and convince me otherwise."

A short while later, the phone rang and Nina answered. Julia could hear Remedios's voice on the line. Nina stepped out of the room to take the call, but this did not prevent Julia from hearing Nina's side of the conversation. In response to Remedios, Nina offered a few "mmm hmms" and "okays" and a "thank you." When Nina came back into the kitchen, she was a shade whiter than usual.

"That was Remedios."

"What did she want?"

"To wish me a happy wedding and say there are no hard feelings."

"You're shaking. Why?"

Nina's eyes returned to Julia from some faraway place. "I think she's planning something."

"*Planning* something?"

Nina shook her head with the vigor of a child refusing a spoonful of medicine. "She was *too* nice. There was something strange in her voice . . . like a warning. Shit, Julia. I think she's going to do something to ruin my wedding."

"Nina, you're just feeling guilty, that's all. She promised me she wouldn't interfere with your plans."

"That was before," Nina said gravely. " 'I hope you'll be very, very happy.' Those were her words. Two 'verys', Julia."

Julia conceded to herself that she couldn't be sure that there wasn't a second meaning to Remedios's words. But she felt compelled to believe what Remedios had told her, that she was no longer the same person who had sought revenge on Claudia Aguilar. "Everything is going to be fine, Nina." The words did not come easily or naturally. But Julia had no choice but to say them. Her friendship with Remedios demanded it.

Nina's wedding day could not have coincided with nicer weather. The December air was dry and pure, and the sky over the Valley was clear. Predictably, however, the beauty of the day did nothing to alleviate Nina's anxiety. Trying to prevent a meltdown, Julia distracted Nina by talking about anything other than the occasion at hand as she helped her do her hair and makeup. She did not tell her that Marta, only just now on her way back from Tijuana, had called to say she'd gotten a flat tire; or that neither she nor Marta had heard anything at all from Concepción in spite of repeated attempts to reach her; or that the photographer Nina had hired had come down with the flu and was sending a replacement whom Nina had never met before and whose work she had never seen. Nor did Julia reveal her own agitation as she anticipated seeing Ime again.

She had no idea what she wanted to say to Ime. The pain of what Ime had done had begun to sink in, and if Ime really didn't think she could remain friends with Julia, then Julia had to accept that. For now, though, the door to reconciliation was still open; there had to be some way of accommodating each other.

Yet if Julia were entirely honest with herself, she would also have admitted that some part of her wanted it to be over. Part of her wanted to be with Ilario.

At about 10:30, Julia helped Nina into her wedding dress. Stepping back to take in the full effect, Julia was overcome with emotion; all her other concerns dropped away. Nina had never looked so beautiful. The dress showed Nina's narrow waist to advantage while creating the illusion of hips where she barely had any. In the soft light coming through the windows, Nina's pallor made her look angelic rather than depressed. Stepping in front of a full-length mirror, Nina, too, appeared amazed. The two women stood side by side, looking at Nina's reflection.

"Shit," Julia said.

"Fuck me, I look good," Nina said.

Julia and Nina arrived at Our Lady of the Holy Rosary, a Catholic church on Vineland in Sun Valley, just before eleven. Julia parked in the lot behind the church and adjacent to the classrooms of the church school.

"Where are Marta and Ime and C?" Nina said. "I don't see their cars."

"We're early," Julia said, though in fact they were cutting the time close. Seeing Nina looking at the clock on her dash, Julia said, "Ignore that, it runs ahead." She got out and helped Nina out of the passenger side, then got her bridesmaid dress out of the backseat. They took the path that ran between the church from the rectory around to the front, to the school. "I'm going to change in here," Julia said, going in. Nina followed her into the first class-room they came to and Julia shut the door and started getting into the dress. The fabric was cheap and the cut of the dress was unflattering to her, but she didn't care. Once Nina had helped her zip up, Julia said, "I'm going to check on Marta and C. Stay here, OK?"

Julia went out past the rectory to the front of the church. Roberto was standing there alone, looking even more nervous than Nina. Seeing Julia, he pulled on the fingers of his left hand. "She's here?" he asked.

"She looks beautiful," Julia said. "Have you seen C or Marta or Ime?"

Roberto shook his head no. "Julia, Nina told me about what happened with you and C. You'll let me know if there's anything I can do to help, won't you?"

Julia ran her hand down Roberto's smooth cheek. He had shaved his beard and mustache. "Roberto, you always say just the right thing."

Julia went back to Nina. Nina flew to her as she came through the door. Panic of a new kind had infected her in the few minutes Julia had been gone.

"It's *her*," Nina said. "Remedios is here."

"She can't be," Julia said. "I just walked through the whole church."

Nina pulled Julia over to an open window that faced the parking lot. "That's her car. Right there! The Corsica. She's here to ruin everything, just like I said."

Julia pushed the classroom window wide open and looked out. Sure enough, a '94 or '95 Corsica sat parked at the free-throw line of the basketball court in the lot. But Julia was pretty sure that Remedios's car was a darker shade of blue.

"Please go check," Nina squeaked. "She's here. I can *feel* it."

With a sigh, Julia left the room a second time to scout the church. What did Nina think she was going to find? Remedios crouching behind a bush? She circled the outside of the church and rectory. Marta was getting out of her car in the lot.

"Thank God you're here," Julia said. "I need you to keep an eye on Nina."

"You wouldn't believe the morning I've had," Marta said, digging through her purse. "First the flat tire, then I spilled a cafecito on this lame-looking dress—"

"Hold on," Julia said. "I thought you were going to pick up C."

"Oh, that's the other thing," Marta said, putting a cigarette to her lips and lighting up. She took a couple of puffs. "I went by C's place and she wasn't there. Well, guess what the Pentecostals next door told me? She's with her lawyers right now getting ready to confess everything to the police in exchange for a reduced charge."

"She came to her senses?"

"Not exactly," Marta said. "Some producer from *20/20* called her saying that John Quiñones wanted to talk to her. She wants to get her face on TV, which means she has to come clean, so she's talking to her lawyers about it now."

Julia pulled Marta close in a taffeta-crushing hug.

"I thought you'd be happy." Marta blew smoke next to Julia's ear. "But Nina's going to shit her gown when she finds out C's not coming."

. . .

Back in the classroom with Nina, Julia assured her that Remedios was not around. "But there is some bad news. C's not coming."

"She can't not be here! My God, first Remedios, now this."

"What about Remedios?" Marta said.

"She's here," Nina said.

"No, she isn't," Marta said. "I talked to her this morning. She's in Oxnard for her mother's birthday."

"What? That's not possible," Nina said.

"She can't be in two places at the same time," Marta said. "She won't be back until Wednesday."

Nina stared. "You're sure?" A strange quiet fell over her. Her chest rose and fell in short breaths.

Marta crushed out her cigarette on one of the school desks. "We need to get this show on the road."

"Of course, but—" Her eyes flicked back and forth between Marta and Julia. "I'm ready, I just thought . . . I must have been imagining things . . . I thought for sure . . ."

Julia told Marta to stay with Nina while she let the priest know they were nearly ready. A few paces from the church vestibule, she saw Ime.

She had done her hair in an elegant nape twist that exposed the angles of her face, making her look younger and more innocent than she had appeared in a long time. The dress, while no more flattering to her figure than it was to Julia's, at least took advantage of her petite frame.

Julia felt a rise of emotions she could not control. She rushed forward in a swish of fabric and broke loose with all the thoughts that had been gathering in recent days. "Ime, I'm glad you're here. Maybe we're not friends anymore, but there's still a lot we have to talk about. It's not like we can just ignore each other forever. We have a history together, and no matter where things stand between us, the fact is we're always going to be connected. We need to find a way to stay in each other's lives, even if—"

"Stop," Ime said. She took Julia's hand between hers and pressed. "Stop for just a minute. There's something I have to tell you."

Sorrow and regret rose in Ime's face. Julia could tell that she was on the brink of another admission. It took Ime a few seconds to gather herself. Then she said, "I'm moving. I've been offered a job up north. I'm going to take it."

Julia stood back. Ime's news crashed through her thoughts, scattering them like pins in a strike. The murmur of voices in the church receded. "What job? When?"

"I'm getting into a new area of real estate. It's a good opportunity. I've lived my whole life in the Valley. It's time for me to make a change."

"My God," Julia said. "I had no idea. . . ."

"I've been needing to do something like this for a long time. The job just sort of came up, but the timing feels right. I've got a buyer for my house and I leave in two weeks."

"Two weeks! But Ime . . . what about your life here?"

"Life here just doesn't interest me the way it used to, and—"

"You're just going to leave? But you have so much built up here in L.A. Your whole life is here. How can you just—"

"I have to," she said, squeezing Julia's hand in a way that seemed to convey an urgent second meaning. "I have to."

Julia had promised herself that no matter what Ime said or didn't say, for Nina's sake there would be no anger, no drama. But she couldn't have prepared herself for this. The straight lines of the vestibule walls seemed to wobble.

"Maybe this is what we need," Ime said. "To get out of each other's way. I'm in your way right now. You know that."

Julia felt the weighty truth of what Ime was saying. As long as they lived in the same city, Ime would be in her way. "So you're doing me a favor by going," Julia said. She'd meant this as a question, but it hadn't come out that way.

The statement floated between them for a few seconds before Ime followed with, "I'm going for a lot of reasons. You don't need me anymore." She let go of Julia's hand. "Maybe someday after you've forgiven me, then we can talk and see where things are, and . . ."

Julia's impulse was to tell her that she had already forgiven her. But this would have been a lie. She was only just beginning to feel angry about what had happened; forgiveness was a long way off. Instead, she answered, "So this is good-bye?"

"It is," Ime said.

There seemed to be nothing more to say. In her heart Julia felt what she had not expected to feel—certainty that this was the right thing. The best thing. She took a step back to take Ime in more fully—this businesswoman on a new career path. "So, this job you're taking," she said. "What could be so great that it would make you leave L.A.?"

"I'm going to be starting from the ground up in commercial real estate."

Julia shook her head. She didn't know what that meant.

"Shopping malls and office buildings. It's where the real money is," Ime said.

"And how did this come up?"

Ime turned red. "Lydia. She knows someone who knows someone."

"Impossible!"

"I know," Ime said, struggling to suppress her embarrassment. "She mentioned the job when Ilario and I were together. Of course I figured she was just trying to get me out of town, so I told her to go fuck herself. But then, well, after Ilario and I split . . . I called her . . . and one thing led to another, and . . ."

Julia could imagine how hard that call must have been for Ime to make. Julia wondered, too, to what extent Lydia had conspired on Ilario's behalf.

"We have a problem," a voice said.

Julia and Ime turned to see Marta. Her lips were pursed with worry.

"What is it?" Julia said.

"I left Nina for a second to smoke another cigarette. I went back to check on her . . . and she wasn't in the room."

Julia and Ime followed Marta. The urgent rustling of their dresses filled the air. When they got to the room it was empty.

"She can't have gone far in that dress," Julia said.

"I checked the bathroom and the toilet stalls, but she wasn't there, either."

"She has to be here somewhere." Julia floated down the hall, opening doors one after another and looking into the rooms. Marta headed down to the far end and peered out the back window, then started opening doors as well. When she pushed open the door to the third classroom at the end of the hall, she let out a scream.

Ime and Julia ran toward her. They looked in. Nina's wedding dress lay abandoned in a pile on a folding table against the wall, but there was no sign of Nina. Julia's clothes were gone as well. Her handbag lay on the table beside the dress, its mouth agape. Looking in, Julia saw at once that her keys were missing. Marta pressed her hand to her forehead and steadied herself on a desk chair. A cool breeze swept freely through the open window.

⁓ 31 ⁓

Obstacles and Opportunities

Julia stepped out of the courthouse and into the hazy February light, her legal troubles behind her at last. She was satisfied with the sentence the judge had just handed down to her: three months of suspended jail time to be erased from her record in a year, and six months of community service to be performed for a Los Angeles service organization benefiting the underprivileged. Along with the sentence, the judge, a mottle-faced old man with pinprick eyes punched into ancient, papery skin, had croaked out a long lecture about civic responsibility—stern words that had produced in Julia's heart an anxious fluttering.

Her heart was still fluttering now as she turned to Brenda for what she hoped would be the last time. "Thank you," she said. "You were wonderful. I'm glad Remedios thought of you."

"You know where to reach me if there's anything else I can do," Brenda said.

"There is one thing," Julia said, flushing slightly. "I'm going to need some time to pay you the rest of your fees. As soon as I'm working again, it shouldn't take me long. . . ."

Brenda regarded her with a comical tilt of her head.

"What's wrong?" Julia said.

"Your money order came this morning," Brenda said.

"What money order?" Julia said.

"The Wells Fargo one."

"I didn't send you anything."

"Somebody did. It had a sticky with your name on it. You're paid up to the penny."

"How can that . . ." Julia spun through the people she knew who might have done such a thing for her. Ime was the only person with that kind of money. Yet Julia hadn't heard from her since her move to the Bay Area two months ago. Perhaps this was her final good-bye. Perhaps guilt or something like it had moved her.

"Well, thank you again," Julia said, not wanting to press her luck.

"I wish all my cases were so straightforward," Brenda said, and with a flirtatious squint added, "and all my clients as smart and pretty."

Julia absorbed the compliment with a smile. She shook her hand. She could not remember the last time she had felt so light.

In times past, a milestone like today's would have occasioned phone calls to her friends to meet at the Revolutionary Cantina, where beer, questions, and opinions would have flowed freely. But today Julia was satisfied to celebrate without them. The cold winter air was soothing, and she chose instead to stroll through the civic center neighborhood, taking comfort in the familiarity of brown faces that brought to mind the better memories of her childhood. Since quitting her job, she had been spending more and more time alone. This was in part by choice, but also out of necessity. Ime and Concepción were out of her life. In the space created by their absence she began to reconsider who she was, and who she wanted to be. It amazed her that for so many years so much of her sense of self had been shaped by her relationship with these two women. No longer caught up in the colorful whirl of their lives, she began to notice the quiet stirrings of a new person, and a new way of living in the world.

While losing Ime and Concepción was necessary and even good, it pained Julia to have heard so little from Nina. In the aftermath of her failed wedding, she had been in touch only sporadically, needing, as she put it, "time alone to figure out what the hell I'm doing."

"Let me come by so we can talk," Julia had said when Nina called shortly after fleeing the church to let Julia know she was all right.

"I can't," Nina, in tears, had said. "I'm so, so embarrassed. I've wasted so many people's time and money."

"Nobody cares about that," Julia said. "Nina, what happened?"

"I don't know, exactly," Nina said. "I was so sure that Remedios was going to disrupt everything. Then, when she didn't, I guess I kind of realized that I wanted her to."

"What do you want me to tell Roberto?"

"Tell him how sorry I am and I'll talk to him in a few days. Please, do whatever you can to smooth things over with him and his family. I just can't face them right now. I'm such a big fat stupid chicken."

Julia didn't know if by "big fat stupid chicken" Nina meant she feared seeing Roberto, or feared admitting she was a lesbian. Sensing that she wasn't ready to explore the question in any depth, Julia assured her, "Just tell me what you need me to do, Nina."

"I just need to be alone," Nina said.

"But I'm worried about you."

"You don't need to be worried."

"I need to see you for myself."

"No. I'll call you later."

Julia didn't wait for her to call. She went by her house a short while later. But Nina wasn't there.

"Of course she wasn't there," Marta said when Julia called her to see if she'd heard from her. "I bet she's with Remedios right now, romping around naked in her bed and having a great old time while the rest of us clean up her mess."

Remedios called later to confirm that Nina was with her. Returning from her trip to Oxnard, she'd found Nina waiting for her on her front step, her face streaked with tears of shame and regret. "I can't believe she thought I would show up at her stupid wedding," Remedios said. "What kind of garbage have you been putting in her head about me?"

"I haven't said anything about you," Julia said. "Whatever ideas she has she came to on her own. But what's happening between you two? Why is she at your house?"

"I told her she could stay with me until the end of the month, but only on the couch," Remedios said. Then, with a sigh so immense it seemed to have been gathering for days, she added, "Nina's hardly the person I pictured myself being with. She needs so much . . . *help.* I'm a busy woman, Julia. I don't have room in my life for someone like that."

Despite these objections, Julia heard in Remedios's voice both tenderness and resignation, suggesting that the question of what was to become of Nina and Remedios was already decided, even if Remedios was not yet ready to fully embrace it.

"A person could do worse than Nina," Julia said.

"A person could do better," Remedios said. Then, a little uncomfortably, she asked, "So, what about this Roberto clown? How is he dealing with all this?"

"Not very well, of course," Julia said. This was an understatement. It was difficult to do justice to Roberto's devastation. When

Julia had gone up to the altar to tell him that Nina had disappeared, the white, gaping look that came over him had frightened her so much that for a moment she'd thought she might faint. She didn't. Roberto did, falling into the arms of the Pacheco brothers after nearly hitting his head on the altar table. A gasp had echoed through the church. Then it had been left to Julia to tell the crowd, consisting almost entirely of Roberto's relatives, that the wedding was off. Julia's stomach still dropped at the memory of Roberto's mother's bull-like nostrils flaring with fury as she made the announcement.

"Roberto will be all right eventually," Julia said. "I think once he understands that Nina's gay, it's going to help a lot."

"How?" Remedios said.

"He'll know that it's not that Nina doesn't love him. The one thing I know about Roberto is that he wants Nina to be happy." Roberto had not said this to Julia, but she believed it to be true. He had always held Nina's happiness above his own, and Julia had no reason to think that had changed.

On the first of March, opening arguments began in the murder trial of Diego Ramirez. Not wanting to be reminded of all that Concepción had put her through, Julia avoided watching or listening to any coverage. This was nearly impossible. For several days in a row it was the top story in the news. And because the judge was allowing TV cameras in the courtroom, live coverage played throughout the afternoon on cable and on the networks.

Stopping at the Cantina for a quick drink with Marta one day, Julia was tempted into watching just a few minutes of the trial on the TV that Marta had installed behind the bar for the sole purpose of keeping abreast of the proceedings. A few minutes became an hour, and an hour became an afternoon.

"I don't see how he's going to get off," Julia said between mouth-fuls of peanuts that she and Marta were munching on at the bar. "It was his gun, and he's admitted he and his manager conspired to kill her."

"Admitting that sounds risky," Marta said, "but it may be the only way to shift the blame to someone else."

"So they're trying to convince the jury that his manager stole the gun from Diego's home and gave it to a hired killer, then got it back after the murder, then snuck the gun back into Diego's gun collection without him knowing it? Who's going to buy that?"

"The defense attorney explained that that's why Diego fled the country," Marta said. "He went to Guadalajara because that's where the hit man his manager hired said he was going to hide once he finished the job."

From that day, Julia was hooked. At home she left the TV run-ning at all times during the waking hours, even while she was busy surfing job sites on the Web and making phone calls in search of job openings.

That night, Concepción called for the third time that week.

"C? Again. This is getting ridiculous." Having decided that she had no room for Concepción in her life, Julia had steeled herself against her attempts to reconcile.

"Julia, I'm really sorry about everything. When are you going to forgive me?"

"We've been through this," Julia said. "It's not a matter of for-giving you. I forgive you. But I can't risk having my life turned up-side down again."

"Don't you think *my* life is turned upside down?"

Julia gave a laugh. Yes, Concepción's life had been turned upside down, but in ways as agreeable as a person could possibly hope for. Shortly after her admitting to helping Diego, her lawyers had convinced the DA's office to drop the charges against her. In exchange, Concepción, with Diego's permission, had agreed to share with them the details of all the conversations she had had with the actor. Three days after this, Concepción had appeared on a special edition of *20/20* devoted entirely to the murder case. Guided by the honey-throated John Quiñones, she had offered a day-by-day account of her time with the actor. Among the many tidbits she offered up for a rumor-hungry public was the fact that Diego preferred boxers during the day and slept in the nude at night, knew the lyrics to every song ever sung by the legendary Mexican ranchera singer Vincente Fernández, and was prone to bursting into tears at the mention of his ex-wife's name—further evidence, as far as Concepción was concerned, that he was incapable of killing her. Through the wizardry of clever editing and heart-stirring music, the show had portrayed Concepción not as a high-strung fanatic but rather as a Madonna-like figure offering comfort, care, and, yes, even spiritual counsel to the actor in his darkest hours.

"Did your lawyer get the money order I sent?" Concepción said.

"That was you? How . . . where did you get . . ."

"*Star* just paid me a bunch of money for an interview and I was able to borrow the rest. Nina told me how much you owed. I'll do whatever it takes, Julia. If that's not enough, then maybe this will convince you: I want you to be my date to the Academy Awards."

Julia wasn't sure she had heard right. It wasn't possible that an appearance on *20/20* had somehow led to Concepción being invited to the Academy Awards.

"Diego felt terrible that he had caused me so much trouble, so he asked his people to ask me if there was anything else they could do for me. I mentioned that I'd always wanted to go to a big movie premiere . . . and the next day they called and said that Diego was giving me his tickets to the Oscars. . . ."

Julia began to laugh—a deep, hearty laugh brought on by a mix of amazement and admiration. Nevertheless, she said, "I'm sorry, C. I have to go. I'll look for you on TV."

When Julia first learned that community service might be part of her sentence, she'd pictured herself in an orange vest spearing trash on the side of the Hollywood Freeway. Brenda had assured her that there were other, less punishing options. As she'd ticked off ideas, one in particular had jumped out at Julia—working at a career resource center that helped poor, unemployed women develop job-search skills.

The more she thought about it, the more the idea appealed to her. Her interest only continued to grow as the woman who answered the phone at the resource center provided her with details: "Some of the women who come to us have never touched a computer or seen a résumé. We teach them basic skills and do practice interviews with them until they're comfortable answering questions. We even show them how to dress to make a good impression. If they can't afford the right clothes, we have a whole roomful of donated clothes for them to choose from. It's incredible to see their reaction when they look in the mirror and realize that they look just like the women they see going into offices every day. We help them develop the confidence they need to take that first step to a better life for themselves."

As Julia listened, a tingling sensation traveled over her skin. It was so easy to picture herself being a part of what this woman was describing. Julia had plenty to offer in the way of advice, plenty of work knowledge and wisdom to impart. She remembered how Ime had helped her prepare for her first successful office interview. Afterward she had felt unstoppable, inches taller, energized. Everything had seemed brighter. She could picture herself playing for other women the role Ime had always played for her—adviser, mentor, motivator—and it excited her. She could almost forgive Concepción for bringing her to this point.

The next day Julia made arrangements through the court to begin her community service. The woman at the center had asked her if she could start right away, so the following morning Julia rose early, dressed, and poured herself a cup of coffee to take with her. She set out far in advance of her 9:30 appointment. The center was located on Van Nuys Boulevard, almost within walking distance of the Revolutionary Cantina. But when Julia reached the boulevard, she did not make the turn. She continued heading south. She had one other stop she needed to make first.

Since the night of her arrest, she had returned none of Ilario's calls. Had anyone asked her why, she probably would have explained that she could not picture herself running into the arms of the man who had been at the center of her problems with Ime. As often as she thought about Ilario, her friendship with Ime, or the memory of it, deserved some respect. She might also have said that she needed time to fully accept the loss of what she and Ime had once had, or what she had thought they'd had. This was not to say that she wanted to see her again; she understood that Ime's moving away was for the best. But such knowledge did not preclude a range of emotions that made a future with Ilario difficult to contemplate.

Such answers would have made up only part of the truth, however. Julia understood that she was also delaying calling Ilario because she was nervous—afraid, really, of what seeing him might mean. In her experience, love had always been accompanied by obstacles. More often than not, these obstacles were self-created; nevertheless, obstacles were what she knew. The fact that every nameable hindrance had now been removed was strange and even frightening. It was as though, having at last cleared a path to a window, she realized that she was expected to leap through it.

But today, buoyed by the prospect of volunteering at something she believed she would excel at, and sensing only opportunities around every corner, she knew that the time had come to talk to him. She did not call first. It seemed fitting given the times he had shown up at her door without warning that she should do the same. Her heart sped up as she followed the directions she had copied from the Web site of the company that had recently hired Ilario, an upstart laser manufacturer in Studio City. She had barely been able to recall the name of the company from her last conversation with Lydia. She hadn't expected to be this nervous. Her heart was beating almost as hard as when she had stood before the judge to hear her sentence.

Pulling up across the street from his building, she was struck by the plainness of the industrial, almost military-looking structure. A single diagonal red stripe painted across the gray, windowless facade was the only hint of cheer. She parked, fed the meter, and went into the first-floor lobby, which was all exposed, chilly-looking concrete. She asked the receptionist at the spacious, curved wood front desk if Ilario was in. When she asked Julia for her name, Julia said, "Tell him it's someone he doesn't have much in common with."

The receptionist frowned but dutifully relayed the message by phone to someone Julia gathered was Ilario's assistant. While Julia waited, she looked up at the small, circular skylight that was the room's only source of natural light, something to concentrate on as her heart pumped even harder. A minute went by. Then another, and another.

Several minutes later, Ilario still had not appeared. A thin film of sweat began to form at the back of her neck. She wondered if it had been a bad idea to catch him off guard this way. In a weakening flash it occurred to her he might not want to see her. Who was to say that she hadn't waited too long, that he hadn't moved on or even started seeing someone else? Two and a half months was a long time to keep someone hanging. Who was to say he didn't hate her? The anxiety in her chest tightened into a fist of throbbing, panicky fibers.

The elevator door opened and Ilario came out. He looked thinner than the last time she had seen him, but only slightly less handsome. He had regrown his beard and was wearing khaki pants and an untucked shirt that fit too loosely on him. She started to walk toward him but stopped. The expression on his face was not at all what she had hoped to see.

Uncertainty was stretched tight across his features. An unfriendly light shone in his eyes. It took Julia a moment or two to manage: "I'm sorry I didn't call first. I thought it would be fun to surprise you. Maybe that wasn't such a good idea. I've been meaning to call you, but with so much going on, it's been hard. I had to deal with the charges, then a bunch of stuff happened at work, and then there was my friend Nina's wedding, which didn't work out, which caused a whole bunch of other problems. . . ." Christ, what was she saying? That all of these things were more important than Ilario? That he was the last item on her list of things to do? She swallowed and tried to start over, but he interrupted her.

"You never called," he said. "Not once."

"I wanted to, Ilario. But I couldn't. Not until I was sure where things stood with Ime."

"You could have told me that."

"It's hard to explain why I didn't. I wanted to, but I was afraid."

"I just wanted to know you were all right."

"I'm fine. All that other stuff is over. I'm here."

In Julia's version of the scene, this would have been the point at which Ilario told her how happy he was to see her, embraced her, flooded her with all the things he had wanted to say but hadn't been able to when he had come to see her. He would have said he understood why she needed to wait, and that the waiting only made him appreciate her all the more. But these things did not come from him. He did not move. Julia squeezed her briefcase handle. She had no idea why she had brought it, unless it was just for this—to have something to hold on to.

With another look around at the lobby walls, she said, "So this is your new work. It's nice."

"It's nice enough."

"And the job is going well?"

"It's an improvement."

"And have you talked to Lydia?"

"I talk to her every day."

She continued to look around at the walls, as if there were objects of interest on them to look at. Were things really going this badly? She couldn't believe this was happening. It was as though she were talking to the old Ilario, the one who was threatened by her and believed things about her that weren't true. She felt a pressure at the back of her eyes, the threat of tears. She took a great gulp of air. "Ilario," she said, "there's something I have to tell you."

She had no idea why she was about to tell him what she was about to tell him. It had been the farthest thing from her mind when she had walked in. But the moment seemed to demand it— some significant truth with which to anchor a drifting situation. She said, "I knew Roger was going to fire you. I wanted to warn you, but there didn't seem to be a way to do it." She looked down as she said this. When Ilario didn't respond, she pushed on: "Roger was going to fire you so I could have your job. He told me about it at the hospital."

When she looked up, Ilario's jaw looked locked in place. With some effort he got out the words, "I know. I found out about it last week. Anne called me wanting to know if there were any openings here because she wants to get out of Ostin. She told me that's what people were saying. That you had conspired with Roger. That you were plotting for my job."

With these words she understood Ilario's demeanor. She felt as if someone had splashed water on her. "It wasn't like that at all," she said. "Roger came to *me*. He'd already made up his mind about what he planned to do."

Ilario's skepticism was painful to behold. She quickly tried to explain to him how things had truly played out, how Roger had warned her not to say anything, implying that her job would be in jeopardy if she did. She tried to make Ilario see how she had suffered with knowledge she wished she hadn't been given, how hard it had been not to be able to say good-bye or tell him how much she had come to appreciate him. She told him about how she had quit, in part because Roger had gone back on his word but also because she'd come to realize how unfair he had been to Ilario. And without Ilario there, what would have been the point? He had been right after all. Ostin was too rigid, too restricted by rules and policies that would never change so long as Roger had his way.

Julia could feel Ilario wanting to believe her. Of course, he had every reason not to. She had deceived him and nearly taken his job and then ignored him. It was just the sort of thing one would expect from someone who would sleep with a boss to get ahead— and she had, hadn't she? Call it the need for security, call it whatever you wanted, it amounted to the same thing, didn't it? Why had it taken her so long to admit it to herself? She had slept with her old boss to get ahead! So why shouldn't Ilario think she was capable of this? Why should he believe her now?

Ilario was still far away. Words could do only so much. She saw now that she needed to put something else on the line, to take a further risk. She set her briefcase down on the concrete floor, then removed her jacket and draped it over the briefcase. She walked up to Ilario and threaded her arms through his and around his torso and pulled herself against him, pressing her cheek against his chest. She held him. She said nothing. She held him. She did not let go.

She listened for his heartbeat but didn't hear it. She felt his shallow breath. She held on.

Slowly, his hands came up and touched her shoulders. Lingered there tentatively, cautiously. Traced the backs of her arms down to her elbows.

Pulled her tight against him.

She felt the pride and anger melt out of his body. It was like a magician's trick. One second she was holding the old, cold, impenetrable Ilario. The next she was holding the man she thought she could love.

She felt him shudder with emotion. Then she heard, "Promoting you . . . would have been the smartest thing Roger could have done."

"You mean that?" she said.

"He made a huge mistake letting you go."

The fact that his words came haltingly did not reduce their impact on Julia. She swelled with feeling, and relief. Creating some space between them again, she looked at him appreciatively. But while his indignation had receded, doubts moved over his face like shadows.

"What's wrong?" she said.

"Ime," he said.

Julia had forgotten that he didn't know Ime had moved away. Knowing that telling him would trigger more questions about her former friend than she cared to answer, she said, "There's so much I have to tell you. Ilario, I didn't really see Ime for who she was, or who she was becoming. I was blind. But I understand everything now. Things are much, much clearer."

Ilario nodded thoughtfully, as though blindness were something he, too, had been guilty of.

"Can we do this?" Julia said.

"I want to."

"You don't sound too sure."

"I'm not."

"Why?"

"I don't know. The last few months . . ."

"What about them?"

"They were hard, Julia. I understand why you waited to call me. But it was hard. I can handle just about anything. But that . . . well, it was just hard, that's all."

She could see now how putting Ime above him had hurt him. She had been doing so for most of the last year. It was going to hurt him even more to find out that she had waited even after her friendship with Ime had ended to see him. So there were still obstacles, after all. Many things would need to be discussed, many mistakes redressed, many assurances offered. But to Julia's mind the obstacles that lay ahead posed no greater challenge than any of the ones they had already faced.

"Are you working yet?" Ilario asked.

"No."

"Any prospects?"

"No."

"Aren't you worried?"

Julia wasn't sure whether Ilario was suggesting that this, too, might somehow be an obstacle for them. But after a moment she saw that he merely was concerned about her. This made sense, given how much work meant to them both. His concern was touching. But it was also unnecessary. If she had learned anything from Ilario, it was not to be quite so afraid.

"I'll be fine," she said. "Really."

With that he took her hands and pressed his forehead to hers. After a moment of intense concentration, he said. "Let's try."

Julia smiled. It was funny, truly funny, that only a couple of months earlier he had come to her door to tell her that he loved her, to sell her on the idea of love. Now it was taking all his focus to simply say, "Let's try." This did not discourage her at all, because despite Ilario's hesitancy, there was also hope in his eyes. She felt the warm glow of it pushing through his doubts. It was less than what she had hoped for and expected. But it felt like enough. It felt real. And that was what she needed.

Julia noticed the clock above the reception desk: It said 9:15. Either the clock was fast or she had misjudged the time it had taken her to find Ilario's workplace. She did not want to risk being late for her appointment. She promised Ilario that she would call him later that day. Before she turned to go, she said, "One more thing."

"Yes?"

"A favor."

"OK?"

"Tell Lydia to call me. I think you were right. She and I could be really good friends."

This brought a smile to his lips, as she knew it would. She turned away quickly before the smile could fade, so that she could carry it with her for the rest of the day.

On her way to her car, an unfamiliar feeling began to overtake her, making her skin tingle. She might have called it joy or optimism. But it was not as heady as joy, and not as bright as optimism. It was something more grounded than that, more certain, more permanent. Trying to put a name to it, she realized it had less to do with her feelings about Ilario than with something Ilario had asked her. "Aren't you worried?" he'd said. Here she was, unemployed for the first time in her adult life, with no prospects that she could name, and as of that morning with just $1,172 in her checking account and nothing in savings. Yet she was not worried. She felt secure. Secure in her ability to get by. Secure in all that she had learned at Ostin. Secure in her talents. Ilario had been right—Roger had made a mistake in not promoting her, in not doing everything in his power to keep her. She felt this truth down to her bones. She felt it for the first time. She was without many of the things she had once thought she needed for her own security, yet she had never felt more secure. It was a strange thing. It was a wonderful thing.

Back in her car, she traced the route she had planned back to the resource center. Her excitement only continued to grow as she considered what lay ahead. Coming to the address on Van Nuys Boulevard, she realized that she had passed it hundreds or thousands of times without noticing it while on her way to meet her friends at the Cantina. The building was nothing more than an old windowed storefront, dilapidated but nevertheless cheerfully painted in welcoming colors. She parked out front, fed the meter, and took the steps up to the front. She followed the signs up the stairs to the second floor, then pushed through the glass-framed door and into the busy atmosphere, where several Latinas were at work at various tables and workstations spaced evenly throughout the room. They all looked up as though they had been expecting her. She felt like a woman arriving.